Frank 'n' Stan's Bucket List #5

Isle of Man TT Aces

By

J C Williams

You can subscribe to J C Williams' mailing list and view all his other books at:

www.authorjcwilliams.com

Copyright © 2021 J C Williams

All rights reserved. No part of this book may be reproduced in any manner without written permission except in the case of brief quotations included in critical articles and reviews. For information, please contact the author.

All characters appearing in this work are fictitious. Any resemblance to real persons, living or dead, is purely coincidental.

Cover design by Paul Nugent

Interior formatting & design, proofreading, and editing by Dave Scott

ISBN: 9798481211428

First printing October 2021

Books by JC Williams

The Flip of a Coin

The Lonely Heart Attack Club

The Lonely Heart Attack Club: Wrinkly Olympics

The Lonely Heart Attack Club: Project VIP

The Seaside Detective Agency

The Seaside Detective Agency: The Case of the Brazen Burglar

Frank 'n' Stan's Bucket List #1: TT Races

Frank 'n' Stan's Bucket List #2: TT Races

Frank 'n' Stan's Bucket List #3: Isle 'Le Mans' TT

Frank 'n' Stan's Bucket List #4: Bride of Frank 'n' Stan

Frank 'n' Stan's Bucket List #5: Isle of Man TT Aces

The Bookshop by the Beach

The Crafternoon Sewcial Club

Cabbage Von Dagel

Hamish McScabbard

Deputy Gabe Rashford: Showdown at Buzzards Creek

Luke 'n' Conor's Hundred-to-One Club

Chapter
ONE

Brad's heart pounded against his ribs as the elevator rose. As he watched the indicator light count out the floors, he took several deep lungfuls of air, in through the nose, out through the mouth, practising the breathing technique he'd learned from his one and only visit to a yoga class. Belly breaths, the instructor had called them. They were meant to be calming, though Brad wasn't certain it was having the desired effect right now. A short time later, a cheery ping announced their arrival at the sixteenth floor, welcoming them to their destination. "Here we are," Brad said, stating the obvious, while running a shaking hand up to his throat to quickly check his navy-blue tie for correctness in the polished stainless-steel door before it slid open. "How are you doing? Are you okay?" he asked his brother, who was standing there beside him.

"No," Chip answered. "My mouth is dry," he said, swallowing hard. "Is yours? Is your mouth dry?" he asked, looking to his brother desperately, but receiving no response one way or the other to his question. "Am I sweating?" he went on, feeling his forehead. "Do I look sweaty?" he continued, following a step or two behind Brad, who'd by this point already left the confines of the lift. "I think I'm sweating," Chip said, scurrying after him.

"You're fine, dude, don't worry," Brad stated, turning around to provide visual confirmation of this. "Remember, buddy, we can *do* this," he said, holding his resolute gaze for several seconds by way of motivation. "It's taken us two years to get this far, Chip. We *deserve* to be here," he added, as much for his own benefit as for Chip's, giving the both of them a little boost of confidence. "What did I just say?" he said.

"What? Oh, sorry. Which part?" Chip replied after a brief pause, upon realizing his brother was actually expecting an answer.

"The last part," Brad told him.

"Oh. Gotcha," Chip replied. "We deserve to be here," Chip said in answer, through gritted teeth, repeating his brother's words of inspiration as he balled his hand into a fist in solidarity.

"I can't hear you," Brad whispered, leaning in, and moving his mouth so it was adjacent to Chip's ear.

"We deserve to be here!" Chip whispered back, perhaps a little too loudly, raising his clenched fist into the air now as he recited their mutual rallying cry with a fair degree more vigour this time.

"Nice," Brad offered, along with an encouraging nod, in the way one might congratulate a small child for drawing a crayon picture of their house. He smiled politely as someone approached, the person likely on their way to the elevator just behind them. The person was giving them a peculiar look, probably because of their little impromptu motivational session. "Reception desk?" Brad asked. "Ah. Thanks," he replied, after receiving a rigid, outstretched finger in return, pointing the way.

"Let's nail this," Brad said, addressing his brother once again, slapping Chip firmly between the shoulder blades as they walked in the direction the extended digit had directed, even though directions were hardly necessary. The whole floor was devoted to the NBC Boston offices, and the very first thing you ran into not too far from the elevator was the reception desk. You couldn't miss it. It was only a few steps away, and had the word RECEPTION written in big letters on the wall behind it.

The brothers did look rather smart, the two of them, and surprisingly so. For two gents who ordinarily dressed in combat shorts and comfortable hoodies, they made an acceptable account of themselves, managing to blend into their current corporate surroundings reasonably well all things considered. "We've got everything we need?" Brad asked, although, as they'd already checked and double-checked, he already knew the answer to his question. But it didn't hurt any to check one more time.

"Yep, sure do," Chip offered, patting the black folder firmly gripped under his arm.

"Good. We've got one chance with this, Chip, so let's provide an outstanding first impression, agreed?" Brad answered. He then offered up a friendly wave in greeting as they approached the headset-wearing receptionist sitting behind a sleek, fancy, modern-design glass desk. "Afternoon," he put forth, in his most affable voice, turning on the charm. "We're here to—"

But his cheerful introduction was ended prematurely when the stony-faced gentleman operating the welcome desk threw him a look like he'd dragged something awful in on the sole of his shoe. "I'm on the phone," the man said, mouthing the words while pointing to his headset.

"Oh," Brad whispered in reply, holding up one hand in both acknowledgement and apology. "He's on the phone," Brad relayed to Chip, although, being stood right next to him, Chip was very likely already aware of this fact.

"Can I help you?" the receptionist added a few moments later, though it wasn't delivered in a manner suggesting that he did, actually, want to render assistance. "Hello?" he said, no more than a half-second later, waiting impatiently, his time clearly more important than theirs.

For their part, Brad and Chip were distracted by their present environment, looking around in wonderment, smiling politely, happy to be there in the first place. A dream fulfilled to be even invited to such a prestigious place.

"*Hello.* Yes, can I help you?"

Brad gradually brought his eyes back around to the reception desk, finding the fellow there staring directly at him. "Oh," said Brad. "You mean me?" he asked, pointing to himself. "Sorry about that. I thought you were still on—"

"NBC Boston, Clifford Tanner's office," said the receptionist, pressing a flashing button on his phone. "Certainly, sir," he said. "Putting you through to public relations," he added, before hitting another button to do just that. "Alright, you've probably got about ten seconds, at the most, before another call comes in," the receptionist suggested, looking to Brad once again. "So, you know," he said pointedly.

"Thanks," Brad said, now that it was evident he was being spoken to, or, as was the case, at. "Um, Brad and Chip Freestone to see Mr Tanner, please."

The receptionist nodded, and was about to reach out to press another button on his phone when his eyes narrowed like he'd just noticed the two of them for the very first time, as in really actually noticed them. He looked back and forth between the pair, staring without blinking, in what appeared to be either suspicion or confusion, or maybe a combination of both.

"We're twins," Brad explained, recognising the look he was being given, as it was something that often happened when he and his brother were standing side by side. "Two peas in a pod, like my mother always used to say," he offered with a smile. "In fact, she also—"

"Fine," said the receptionist, satisfied enough with Brad's answer, not returning Brad's smile, and nor, it would seem, interested in what other endearing expressions Brad and Chip's mother might have used to describe them. "I'll let Mr Tanner and the team know you're here. Take a seat on the leather couch over there, and his personal assistant will invite you in when they're ready for you," the man said curtly.

"Okay, thanks," Brad said. "And by the way, I just wanted to say how very thrilled we are to—"

"Yes, NBC Boston, Clifford Tanner's office, how may I direct your call," the receptionist recited into his headset, swivelling around in his chair just a tad, but enough to clearly declare that his conversation with Brad had concluded and he'd moved on to other matters.

"Oh," Brad said. "So, we'll just..."

"I guess he's finished with us," Chip suggested, giving his brother a wry smile as they turned to make their way to the waiting area. "Oh, and Brad. Just so we're on the same page here. Was that the 'outstanding first impression' you mentioned earlier? Just so I can file it away for future reference."

"Hardy har-har, very funny," Brad answered, rolling his eyes. "But yeah, look, things can only get better from here on in, right?" Brad added, turning slightly more serious again, and trying his best to sound optimistic as they headed towards the couch in the seating area as instructed. Nothing was going to dampen his spirits on this special day, no siree Bob. "Wait, did you hear that?" Brad said suddenly, his bum hovering an inch or two above the sumptuous leather, his dress trousers not yet making contact with it. He held this awkward squatting position for a moment as he directed his attention to the imposing mahogany door, identified as the boardroom by the shimmering brass plaque affixed to it.

"Hear what?" Chip asked.

"I could've sworn I heard somebody screaming behind that big door..." Brad offered, angling his ear, still squatting, positioned there like he was just about to attend to some business on the porcelain throne. He listened intently for several seconds, tightly closing one eye, like this would somehow improve his hearing acuity or aid his concentration. "Naw, I guess I don't hear it anymore," he said with a shrug, before finally sinking his bottom down onto the soft, welcoming leather of the couch.

But just then, the large door flew open, scaring the bejesus out of Brad and Chip in the process. "They'll eat you alive!" a certain agitated man emerging with a horrified expression declared, stumbling into a nearby water dispenser as he rushed out of the room. "Watch where you're going, for the love of God!" he said, angrily rebuking the water dispenser as he continued along, as if it was somehow the water cooler's fault for allowing itself to be bumped into.

"Is he crying?" Chip asked, watching the distraught fellow hurry across the floor of the office. And yet despite the man's obvious distress, not one person looked over from their desks, suggesting this emotional outburst was commonplace and just another business-as-usual moment in their working day. Even as the poor man started slapping the lift call button frantically and repeatedly, wailing loudly in despair as he did so, did it fail to evoke any reaction.

"Sobbing, I think, yeah," Brad agreed. But they didn't have much time to dwell on the poor unfortunate soul in any case, as the man was soon on his way, cradling his face in his hands as he disappeared into the lift.

"Brad and Chuck Freestone?" said a sharply dressed woman, appearing from the boardroom not too long after, eyes down on her notebook. "Good afternoon, gentlemen. I'm Clara," she said, looking up at them now with the assumption that they were indeed who she thought they were.

"It's Chip, actually," Chip said in response, rising to his feet and offering out his hand as Clara approached.

"Hmm? What is?" Clara asked, looking straight at him but not seeming all that interested, and either ignoring or choosing not to accept his handshake.

"My name. Sorry, it's Chip, not Chuck like you said," Chip explained, reholstering his hand by placing it back into his pocket when leaving it hovering in the air unattended started to get a bit awkward.

"Alright, then," said Clara, using her pen to score through her notes accordingly, with no apology given, nor any apology even considered judging by the speed she then moved the conversation along. "So..." she continued, now addressing the both of them, and speaking slowly and deliberately like a teacher giving instruction to her class. "So you've got ten minutes to make your pitch. Please don't go a minute over, or they *will* cut you off. We have back-to-back proposals today, and they've already been at it for five hours, so if they come across as a little abrupt, please don't take it too personally like our last appointment did." Clara turned her back, stepping towards the boardroom. "Walk this way," she said.

"If I could walk that way..." Chip mumbled under his breath, chuckling to himself.

Brad chuckled as well, but quietly shushed his brother lest their kind host overhear and take offence. "Can I ask who we're pitching to?" Brad quickly asked to Clara, catching up behind her.

"Everyone," Clara whispered over her shoulder, holding the door ajar. "The entire team is sitting around the boardroom table. Try not to be too nervous, since there are quite a few of them, and some people can find this somewhat intimidating," she told them, being a little more helpful now. "Be clear, be concise, and above all, convince them why they simply *must* commission your new series," she offered with a wink. "I received your PowerPoint presentation via email, so that's already displayed for you up on the screen. You just need to indicate to me when you want to move between the slides, and I'll take care of that for you. Ready?"

"Ready," the two brothers replied in unison.

"Gentlemen and ladies," Clara intoned with authority, fully opening the door now and addressing those inside. "Next up, we have Brad and... Chip Freestone," she announced, stepping to one side and ushering the pair in.

Brad and Chip immediately appreciated why some people might find this environment intimidating. Several acres of rainforest must have been sacrificed to create the enormous hardwood table, for instance, and adding to their sense of panic was the vast array of faces positioned around it, staring over at them expectantly.

"Good morning. Or, um, afternoon, as the case may be," Chip offered weakly, his voice breaking under strain, unzipping the black leather folder that'd been tucked under his arm. "We've brought along printed-out copies of our presentation," he told them, pulling out a stack of collated pages even though the same presentation was presently displayed on a very large TV monitor, large enough, in fact, that it wouldn't have seemed at all out of place in Times Square. "I hope I have enough," Chip remarked, glancing around the table. "Would anybody like a copy?" he asked, running his eyes around the table again, his stack of presentations readied for distribution. "No...?" he asked, after a long pause in which there seemed to be no takers. "Okay, no problem, I guess," Chip concluded with a shrug, placing the unrequested presentations back inside the leather folder.

"Jumpin' Jehoshaphat!" yelled the man at the head of the table as he suddenly looked up for the first time at them, reaching for his glasses as he did so. "Am I seeing double, or are there two identical-looking blond-haired gentlemen standing there? Am I possibly having a stroke, or do I need new glasses?" he joked, putting his glasses on, taking them off and examining them for a moment, and then placing them back onto his face again.

"We're twins, Mr Tanner," Brad was happy to explain, once more now, instantly recognising the Oscar-winning producer Clifford Tanner and calling him by name.

"Cancel the ambulance, Clara. Looks like I'm not having a stroke after all," Clifford said, taking a mouthful of coffee from his cup, pulling his glasses off, and then running his hand across his forehead in relief. "For a moment there, I thought maybe scientists had finally perfected human cloning or something," he mused aloud. "Jenkins, have scientists finally perfected human cloning yet?" he asked, glancing around the table. No one answered, however, as the question was largely rhetorical, and plus there wasn't anyone there named Jenkins anyway. Mr Tanner just liked to occasionally pose questions to a Jenkins, because he felt that there really *ought* to be someone named Jenkins there at the boardroom table.

"Well, then. Let's hear what you've got for us, boys!" Clifford Tanner said amiably, leaning back in his chair and moving the proceedings along.

"Yes, sir. Thank you," Brad answered, encouraged by their host's unexpected friendliness (considering the way the last person visiting the room had exited), and turning to face the colossal screen hanging on the wall at the far end of the room. He cleared his throat before commencing with his polished pitch. "The image on this first slide is my brother and I climbing the Matterhorn," he said. "That was seven years ago, on my twenty-first birthday. Well, *our* twenty-first birthday, I should say, since we're twins. Anyway, as well as being accomplished mountaineers, we're also adventure documentary filmmakers with eleven productions so far to our credit."

"That's right, Brad," Chip jumped in, his turn to speak in their well-rehearsed routine. "And for our next project, we're teaming up with three individuals hungry for adventure. And not just *any* adventure..."

"You're not wrong there, Chip," Brad said, taking up the reins like a seasoned double act. "And the adventure doesn't come any more prominent than mankind's toughest challenge... Mount Everest."

Brad paused, waiting for the audible gasp that was certain to come their way. Any second now. Yup, right about...

"Is this guy pulling my leg, or what?" Clifford Tanner asked, throwing his colleagues a look. "You're the third person in here today pitching to us about Everest," he said to Brad with a weary sigh, rubbing the bridge of his nose with thumb and forefinger. "What's this sudden obsession with Everest everyone's got?" he asked, shaking his head sadly. "It's been climbed more than once, you know."

"You're *absolutely* right," Brad said with a gulp, sensing he was losing the room before he'd really managed to get into his stride. "The thing is..." he pressed on, looking to Chip, who appeared very much like a deer caught in the headlights of a large oncoming vehicle. "Well, Mr Tanner," Brad continued, fumbling with the knot on his tie, buying himself some thinking time. "Ours isn't *just* a trek up Everest," he suggested, raising his finger in the air to emphasise the point.

"It isn't?" Clifford said, perking up slightly, and then motioning with his hand to invite further explanation.

"No, sir," Brad said, shaking his head. "You see, our three colleagues..." he went on, pausing momentarily. "Well, what makes our project unique is that our three colleagues only have one leg."

"Oh?" said Mr Tanner, tilting his head to one side.

"Uh, I mean they *each* have one leg," Brad clarified. "I don't mean they have only one leg among the three of them."

Clifford rested his arms down on the table, absently twirling his pen around like a spinning top. "You know what the only thing worse than watching someone climb a mountain through a snowstorm is, boys?" he asked, in a tone suggesting he already had the answer lined up.

"Um... no, sir," Brad replied with a nervous laugh. "Maybe... stepping on a piece of Lego in the middle of the night on your way to answer nature's call?" he offered, hoping for a laugh.

"No," said Mr Tanner. "No, actually, the only thing worse than watching someone *climb* a mountain would be watching three people *hopping* up a mountain."

"Oh," Brad said simply, lowering his head and hoping for a hole to open up on the floor that he could possibly dive into.

"What else have you got for us?" asked Mr Tanner, glancing at his watch, the pen still spinning under its own momentum.

"Well..." Chip entered in, much to the immediate relief of his brother. "Well, we were approached by four adventurous nuns," Chip offered with a sunny smile.

"Nuns?" Mr Tanner repeated, steepling his hands together as if he were praying. "As in *nuns*, nuns?"

"That's right," Chip answered. "They approached us and said they're planning on walking across the, um... yeah, across the, uh, Atacama Desert in Chile, I think they said."

"Nuns walking across the Atacama Desert in Chile," Clifford repeated back. "This is your pitch for a documentary series? Just so I'm sure I've got this right?"

"Yes, sir," Chip said, heartened by the perceived interest coming his way. "The kicker is..." he continued, building up to his big reveal. "The kicker is, they're planning to complete the trek with no shoes on," he said, appearing to take inspiration from his brother's Lego remark.

In response, Brad placed his face in his hands, offering up a groan, as he imagined it must be painfully obvious that they were just making things up by this point. "Should we just go?" he asked through splayed fingers.

"Probably for the best," the lady sat nearest to them answered on behalf of the room, offering a sympathetic smile. "At least while it's still your choice."

The brothers could now appreciate why the unfortunate soul from earlier had left the boardroom sobbing, though at least their own demise was largely of their own making. "One-legged mountaineers?" Chip scoffed once they were outside the room, making no attempt to hide the disdain written all over his face. "Since when did our pitch involve one-legged mountaineers?"

"I had to think fast," Brad suggested. "I could sense I was losing the room and needed to up the ante. Anyway, four shoeless nuns walking across some freaking sand dunes in Ecuador or something? Where the heck did that nonsense even come from?"

"Across the *Atacama Desert in Chile*," Chip corrected him, disappointed his brother wasn't appreciating his cleverness for having come up with that on the spot.

"Whatever," Brad answered, loosening and then removing his tie. "Come on, I need something strong to drink," he said, letting out a deep sigh.

Brad walked forward, past the water dispenser the fellow before them had bumped into, and on towards the reception desk. "Shoeless nuns," he muttered. "One chance we had, and we go and..." he said, trailing off when it suddenly became apparent he was now walking alone. Brad turned on his heels, spotting his brother back by the leather couch, for some reason lingering there. "What are you doing? C'mon, let's go," Brad called over. "Chip...?"

"We've only got this one chance. You said it yourself, Brad," Chip answered with a determined smile, a smile that belied the fact that they'd just made prize turkeys of themselves in front of NBC Boston's senior management team.

"Okay," Brad said, after heading back over to his brother. "So? Have you got something in mind?"

"So," Chip replied. "Follow me."

Chip spun around, and then walked over and threw open the boardroom door without looking back. "It's only us again," he said once inside, offering a cheerful wave to the collection of startled, now-familiar faces.

"Do I need to call security?" asked one of the nearby board members, reaching for his phone.

"What? Oh, no, we're not crazy or anything, I promise," Chip answered. He stepped up to the boardroom table, glancing around the room for the particular person he was looking for. "Ah," he said, upon finding Clara frowning back at him. "Is that big-screen monitor of yours connected to the internet?"

"Of course, but..."

"May I?" Chip asked.

Clara glanced over to Mr Tanner, unsure if her boss had already seen quite enough of these two characters or if he perhaps wanted to hear more. She received a raised eyebrow and a slight shrug in response, taking this as a green light to accommodate Chip's unusual request.

"Follow me," Clara said, getting up and leading Chip over to where the various controls could be had for what showed up on the large, wall-mounted screen.

"You know, you two have got some real major cojones for coming back in here after that previous trainwreck of a presentation you just gave," Mr Tanner called over, as he waited for Chip to do whatever it was that Chip was about to do. "I like that," he added with a laugh.

"Things can only get better, Mr Tanner," Brad suggested, grinning nervously, as intrigued to see where this was going as the rest of the room.

"Okay, here we go," Chip said, loading YouTube up on the screen. "We appreciate your indulgence," he offered, talking while typing. "What I'm about to show you is an event that's a huge deal across the Atlantic, really very widely appreciated over there, but not so well-known at all over here in the United States, unfortunately. When we were travelling in Europe, we had the great fortune of catching this thing first-hand when we passed through the British Isles. It's the quickest, craziest, most unbelievable sporting challenge you'll ever, ever hope to see." Chip then shifted his attention up to the screen, locating the exact video he was looking for. "Ladies and gentlemen..." he announced, clicking the mouse button. "This is Guy Martin running through a lap of the Isle of Man TT course with an HD camera attached to the front of his racing motorcycle."

"Holy shit!" exclaimed more than one viewer present in the room when the sound of a race-tuned engine erupted through the expensive speaker system, nearly shaking the large screen loose from its anchor fittings.

Chip had enjoyed the video dozens of times previously and looked on carefully as those sitting around the table watched it as well, hoping for the same amazed reaction he'd had when viewing it for the very first time.

"That's got to be a computer game," came one sceptical voice in response to the motorcycle onscreen hurtling down the island's Bray Hill at warp speed, the faces of the watching crowds blending together in a blur.

"There *are* two video games featuring the race, actually, if I recall," Chip said in answer. "But this video here, what you're watching right now, is totally real," he promised.

"But surely this footage has been sped up for effect?" added another incredulous voice. "He can't possibly be moving that fast, can he? I mean..." the person went on, but then trailing away, watching as Guy appeared to wobble under braking on the approach to the Quarterbridge roundabout at the bottom of the hill and then shoot off like a rocket again up Peel Road.

Chip glanced over to his brother, receiving a furtive thumbs-up in response. He didn't want to be too optimistic, but the fact that every set of eyes in the room — including Clifford Tanner's — were presently glued to the screen, some with mouths wide open, he hoped was a positive sign. Chip couldn't resist a smirk, noting several men in suits leaning over each time Guy's bike negotiated the next treacherous corner onscreen.

Conscious that the ten-minute mark — pitch limit — was rapidly approaching, Chip raised one hand, indicating he wished to pose a question. "Should I?" he said, his other hand holding onto the mouse and hovering the cursor over the pause button.

"Stop? Hell, no!" Mr Tanner answered, quickly waving the suggestion away, eyes in danger of drying out such was his intense concentration on the action unfolding before him.

With Guy approaching the town of Ramsey's Parliament Square at speed, a slower rider appeared into shot just ahead, resulting in an audible gasp in the room as Guy safely nipped through on the inside. Once through the right-hander at the Square, snaking under the force of braking, the throttle opened back up again, sending him on his way through Ramsey on his ascent towards the area of the circuit known as the Mountain section of this most challenging and spectacular course.

Chip's optimism was dealt a further boost as the captivated group watched the lap in its entirety. Indeed, there was even a collective round of applause as Guy crossed the start/finish line back on Glencrutchery Road, before he slowed to head up the return lane towards the pit area. Chip allowed the video clip to continue even though the lap itself was complete. "You'll see Guy himself in just a second," he explained. "Or in just a tick, as I think they might say over there."

Guy Martin drew up outside his awning — an impressive canvas structure which served as his team's headquarters — removing his helmet just as a microphone was thrust under his chin. For several minutes or more Guy prattled on, talking about his lap but digressing into bizarre, unrelated topics (in his own inimitable fashion, as he so often did) multiple times during the course of the interview.

"I haven't got the faintest clue what that Martin guy was talking about at the end, but I like him," Mr Tanner announced enthusiastically once the clip had finished, and then rising up from his chair to stretch himself off.

"Yeah, that's Guy Martin for you. He always talks that way, from what I hear," Chip said with a laugh, emerging from his position behind the controls.

"He's got magnificent hair," one of the female board members remarked admiringly.

"He certainly does," one of her male colleagues promptly agreed, rounding out the unofficial Guy Martin Admiration Society to include members of both sexes, all-inclusively.

"And you're completely certain that footage wasn't sped up for effect?" asked Mr Tanner, referencing the same question that was posed earlier.

"No, sir," Chip confirmed once again, shaking his head. "In fact," he added, pointing over to the screen, "that lap I just showed you was from a *practice* session. So, on a race day, they go even *faster* than that, believe it or not. Trust me, we've had the pleasure of watching the race right up close and personal, and it's pretty amazing."

Mr Tanner walked up to Chip, waving Brad over as well. "You were just toying with us before, right?" he asked them confidentially, placing a hand on each of their shoulders and pulling them in close. "You can tell me," Clifford said, pursing his lips, and looking at each of them in turn. "When you two were throwing that bullshit around about one-legged nuns climbing Mount Everest or whatever, you were just yanking my chain, am I right?"

Chip started laughing. "Yeah. Yeah, of course," he answered, nodding along as he spoke. "We were *totally* just yanking your chain. Absolutely," he said, while also graciously ignoring the fact that Mr Tanner was mixing their respective pitches up.

"Purely as a warm-up," Brad entered in, taking his brother's lead and picking up where Chip left off. "You know, to break the ice. Before we told you our *real* pitch."

"Before we told you the real one," Chip agreed.

"So what exactly *is* this pitch of yours, gentlemen?" Clifford asked, releasing his grip and taking a step back, ready to hear what the two of them had to offer. "So far I like what I've seen. So lay it on me."

"Well, sir," Chip began. "Well, sir, what you've just watched..." he continued, now speaking up so that everyone in the room could easily hear as well, "is the Isle of Man TT, one of the most spectacular motorsport events on the face of the earth. And what makes it unique, among other things, is that the course is just an ordinary set of roads, used by regular traffic right up until about an hour or two before the race when they're closed off in preparation for letting the riders do their thing."

"Mm-hm. Interesting. Go on," said Mr Tanner, urging Chip to continue.

"Well, when we were over there, we both talked about how great a documentary about the race would be. You see, many of the folks racing prepare their own machines, funding most of the expense themselves. In fact, some of the racers invest *years* of their lives just to be able to get to the starting line of this thing," Chip explained. "So in other words, I'm pretty sure there's a great human-interest angle here, I would think."

"Mm-hm, mm-hm. Yes. Go on," Clifford agreed, motioning for Chip to carry on.

"Well, as I said, the race isn't very well-known over here. But, as I see it, that's actually a *good* thing, a positive rather than a negative, because we'd be introducing something totally new to a U.S. audience, something most of them have never ever seen before. And you saw the reaction just in this room alone, right? So now imagine how big this could be if a documentary TV series was made and we brought this really, really cool event to the broader attention of our great American viewers?"

Clifford Tanner certainly seemed intrigued, swallowing the premise of the pitch hook, line, and sinker. Brad was going to enter in again and say something, but then decided to just let his brother keep on talking since he seemed to be doing such an effective job of it.

All of Chip's earlier nervousness was definitely gone now. "And we were thinking of calling it..." he added, clearly enjoying himself, and purposely pausing here for a moment or two for proper dramatic effect. And in fact all eyes were upon him, waiting for him to reveal the name. *"Isle of Man TT Aces,"* Chip declared proudly, savouring the moment. "It's like Isle of Man TT Races, you see, but without the R," he explained to them, lest the sheer brilliance of the name should escape anyone's notice. "You know. Aces," he said, after receiving several blank looks. "As in, experts? So, Isle of Man TT *Aces*." The blank stares then turned to nods of understanding and approval, and with one of those nods of approval coming from Clifford Tanner himself.

"Six one-hour episodes?" Mr Tanner suggested, looking to his colleagues around the room for concurrence.

"Sure, sounds good," Chip said, rather excitedly, in perfect agreement and finding this entirely acceptable.

"Can we get this Martin guy as our lead focus?" Clifford asked.

"Guy Martin?" said Chip, considering the request.

"Right. This Martin guy," Mr Tanner replied.

It suddenly occurred to Chip that Mr Tanner was perhaps a little confused by Guy Martin's name, with him apparently not quite understanding that *Guy* was Martin's first name. Chip didn't dare correct him. That wasn't the only problem, though. "Uh, thing is..." Chip hesitated to say, not wishing to dampen the flames of enthusiasm at this critical juncture. "The thing is, Mr Tanner, I'm pretty sure Martin's already retired at this point. So I'm not sure that'd really work. We might really want someone who's actually, like, actively, currently participating in the races..."

"Oh," Clifford answered, shoulders dropping. "That's a real shame. I loved the sideburns," he said. "Great for the camera."

"Yeah, I agree," said Brad, finally entering back into the conversation again. "But with your kind indulgence, I'm sure we can find someone equally as charismatic, or close to it. Someone the audience can invest in, someone they'll care about. They'll be with them every step of the way, on every twist and turn of their journey and of the race itself." Brad paused, running his hand through the air, allowing those seated around the table to visualise it for themselves. "The viewers will be so engrossed that it'll be just like they're sitting on the back of that motorcycle themselves."

"Yes!" Clifford said. "I love it! So have you got anybody else in mind for our main guy?"

"Um..." Brad answered, not really having had the opportunity to think this far in advance.

"We've got a shortlist, sir," Chip offered confidently, coming to his brother's rescue.

"Yes! Let's do this thing!" Clifford said. "We're going to make this happen!" he said, slapping his hands together in delight. "Oh, and boys? Just one thing..." he added.

"Sure. Anything," Brad said.

"We need our lead racer fella to be dynamic, yes? Someone the viewers are going to absolutely love. Someone they're going to get absolutely hooked on. Women will want to have sex with him, and men will want to *be* him, if you get what I'm saying. Assuming you opt for a male racer, of course."

"Excellent, Mr Tanner, sir," Brad replied, removing a small notepad from inside his suit jacket pocket and diligently jotting down the following: *Find someone with raw animal magnetism and definite sex appeal.*

"Don't worry, sir, we'll find the perfect candidate for our series," Chip assured their new boss. "I can see him now," Chip added, eyes drifting away, picturing the person in his mind. "Overflowing with charm. Dashing, rugged good looks..."

"And funny," Clifford suggested.

"And funny, yes," Chip answered. "Basically, Mr Tanner, we need to find the Hugh Jackman of the Isle of Man TT races.

"Right, right! Exactly! A huge, jacked man!" Mr Tanner happily agreed. "Big muscles! Absolutely jacked!" he added.

"Don't worry, sir. We'll find him," Chip answered.

"We're on the case, sir," Brad chimed in.

Chapter
TWO

Spare time was a commodity Dave Quirk didn't generally enjoy much of these days, what with him now promoted to positions of executive management. The stresses from being at the operational helm of both the TT Farm and Jurby Raceway might have placed an impossible burden on a lesser man, but not Dave. No, he was taking his new responsibilities entirely in his stride, remaining unflappable, and being ably assisted, of course, by his trusted wingman Monty (although if you'd asked Monty, Monty would've probably described Dave as *his* wingman rather than the other way around).

Still, being this busy, when the opportunity arose to relieve some of the executive pressures with a rare afternoon to himself, Dave was eager to avail himself of it and allow his management batteries a chance to recharge, leaving his trusted wingman to stay the course in his absence. Although it wouldn't be easy to relax, necessarily. With balance sheets, profit and loss statements, and complex business strategy constantly in the back of his mind, Dave was a man who could rarely be classed as ever being officially off-duty at any given time.

"Has someone fallen down the well again, Lassie?" Dave asked, deep in slumber on his couch, slobber pooling on his unshaven chin. "I'm coming, boy," Dave confirmed with a twitching right leg. However, Dave would never get to find out who had fallen down the well this day, sadly, due to his mobile phone vibrating on the nearby coffee table, rousing him from the land of Nod. "What the...?" he muttered, peeling one eye open, wondering what had woken him and taken him away from he and his canine pal's grand adventures.

Rubbing the sleepybugs away, Dave was impressed to find his empty pre-snooze Pot Noodle still resting upright on his belly, rising and falling like a ship on the tide with each breath. Unfortunately, the cord on his SuperTed dressing gown had worked its way loose during his nap, resulting in the left flap hanging down, leaving half his naked torso exposed and chilled. "Hang on, hang on," Dave said as his head cleared and he came to the realisation the strange noise he was hearing that sounded suspiciously like his phone ringing... was in fact the sound of his phone ringing. He swung his legs around, pushing himself upright and slapping his Pot Noodle down on the table before reaching for his phone.

"Dave Quirk, International Love Doctor. How may I service you?" he answered cheerily, phone pressed to his ear, stretching his free arm high above his head with a stifled yawn. "Yes, this is he. Sorry," Dave said, upon realising this was a business call. "How can I help you?" he asked. He ran his hand through his erratic bed hair that was long overdue a trim, and then took to his feet, listening intently. He always liked to pace when engaged on any type of business-related call. Pacing focussed his mind, rendering him much better able to make critical decisions at a moment's notice. At least that's what he'd often suggest to Monty when found wandering about, be it with phone in hand or otherwise. The truth was, he'd once heard someone very famous offering the same advice about pacing around when formulating strategy. Bill Gates, perhaps, though Dave wasn't entirely sure. Whoever it was, though, they were extremely, ridiculously rich, so who was Dave to argue with the wisdom of their words.

"Okay," Dave said as he listened on, letting the caller know he was still on the other end as he walked over to his living room window, eager to see what the weather was currently doing this fine Tuesday afternoon, and then glancing up and down the street outside. "Uh-huh. Yup," Dave added as the person spoke, letting the caller do most of the talking. "Ah. So you found my phone number on my *website*, did you?" he entered in, with a half-laugh. Dave rolled his eyes sceptically, suspicious now as to the caller's credibility. He held the phone away from his ear for a moment, appearing as if he were about to drop-kick it across the room, even. However, the voice on the other end rattled on, relentless, barely allowing Dave the opportunity to say much else.

Dave's attention drifted, with him now looking skyward as he checked for any signs of rainclouds outside, worried about the paving slabs they'd laid at the TT Farm that morning for their new BBQ area. He needn't have been concerned, however, as the lovely blue stuff stretched as far as the eye could see and without a cloud in sight.

Mrs Timpson, Dave's long-suffering neighbour, was out enjoying her afternoon walk, leisurely wandering up the pavement with her chihuahua, Frodo, glued to her side as usual. It's fair to say that Dave hadn't been the model neighbour to her over the years, what with late-night parties, drunk Monty snoring on his modest lawn, defiled garden gnomes and empty beer cans and whatnot strewn about. But Dave was eager to rectify his bad-boy image. After all, he'd done a lot of growing up lately, had a steady girlfriend, and was now a respected businessman. As a peace offering, Dave and Monty had even been around recently to offer Mrs Timpson their assistance in mowing her lawn and cleaning her windows. Yes, it may have been true that she'd told them both firmly to sod off in response, but at least the communication lines were now open, more or less, which was something to build upon, Dave hoped.

Dave tapped his finger on the window, waving when Mrs Timpson turned to see what was causing the noise. He offered up a smile so large it was in danger of breaking his face, accompanying this with another friendly wave. "Afternoon," he said, mouthing the words for her benefit through the glass.

Despite his double-glazing and the sound of the energetic voice on the phone prattling away in his ear, there was no mistaking the vocal reply offered by Mrs Timpson outside. "You dirty get!" she shouted, loudly enough to wake the dead. She tugged on Frodo's lead, doubling her pace, and could be seen shaking her head gravely as she hurried away.

Dave grinned simply in response as he watched her go. She was, after all, often animated at times. Part of her natural charm, Dave supposed. "Aww, bollocks," Dave then said, feeling a draft around and about his gentleman's area. He looked down, confirming his fears, realising this to be the very probable reason for the lively reaction on Mrs Timpson's part.

"Are you just about finished, dipshit?" Dave barked down the phone, taking his frustration out on the caller, and not being entirely happy with the caller in the first place anyway. He pulled his SuperTed dressing gown flaps together, concealing what poor Mrs Timpson had just witnessed, showcased there in his front window like a rent boy promoting his merchandise for sale. "So, if I've understood correctly..." Dave went on, phone tucked between his shoulder and ear, thus freeing his hands to secure the cord on his dressing gown. "Right. So if I've understood correctly, you've found my phone number on a website I *don't even have*, and you want to pay me *thousands of pounds* to follow me around with a camera and make me famous? Is that what you're telling me? Just so there's no misunderstanding on my end."

Dave took the phone in his hand again, nodding along as the voice on the other end kicked into overdrive once more. "Seriously?" Dave said, voice raised, cutting across what he was listening to. "Do you think my head buttons up at the back? And what's with that bloody stupid accent, anyway? What even *is* that, Canadian or something?"

Dave listened to the response, appearing to be on the cusp of bringing this conversation to a swift conclusion. "Well, it doesn't *sound* American," Dave suggested, being quite the authority on the subject despite having never visited the country. "Hold up, is that bloody you, Monty?" Dave then said, slapping his hand against his forehead in a eureka moment. "I *know* that's you, Monty. Doing that stupid, rubbish Ray Donovan accent of yours. Well, you've ruined a pleasant afternoon, Monty, I won't lie. I was just having a lovely nap in between watching classic Baywatch episodes, and now you've gone and spoiled it for me. If that's what you'd hoped to achieve, then mission accomplished, my friend. Is this little charade all because I stuffed a live mackerel into your sleeping bag when we went camping recently?"

The voice on the other end fell silent, only adding weight, in his mind, as to Dave's suspicions about the caller's identity. "Ah, got you there, Monty. Not so clever now, are you?" Dave went on, but it was more likely the caller had simply dialled off by now, weary at listening to the ramblings of a madman. "Yeah..." Dave added, for no real reason at this point. "Yeah, well anyway, lifeguard Mitch Buchannon is just about to rescue a seal or something, so..." Dave concluded, mashing his phone's keypad with his paw, terminating the call.

"Bloody Monty," Dave said with a chuckle. "I'll get you for this. You see if I don't."

For many, the thought of hauling your sorry carcass to work every morning was, at best, a struggle. That unshakable, Sunday-night feeling of dread, knowing you'd have to get up and do the same thing all over again, counting down the days until the blessed relief of Friday afternoon gratefully presented itself.

Indeed, there were periods in Dave's own illustrious career where he felt precisely like that, forcing himself through the drudgery in return for a paltry paycheque that disappeared quicker than the will to live. And it was for this very reason that Dave now grinned each time he drove past the Railway Inn pub in Union Mills, as it meant — more often than not — that he was on his way to work at the TT Farm, the most splendid of all places. Or, if he was sat atop his sidecar at this iconic spot on the TT course, it would mean he was racing. And both those options were, of course, most palatable to Dave.

Granted, the salary from his new position wasn't up there with Gordon Gekko's, but that simply didn't matter to Dave. So long as he had a few more quid than he could spend each week, he was perfectly happy. He'd even managed to scrape enough dosh together to purchase a new car for himself: a lime-green Honda Civic Type R, sporting an exhaust pipe like a chimney pot. Young Tyler, his girlfriend Becks' son, adored going out for a drive in it as you could hear them coming from at least a mile away. With the retina-melting lime green paintwork, you could also see them coming from at least two!

Being on the management team of both the TT Farm and the Jurby racetrack was hard work but, ultimately, a complete joy. For Dave, it simply didn't feel like he was going to work. He was outside in the glorious Manx countryside for most of the day, spending time with his mates and getting paid for the privilege. Every morning when the TT Farm came into view, he smiled. It didn't matter how many people may have pissed him off on the short commute because everything was forgotten the moment he slowed the car, turning into the gravel carpark with a cheesy grin all over his chubby chops.

The first phase of the ongoing farm refurbishments was also coming along quite nicely. The guest accommodations were nearly all fitted out and equipped, meaning the charity could soon extend its reach further, providing a warm, comfortable, and safe environment when it was needed the most. For some of those guests, it would offer a temporary situation for a week or two. For others, the TT Farm would remain their home until a more permanent solution could be found, providing a sanctuary from whatever challenges they faced in their previous life. Just like Becks and Tyler.

The vision of a bustling rural education centre was also coming to fruition. Several talented volunteers created a curriculum of classes using the newly completed barn conversion. Farm skills, traditional crafting, ironmongery, and signwriting were among the plethora of courses available to the Manx public eager to avail themselves of this exciting new resource at their disposal. As such, Dave and Monty were now experienced in the art of coopering, amongst other things, and had the confidence and ability to reshoe a horse should the requirement present itself.

This rural hive of activity coupled with a menagerie of animals who also called this place home resulted in a vibrant community hub situated in the heart of the Manx countryside.

As an added bonus, Dave and Monty's roles were relatively flexible, flexible in that it didn't matter quite when their work was completed so long as it was. This meant that they could juggle their hours, giving them the time to prepare their big blue boiled sweet ahead of the upcoming TT races, which would be here before they knew it. It also didn't hurt that they also had two understanding bosses in Frank and Stan, who were equally passionate about Dave and Monty's racing ambitions. Indeed, Frank and Stan offered to step in and cover their duties whenever the boys needed to travel off-island for qualifying race meetings and such. However, that usually didn't go quite to plan, as Frank and Stan would often end up joining them, desperate to coat their nostrils with the smell of burnt Castrol in the air and savour the sweet sound of horsepower shaking loose their fillings.

Yes, life was good, and Dave had the pleasure of calling this place work. It really didn't get much better, Dave thought.

"Morning, handsome!" Monty called out from his elevated position perched up a wobbling ladder in the courtyard, with little regard for health and safety, apparently. "The airport just phoned for you, Dave!" Monty added cheerfully, watching on as his friend advanced.

"Oh they did, did they?" Dave replied in a tone dripping with sarcasm and scepticism.

"Yeah," Monty said, stifling a laugh. "They asked if you could dial down the brightness on your new car," he said, pointing skyward. "Only they've had a few pilots complain about being dazzled."

"You do know I could kick that ladder away from under you and make it look like an accident, right?" Dave said, swinging his foot through the air to illustrate. "Anyway, what exactly are you doing up there?"

"Frank texted over a reminder of the to-do list he'd left us," Monty explained. "I was surprised to hear from him, you know, what with him being on his honeymoon and everything, where he probably has his own to-do list to administer, if you take my meaning," he added. "Yes, *very* surprised," Monty reiterated, after receiving no reply. "Very surprised indeed, Dave, what with it being his honeymoon and all... Are you listening, Dave? I said I was so surprised to hear from him because I thought he'd have more *important* things to attend to. Other matters on his mind. Matters requiring *vigorous attention* and at *regular intervals*. Several times daily, I'd reckon. What with him being on his *honeymoon*, Dave... Dave? Dave. What do you think, Dave? ... Dave?"

"I'm not listening to a single word of your bawdy locker-room banter, Monty!" Dave insisted, although he clearly *had* heard every word, shuddering as he was at the prospect of what matters Frank might be attending to with his new wife, a wife that also just so happened to be Dave's dear old mum.

Monty sighed merrily, pleased at his delivery of the razor-sharp, humorous repartee he'd been preparing and waiting for the opportunity to serve up ever since he'd awoken that morning. "Anyway," he said, returning his attention to the job at hand. "First up was to take a look at the gutters, because the other..." he started to explain, but trailing off. "Hang on, what's that smell?" Monty asked, in appreciation of the wonderful fragrance that had suddenly made its way up and introduced itself to his now-flaring nostrils.

"What's *what* smell?" Dave teased, knowing full well what Monty was referring to.

"You've got something behind your back," Monty suggested, glancing down. "And..." he added, moving his head in a circular motion, sniffing the air furiously. "And if I'm not mistaken..."

he went on, tasting the air, smacking his lips together. "If I'm not mistaken, that's a McDonald's breakfast!" he ventured, his scent-based investigation now complete. But then his joy quickly washed away. "You haven't been to McDonald's without me?" Monty pleaded, pressing out his lower lip like a sulking schoolgirl. "We both agreed that would never happen, Dave. We even made a pinkie promise, Dave. A *pinkie* promise."

Fearing Monty was close to jumping from a great height, such was his pain, Dave opted to put him out of his misery. "Would I forget about you?" Dave asked, revealing the characteristic brown paper bag with red lettering and golden arches printed on it that he'd been concealing behind his back. "Yes, I did go. But I've brought along some for you as well, haven't I?"

"I bloody love you, Dave Quirk," Monty declared, leaning back, and then sliding down both sides of the ladder on the instep of his feet with the grace of a career submariner.

"Monty, that was impressive," said Dave, looking his friend up and down, checking for injury or signs of smoke rising from his trainers. After all, he'd just descended nearly twelve feet or more quicker than falling rock.

"Sausage and egg McMuffin, if my nose hasn't deceived me?" Monty asked with hope-filled eyes, unconcerned by any potential injuries the soles of his feet may have suffered.

"Of course," Dave said, shaking his head, as if any other menu option was an insult to their friendship. "Becks about?"

"Dunno," Monty said, his gaze fixed on the bag like a dog stalking the dinner table. "I saw her walking Tyler to the bus for school a while ago," he added, but his attention really was elsewhere. "Should we head inside?" he asked eagerly.

"Yeah," Dave said, leading the way inside and towards the kitchen. "We'll have some breakfast and then get to work on our TT chariot," he suggested, referring to their sidecar. "Oh," Dave said, recalling something that was still pressing on his mind. "And there's something else I need to speak to you about, Ray Donovan."

Monty made short work of his breakfast, taking as long to

FRANK & STAN'S BUCKET LIST #5: ISLE OF MAN TT ACES

demolish it as it did for him to descend the ladder a few moments before. In other words, mere seconds. Indeed, Monty eating often put people in mind of watching seagulls sweeping in at the fairground to dispatch a discarded portion of chips without landing. It was often strangely hypnotic to witness.

"Those hash browns were absolutely magnificent," Monty declared, running his tongue around his lips and appearing like he was about to break into a round of applause for the chef.

"So it wasn't you who phoned the other day?" Dave asked, bringing up his previously laboured point once again, while wiping away the muffin crumbs of his own breakfast from his stubbly chin.

"How many times do I need to deny it, Dave?" Monty said. "There are several reasons I would never disturb a man on his afternoon off. Topping that list of reasons is potentially disturbing a nap. And I'm also confident that watching Pamela Anderson Baywatch reruns made it to my shortlist. Though I'd need to double-check to be absolutely confident."

"Hmm..." Dave said, looking deep into Monty's good eye, hoping to see any flicker of guilt.

"Which one was it?" Monty asked. "Which Baywatch episode, I mean."

"I'm not sure because that bloke on the phone broke my concentration," Dave said with a sigh. "But I think Mitch was about to rescue an abandoned seal, if I remember correctly."

"Ah, yes," Monty answered, nodding smartly. "Series four, episode six," he added, with impressive instant recall, his eyes drifting away fondly at the mental image forming in his mind's eye. "However, I think it was a manatee rather than a seal, if memory serves. But there was an awful lot of flesh on display in that particular episode, so you'd be forgiven for confusing the two creatures."

"We need to get you on Mastermind," Dave marvelled, unscrewing the cap on his orange juice. "So, if it wasn't you, Monty..." said Dave, moving the conversation reluctantly away from Pamela Anderson and Co. "Then who's this joker, Chip, and how did he even get my contact details?"

"Your website, dopey. You already said," Monty was only too happy to point out.

"I don't have a website, *dopey*," Dave shot back, scrunching up his greasy hash brown wrapper into a ball, sending it across the table towards Monty's forehead.

"Yeah, you do," Monty was quick to remind him. "I set you one up when you won the TT, remember? I did tell you at the time."

"I have a website?" Dave asked, clearly unaware of this fact until right then.

"Yes! Only I didn't actually get around to doing much with it other than adding a photo of you in the hot tub and your phone number for press enquiries."

"You put my personal phone number up on the internet for all sorts of idiots to access?" Dave admonished, although not overly concerned with the part about using a photograph of him in the hot tub. "Honestly, Monty. I could have all sorts of crazed stalkers bothering me like this Chip wazzock. Have you not heard about this phone hacking scandal that celebrities fall victim to?"

"That website's nearly a year old," Monty pointed out. "How many people, stalkers, or idiots, have found your website and phoned you in all that time?"

"Including Chip?" Dave asked, tapping his finger on the kitchen table as he counted out in his head, tallying up the final figure for the very large number in question. "Okay, one," he admitted eventually. "But that's not the point, Monty."

"Wait, hold on," Monty said, a particular realisation suddenly dawning in regard to Dave's caller. "The guy's name was Chip, yeah?" he asked, removing his phone from his oil-stained work pants.

"Yeah, that's right," Dave confirmed. "I clearly remember it because hearing the name that first time made me think of the food item and got me hungry."

"Understandable," Monty offered. "But the thing is, I think I might have had an email from him submitted through your website," Monty advised, pressing a finger down on his phone's display and scrolling through.

"You're receiving emails from my website now?" Dave asked, folding his arms over his chest. "What's all that about?"

"Dave," Monty said with one eye fixed on the phone screen and the other wandering over in Dave's direction. "You're not exactly one to embrace new technologies," he said, pointing to the Nokia brick lying next to Dave's orange juice that even now remained largely a mystery to Dave.

"Fair point. So...?"

"I'm looking for his email now," Monty explained. "When I saw the word Chip, originally, I assumed it to be from some poxy gambling website or something, so I sent it to my spam folder, and... Ah! Here we are."

"Well?" asked Dave, placing his arms down onto the tabletop and leaning over.

"Hang on," Monty said, moving his face closer to the screen, first skim-reading a variety of spam emails offering marriage proposals from Russian mail-order brides, inheritances from dead Nigerian royalty, and cute puppies for sale, amongst other things. Monty moved the message about the cute puppy to his Inbox, labelling it as "Not Spam," and then... "Ah. Here we are. Chip Freestone," he said, pleased with himself as he opened the specific message under present discussion.

"What's it say?" asked Dave.

"How bloody quick do you think I am? Give me a chance to read it!" Monty protested.

"I heard you were *very* quick," Dave suggested with a childish smirk that was promptly ignored.

Monty hummed to himself, running his thumb along the length of the display, engrossed in the contents of the email. "Ooh," Monty offered, breaking the brief silence momentarily before continuing what he was doing. "Right. Okay, the email is from the same bloke who spoke to you," Monty confirmed, a few seconds later. "And according to his auto-signature at the bottom of the email, he's a documentary filmmaker from over in Boston, Massachusetts. That's in the United States, just in case you didn't know."

"Yeah?" Dave said, sidling over, taking up a position next to Monty with his chin resting on Monty's shoulder.

Monty continued reading through the email. "Jesus, Dave!"

"What? Did I dribble on you?" Dave asked, lifting his head enough to check.

"No. This," Monty told him. "Did you seriously call this guy a dipshit?"

"Mmm... yeah. Sounds like something I might've said," Dave answered. "Either dipshit or dickhead. One of the two."

Monty shook his head, setting his jowls wobbling. "It's lucky this bloke thought you were inebriated when you both spoke," Monty informed him. "Because that's the only reason, according to his message here, that he bothered sending this follow-up email, hoping to catch you once you'd sobered up and were in a more coherent state of mind."

"So what's he offering us, and how much does it cost, then?" Dave asked with a weary sigh, still unconvinced that this was anything other than a scam, certain they were on the receiving end of the sleazy approaches of some kind of rubbish snake oil salesman. "Let me guess, he films a promotional video of us and then sends us a large bill for the pleasure?"

But before Monty could answer, Becks wandered into the kitchen. "You two look very cosy," Becks remarked about Dave positioned like he was about to start licking Monty's neck. "Whatcha doin'?" she asked, snuggling in herself, and placing her chin on Monty's spare shoulder.

"Ah, nothing much. Just reading about some American chap trying to swindle us," Dave replied. "I bought you a Maccies," he added, leaning around Monty's back with his lips puckered to steal a quick morning kiss from Becks.

"Ooh, nice," Becks said, leaving Monty to his reading, and then taking a proper seat. "Sausage and egg McMuffin?"

"But of course," Dave was happy to confirm, returning to his own seat as well, bored with the progress Monty was making.

Dave watched Becks unwrap her breakfast, smiling away to herself like she'd just been handed a Tiffany bracelet rather than merely a McMuffin. Seeing her happy always gave Dave a warm fuzzy feeling down south. In his tummy.

It was difficult for Team TT Farm to imagine the place without Becks and Tyler, even though it'd only been a few short months since they'd arrived, and Becks herself was thrilled beyond belief when Frank and Stan had offered her the newly appointed role of administration manager. She was tasked with organising the farm's hectic schedule of events, making sure everybody was precisely where they were supposed to be, Dave and Monty included. Which was commendable in itself. The ongoing fortunes of the farm was a team effort, of course. But the education centre's unbridled success was firmly down to Becks and her impressive grit and determination to drive it forward.

She definitely seemed happy, Dave observed, and Tyler as well, who'd settled into island life with consummate ease, eager to spend his days traipsing through the endless countryside or skimming stones down at their favourite beach, soaking up what this magical location had to offer. But as happy as Dave was with the two of them in his life, he couldn't shake the realisation that Becks and Tyler were, ultimately, only visitors to this place he called home. He knew that she could up sticks and decide to return to the UK at any given moment, if she so desired. And this worrying possibility, however likely or unlikely it may have been, played heavily on Dave's mind.

"Sweet cheese and crackers!" Monty piped up, having finally processed the entire contents of the email. He placed his phone gently on the table, forcing air outward through pursed lips in a steady stream, sounding like a deflating balloon.

"Well?" Dave pressed, prompting Monty to start speaking again before exhaling all of his oxygen entirely.

"F-f-five... grand..." Monty offered up, placing a knuckle in his mouth, chomping down on it like he was bracing himself to have a limb amputated.

"See? There you go!" Dave declared confidently, thrusting his arms into the air in triumph. "Dave Quirk can weed out a bloody flimflam artist from a thousand yards! Or from all the way across the Pacific, even, as in this particular instance. Charging us five grand for a glorified promo video? *Pfft*. The brass neck of the man! I'm glad I called him a dipshit and sent him away with a flea in his ear, the bloody charlatan. If I was paying five grand to be in a video, Jet from that Gladiators show would need to be in it, along with some mood lighting and a bottle of baby oil."

"Oh, is that right?" Becks entered in, raising one eyebrow in response.

"I'm only kidding," Dave added, with a playful rolling of the eyes. "It'd be melted chocolate rather than baby oil," he said with a wink, and with this cheery wink suggesting he wasn't being entirely serious and hadn't given the scenario all that much consideration (even though he had).

"Ehm... Dave. Firstly, I think it's actually the *Atlantic*," Monty advised, happy to score points over his chum. "And, secondly, this bloody charlatan, as you refer to him, wants to *pay* us five grand, not *charge* us five grand. And just to be clear, that's five thousand *pounds*. Not dollars."

"Oh? Oh, yeah," Dave admitted, feeling more than a little embarrassed. "Now I think on it, I believe that's what he said to me when I spoke to him originally. I just didn't, ehrm... Sorry. Sorry, Monty. Go on."

"Apparently, this guy and his brother are making a documentary series about the TT for the American market," Monty continued, relating the details contained in the email. "In his words, he wants to feature the two of us in his story and document our struggle to reach the start line of this great and wonderful race, introducing it to an American audience which largely knows nothing about it," he said. "So, then. What d'ya think about that?"

Monty eased back in his chair, fingers wrapped together behind his head, listening out for the cogs whirring inside of Dave's skull.

"Well, let's not keep the guy waiting, Monty!" Dave suggested with a laugh, having suddenly, miraculously concluded that the chap in question wasn't a flimflam artist or charlatan after all. "Honestly, Monty. Time is money, don't you know?"

"You're right, as always, of course," Monty replied, casting a discreet head shake over to Becks for her benefit. "Oh, and you should know," Monty continued, with a smile implying there was more to come. "This five grand...?"

"Yeah?" Dave said, placing his palms together in prayerful fashion.

"That's *each*," Monty clarified, rubbing his thumb and forefinger together to count out the imaginary wad of cash held in his mitt.

"Holy crap!" said Dave.

"And you called this guy a dipshit. And told him to piss off," Monty couldn't help reminding his friend. "So who's the real dipshit here?" he asked.

"*I'm* the dipshit," Dave replied, head lowered in shame. "But five grand each!" he squeaked, looking back up again, his shame not lasting too terribly long at all, overcome as it was by his sheer excitement.

Chapter
THREE

"Surprise!" Frank yelled, throwing the front door of the taxi office open and waving joyfully.

For such a generously proportioned lass, Stella could still fair shift when required. Despite her large size, she leapt from her seat like a gymnast, vaulting effortlessly over the front counter and arming herself, in mid-air, along the way, with her cricket bat secured underneath before her feet had even landed back down onto terra firma. It was such an impressive, graceful, and seamlessly executed routine that, had any Olympic judges been present, she no doubt would have been awarded a 10/10 score.

"Come at me!" Stella screamed, eyes bulging ten millimetres from their sockets and cricket bat poised and ready to strike.

"Told you it wasn't a good idea to startle her," Stan smugly suggested from his position of relative safety, having taken cover behind Frank.

"It's only us!" Frank pleaded, pulling back his sleeves and holding out his hands to show that he was completely unarmed and posed no threat. "Stella, it's only us... Please put the cricket bat down, all right? ... It's okay... It's only us," he said slowly, lowering his hands gradually, and speaking in gentle, soothing tones, as he often found best when communicating with Stella, especially under such circumstances.

Stella's ample bosom continued to wobble long after her abrupt landing. "I should crack your head open like a boiled egg," Stella declared flatly, finally placing the bat down on the countertop and returning her shoulders to a more relaxed state.

"Is it safe to come all the way in, now?" Frank asked of her, advancing cautiously like he was clearing a minefield. "Sheesh," Frank added, once Stella was back in her seat and pulling out a ciggie. "Is that how you welcome anybody that surprises you?"

"You didn't surprise me," Stella told him, running her thumb over the well-used flint wheel of her Zippo to spark up her fag. "I saw you two soppy sods walking across the street."

"Wait, hang on," Stan entered in, now that the threat level had decreased to amber. "If you saw us coming, then why on earth did you deploy the cricket bat and do that crazy thing you do with your eyes?"

"Oh, I dunno," Stella said, sucking in a generous lungful of Virginia's finest blend. "Bored, I s'pose? Besides, it's always fun scaring the shit out of you two gormless dipsticks."

"On that bombshell note, I'm just going to check in with the boys back at the farm," Frank suggested, stepping towards his and Stan's office, giving Stella a stern glare as he advanced at a safe distance, giving her a wide berth.

"So, anyway, what do you want?" Stella asked casually, as if nothing unusual had just transpired, dispensing with the small talk and taking a noisy slurp of her tea.

"What do we want?" Stan said, repeating her words back to her. "We came to see you, of course," he explained. "We're on our way back from the Lake District and thought we'd spend the day shopping before catching the ferry home. Thought we'd take you out for lunch?"

Stella glanced over to the empty seat next to her, staring at it for impact. "I'm presently on my *own*," Stella said, just in case Stan hadn't picked up on her subtle cue. "Besides, I've brought along some leftover chicken legs and such from last night's supper, so I'm fine," she added. "And speaking of chicken legs, why are you wearing shorts?" she asked, noting Stan's present attire.

"Because it's exceptionally warm?" Stan suggested, turning his attention to the stylish baby-blue tailored shorts he had on. "And what's wrong with my shorts?" he asked, sensing the disapproval in her voice.

"Nothing," Stella said with a disinterested shrug. "They look fine... if that's your thing," she added, returning her attention to the sudoku puzzle she'd been diligently working on when the two of them had interrupted her.

"Wait..." Stan said, not quite finished on the subject of his new shorts. "Do you not like them?" he asked, running his hand over the cotton fabric.

However, Stella's greatly anticipated critical fashion analysis was interrupted by the sound of Frank's feet stomping around in his office, the footsteps drawing somewhat nearer, and then Frank appearing in his office doorway. "Stella," Frank called over, resting up against the doorframe, arms crossed.

"Christ almighty, what is it now?" Stella said, angrily closing her puzzle book over. "I'm kinda busy over here, just in case you hadn't noticed?"

"Stella," Frank pressed on, undaunted. "Where in hell are our bloody chairs?" he asked, glancing back at his lonely, chairless desk.

Stella released a frustrated sigh, the bother of responding to such questions obviously a terrible inconvenience. "Well the biscuit barrel was empty last week, wasn't it," she said rather cryptically, as if this little bit of information should have been explanation enough.

"And...?" Frank said, when no further elaboration was offered. "So how does that in any way relate to our missing chairs?" he asked, looking over to Stan for moral support.

"The bank had closed for the day, and we needed petty cash," Stella answered.

"And...?" Frank said again, not following.

"And I sold them."

"Wait, you sold the chairs so that you could replenish the contents of the *biscuit* tin?" Stan asked, incredulous.

"Now you're catching up," Stella answered.

"Are you serious?" Frank said, leaving his office and drawing nearer. "You actually sold our chairs so you could restock the biscuit tin??"

"Yes, that's what I said," Stella replied with another sigh of annoyance, as if this line of enquiry were a complete drain on her precious, valuable time. "And I'd offer you two a biscuit, but sadly, the tin is empty again, so..."

Frank ground his teeth, trying his best to get his anger moderately under control before responding. "Stella, my chair was specially designed to support my lumbar region," he informed her. "It cost me a lot of money, and I had to have it made to measure."

"You weren't even using them," Stella shot back. "Besides, it's not all about you two, you know, you bunch of selfish gets. Did you not think about the joy that they would bring to Alesha? The poor woman couldn't even sit down before I stepped up to help."

"Right. Alesha. Of course. How silly of me," Frank said, giving Stan a look suggesting they should have headed straight to the ferry. "And who's Alesha?" Frank asked reluctantly.

"The one who bought your chairs, obviously," Stella replied, raising her thinly drawn eyebrows in frustration. "Do I need to paint you pair a picture? Alesha owns the Caribbean chicken takeaway. You'd know that if you were around here more often. The poor thing was on her feet all day, struggling, until yours truly offered a helping hand. So you should be *thanking* me."

"Stella," Stan said, exasperated. "What Frank's trying to say is, if you could please arrange for the return of our chairs, we'd both be very grateful. That's all. You're correct that we weren't using them, but we do intend to use them each time we pop back, yeah?"

"Hmm, I might be able to get you *one* of them back," Stella offered, like she was doing them both a hugely massive favour by even considering the idea at all. "And don't say I don't do anything for you two, yeah?" she added, dispatching the precariously balanced ash from her fag into the empty Diet Coke can sat there, next to her stapler, with practised precision. But then the phone rang, and Stella needed to answer it. "Frank and Stan's Cabs," she announced gruffly, after picking it up. "Sure," she said, fag glued to her lower lip, moving each time she spoke. "Right," Stella continued, inputting the details of the request up into her computer with the nimble fingers of a concert pianist. "It'll be with you in ten minutes," she advised in an assured tone.

Frank and Stan hovered around in the reception area, but Stella soon became occupied by a steady stream of calls, so she was genuinely busy now as opposed to just sudoku-puzzle busy. "We should really think about going, I suppose," Stan suggested after a bit, glancing at his watch. "The others will be famished," he told Frank.

"Well hello, you two," Susie cheerily announced, suddenly arriving and using her back to ease open the door, hands laden with an armful of office supplies.

"Oh, let me help," Stan said, darting over to relieve her of her load, ever the gentleman.

"It's so lovely to see you both," Susie said, shaking out her fingers to restore the blood flow to her digits. "And so how's married life treating you, Frank?" Susie asked with a radiant smile.

"Marvellous," Frank was happy to report. "And it meant a great deal to us all that you were able to attend the wedding," he added warmly.

"Oh, I had a wonderful time, Frank. And I hope to get over for a visit with the rest of the family soon. I was also so pleased to see Becks settling in so well. Please tell her I was asking after her?"

"Of course," said Stan, answering for Frank. "And you know that we'd always make you welcome anytime," Stan added, while wondering where he should set down the items he'd taken from her.

"Ah, anywhere right over there," Susie instructed, pointing to an area behind the counter. "So," Susie continued, removing the bag draped over her shoulder and addressing the both of them. "Not that it isn't an enormous pleasure, but what brings you here?"

"We're just on our way back from honeymoon," Frank told her, a contented smile emerging.

"The Lake District was lovely," Stan chipped in. "Beautiful scenery, long walks in the countryside, and chilled wine waiting for us to enjoy in the hot tub."

"Oh?" Susie answered, looking first to Stan and then over to Frank, confused as to why Stan would be present on Frank's honeymoon. Of course, she knew they were close, but...

"Ah," Frank entered in, picking up on her quizzical expression. "Jessie and I had booked a log cabin for a few days, but we didn't realise it had three large double rooms. So, we asked if Stan and Edgar fancied joining us, and here we are."

"Right," Susie said, looking around for the rest of their party.

"We've all been shopping," Stan explained further. "Edgar and Jessie are meeting us in that new French restaurant that's opened up around the corner. So we just nipped over, hoping to steal Stella away from you for an hour or so?"

"Yeah," Frank continued, "Edgar and Jessie didn't really have much time to chat to her when we were all together. So we thought lunch would be a good opportunity to catch up. That is, if we can pry her out of here."

"Sure, I can cover things," Susie offered without hesitation. "Wait," she quickly added. "When you said French restaurant, do you mean Raphaël's?" she asked with a grimace.

"Yes," Stan answered, throwing Frank a worried look. "Yes, why? Is the food terrible?"

"What? No," Susie replied, shaking her head in the negative. "No, no. In fact, the chateaubriand is to die for," she informed them, running her tongue over her top lip in fond remembrance of said chateaubriand.

Frank appeared confused by this apparent contradiction between her initial reaction and her positive food review. "It's just that you pulled a face, which suggested...?" he said.

"Ah, yes," Susie said, edging away from Stella, who was presently still engaged on the phone. "The thing is..." she began, taking a quick, cautionary glance over her shoulder. "The thing is, Stella's not allowed in," she quietly advised.

"She's not allowed in?" Frank asked.

"No," Susie told him, bowing her head a little, slightly embarrassed on Stella's behalf. "They barred her a couple of weeks back."

"Okay, then," Stan said, not appearing too surprised by this revelation but choosing not to enquire further as to the whys and hows of it.

But Frank, being under no such prohibition, couldn't resist digging just a little further. "How does one get barred from a French restaurant, exactly? I mean, this is Stella we're talking about, so it's not like this comes as a shock, but..."

"Did Stella inform you of our toilet backing up recently and then being unable to find an available plumber?" Susie asked, flicking her eyes between the both of them. "Or, I should say, finding a plumber who wanted to attend?"

"Oh, yes," Stan was delighted to confirm. "She didn't bother telling us when one of our drivers was robbed at knifepoint a while back, but with the toilet situation, she was sure to notify us immediately and didn't spare any of the gory details."

Susie nodded. "Yep, that's our Stella," she agreed. "Anyway, we were without a toilet for three days," Susie continued, in a hushed voice. "If I needed a bathroom break, then I'd just walk up to the public toilets in the supermarket," she explained.

"Okay...?" Frank said, wondering in which direction this little anecdote could possibly be heading but concerned enough to find out.

"Well, Stella decided she didn't want to walk all the way to the supermarket, saying it was too far, especially if things got urgent," Susie explained further. "So she started using the loo in the French restaurant, as Raphaël's is only right around the corner. Anyway, if you've ever been there before, you'll know it's a rather intimate restaurant. They've got only one individual toilet to sit on for the gents, and one for the ladies. So the owners soon started receiving complaints about the length of time Stella was in there, occupying the small women's loo."

"I can imagine," Stan said with a shudder.

"Yeah," said Susie. "It was okay if she was just going for, you know, a widdle, as she'd be in and out in the span of a few minutes. But, if she was going to... you know... well, she liked to take her copy of *Hello!* magazine along with her. So she could be in there for a good twenty minutes or more, between doing her business and reading, and longer if there'd been a celebrity wedding she was interested in. And it was at this point that the owners reminded her the toilets were really only meant for patrons, only people eating there."

"I feel their pain," Frank said. "However, that doesn't sound like she's been banned, necessarily, does it?" he asked, looking around for answers. "Just set straight on their house rules?"

"She wasn't banned at that point, no," Susie disclosed. "But then Stella started bringing her sandwiches along with her to eat on the toilet, in addition to her copy of *Hello!* magazine to read. She pointed out to them that she was now eating in there, as requested, so the matter was fully resolved as far as she was concerned. As you can likely imagine, that's when they really took exception."

"As you would," Stan said, struggling to keep out the mental image forming inside his head.

"But, it still didn't stop her from going," Susie added warily. "With no other options, the waiters had to take it in turn to keep watch. If they saw Stella coming, they'd run inside and hide all the bog rolls. The restaurant owners were so desperate to get rid of her that they eventually paid for a plumber out of their own pockets to come fix our toilet. Apparently, that was a cheaper option than paying the waiters to take turns sitting outside theirs on StellaWatch."

"Are you telling them about those stuck-up French twats?" Stella enquired ever-so-eloquently from behind the counter, apparently overhearing just enough of their conversation to place two and two together. "How's it my fault?" Stella asked.

Worryingly, she still appeared to have a caller waiting on the line with their booking only partly processed, judging by the position of her nicotine-stained fingers hovering over the keyboard. "If a restaurant invests in a cheap extractor fan to remove odours, then how's that my fault when it overheats, exactly?" Stella asked, tapping the keys on her keyboard again. "That's booked for you, luv," she then said down the phone. "Ten minutes or so and they'll be there."

"No, I was just telling them about the sandwiches, actually," Susie admitted to Stella in answer. "I didn't even know the part about the issues with the extractor fan."

"Can we just go?" Stan asked, edging closer to the door.

Frank followed his lead. "Absolutely, we can. Stella, perhaps we'll take you out to lunch another time, all right?"

"Fine with me!" Stella replied, rising up from her seat to call after them. "If you think I'd go anywhere with him wearing those stupid bloody shorts, you've got another thing coming anyway," she said, whilst shoving her hand down inside the rear of her black leggings and rooting around for a good scratch and to rearrange the fabric. "I've got standards, you know!"

Stan staggered through the bar area of the Isle of Man Steam Packet ferry, careening from side to side like a punch-drunk boxer. "Please excuse me," he said, offering an apologetic smile to the lady whose personal space he'd just infringed upon. "Awfully sorry," he offered to another, snaking his way back to the rest of his party. "Edgar, you're sure you wouldn't like something stronger than an orange juice?" Stan asked upon arrival, laying the tray he was carrying down on the table and hoping nothing on it had been spilled along the way.

"Not just now, but thank you," Edgar answered, dabbing his brow with his white linen handkerchief. "Perhaps when the swell subsides, and the rocking eases," he indicated, swaying in his seat and appearing decidedly green about the gills. Edgar's sensitivity to the increased motion of the Irish Sea came as something of a surprise to Stan. Admittedly, it may have been an irrational conclusion to draw, but Edgar's attire of tailored navy blazer, crisp white shirt and smart, cream-coloured slacks brought to mind that he was no stranger to life on the high seas, as it made him look just like a sailor. That, coupled with the decidedly nautical-sounding surname of Seaforce, and one would suspect him to be more of an accomplished mariner than his current ghostly expression suggested.

Frank reached over for his drink, snatching it up before the contents of Stan's tray were dispatched out onto the tabletop. "Edgar deserves a large brandy after meeting Stella," he put forth. "I'm glad we were able to convince her to come out with us after a slight change of plans, though poor Edgar here may not be."

"I did have the pleasure of a brief introduction at the wedding," Edgar was happy to correct. "But it's when sharing a sumptuous meal that you genuinely have the pleasure of getting to know someone's most endearing character traits," Edgar offered generously.

Spending any length of time in Stella's company was often eventful. Even to those closest to her. For a novice, it would undoubtedly be considered something of a challenging experience. Throughout their lunch, however, Edgar had remained polite and attentive throughout, despite being a relative newcomer to her idiosyncrasies. Even when Stella suggested that with a name like Seaforce he'd be well used to blowing sailors off course, he smiled, laughing along for a time. "She's unique in her ways," Edgar added, having given the matter some reflection. "Eccentric, one might say," he remarked, reaching into his blazer pocket. "And I for one can appreciate eccentricity," he added with a wry smile, exaggerating the placement of his imaginary monocle to consider the wine list. "She's a lady I very much look forward to meeting again," he said, a sentiment that was delivered with apparent sincerity, and even, remarkably enough, a sense of genuine anticipation.

"Oh? And what's got you tickled all of a sudden?" Frank asked of Jessie as he stirred his gin & tonic, noticing the mirthful smile spreading across the face of his new bride.

Jessie's grin developed into a giggle as she remembered what she was remembering. "I was just thinking of the waiters in the French restaurant where Edgar and I were sat waiting," she explained. "When you phoned us to come outside and meet you, I caught a glimpse of the staff in a state of complete panic when they noticed Stella stood with you across the street," she went on, the laugh intensifying. "Oh my," she said. "They all looked horrified, and then they started running around like madmen, shouting at each other frantically."

"Go on!" Stan pressed, eager for further details, edging closer in his seat. "Shouting what?"

"Well, my French isn't what it was, mind you," Jessie felt obligated to point out. "But, roughly translated, it was, I think, something along the lines of, *Shit! It's the phantom crapper! Hide the bog rolls!*"

"With all the commotion, a couple near us thought a fire had broken out," Edgar entered in, a smile of his own emerging through his nausea. "The maître d' dropped an entire tray of tarte Tatin in his haste to secure the front door."

"Fortunately, we hadn't been seated at a table yet," Jessie added. "And the waitstaff were much relieved when we told them we were going out, while assuring them that Stella was *not* coming in."

"Ahh," Frank sighed fondly. "You know, being over on the island much of the time now, I really do miss her," he said. "Warts and all."

"Life's never dull when Stella's around," Stan was pleased to report, struggling to open his packet of peanuts. "Bugger. Ah, well. It must be a sign to reduce my salt intake," he remarked, disappointed yet graciously accepting of defeat, and placing the snack back on the table unopened. "Fresh air, anyone?" Stan asked, running his eyes around the table, searching for a daring companion brave enough to step outside into the driving wind.

"I think I'll pass," Edgar replied, gripping his chair, a chair that was bolted to the floor, in fact, to prevent it sliding about in choppy weather. The thought of a stroll out on the pitching deck appeared to be the very last thing on poor Edgar's mind as he closed his eyes over, offering a pained sigh.

"Jessie? Entice you into enjoying some bracing sea air?"

"Tempting," Jessie suggested with a sour expression, noting the wind-ravaged woman presently appearing from outside. "But I think I'm best staying here, in the warmth," she advised, raising her drinks glass to toast her wise decision.

"Oh," said Stan, half-seated, half-standing, and unsure as to whether he should venture off after all.

Frank pushed himself up from his chair. "Come on, then, I'll keep you company, Stanley. Make sure you don't get washed overboard and swallowed by a basking shark or something."

"You don't think it's too cold, Frank?" Jessie fussed over him, as she often did. She reached for and retrieved a knitted scarf from her travelling bag quicker than an F1 mechanic reaching for a wheel gun. "Here," she said, reaching up and lassoing his neck with her toasty, home-crafted apparel.

When the Irish Sea was still as a millpond, there was no better way to travel to the Isle of Man than by ferry. However, throw in a force 5 or 6 weather system, and the journey could be described as a less than pleasurable experience, torture for those poor souls spending hours with their nose pressed into a sick bag, willing the minutes along, vowing their next journey would be completed in the air. Still, it was a burden worth bearing, knowing you were either returning home to that magnificent island or, possibly, relishing the prospect of a holiday there. Either way, the sacrifice was worth it.

Frank and Stan leaned on each other for support, wandering precariously towards the exit like two drunkards staggering home after a night on the ale. "Brace yourself," Frank suggested, pulling open the cumbersome watertight door.

"It's blowing a hooley!" Stan shouted after climbing out on deck, his once impeccably-styled hair in complete disarray almost immediately. He ventured onward, now on the receiving end of a temporary facelift such was the force of the wind battering against his mush. "Over there!" Stan said, hurrying towards a metal bench, rusting in parts due to its regular pitched battle against the elements. "The width of the funnel should give us some protection from the weather!" he added. "Ah, yes, that's better," Stan said, lowering his voice to normal levels now he was no longer competing against the stiff breeze, plonking himself down on the cold metal under shelter of the exhaust stack. "Good thing I had the foresight to change out of my shorts into something else. It can get cold out on the water!"

"Yes, and there's some lovely warm air coming from the vents of this chimney thingy," Frank told Stan, rubbing his hands together briskly, taking advantage of this present find. Then, with his hands heating up nicely, Frank observed those hardy souls scattered about the deck, some having a crafty fag, others watching the industrial seaport of Heysham gradually disappearing from view behind them. Car alarms rang out incessantly from the vehicle deck below, triggered by the motion of the waves, and possibly resulting in several flat batteries for some poor unfortunates on arrival in Douglas four hours hence.

"You remember catching the ferry for our first trip to the TT races?" Stan asked, lifting the collar of his jacket, hoping to protect his chilled ears from further punishment.

"Of course," Frank replied with a nostalgic smile. "I recall us having no hotel accommodation booked and you remaining confident that we'd find something when we landed," he remarked, rolling his eyes, the pain of that particular detail still fresh in his mind.

"Well how was I to know that hotels were booked up years in advance for the TT?" Stan replied, anxious to deflect the blame. "Remember we also had the pleasure of meeting Henk for the first time in the ferry terminal," Stan pointed out, eager to move the conversation away from his accommodation mishap.

"I dare say nobody forgets meeting Henk for the first time," Frank joked, tucking his chin inside his scarf. "You know, it's funny that the Isle of Man's not been in our lives for too long, yet it doesn't half feel like—"

"Home?" Stan ventured.

"Yes," Frank said, turning to face his old pal. "Home. Exactly."

Stan placed his hand down on Frank's knee, patting it gently. "A lot's happened in a short amount of time, my friend. You're married to the lovely Jessie. The TT Farm is coming on a treat. And on top of that, we've somehow ended up with a racetrack."

Frank nodded along contentedly at what Stan was saying. "And, you had the pleasure of meeting Edgar, so there's that as well," Frank offered. "I do like him, Stan. He's a terrific bloke, and if he can put up with all of us and our various baggage, then the guy deserves a medal."

"He is something special, isn't he," Stan said, eyes drifting away dreamily at the mere mention of Edgar's name. "Oh," Stan said, returning to the present. "And don't forget about us being blessed with two amazing children, also."

"Two children...?" Frank asked. "Ah, I see," he quickly added, with a knowing expression. "You mean our dear boys Dave and Monty."

"They're growing up so quickly, aren't they?" Stan observed drolly. "They'll be off to school before we know it."

Frank and Stan sat quietly for a minute or two, occupied by their own thoughts outside in their temporary shelter against the howling wind. It's fair to say that the lives they were now living were poles apart from where they'd been not too long ago. It wasn't that they entirely disliked their previous lives, necessarily. (Well, in Frank's case, excluding promiscuous and expensive ex-wives, of course.) It would have been easy enough for Frank and Stan to continue drifting along, relatively happy with their lot as they knew it. Frank often reflected that a cruel twist of fate in his health issues and then catching his wife in the act had ended up changing the direction of his and Stan's lives, though for the better. Sure, there were dark days when tears were shed when thinking about certain events, but Frank was a firm believer in things happening for a reason. After all, if Frank hadn't been to the doctor on that fateful and memorable day, he'd probably still be living with his lying, cheating, plastic-infused wife, plodding along for the rest of his days (though with Stan still likely by his side, keeping him company on the journey and listening to him grumble).

However, fate had thankfully intervened. If Frank and his disorganised travelling companion hadn't climbed aboard the ferry destined for the Isle of Man TT as they did, he shuddered to think about how much of life he'd now be missing out on. It's funny how being told you're potentially dying could be the kick up the caboose needed to actually start living. It was a twist in his life's tapestry that Frank often gave thought to. Now, if he ever spoke to somebody agonising over a new career or general change of direction in life, he'd tell them to just bloody go for it. Jump feet-first into whatever opportunity life presents you with, he'd say, because ultimately, what really is the worst that can happen? And if things go tits-up? Well, you hopefully learn from it and move on. This was very much Frank's new mantra. And, while it may have been in his later years that he'd come round to this way of thinking, he was thankful that he had, and that things had in fact happened the way they did. It was something he was grateful for each and every day.

"So," Stan said, bringing them both back into the moment. "Do you think she'll come around to the idea?"

"Who?" Frank asked. "Oh, you mean Stella," he added, upon working out who Stan was referring to, his brain catching up with the question posed. "I'm honestly not sure, Stan," Frank offered, with a solemn shake of the head. "If her first reaction is anything to go by, then no."

"I suppose saying we can stick the offer right up our scrawny arses as a response doesn't really suggest she was champing at the bit," Stan agreed. "She did warm to the idea a little after creating her potential new job title, though. So there's that, at least."

"Yeah, but is Commander-in-Chief even a job title other than in the White House? I'm not sure it's really appropriate

FRANK & STAN'S BUCKET LIST #5: ISLE OF MAN TT ACES

for a new car hire company on the Isle of Man," Frank said in answer.

"I expect it makes her feel important?" Stan ventured. "She already bosses us around now as it is, so whatever job title she holds would make no difference to us, I suppose," he advised. "Did you mention the idea to Jessie?" Stan asked, slightly changing direction for a moment.

Frank shook his head in the negative. "I've mentioned the general idea of selling up the taxi business in passing. But nothing definite. I didn't want to set too many hares running at this stage."

"We *are* doing the right thing, Frank?"

"I think so, Stan," Frank answered, wiping away the sea spray from his rosy cheeks. "We're not getting any younger, and it's a generous price we've been offered. And it's not like we're in the UK that often to keep our eye on the ball, either. Plus, thanks to Stella, we don't even have any blooming chairs to sit on. So, if that's not a sign, then I don't know what is."

"Only Stella could sell our chairs from under us so she could restock her biscuit supply," Stan said with a laugh, amused by the thought. "Oh, and you know what's ironic about our present situation?"

Frank didn't respond, turning his head to receive the answer.

"I was thinking about that tosspot, Rodney Franks," Stan told him, smiling warmly, a reaction not typically associated with thinking about that particularly loathsome chap. "If it wasn't for old Rodney, we probably wouldn't have even considered selling the taxi firm until he went and put the idea in our heads. So we must thank him the next time we see him."

"We'll do no such thing," Frank shot back, although he knew his friend was of course only joshing about the thanking him bit. "I've still not forgiven the odious little maggot for that whole blackmail situation over Lee's video, with him offering us the Jurby racetrack for an exorbitant price in return for his silence, and then still releasing the video anyway."

"Yeah, he's a piece of work, all right," Stan concurred. "I'm quite looking forward to bumping into him at the TT this year," Stan said with a growl. Though, coming from Stan, who was anything but a fighter, the physical threat level was modest at best and unlikely to disturb too much of Rodney's sleep if he were aware of the imminent danger, such as it was.

"We'll steer well clear of Rodney Franks, thank you very much," Frank was quick to suggest. "He'll only end up trying to sell something to us, steal something from us, or gamble on the result of something. I've had it with that... that..." Frank said, looking for the appropriate words to describe Rodney Franks.

"Shortarse piss wizard?" Stan offered up, though unsure if he'd perhaps overstepped the bounds of what Frank was hoping to achieve.

"Nicely done, my friend," Frank replied, nodding his head in approval. "So we're agreed then, pal? If we can get Stella to come and work for us on the Isle of Man, we'll accept the offer for the taxi firm?"

"Yeah, let's do it," replied Stan. "Although maybe the new owners would like to keep Stella on?" Stan added with a smile, though not mean-spirited.

"Ha-ha!" Frank laughed, but again, not entirely unkindly. "Can you imagine their first management meeting with her, with her wandering in, fag in hand, scratching her arse? I'd certainly like to be a fly on the wall for *that* introduction."

"So, we'll give her a couple of days to mull things over, see what she thinks?"

"Yeah," said Frank. "Lee's already said he'd love to move over to the island. So I suppose the burning question, then, is whether or not *Stella* is ready for it."

"Oh no, my friend," Stan was quick to enter in. "The real question, Frank, is whether the *Isle of Man* is ready for *Stella!*"

Chapter
FOUR

For Frank and Stan, the thought of lining Rodney Franks' pockets was about as palatable a prospect as wiping your bottom with sandpaper that'd been dipped in acid. Despite the over-inflated purchase price paid for the Jurby raceway, Rodney had still reverted to his true snake-like nature, double-crossing them at the earliest opportunity and releasing Lee's video to the press despite assurances to the contrary.

However, now owning the island's only short-circuit racing track was not without its advantages. Under their stewardship, Frank and Stan could secure its future as a premier venue for motorsport activities. If Rodney were still at the helm, the area would have either been left to rot or flattened to use as a building plot, a grim fact Rodney himself had confirmed previously.

There was no overriding desire to profit from their investment. But Frank and Stan still needed the circuit to cover its running and maintenance costs. And so, in addition to the regular bookings in the diary, such as track days and go-karting, the new management team was tasked with thinking outside the box to drum up new revenue streams — a challenge that both Dave and Monty had eagerly embraced, setting their creative juices running at every available opportunity, diligent captains of industry that they were, never shirking, never off-duty...

"Wait, hang on," said Dave, twirling the cord attached to his whistle so it coiled around his index finger like a boa constrictor. "You mean as in... *forever*, forever?"

"Yup," Monty was happy to confirm, following behind a couple of paces, having dropped his own whistle whilst unsuccessfully attempting the same manoeuvre as Dave. "Forever," he added gravely, lest there be any doubt.

Dave continued walking the tarmac of the Jurby racetrack, affectionately known to many as the Jürburgring (in homage to the famous circuit in Germany). "Keep going!" he shouted, fist raised, offering words of encouragement to the group of young cyclists pedalling furiously by. "Well, it's not an easy decision," Dave suggested after a moment, speaking to Monty again and in explanation of the delayed response to the question posed. "And which would *you* go for?" he asked, turning and walking backwards, scouring his pal's face for any form of clue.

Monty shook his head vigorously. "Nah-ah," he said. "If I tell you, then that might influence your decision."

"Right," Dave replied, twirling his finger round, uncoiling his whistle this time. "Spend the rest of my life talking like Yoda or breathing like Darth Vader, is it?" he said, muttering to himself, and then running the various pros and cons of either option through in his mind. "It's a pickle, Monty," Dave said eventually. "My initial feeling is to opt for breathing like Vader, but then I'm picturing myself sitting in the cinema, listening to everybody moaning at me for breathing too loudly. Also, every time you had to phone someone, they'd probably call you a pervert. So, all things considered, young Monty... I'll have to select the Yoda option in this hypothetical of yours."

"*Hmmm*," Monty replied, adopting his most passable impression of the little green Jedi fellow under discussion. "Same as me, you were. *Hmmm*," Monty said, loudly enough that it attracted the attention of the mums operating the nearby refreshments stand.

One of the first new initiatives the dynamic duo instigated in their present roles was hosting a cycling league on the circuit. It was the ideal venue for the younger audience, with there being no danger posed by passing traffic. Furthermore, with it being a circuit — starting and finishing at the same spot — parents could relax by the start line, with no need to chase behind their children as they likely would if out on the busy roads. For that reason, the take-up from the local cycling clubs was impressive. Seven separate organisations had signed up, with over two hundred kids happily attending every Saturday to challenge themselves on the 1.7-mile track. Parents brought along snacks for the refreshments stand, and if the weather obliged, it was a jolly pleasant morning in the north of the island. Also, the modest two quid admission fees gathered into the track's coffers were certainly not to be sneezed at, either, when all tallied up, and were most welcome, as far as Dave and Monty were concerned.

Dave and Monty were on hand as marshals for the present day, patrolling the circuit, attending to the occasional grazed knee and assisting with punctured tyres should the need arise. As an added bonus, the two of them had brought the sidecar down for some track time to make valuable adjustments once the children had packed up and left for the day. With the TT races less than three weeks away, having this facility available for use to them was a godsend.

"I'm a little nervous about this fly-on-the-wall type of documentary thing," Monty confessed, looking over to his pal for some much-needed encouragement on this particular matter. "From what Chip was saying, their programme is going to be shown all over America and beyond."

Dave grabbed hold of a nice, plump-looking cheese sandwich from the refreshments table, offering a cordial smile to the parents crewing their station. "Much appreciated," Dave said, offering a quick salute for keeping them nourished during their shift. "Ah," said Dave, turning his attention back to Monty. "Nothing to be worried about, old chum. If we make complete idiots of ourselves, then when are we likely to be in the US of A to find out anyway?"

"I s'pose," Monty said, throwing an entire Scotch egg into his gob. "Although word could still make its way round to us," he added, between chews.

"Wait, weren't you the one who was all for this before?" Dave pointed out. "In fact, you were the one who had to convince *me* that it was a good idea, and not a scam, if I recall."

"Yeah, but I've been thinking," Monty explained.

"Ah," replied Dave. "Well you know what I've told you about that, Monty," he cautioned. "Too much of that sort of thing can be dangerous."

"True, true," Monty said with a laugh. "Any ideas as to what you're going to do with your portion of the money we'll be getting?" he added, turning slightly contemplative again.

Dave wandered leisurely along the edge of the track, safely away from the passing cyclists, chomping down on his cheese sarnie. "I was thinking about buying a house," he offered, once his mouth was clear. "Maybe I'll put the cash towards a deposit."

"Oh," said Monty, this revelation being news to him. "Are you fed up with renting?" he asked.

"Well, I'm not getting any younger, Monty, my old son," Dave told him, sighing heavily. He lowered his head, kicking a loose stone along the tarmac as he walked along, deep in his own thoughts.

"What's up, buddy?" Monty asked, drawing up alongside.

"Hmm? Whaddya mean?" Dave answered.

Monty looked him up and down, concern evident across his face. "You're not yourself this morning, buddy. You've been fairly quiet," he said. "And just now, I couldn't help noticing you only took one sandwich from the ladies at the table as opposed to your usual two," he pointed out. Dave suddenly reducing his caloric intake was like a dog with a dry nose, Monty reckoned — a sign that something was seriously amiss. "Is this just about you getting older, as you said? A little long in the tooth? Is that what's playing on your mind?"

"No, not at all," Dave replied with a laugh. "I'm a magnificent specimen, only improving after each and every day on planet

Earth, ageing like a fine wine."

"Daaaave," Monty added, badgering, persistent bugger that he was, moving in front of the big man and preventing Dave from progressing further. "What's going on in there?" Monty asked, reaching up and gently tapping Dave on the side of the noggin.

Dave took a step to his left, in an attempt to circumnavigate this present obstacle in his path, but his evasive manoeuvres were countered immediately by Monty, who adjusted his position accordingly. Undaunted, Dave repeated the process, this time taking two steps to his right. Again, however, his path was blocked by Monty, who mirrored his movements precisely. Indeed, the parents behind the picnic table may well have thought the two of them were practising a waltz due to the impressive choreography on display, or perhaps studying to be mimes in order to see who could be the next Marcel Marceau.

"Dave...?" Monty said, cocking his head.

"Ah, you know me too well," Dave said wearily, shoulders sagging under the weight of the baggage inside his head. "It's women trouble, Monty," Dave confessed, in a rarely witnessed display of emotional vulnerability.

Monty nodded in response, staring up at Dave intently. So intently, in fact, that for a brief moment his eyes sat uncharacteristically uniform, both focussing on the same thing, before saying their long goodbyes and going their separate ways once again, as per their usual misaligned configuration. "I thought you and Becks were getting along?" Monty asked softly.

"We are," replied Dave. "And therein lies the problem."

"That's the problem?" Monty asked, not seeing the problem. "How's that an issue? That's often an indication that things are going *well*, Dave, not poorly."

"Becks and Tyler are only staying at the TT Farm due to the domestic issues she was having at home," Dave explained, pointing in the vague direction of where home might be. "She keeps talking about how happy she is and how, finally, her life's getting back on track." Dave slowly shook his head in summary.

"So, you can see the problem?"

"Yeah," Monty said, appeasing the big guy momentarily, but then, "Actually, no. What the hell are you on about, Dave? If Becks had told you she was running off with the milkman, I could understand that being a bad thing. But what you're describing is a good thing, David J Quirk. A *good* thing."

"She told me she's hoping to move out of the TT Farm," Dave confided, walking around Monty successfully this time, and kicking out at a loose stone once more. "Said she wants to free up her room for someone else who'd benefit from it. Which makes sense, I suppose. But, Monty, I'm worried in case she decides she's ready to return to the UK. I'm worried they're both going to leave me."

"Oi, you silly sausage," Monty said, skipping alongside, eager to put a positive spin on things. "You always knew she was going to leave the TT Farm eventually, Dave. After all, that's the entire *purpose* of it," he told him. "You check in when life deals you a lousy hand, and when things hopefully pick up, you move on to bigger and better things. And that's precisely what's happened to Becks and Tyler, yeah? The things getting better part, I mean. *But*, she's found herself a new job, new friends, and a new home all in the Isle of Man. So why would she want to up sticks and head back to the UK now?"

"You could be right, Monty, thanks," Dave answered, placing his meathook hand over his mate's shoulder, pulling him in closer so his head tucked in next to his armpit. "You're a real pal," he added, perking up and finding the strength to polish off what remained of the half-eaten sandwich still safely housed in his spare hand. "It would still be nice to have a place of my own," Dave added dreamily, pressing the last of his sandwich into his gob, spilling crumbs down into Monty's hair.

"And plenty room for the three of you?" Monty ventured, enjoying his cuddle. "Possibly *more* than three, eventually, if things go especially well...?" he added cheekily.

Dave chose to step right over that expanding family comment. "And if I did happen to own my own home, then it might be another solid reason for them both to stay here," he said, thinking aloud.

"It could," Monty agreed, without removing his head from Dave's armpit area. "But would the cash from the TV episodes be enough for a deposit?"

"Nah," Dave sighed. "It's a good start, of course. But I reckon I'd need at least another eight to ten grand," he explained, releasing Monty from his vice-like grasp, giving his hair an affectionate ruffle both for good measure and to shake away the remnants of his sandwich stuck in there.

Dave turned towards the racing action, offering an enthusiastic cheer of encouragement to the next cyclist pedalling furiously by, legs going like the clappers. With the 600-cc engine powering Dave and Monty's sidecar, a lap of the Jürburgring would have been completed quick as a flash. But for these plucky kids, some of whom were in the under-eights category, it must have presented itself as rather more daunting, especially with a headwind as was in attendance today.

"Go on!" Dave yelled, full of admiration for the little tykes on their bikes. "They're probably going around here quicker than us, Monty, whaddya reckon?" he asked his cohort stood beside him.

But Monty didn't respond, instead staring vacantly towards the ground like a man with things on his mind. "I can loan you some dosh," he said, running the sums through his head and using his fingers to confirm the calculations as to what he felt he could safely part with.

"What, now?"

"Out of my share of the money," Monty told him. "I've got at least two grand spare that I can give you towards your house deposit. I'd happily let you have the full five, but I've already paid a deposit to get these removed at a private surgery," he went on, pointing in the general direction of his buttocks. "So the rest of my money is already earmarked, I'm afraid. Or then again, it's *rear*marked, I should say."

"You're getting the piles removed?" Dave asked, delighted for his chum, and also for his chum's bum. "Monty, that's amazing news."

"I was going to surprise you," Monty explained, although precisely what element of this impending surgical procedure was going to be a pleasant surprise to Dave would be anyone's guess. "I was speaking with Stella at the wedding," Monty went on, moving on from merely pointing at, to now enthusiastically caressing, his right bum cheek. "It turns out she shared the same general affliction as me, Dave. But from what she was telling me, hers were the size of conkers," he said, with a pained, sympathetic wince. "Stella's given me the number of the private practice who specialise in this sort of thing. It's not cheap, but it'll pay for itself inside two years just from the cash I'll save on medicated cream and lubricated toilet roll."

Dave shuddered at the mental image being painted for him. "Firstly, I'm genuinely pleased you'll soon be saying goodbye to your unwanted lodgers, Monty. Secondly, your offer is greatly appreciated, my friend. But that's your money, and I wouldn't feel right about taking it. Though I do sincerely appreciate the offer."

Monty went to speak but held himself back for a moment, wavering, uncertain as to whether to continue with what he was about to say. "Dave," he offered eventually, after a bit of contemplation, pressing his hand to his head and massaging his scalp. "Dave, there could be another option," he suggested.

But before Monty could elaborate or give any further details, a child's voice, tinged with emotion, attracted both of their attention. "Mistermunty!" the young lad called out, having possibly misheard Monty's correct name at the earlier pre-race briefing. "Mistermunty!" the boy called out again, and judging by the size of the little guy, he was likely one of the campaigners in the under-eight category.

"What's up, little dude?" Monty answered, stepping out onto the live track once it was clear no other cyclists were approaching.

It was evident the young lad was suffering from some form

of technical malfunction on his sprocketed steed, as his cheeks were scarlet, and he was struggling with every rotation of his pedals like he was cycling through beach sand. "Something's... wrong... with... my... bike... Mistermunty...!" the lad explained, taking a large gulp of air between each word. And then he came to a halt, the required effort of his endeavours simply too much to endure.

"Fear not!" Monty called over, quickening his pace to cover the short distance between them. "What's your name, son?" he asked upon arrival at the scene, placing his hands on the lad's handlebars.

"Oliver," replied Oliver, dismounting his wounded beast and throwing it a look of contempt. "I'm going to be in last place," the boy said, throwing his arms across his chest and pushing out his bottom lip. "Stupid bike."

"Hey, now," Monty said, flipping the bike upside down so it was resting on its saddle. "Let the dog see the rabbit, and we'll have you on your way in no time," he advised, sensing that a downpour of boohoos was imminent.

Monty adjusted his position, lowering himself down onto one knee next to the rear wheel. He gripped the tyre, spinning the wheel, but the pathetic amount of distance it travelled suggested the issue was potentially a sticking brake. "Right," he said, sounding confident now he'd diagnosed the problem. "We just need to whip the rear wheel off," Monty explained, expertly loosening the quick-release mechanism holding the wheel in place and removing the wheel in less time than it took to say he needed to remove the wheel.

Oliver unfolded his arms, leaning over Monty's shoulder to see what was going on, tears on hold for now. "That's the problem there, see?" Monty told the boy, taking a flathead screwdriver from his waist-mounted toolbelt and then moving his nose in for a closer inspection.

Several quick adjustments later, Monty replaced the wheel, reattached the chain, and span the tyre to show it was now moving freely and without interference. "Bingo," Monty said, pushing himself upright again. "That should get you to the finish line," he suggested, flipping the bike over so it came to a rest on its tyres, right-side-up. "Now, go get 'em, Oliver!" Monty said, stepping to one side and inviting the lad to climb aboard and be on his way.

"Thanks, Mistermunty!" Oliver replied, mounting up and pushing off. He pressed down on his pedals with fury, head buried, bum in the air, desperate to catch up the guys in front.

Monty sighed a contented sigh, rubbing his hands together in a satisfied, *that's-taken-care-of-that* manner.

"I'm impressed," Dave remarked, watching as Oliver disappeared from view. "Mistermunty," Dave added with a chuckle. "That nickname might just catch on."

"I've been called worse," Monty replied. "Anyway, about what I was saying before attending to that impromptu pitstop."

"Yeah?" Dave said, giving his undivided attention to Monty. "Go on..."

"Well," Monty said. "Firstly, Dave, before I begin, you need to understand there's a reason why I didn't tell you this earlier, okay? So you won't be angry?"

"Never," Dave offered with a cheery smile. "Just spit it out, man. I'm starting to get my appetite back and want to take full advantage of the refreshments table before the kids get to it."

"Okay," Monty said, taking a precautionary step back, just in case. "Okay, I won't beat around the bush, Dave, so here it is. A large online gambling company heard about our upcoming appearance in this documentary series."

"All right?" Dave said, swirling his fingers in the air, inviting further detail.

"They said they wanted to sponsor us for the race, Dave. They think it'd be great coverage for them and were excited about the partnership opportunities."

"Oh-kay," Dave said, his eyes narrowing a little bit. "And just how much sponsorship money are we talking about, Monty?"

Monty suddenly found his mouth dry. "Ehm..." he said, running his tongue over his top lip. "You mean from this gambling company?" Monty asked, even though that was obviously the information Dave was attempting to glean, as Monty himself was the one to have just brought it up. "Thirty grand," Monty revealed, lowering his head like a naughty dog who'd just pissed on the carpet, despite this seemingly good news.

Dave started to laugh, eager to hear the inevitable hilarious punchline to this little anecdote. That is until he could see that Monty was deadly serious. "You're kidding?"

"No, but here's the thing—"

"Thirty grand!" Dave shrieked, with the ear-splitting pitch of a man suddenly catching himself in his zipper. "Please tell me you accepted it?" Dave said, staggering forward like a zombie, arms extended. "Monty...?" Dave said, placing his sausage fingers on Monty's shoulders.

"I declined," Monty said, almost inaudibly. "But, Dave, just listen for a moment, yeah?"

Dave tightened his grip just a smidge. "I'm listening," he confirmed, forcing a smile. Well, if exposing his front canine teeth and his left eye twitching madly could be considered a smile.

"Right," Monty began. "Right, okay, so this company wants maximum exposure in return for their sponsorship funding, Dave. Which is fair enough."

"Fair enough," Dave said in agreement.

"So," Monty continued. "There was a major condition to us getting the bulk of the cash."

"Which was?"

"Well, we have to qualify for and then participate in at least one of the two sidecar races," Monty explained. "They proposed giving us an advance of two grand in return for placing their logos on our bike and our leathers. So the advance would be ours to keep, regardless. But the remainder and bulk of the dosh is incentive-based to maximise their coverage."

"Makes sense," Dave suggested. "They don't want to give us a load of cash if we then blow the engine on the first night of practice, I suppose. However, I'm struggling to understand why

FRANK & STAN'S BUCKET LIST #5: ISLE OF MAN TT ACES

you'd decline such a generous offer, Monty. But I'm looking forward to finding out why."

"Ah. Well," Monty pressed on. "You see, the other and most challenging part of their conditions is that we'd need to finish at least one race in the top ten to secure the moolah."

"Top ten," Dave said, deflating like a car tyre with the fill valve pulled out. "That's a bit tricky, Monty," he added, releasing his firm grip, suggesting Monty was no longer in any imminent danger.

"That's why I declined their generous offer, Dave. We'll be giving it everything we have just to break into the top twenty, let alone getting anywhere near the top ten. So with the temptation of all that cash on the table, I suppose I was worried we'd do something stupid and push ourselves too far beyond our limits."

"I completely agree," Dave agreed, catching Monty off-guard.

"You do?"

"Sure I do," Dave replied. "And as much as I love our sidecar, Monty, the simple fact is that it's just not in the same league as the other outfits that will be in the top ten. For that reason, it's definitely a distraction we don't need, Monty. You made the right decision, my son."

"Ah, bugger," Monty said. "I didn't think you'd agree with me so readily, Dave. I was expecting you to go all gung-ho on me and tell me how we'd spend countless nights working on the bike so we could break into that top-ten position and bag the cash, convincing me we could overcome the impossible like something from a Rocky movie."

"I'm starting to get mixed messages from you, Monty, I really am. You know as well as I do that the only way our sidecar could finish in the top ten is if we strapped a jet engine to our backs like in a bloody cartoon. Aside from that, we've not got a snowball in hell's chance."

"But..." Monty suggested, changing tack, teasing Dave with a flurry of eyebrow flapping. "But just imagine if we *could* do it," Monty said, allowing Dave the opportunity to imagine that very outcome for a moment. "Dave, you're a TT winner, after all. So, with a bit of extra work on the bike, maybe we could dare to dream, you know? Dare to dream."

Dave ran his fingers upwards through his hair, following the trajectory of Monty's eyebrows. "Monty, have you *actually* told this gambling company we're not interested? Because, from the way you're talking, I'm starting to think—"

"I've not categorically declined their offer as such, no," Monty admitted. "I wanted to tell them it was a no, yeah? But then I kept thinking of all that lovely lolly, Dave. Lovely lolly..." he said, repeating himself again.

"So why did you *say* you'd declined them, man? I'm getting right bloody confused, Monty."

"I told them I'd get back to them, Dave. I wanted to sound you out first. So whaddya reckon, then? Should I tell them that we're in?"

"Yes, Monty. Yes you should," Dave said firmly, suddenly reconsidering. "We've nothing to lose, and thirty thousand reasons why we should give it a go," he added. "We've just under three weeks to figure out how we're going to get that big blue boiled sweet of ours into the top ten, but it can't be *that* hard, can it?" Dave asked with a friendly wink.

Although, of course, what they were proposing was indeed hard, and exceptionally so. To even finish a race at the Isle of Man TT was a monumental task in itself, due to the physical and mechanical challenges that the circuit was ready to throw at you. This they both knew. Yes, Dave had won a TT, but that was on a professionally outfitted bike, with no expense spared. That was certainly not the case with their own machine, where they, like many other teams, operated within the confines of a shoestring budget.

But what they didn't have in cutting-edge technology was more than made up for in passion, grit, and experience, or at least so they hoped. After all, you could have the fastest machine on the grid, but you still had to know your way around each and every intimate twist and turn of the 37.73-mile track.

FRANK & STAN'S BUCKET LIST #5: ISLE OF MAN TT ACES

Only those seasoned campaigners knew where to keep the accelerator pinned in top gear when others may roll off a little, losing vital seconds in the process, for example. The knowledge gathered from returning to this magnificent racetrack each year was just as valuable as, say, the precision of the suspension set-up or the quality of the rubber on your tyres. If you wanted to even consider crossing the finishing line, everything had to go in your favour as the variables conspiring against you were considerable. Races had been lost due to issues such as a wire shaken loose or an empty fuel tank with the finishing line agonisingly in view. The margins for error were razor-thin. There was a well-used saying around the isle that in order to finish first, you first had to finish — a statement that would have been on most competitors' minds. And also just another contributing factor making the Isle of Man TT the greatest and most challenging road race on earth.

"We can *do* this," Monty said, pacing around Dave like a matador goading an angry bull, though Dave didn't really need any goading at this point, nor was he angry. "We'll use all our years of experience to get the bike purring like a kitten," Monty advised, smiling confidently. "I'm going to use every ounce of my mechanical brilliance to squeeze out every last drop of horsepower from our engine, Dave. She'll be like a rocket ship by the time I've finished with her!" he declared. "And our only problem at that stage will be how we can manage to hang onto her!" he said, coming to a triumphant halt in front of Dave.

"Mechanical brilliance?" Dave said, impressed by Monty's modesty. But then Dave was distracted for a moment, spotting something on the tarmac behind where Monty was standing. "Okay, Monty. If you're such a mechanical genius, what does that thing lying next to your feet do, then?" Dave enquired.

Monty jumped at the opportunity to showcase his extensive knowledge on such matters, crouching down to retrieve the item in question. He ran his good eye over the piece as he gradually straightened to normal height. "Hmm," Monty said, murmuring to himself as he considered options, weighing up the various possibilities, until finally a magnificent moment of realisation presented itself to him. "Yes!" Monty said, victory at hand, looking confidently at his buddy and fully prepared to cover himself in glory. "This, Dave," Monty said. *"This* is a quick-release mechanism from a *bicycle*," he proudly declared, shifting the item held in his palm closer to Dave's face for his inspection.

"Yeah," said Dave, nodding. "Yeah, I would completely agree with your analysis."

Dave stared intently at Monty, listening out for any gears that might be turning inside of Monty's head, clicking into place. But, alas, there were none.

"*And...?*" Dave prompted, when there was no flicker of recognition evident on Monty's face, a face which was presently smiling back at him simply, smug in its own satisfaction. Several seconds later, Dave could see the moment of horror on Monty's mush upon realising precisely what it was that he was holding in his grubby little mitt.

"No!" Monty said, looking at the item, up to Dave, and then back to the item. "Dave, this is from..." he began to say, but what he was about to say was a fact Dave was already obviously well aware of. "Ah, crap," Monty added, in a state of panic now. "His wheel could come loose at any moment!" Monty cried, turning on the spot, and then sprinting up the tarmac while waving the part above his head. "Olllliiiivvvveeeer, slow dowwwnnn!" Monty screamed, running as fast as his chubby little legs could carry him.

"What a plonker," Dave said with a chuckle, folding his arms across his chest and shaking his head sadly.

Chapter
FIVE

"So much for taking things easier," Stan remarked with a wry smile. "Sign here?" he asked, seeking clarification, looking up, fountain pen poised above the document.

"Yes, please," the solicitor confirmed from her side of the table. "So," she said, once Stan had taken his turn signing the form. "That's everything finalised for you," she was pleased to report.

"The business is ours?" Frank asked, receiving a confident nod in return.

"It certainly is," the solicitor added. "And may I be the first one to formally congratulate you both on what I hope is a rewarding venture."

"Thank you, Catherine," Stan answered. "You've been wonderful throughout the entire process," he told her, sharing a giddy grin with Frank, sat next to him. "Frank, we own a car hire company!" he said, though this was naturally information Frank was already happily aware of. "We should celebrate with a glass of something fizzy," Stan suggested. "Catherine, you're most welcome to join us?" he offered, raising an imaginary glass to his lips.

"Thanks, but it's a little too early for me," she said with a gentle laugh, looking over to the wall-mounted clock telling her it was well before noon. "Plus I'm still on duty, of course."

"Okay, then," Frank said, pushing his chair back. "Thank you again, Catherine. And, if you ever need to hire a car, Frank 'n' Stan's Hire is ready to cater for your every need," he cheerfully advised. "So, come on, Stan, tell me more about this drink," he told his chum, as the two of them headed towards the door.

Frank and Stan skipped out of the solicitor's office, each of them with a spring in their step. "It's rather scary how you can spend that amount of cash with the swipe of a pen," Stan commented.

"Where to now?" Frank asked, looking up and down Athol Street, an area of Douglas frequented by the business community.

"How's about we wander down to the quayside and get a nice little table somewhere outside. Soak up some of this glorious sunshine over a spot of early lunch?" Stan suggested.

"I could eat," Frank replied, following Stan's lead as they turned in the direction indicated. "What about the fish restaurant over by—"

"Yes, hello!" a familiar voice called out from behind them. "Mr Sidcup!" it sounded again, loud enough to attract the pair's attention.

Stan turned on his heel, wondering why someone was calling his name. "Oh, hello," he said, as a waving Catherine approached. "Did you reconsider our offer of that drink?" Stan asked, raising the imaginary glass to his lips once more.

"Oh, no," Catherine said with a half-laugh, and somewhat breathless from her exertion running down the flight of stairs and chasing after them. "No, still too early for me," she said, presenting herself before the two of them. "I think you've accidentally taken my fountain pen," she explained, in a tone that didn't come across as too accusing, but firm enough to suggest she absolutely *knew* Stan had absconded with her pen.

"Have I?" Stan asked, patting himself down to locate the contraband in question. "Oh, bugger," he added, feeling a pen-shaped implement inside his jacket pocket.

"Tut-tut," Frank said, shaking his head from side to side in a sort of amused disapproval. "He's always doing this," he told

Catherine, the solicitor. "It's because of his sticky fingers he got himself barred from the florists, for instance."

"What?" said Stan, laughing nervously. "That wasn't because I was stealing, Frank," he said, choosing not to elaborate on the actual reason. "Ah, here we go," Stan said, retrieving the elegant, expensive-looking pen from its hiding place and returning it to its rightful owner. "Terribly sorry."

"Enjoy your drink, gentlemen," Catherine said, heading back to her office with her property recovered.

"Why did you tell her about the florists?" Stan grumbled, after she'd gone. "That was all a misunderstanding, Frank, and you know it."

"Come on, flower boy," Frank said. "Let's get out of here before you get us both arrested."

A gentle sea breeze kept Frank and Stan cool while they wandered casually around the quayside, running their eyes over the array of boats bobbing gently on the tide. "We are indeed lucky to live here," Stan observed, as he and Frank paused to appreciate one impressive, magnificent craft berthed up beside them in particular.

"I wouldn't fancy having to climb that mast, though," Frank remarked, tilting his head skyward. "Mind you, if you could afford to buy something like that, I'm sure you'd have staff to attend to such matters," he considered.

"Oh, I don't know. I've climbed a mast or two in my day," Stan commented, though mostly to himself. "Anyway, yes, she's a stunner, alright," Stan agreed, appreciating the polished brass fittings and luxurious appointments laid out on the rear deck of the especially large vessel. "You'd feel a little inadequate if you had to park your boat up next to *this* beauty, wouldn't you?" Stan said. "A bit like the owner of the HMS Heap right over there," he remarked with a laugh, looking down his nose at the tiny-by-comparison vessel moored directly behind the rather-more-impressive ship in front of it. "It's like Beauty and the

Beast," he added, chuckling away at his own impeccable wit.

"I can bloody hear you, you know!" the owner of the good ship *Heap* shouted from inside his wheelhouse, presently obscured from Stan's field of view. "So," the shaven-headed captain said, now appearing out on his humble deck, wiping his hands on an oily rag. "This heap, as you call it, is what puts food on my table."

Frank took a judicious step to his right, away from Stan, leaving his mate to dangle in the wind and squirm his way out of this one alone.

"I-I-I... That is..." Stan stammered, caught off-guard by the man's sudden appearance.

"I-I-I," the angry captain stuttered back, mocking Stan.

"I didn't mean to cause any offence," Stan pleaded, feeling embarrassed now and hoping to appease the situation. "Look, Captain. Please accept my apologies," he said, drifting over to where the smaller boat was docked, tail between his legs. "If there's anything I can do to make amends, then—"

"Paint my boat," the captain replied without any hesitation whatsoever, accepting Stan's offer immediately.

"What's that?" said Stan, jerking his head back in surprise.

"You just said you wanted to make amends," the captain answered, tossing his rag down on the deck. "So, you can help me paint my wheelhouse. That will make up for hurting both my feelings and the feelings of my boat. Unless you didn't mean what you said by your apology, which would cause me even *more* offence."

Stan offered an uneasy laugh, looking to Frank for some form of support that was unfortunately not forthcoming. "Wait, you mean right *now*?" Stan asked, after returning his attention to the boat and noticing the captain waiting there impatiently, arms crossed. "But I'm wearing a *suit*," Stan protested. "And these are my *good shoes*," he added, lifting one leg slightly into the air so that the shoes mentioned could be fully appreciated by the irate skipper. "They're from *Italy*."

"There are overalls in that box," came the reply. "And you don't need to wear shoes to paint, now do you?"

"Well... no," Stan conceded, wondering if he should just start running, though deciding that probably wouldn't be an easy task in designer Italian shoes. "Frank?" Stan said in desperation, hoping for some assistance.

Giving a lick of paint to an old weather-beaten 1970's boat, wearing his good trousers, certainly wasn't what Stan thought he would be doing when he'd woken up that morning. But paint he did, with Frank eventually pitching in and lending a hand as well, not letting Stan have all the fun. And despite initial concerns that the captain was more than a little bit unhinged, the two of them had a most agreeable couple of hours working up a sweat in the Manx sunshine. Captain Gary — or simply Gary to his friends — was actually a thoroughly decent chap, as it turned out, even making them a nice cuppa to keep them all hydrated.

"I think I want to buy a boat," Stan confidently declared, wandering over and placing his hand on the wheel after finishing up his portion of the work. "I reckon I'd look quite splendid in my captain's outfit."

"Like I do?" asked Captain Gary, bending over a lobster pot, his builder's bum on full display.

"I've no comment, Gary, as I'd probably end up mowing your grass if I offended you further," Stan joked.

"That's us all done, skipper," Frank said, applying one last finishing touch to the spot he was working on and then taking a step back to admire his and Stan's collective handiwork. "I bloody well enjoyed that, Gary," Frank added, taking a lungful of the heady mix of salty sea air and paint fumes. "And, I think I've worked up even more of an appetite now, Stanley," Frank remarked, checking his hand was clear of paint before rubbing his tum. "Gary, would you care to join us for lunch?"

"No thanks," Gary answered, continuing what he was doing. "I've been collecting lobster pots this morning, and I smell like rotten mackerel, so I'm not exactly company-ready."

"Yes, you do," Stan ventured bravely, climbing out of his overalls, inspecting himself for any splashes of paint that may have broken through the lines. "Though I'd have suggested herring rather than mackerel," he added, giving the air a little sniff.

"The scent of a hard day's graft," Gary mused, taking a seat on the capstan on deck to savour the rest of his brew. "So, I'll give you a ring to come out fishing soon?"

"Love to," Frank said. "And that would be very kind of you."

"Only if it's not too much of a heap for you to be seen sailing aboard?" Gary asked, looking directly to Stan.

"Well, it's certainly better since we painted the wheelhouse," Stan observed. "But would it kill you to put an air freshener or two around the place?" he added, although offering a smile to show he was only giving a friendly ribbing. "Permission to head ashore, Captain?" Stan asked with a sharp salute.

"Right. Piss off, you lot," Captain Gary playfully replied. "It was a pleasure to meet you both, all things considered," he said with a chuckle. "Now off you two landlubbers go."

A little later than originally planned, Frank and Stan had parked their bums outside a lovely seafood restaurant on the quayside, enjoying the outdoor seating. "I guess we'll be getting a taxi home, rather than driving ourselves?" Stan suggested, swirling the ice cubes around in his drink and entirely hopeful of another alcoholic beverage or three.

"Paint my boat," Frank said, relaxing back in his chair, taking a thirsty gulp of his gin fizz. "Ahh," he said, with a happy sigh. "Your face was a picture, Stanley," Frank added as he recalled Stan's bewildered expression at the time, which set him off chuckling once again at the very thought of it. "Paint my boat... Brilliant."

"Yes, well you ended up painting it as well, lest you forget," Stan commented, feeling the need to point this out. "But he didn't look too happy there at the beginning, did he?" Stan added. "I thought he was going to throw me in the harbour!"

"He turned out to be a smashing bloke, though," Frank said, still smiling in fond remembrance. "I'm quite looking forward to heading out on the boat, as well," he went on, casting off with his imaginary rod, jiggling it about before reeling in a whopper, even though that's not the way one ordinarily catches a lobster. "If we do enjoy it, Stan, we could think about getting one of our own? A boat in general, I mean, not a lobster boat specifically."

"Sure, I suppose we could," Stan agreed, just at the same time as something caught his attention, looking over the rim of his sunglasses to a small group of people walking in their general direction. Stan leaned forward in his seat, placing his drink down on the tabletop. "Is that not...?" he added, holding his gaze.

"Dave and Monty?" Frank replied, after following his friend's eyeline.

"I *thought* it was them," Stan said, removing his sunglasses and waving them over, though the pair didn't immediately see them. "Who are they with?" he asked Frank through the corner of his mouth, noting the two gentlemen walking beside them.

"Dunno," Frank said with a shrug, before quickly adding, "Wait. Was it today those TV documentary fellows were flying in? Perhaps it's them."

"Hi, boys!" Stan called out, rising up out of his chair. "Dave! Monty!" he shouted, receiving quizzical glances from those out enjoying a stroll in the sunshine. "Over here!"

Dave, finally alerted as to Frank and Stan's presence by Stan's caterwauling, strolled leisurely over to the restaurant's outdoor seating deck, entourage in tow. "Early start?" Dave surmised, noting the two bulbous gin glasses.

"It's never too early for a gin," Stan advised, before then glancing over to the two chaps accompanying their friends.

"Oh," said Dave, noting Stan's wandering attention. "Frank? Stan? Allow me to introduce you to Brad and Chip from the mighty USA."

Brad stepped forward with his hand extended. "Dave and Monty have told us all about you. It's a pleasure."

Frank stood to return the welcome. "Ah. Twins," Frank remarked (as nothing at all got past the ever-observant Frank). "Please, join us," he said, introducing the empty table adjacent to theirs. "How about a beer to welcome you to the island?"

"Or a gin fizz?" Stan suggested. "They're delicious."

The waiter soon appeared with a large tray of gin fizzes and a cheery smile. "Something to eat, gentlemen?" he politely enquired. "Our lunchtime special is a delicious golden beer-battered fish accompanied by twice-cooked chips."

"Sounds lovely," Frank said. "A bite to eat?" he asked, running his eyes around the wider group, receiving energetic nods in response. "Fish and chips all around, please," he declared.

Once the waiter had headed away with their food order, Stan adjusted his seat to face the new arrivals. "So, you're going to make stars of Dave and Monty?" he asked, but before a response could even be offered, Stan quickly added, "I've some experience on the screen myself, and I've been told the camera loves me."

Stan's rather bold, forthright claim resulted in both Dave and Monty erupting into laughter. "Told you!" Monty said, slapping the top of his thigh in mirthful delight. "Didn't I tell you?" he added, looking to Brad and Chip for confirmation of his prognosticative prowess.

Brad and Chip, for their part, smiled courteously. "You did," Chip answered politely, not wanting to return the frivolity for fear of offending someone he'd only just met.

"Oh? What's this?" Frank asked, hoping to get in on the joke, especially now that he didn't appear to be the butt of it.

"Clark Gable over there," Monty explained, reaching over and nudging Stan playfully on the arm. "I said that the minute he met Brad and Chip, he'd be telling them how he'd once been in an advert."

"It was a *commercial*," Stan replied with an air of sophistication about him, as if saying it that way made it much more impressive somehow. "And, I'll have you know that my performance was very well received by the critics."

"What critics?" Frank entered in jovially. "It was an advert for eggs, wasn't it?"

"Yes, but one that would have been seen by at least four thousand people," Stan was eager to point out. "Both my teacher at the time *and* my neighbour each commended my performance, saying that I had real star quality, I'll have you know," he said, crossing his arms, and looking directly over to Brad and Chip, allowing them time to appreciate the glowing critical reviews he'd received. "I was told egg sales increased by eleven percent," Stan added after a moment. "Now, I'm not saying the uplift was all down to me, but..." he said, trailing away dramatically in a manner suggesting that this was precisely what he *was* indeed saying.

"I'm sure our camera is looking forward to meeting you," Chip said, happy to appease his new friend. "So," he added, moving the conversation along, "I have to pinch myself, because it seems like a dream that we're back here again," he said, looking around him, soaking in the environment.

"It's a magical place for sure," Frank said, happily sharing the sentiment. "Stan and I haven't lived here for too long, but the beauty of the place takes my breath away."

"Whereabouts are you both staying?" Stan asked, by way of conversation.

"We rented a house in Douglas," Brad replied. "We were just there dropping our recording equipment and luggage off, as a matter of fact, when Dave and Monty so graciously offered to show us around town. We've been to the TT once before, but didn't get to see much of Douglas when we were here previously. Anyway, with the TT coming up again soon, we were real lucky to find someplace to stay on such short notice, since all the hotels were booked up when we phoned around."

"Yeah, you'd be crazy to turn up without anything booked," Frank answered, casting a smile in Stan's direction.

Stan scowled briefly at Frank, knowing precisely what was implied by Frank's pointed comment and sideways, grinning glance, though aside from that not giving his chum the benefit of a response.

Brad and Chip's guided tour of Douglas was put on hold, for the time being, when a further round of drinks arrived to wash down their delicious lunch, which also arrived in short order.

FRANK & STAN'S BUCKET LIST #5: ISLE OF MAN TT ACES

Frank and Stan didn't mind, however, as it was a delight to listen to the way they spoke passionately about their upcoming documentary project. The brothers explained how the Isle of Man's TT wasn't known by many in America, other than a select group of motorcycling enthusiasts for whom the very mention of the place sent shivers running down their collective spines. Brad and Chip felt confident they could bring the event to a broader audience by telling the story through both the eyes of those competing and the diehard fanatics who returned to see the race each year. The intention was to keep the footage real, in their words. They weren't looking to create a polished feature, but rather a travelogue video diary format that'd been their modus operandi on previous projects to date and one that worked well for them. They described how the raw, unscripted footage often proved to be the most effective, and made for more compelling viewing.

In addition to Dave and Monty appearing as competitors, they'd also secured the participation of several regular, visiting spectators willing to share their love of the event, with a few of them travelling thousands of miles to be there each and every year. By their own admission, Brad and Chip weren't working to a rigid script, choosing to just go with the flow and roll with any punches, confident the compelling story of the Isle of Man TT would present itself to them. They were also happy to point out that Dave and Monty securing a TT victory during their upcoming campaign would undoubtedly help raise the profile of their documentary. Of course, neither Brad nor Chip wanted to tempt fate, but both remained quietly confident in this regard concerning Dave and Monty's impending win.

"Right, you two. What the dickens is going on?" Frank asked, glaring across the table once Brad and Chip had gone off to the bathroom temporarily.

"What?" Dave and Monty both replied innocently, in unison.

Frank looked over his shoulder, making absolutely sure their new American friends were still out of earshot. "Why do Brad and Chip..." Frank began, taking another precautionary glance.

"Why do they keep talking about you two dipsticks like you're contenders for a TT victory?"

Monty shifted uneasily in his seat, pushing his fork around his plate. "Yeah, ehm..." he replied eventually. "Yeah, I suppose they *are* quite optimistic now you come to mention it," he suggested with a nervous laugh.

"Quite optimistic?" Stan said, jumping on Monty's words and playing them back to him. "You just promised them, only moments ago, that you wouldn't spray their camera with the winner's champagne, Monty! So you weren't exactly dampening their expectations, were you?"

"Yeah," Dave entered in, shaking his head. *"Honestly*, Monty," he said, followed by an audible tut-tut in regard to his friend's disgraceful behaviour.

"I think..." Monty offered, thinking. "That is... I believe Brad and Chip may have assumed our chances of appearing on the podium are a little higher than they perhaps actually are."

"And you've not put either of them straight on that point?" Stan asked.

"Well..." Monty said, considering his response for a moment or two. "Not exactly, no," he eventually offered. "You see, apparently, they've told their bosses back in America that they've signed up one of the lead favourites to win the sidecar race. So I didn't really want to disappoint them."

Frank looked over to Stan, and then back to Monty. "And why would they assume you're one of the lead favourites to win?" he asked, incredulous. "Surely they must have looked into the two of you and done their homework in advance? I mean, surely?"

"You would think," Dave chipped in, happily chuckling away at the unfortunate misunderstanding (though not really *that* unfortunate, considering the amount of money he and Monty stood to get paid).

"They *have* done their homework," Monty insisted. "Well, to a certain extent, at least. You see, they'd read all about Dave Quirk, glorious TT winner, and must have assumed from that information that he's one of the current leading contenders. I mean, you would too, wouldn't you?"

"Yeah, but that TT win was with a completely different passenger, and more importantly, riding one of the finest bikes money can buy," Stan said. "They're not aware of that fact?"

"No," Monty offered flatly. "But I didn't deliberately mislead them when they first made contact," Monty was eager to point out. "They wanted to sign up a TT winner for their docuseries, and, technically, that's precisely what they've done," Monty said, pointing to his chum and former TT winner sat next to him.

"It's like hiring a Grand National jockey and finding out he's presently riding a donkey," Dave suggested with a shrug.

"Wait, who's the donkey?" Monty asked. "Me or the bike?"

"I dunno," Dave said with a chuckle. "Either would work?"

"Don't you think you should at least try and manage their expectations?" Frank whispered, catching sight of Brad and Chip returning from their trip to the loo.

"Nah," Monty answered. "Anyway, who knows, we may end up *actually* contesting at the top of the leaderboard," he added, full of enthusiasm. Or, more likely, gin fizz.

"That's the spirit!" Dave added, offering his dinner-plate-sized hand out for a motivational high five. "Let's aim for the stars, buddy," Dave said. "Only losers understand the true value of a win," he added, with sage-like wisdom.

"What's that supposed to mean?" Monty said, turning up his nose. "Hang on, wasn't that a saying from one of the fortune cookies after last week's Chinese?"

"Yes, it is," Dave said serenely. "And the fortune cookie knows all."

"Waiter!" Stan called out. "I think we're going to need another round of drinks over here!"

Chapter SIX

During the build-up to the TT races, the Isle of Man experienced something of a transformation, and with several familiar signs indicating it was nearly that wonderful time of the year again. Beer tents started to spring up, ready to cater to the thirsty hordes due to shortly invade these ordinarily sedate shores. Safety fences were also deployed around the length of the course, indicating that it would soon morph into one of the world's most famous racing circuits. Additionally, the TT Grandstand area became a hive of activity, with dozens of trucks and vans arriving to occupy their place in the paddock, ready to turn this ordinarily grassy expanse into the most exhilarating, motorsport-themed campsite anywhere on earth for at least the next few weeks.

Of course, there was also a significant unseen effort behind the scenes throughout the year, as the logistical challenges of organising an event on this scale were simply mind-boggling when considering ordinary public roads would be converted into a racetrack for the better part of two weeks. Fortunately, the race organisers were like a well-oiled machine, and ably supported at the time of the race by an army of volunteers, without whom the event simply couldn't happen. Doctors, paramedics, marshals, and many other unsung heroes selflessly contributed their services and talents on each occasion.

When the appointed time approached, it was difficult not to

FRANK & STAN'S BUCKET LIST #5: ISLE OF MAN TT ACES

get caught up in the sense of anticipation, knowing that in only a few short days the island would awake from its usual tranquil existence, roused into life by the arrival of thousands of race fans and the sounds of raw horsepower lingering in the air.

Two of those people counting down the hours until the start of the current TT festival were Dave and Monty, pulling into the paddock in Dave's trusty rust-speckled van.

"I'm that excited that I've got a bulge in my pants, Dave, and I'm not ashamed to admit it," Monty declared cheerfully, while winding down his passenger-side window. "It's down there," he added.

"I'm not bloody looking!" Dave shot back, cringing at the suggestion.

"I'm talking about our pitch now," Monty advised, extending his finger in the direction Dave should proceed. "Park up next to that yellow van. Just there."

"Good!" said Dave, heading as directed. "Because you'd need to buy me at *least* several beers before I looked too closely at Little Monty, if that had been your intention."

It was still three days before the start of the TT festival, but the paddock area was already heaving with vehicles, covering almost every blade of available grass. Giddy faces were happily unloading vans and erecting awnings that would serve as their nerve centres over the next couple of weeks. Some of those early-bird arrivals enjoyed a beer in the sun, catching up with friends and colleagues they may not have seen since the previous year. It was truly an international affair as well, with flags displayed in motorhome windows announcing where the occupants had travelled from in order to complete their various pilgrimages.

Even for those who'd experienced it all before, the thrill of unpacking your machinery at the Isle of Man TT would never wane. Each and every competitor had their individual goals and ambitions. For some, it may have been to complete, for the very first time, a race over this most challenging of courses. For others, who might have raced here before, it may have been to improve upon their personal-best time, and perhaps, daring to dream, even earning a spot up on the coveted winners' podium. Whatever their motivation, whether they were newcomers or seasoned campaigners, their journey to this point would have involved months of diligent preparation, including financial hardships, late nights hunched over their bikes in a freezing cold garage, praying to the mechanical gods in the early hours, and wondering what the hell they'd signed themselves up for. All of that pain, all of the sacrifices, were usually forgotten about the instant they drove their van off the ferry in Douglas. At that moment, all of their blood, sweat, and tears were rendered a distant memory, for they'd arrived. They were soon to become members of an elite racing group of men and women who could say they'd done it, that they'd raced at the Isle of Man TT — a spine-tingling prospect that made it all worthwhile.

"Careful!" Dave shouted, shuffling slowly backward on the ground, his reddened face beginning to show the strain. "Keep it coming, Monty! Careful!" he said, arms shaking under the weight. "Careful!" Dave shouted up to Monty, who stood in the rear area of the van lowering down their critical cargo.

"How about I remain careful until further notice?" Monty snapped back, edging a little bit forward each time Dave moved a little bit back.

"Sorry, mate," Dave offered up. "But if we damage this, it could be curtains for the success of our TT campaign, right?"

"It's a bloody sofa, Dave!" Monty shouted over the armrest positioned inches from his nose. "And it stinks, too," Monty noted, stupidly placing his beak even closer to the well-worn leather. "It's like..." Monty said, searching for the words to best describe the overpowering stench filling his nostrils.

"Wet dog?" Dave suggested, as Monty climbed down from the rear of the van.

"Yes," Monty said in response, placing his side of the sofa down on the grass and then shaking out his fingers, which he then proceeded to sniff. "Wet dog. Exactly. And I've now got the smell stuck in my nose. Please tell me you didn't pay much for this thing?"

"Of course not," Dave replied, lowering his side of the heavy load. "In fact I didn't pay anything at all. Kenny down the road from me was taking it to the tip," Dave explained, tapping the side of his nose, shrewd businessman that he was.

Monty sniffed his digits once more. "I'm guessing he was taking it to the tip because the leather looks like it's worn down to practically nothing, and it bloody reeks?"

"Exactly!" Dave said, as if this was in some way a glowing endorsement of his shrewd acquisition. "We'll just leave it to air out, Monty. And in no time at all, it'll be fresh as a daisy, ready to welcome the visitors to Dave and Monty's hospitality tent."

Monty eyed the sofa with suspicion. "I'm sure I've just seen something jumping around on it."

"That's because it's so comfortable!" Dave countered, tapping his nose once more.

"No, Dave. That's more likely because it's probably infested with fleas?" Monty protested.

But Dave wasn't listening at present as he'd already started in on assembling their canvas headquarters, and with Monty soon lending a hand as well.

Despite the fact that they'd successfully erected their awning numerous times previously, it didn't prevent Dave and Monty from forgetting how and where several of the poles should be placed. And such was Dave's frustration at one point that he was threatening to insert one of those poles up into someone's, anyone's, opening — a particular type of opening certainly not specified or approved of by the manufacturer. Still, a couple of hours later, with two or three cold beers quaffed, their camp was finally complete, looking resplendent, like a sailcloth palace (in Dave and Monty's eyes, at least).

The amply-proportioned awning was divided into two separate areas courtesy of an internal dividing fabric wall. The large section on the right — and closest to the van — was designated as their workshop. This would be home for their bike, and where they would make adjustments and repairs as necessary.

And the equally large space to the left was essentially their lounge/hospitality suite, housing their microwave, beer fridge, new sofa, and additional plastic seating, amongst other appointments.

Being the friendly pair they were, the front access flap to their lounge was rolled up, leaving it open to the elements so that they could chat to those passing by, inviting the more interested of the passersby in for a cuppa or a beer. The motorsport family were generally sociable, so the temporary village that was the paddock became a popular place for visitors to visit and wander through. Here, they could chat with the riders and even observe them making adjustments to their machinery if they wanted to. There was up close and personal access on offer that you rarely found in other sporting events of this scale. And whilst it was, of course, a competitive sport, the teams and competitors involved would happily help another crew out if required. Tools and spare parts often changed hands throughout the festival, and if technical assistance or even a second opinion was needed, well, you just needed to shout.

"Ah!" said Dave, relaxing on the grubby sofa, feet resting on a plastic chair. "Look at this, these two turn up just as the hard work's finished!" he joked, waving to the approaching Frank and Stan.

"Yes, boys!" Frank said, running his eyes around the awning. "The TT is finally here!" he added, punching the air in jubilant delight.

"Sorry we're late," Stan offered, wearily following Frank inside. "The buyers of the taxi business asked for a conference call. Unfortunately, Frank and I aren't close to some of the finer operational details, so we had to invite Stella to join the call to fill in the blanks," he explained.

"So you're definitely going ahead with the sale, then?" Monty asked.

"It looks that way, Monty. The price they're offering is just too generous to turn down," Frank said, though his reply was tinged with a bit of guilt for even considering selling the business they'd nurtured for so long. He massaged the tension away in his head as he started to laugh to himself. "Stella..." he began, incredulous. "Well, first, she dialled in ten minutes late before telling us she couldn't talk for too long as she had a colonic booked."

"An overdue luxury, apparently," Stan chipped in. "It's the first one since she had her piles removed, a fact she was only too happy to divulge to people she'd never spoken to before."

"Fortunately, we warned them in advance that Stella can be a little unorthodox," Frank added, reaching towards the well-stocked beer fridge. "I suspect she was just playing up, though, because she doesn't want us to sell. But at least now we can be pretty confident Stella won't be remaining under the new owners after that little introduction."

"We're hoping she'll come and work with us at the new car hire company," Stan explained to the others. "Frank, we'll call her later once she's had the clearing-out she was briefing us all on," he advised to Frank.

Stan took a seat on the sofa, settling in between Dave and Monty, patting both their knees. "I've missed all of this," he said, smiling broadly, revealing his recently bleached teeth. "So where's the sidecar?" Stan enquired, having noticed the empty workshop area on his way in.

"It's with the graphic design company," Monty replied. "The new sponsors are having their logos placed on the bodywork."

"And," Dave enthusiastically jumped in, "I was moaning to them about how my old leathers have a hole right there," he explained, pointing to his crotch. "So, they've offered to supply us with a brand-new set apiece."

"Perfect," Frank said, happy for the two of them.

Dave looked directly at Frank, and then over to Stan. "You're sure you don't mind? You know, what with you being our original sponsors, and us now getting another company onboard also?"

Frank swatted away the suggestion. "Of course not. If they're offering you all of that cash, then go for it, I say."

"Seconded," Stan added, in happy agreement, after which he then rather abruptly reached around behind him to scratch the small of his back.

"You okay?" Frank asked, noting the pained expression on his mate's face.

"I dunno," Stan replied, clawing furiously. "I just feel really itchy all of a sudden," he said, running his fingernails over the base of his spine. "Also, it stinks of wet dog," he remarked, glancing accusingly at both his neighbours seated next to him on the couch.

With the skin on Stan's back soon raw from scratching, he suggested a return home so he could apply some moisturising cream and hopefully escape from the pungent odour of damp pooch clinging to the hairs inside his nostrils. Frank and Stan's house was only a short walk from the paddock, fortuitously enough, ideally positioned for them to wander over to racing HQ as the mood took. Which it often did this time of year. Another reason for leaving the boys to it was that Brad and Chip, they were told, were eager to get some footage recorded against the backdrop of the newly erected awning.

As far as lodgings went, Dave and Monty, for their part, pretty much moved out of their respective homes for the duration of the TT festival, choosing to kip in the back of the van most nights, immersing themselves entirely in the incredible atmosphere. The excuse offered for their extended camping trip was they were keeping an eye on their bike. Fortunately, those closest to the boys understood what the TT meant to them both and were happy to extend some leeway in their direction come racing season (including Frank and Stan, as their employers).

It was these types of sacrifices — the disruption that people willingly made to pursue their dream — that Brad and Chip hoped to capture in their project, and was the human element of the story to accompany the adrenalin-fuelled action shown out on track.

"Look at this lot," Frank said with a laugh, as he and Stan were making their way home, watching as a pair of excited schoolchildren wandered towards them laden with various motorsport-themed merchandise they'd blagged from the larger race teams. The youngsters beamed with delight, with one young lad wearing several hats, stacked one atop the other. Meanwhile, his mate was busy adjusting his oversized Honda t-shirt that went down as far as his knees, with a Dunlop sticker displayed proudly across his forehead.

"They'll be disappointed if they're heading down Dave and Monty's way," Stan remarked. "The only souvenir they'll find is an empty packet of HobNobs, or maybe, if they're lucky, a dried-up cheese sandwich."

"Slim pickings indeed," said Frank.

Just then, the kids came to a halt, gawping at the posh, expensive-looking blue Bentley slowly coming into view. The car slowed further, turning off the main road and onto the gravel track that formed a temporary access route through the paddock.

"Look at that!" one of the lads shouted, removing his tower of hats and tucking them away under his arm. "Come on!" he suggested, tugging at his mate's oversized shirt. "It might be someone famous!"

"And rich!" advised the other, reaching for his phone, hopeful of a selfie for bragging rights at school.

Despite the obvious placement of several 5-mph warning signs, the Bentley picked up speed along the track, kicking up gravel and covering everything in its wake in a cloud of dust.

"The *nerve* of that tosser," Frank remarked, watching on, offering an exaggerated shaking of his head to let his feelings be known to anyone within visual range.

"And with *kids* about," Stan added, now also shaking his head. "I'll jolly well give him a piece of my mind," Stan insisted, with a threat straight out of the 1950s.

The Bentley slowed again. Not through courtesy or concerns

of safety, but primarily because the young lads had rushed onto the temporary road in order to intercept the majestic motorcar, waving excitedly, and moving to block the vehicle's path.

"Nice motor, mister!" the lad with the multiple hats said once the car had stopped, caressing the vehicle's stately lines with his fingertips. "Bet this cost a fortune?"

"Are you a rider?" the other of the lads asked, his arrival slightly delayed from picking up one of his mate's hats that'd been dropped during their mad dash over.

The car's windows had remained rolled up, so the driver now lowered the passenger-side glass with a push of a button before scowling across to the happy face nearest outside, a face which was staring back optimistically. "If you've left greasy fingerprints on my paintwork, you'll be washing this car," the driver said coldly, rattling his fingers impatiently on the steering wheel. "Now *shift* it," he added abruptly, having been thoroughly inconvenienced by this minor delay.

"I'll wash your car for a tenner," Hat Lad offered helpfully, spotting an opportunity to make some quick cash.

"So, are you a famous rider?" the lad drowning in his freebie t-shirt asked, ambling up and placing his elbows casually on the passenger side door, peering inside the car.

"*No*," the driver said, impatiently. "I'm *not* a famous rider."

"How did you afford this, then?"

"None of your bleedin' business," snapped the driver. "Now, get your grubby, filthy, wretched hands away from my car, the both of you!"

"What about the car wash, then?" the entrepreneurial lad pressed on, undeterred by the frosty reception. "I could reduce the cost to a fiver?"

"I've just *had* the car washed," came the firm rebuttal. "Now bugger off out of the way, I don't have time for this nonsense!"

"What about the bit they've missed?" the lad asked, disappearing from the driver's view for a moment.

"What bit?" came the curt reply, delivered in a tone suggesting the previous cleaner would soon be whipped if any sections having been missed should prove to be true.

"*This* bit," the lad said, throwing the handful of dirt he'd just retrieved from the road onto the shimmering bodywork.

"You little...!" the driver responded, reaching to unfasten his seatbelt. "Wait till I..." he said menacingly, and yet oddly enough, for all his bluster, ultimately doing nothing, his threats remaining idle, just like the engine of the car at the present moment.

The lads took no chances and quickly made good their escape, sprinting back past Frank and Stan, delighted at their successfully executed retribution towards the especially grumpy driver and taking care this time around not to drop any of their recently acquired swag.

"Oi, Stirling Moss!" Stan said in a raised voice, wagging his finger forcefully and marching over before the driver had a chance to put his vehicle into gear and drive off. Frank followed close behind, surprised that Stan was actually following through on his aforementioned proposed reprimand. Stan wasn't usually one for conflict, but throw in a couple of beers and an irritatingly itchy back and there was no holding him back, it would appear.

"You know the five-mile-per-hour signs you just raced past?" Stan asked rhetorically, approaching the car from behind, eyes fixed on the back of the driver's head.

Just then, in answer, the driver threw open his door. He hadn't responded this way to the kids, but apparently enough was enough. After all, he'd just had his car defiled, and now he had an aggressive Stanley Sidcup advancing towards him to contend with.

"Stan," Frank cautioned, catching up and placing his hand across his friend's chest, holding him back. "Stan, look at the number plate."

"What?" Stan said, looking to where Frank was pointing, not sure what he was talking about. "FRANKS 1," Stan said, reading the number plate aloud. "Oh, you've *got* to be kidding me," he added, once the penny dropped. Stan looked up again, turning his attention to the cravat-wearing shortarse climbing out of the car.

"Rodney Franks," Frank announced. "What an enormous pleasure. An antisocial oaf speeding through the paddock, nearly wiping out a group of innocent autograph-hunting children. I mean, who else could it really have been?"

"Well, well, well. If it isn't my good friends who so kindly overpaid me for that strip of tarmac in Jurby," Rodney said, presenting himself before the two of them. "Did I thank you for that?" Rodney asked. "Because if I didn't, I should. Your generosity helped me to buy this new car."

"And you still went ahead and released the video of Lee, didn't you?" Stan replied. "That really does sum up your character, the slimy little weasel that you are," he said, adding, "Can you hear me down there? I can crouch down to your height if that would help?"

"Now, hang on," Rodney said, holding his hands up in protest, though ignoring the height-related insults which were likely water off a duck's back to him as he was so used to them. "That was a genuine mistake, gents," he explained.

Frank laughed at the suggestion, though of course finding little humour in it. "Okay, so you just *accidentally* released the video of Lee to the press? Is that what you're saying?"

"Exactly!" Rodney answered. "I asked my assistant to delete the footage, and she must have misheard my instructions somehow," he insisted. "It's so terribly hard to find good help nowadays. I'm sure you understand."

"Yeah, it's *such* an easy mistake to make," Stan said, voice dripping in sarcasm and eyes rolling. "But, you'll be pleased to know that the police didn't end up pressing charges against Lee," Stan was delighted to advise.

"Brilliant. So that means we're friends again?" replied Rodney.

"Not on your bloody nellie," Frank told him.

"And we were *never* friends," added Stan.

"Ah, shame," said Rodney, taking a glance down at the gaudy, overly ostentatious gold watch he was wearing. "Wait," Rodney continued, a thought suddenly occurring to him. "Your team aren't racing again this year, are they? Is that why you're here skulking about?"

"What of it?" Stan replied, folding his arms across his chest, certain some barbed comment or another was on its way.

"Oh, nothing," Rodney said, inspecting the state of his manicured fingernails. "I just wanted to wish you good luck, is all. I'm sure those two chubby freaks you've got racing for you will knock it right out of the park," he said, laughing to himself. "Bunch of losers," Rodney added, turning round towards his opened door.

"Now... now you look here, Franks..." Stan said, jabbing his finger in the air, speaking slowly, like a man searching for what to say next (and which was, in fact, and coincidentally enough, precisely what was happening). "You just... you just..."

"Just *what?*" Rodney taunted, as he climbed back into his car.

"Your card is marked," Stan replied, finally settling on what he wanted to say. "You mark my words, Rodney Franks. Your card is marked."

With that fearsome declaration of war delivered, Rodney sped away, happily waving over his shoulder, creating another cloud of dust that briefly obscured Frank and Stan.

"Your card is marked?" Frank said as the dust settled and the air cleared. "That's the most threatening insult you could come up with?" he teased, rubbing grit away from his eyes.

"You know I'm rubbish at that sort of thing, Frank," Stan replied. "I'll probably wake up at two in the morning with the perfect insult in mind. But a fat lot of use it'll be at that point, of course." Stan dusted himself down, cursing his meagre attempt at intimidation. "You know who I wish was with us, just then?" Stan said, thinking aloud.

"Who?" asked Frank.

"Stella," Stan answered, smiling at the very prospect. "All of her foibles aside, she wouldn't have been talking about marking anyone's card, would she? No, I expect she'd have been marking his bloody eye socket with a good right hook, is what she'd have been doing, and without hesitation."

"You're probably right, Stan," Frank replied. "Oh, and that reminds me. We still need to phone Stella to discuss that job offer. So you can tell her all about it then, yeah? And ask her advice on issuing threats at the same time?"

"Yes, I will," Stan heartily agreed, thinking this a very good idea. "Wait, hang on," he said suddenly, temporarily distracted. "I can still..." Stan added, lifting each arm in turn and taking a sniff. "Can you smell it, Frank? I've still got that smell on me! That smell of wet dog!"

Chapter
SEVEN

With the entire TT course being just shy of thirty-eight miles in length, there were numerous vantage points from which the eager race fans could appreciate the action. One of the more iconic spots was at Quarterbridge, located a mile and a quarter into the circuit. It certainly wasn't the quickest area of the course for spectators to observe due to a sharp right-hand bend the riders had to brake hard for and navigate. But the technical nature of the section made for some magnificent viewing. Having the benefit of a popular pub on hand was also a distinct advantage and a welcome distraction on a warm summer's afternoon for those there to spectate.

The TT festival usually took place during the last week in May and the first week in June, with the first week allocated to practice/qualifying, and the second to the racing. A distinct advantage for those early birds arriving during practice week was that the majority of the screaming hordes had yet to arrive. For that reason, the queue at the Quarterbridge pub — appropriately named The Quarterbridge, and often referred to as simply the QB — wasn't too chaotic, and there was a little more room to manoeuvre when securing the plum viewing spots.

Among those enjoying the atmosphere and eagerly awaiting the first practice session at the QB were Brad and Chip, armed with their camera and microphone, mingling amongst the fans. Their focus today wasn't on filming the racing, but in-

FRANK & STAN'S BUCKET LIST #5: ISLE OF MAN TT ACES

stead, it was on getting to know those who were watching. Of course, they would still turn their camera trackside on plenty of occasions. But their desire and mission, to a very large extent, was to capture the event's passion and emotion through the spectators' eyes. And so, while most other journalists/media crews would have their cameras trained on the bikes, the boys' plan was to have their cameras aimed at the people *watching* the bikes, anxious to capture the raw emotion they hoped would be on display in abundance.

After not too long a time, those riders on their debut TT outing had just ridden past on their first, speed-controlled lap, offering the newcomers an opportunity to experience first-hand what they'd likely been dreaming about for months, or possibly years. Though they were moving at a relatively sedate pace, what with it being their very first outing, it still provided those spectating a tantalising preview of things to come.

Enjoying a cold pint in the sunshine just outside of the QB were three twenty-something lads from Runcorn, a town near Liverpool, who Brad and Chip had spoken to a bit earlier in the day. Apparently, from what Chip and Brad had learned, the TT hadn't been the destination of choice for two doubters in the group. They'd first set their sights on a week on the beach in Ibiza rather than sharing a cosy tent in Douglas. But their persistent mate proved particularly persuasive, by all accounts, bombarding them with videoclips of the TT and endless tales of his previous visit until they reluctantly agreed to surrender their suncream and swimming trunks, abandoning their trip to the Mediterranean and hopping across the Irish Sea to the Isle of Man instead.

Coming up shortly, the Runcorn lads would experience the 'big bikes' in the form of the Superbike and Superstock solo machines soon due to get underway on their first run around the circuit. Whilst the practice sessions were designed to get the riders up to speed and fine-tune the technical settings — such as gearing and suspension — there was still the matter of ensuring qualification for race week. For that reason, while the riders would likely be taking things relatively easy on their first outing of the year, they certainly wouldn't be plodding along either.

Those spectators listening intently to the radio commentary team on the loudspeakers were first to stir, alerted that the action would soon commence and the afternoon tranquillity would shortly be shattered by the roar of horsepower. Noting the shifting attention of those standing around them, the Runcorn lads wandered casually over to the safety barrier, pints in hand, staring intently up Quarterbridge Road from whence the bikes would appear.

Standing roughly a dozen feet away, Brad gently nudged his brother. "Let's get our lens on those guys we were talking to before," Brad whispered, nodding in the direction of the three young men in question.

Chip positioned his camera just as the commentary team announced the first two bikes leaving the start line, away from the grandstand, bikes that would now be accelerating towards the crossroads at St Ninian's before descending down the daunting arse-twitcher that was Bray Hill.

With cold tyres, a heavy fuel tank, and their reactions days away from being considered anywhere near up to race speed, the riders would be forgiven for exercising a wee bit of caution on their first run-through. In addition to their own mental preparation, there would be concerns about the bike: *How would it handle? How does the engine sound? How was the gearing?* These were just some of the many considerations, and would be tinkered with over the next few days. They would also be acutely aware that the TT course was a public highway in constant use. That meant that whilst the layout of the course remained very much the same as the previous year, there might well be subtle differences this time around. Roads may have been resurfaced, for instance, therefore changing the level of grip from how they remembered. Or, the yellow wall they once used as a braking marker may have been painted white. Additionally, houses may have sprung up where once was only open countryside. In this respect, it was constantly evolving, and riders thus had to refresh their knowledge of the course. Because the one thing you didn't need while driving around this track was any doubt in your mind.

And speaking of that track, on it, directly in front of the Runcorn lads, two pigeons could presently be seen fighting over a discarded chip. Neither seemed ready to surrender the greasy treat, with wings flapping furiously and beaks clashing like swords. Just then, however, the feathered fellow on the right raised its head, looking to the heavens. Appearing surprised by this unusual tactic, his fellow dining rival followed suit, leaving the violated chip lying unattended for a moment to enjoy a temporary stay of execution. Both birds were now aware of a rumbling noise carried on the breeze and a firm vibration underfoot. Its cause was surely unknown to the two of them, but the disturbance must have been severe enough, and troubling enough, that they didn't care to hang about long enough to discover its source. In short order the two of them took flight, leaving their free lunch behind. Some risks weren't worth taking, they must have realised, flying towards the rugby fields across the road.

The rumbling noise became more and more thunderous, increasing in intensity as it progressed along Quarterbridge Road, where all heads in the immediate vicinity were now directed. The three Runcorn lads gripped the safety fence, jaws slowly lowering like opening drawbridges. Watching. Waiting. Hearts racing. Mouths dry.

You could hear the chaos getting closer, but there was nothing to see right yet. Like St George standing outside a darkened cave, you could hear the dragon coming but you didn't know just when it would appear.

Startled birds evacuated the surrounding trees en masse, heading in the same direction as their pigeon brethren. The assembled press pack knelt behind their cameras with their trigger fingers poised.

And then...

"Holy effing shit!" one of the Runcorn lads shouted ever-so-eloquently, instinctively jumping back a pace as local hero Conor Cummins burst into view like the aforementioned angry dragon emerging from its cave, braking hard, banking over to negotiate the sharp right-hander before pinning the throttle and roaring away towards the Jubilee Oak Tree that sat right smack dab in the middle of the street before Braddan Bridge. The boys didn't even have time to catch their breath when Dean Harrison appeared less than a second later, rear wheel snaking under braking, his angle of approach very nearly flawless.

There was just so much going on at this point that it was difficult to understand which of one's senses were presently under assault. Ears were ringing in response to the race-tuned engines, nostrils filled with the glorious smell of horsepower, and your eyes... well, your eyes didn't have a bloody clue what they were supposed to be telling your brain. And if anyone had any old metal fillings in their teeth, they were in real danger of being shaken loose.

A steady stream of bikes came and went, arriving quickly, and then accelerating away just as quickly, in rapid succession, resulting in spectators' heads moving back and forth like they were observing a particularly fast-paced tennis match. One of the Runcorn lads had his pint in front of him, frozen in the air, having not taken a sip of it in minutes. His plastic cup was held at an awkward angle, its contents dribbling onto the pavement — although he had no way of knowing this at present, as he hadn't dared break his concentration long enough to notice anything else for fear of what he might miss. He hadn't blinked for what felt like ages, in fact, and his jaw muscles were starting to ache.

The lad who'd originally suggested the idea of a visit to the Isle of Man indulged in a sneaky glance over at his friends' faces. "You don't get *this* in Ibiza," he remarked, smugly raising his own pint aloft, and then pressing it to his waiting lips.

"Ibiza can kiss my arse!" came the immediate, enthusiastic reply from one of the lads.

FRANK & STAN'S BUCKET LIST #5: ISLE OF MAN TT ACES

"This is absolutely mega!" said the other, wide-eyed, shaking his head in disbelief.

It certainly hadn't been planned, this chance encounter with the young gentlemen from Runcorn earlier today, and again now. But it was a happenstance that worked out wonderfully for Chip and Brad, enabling them to successfully capture some powerful footage for their documentary. They'd agonised previously over how best to convey the raw emotion that the Isle of Man TT evoked in people. Sure, they could have waxed lyrical about the majesty of the event. But any descriptive narration would realistically have fallen well short. Setting their camera rolling on the lads from Runcorn, then, fit in perfectly with their plan to apply their focus on the reactions of fans. And so, in five minutes of film footage, they'd quite serendipitously managed to showcase what they might otherwise have spent a lifetime attempting to describe to their viewers (and likely still failing miserably to achieve). The awestruck faces on the Runcorn boys were the case in point that a picture really does paint a thousand words.

Quarterbridge was proving to be something of a valuable recruiting ground for Brad and Chip overall. Here, they'd stumbled upon an eclectic mix of race fans, featuring a wide range of ages and representing a considerable geographical footprint. But while they may have come from all different directions, and some even speaking different languages, the one thing they all shared was a common passion: a collective appreciation of motorsport in general, and the Isle of Man TT in particular.

There was Klaus from Dresden, for instance, who'd revealed how he'd first reluctantly come to the TT with his father in 1963. Not particularly fond of motorsport as a young boy, Klaus had resigned himself to a week sat bored in a field. However, he described the time he first set eyes on the great Mike Hailwood securing victory in the Senior TT race on his magnificent MV Agusta, and from that moment on, he was hooked. Apart from

2001, when the TT was cancelled due to the foot-and-mouth disease outbreak in the UK, Klaus had returned every year since. Sure, there were a few more wrinkles on his face these days, but when he spoke about his lifelong passion, you could still see the fire in those eyes. A fire that'd initially been ignited by the spark of Mike Hailwood all those years before.

Other spectators Brad and Chip interviewed were relative newcomers in comparison to Klaus — two, six, thirteen years served, for example — all of them returning each year without hesitation. Some had partners who simply didn't understand their mate's annual pilgrimage, frustrated that any alternative travel plans were ruined by their spouse's insistence at heading back to the Isle of Man like migratory birds every year. With the option of a new partner a distinct possibility, many TT enthusiasts gave their significant others one final chance, convincing their doubting spouses to see for themselves what all the fuss was about. Often, like Klaus, the doubters became instant converts once they saw it with their own eyes, and would from that point forward accompany their loved ones the following year, and the next, and the next, with no further explanation needed or coaxing required. It was a given. It was happening.

Also, as was related to Chip and Brad, it mattered not if you were a relative newcomer to the island or a seasoned campaigner. Either way, you were made welcome by your fellow pilgrims regardless. The highlight of your visit would undoubtedly be the racing, but the lifelong friends you'd meet, the stories you'd share, and the sense of belonging you'd feel would indeed come a close second and live long in your memory.

Presently, with the practice session for the solo machines reaching its conclusion for the day, it was time to hand the tarmac over to the sidecar outfits. Blaring out over the loudspeaker system, the radio commentary team chatted to some of the riders, trying to glean some insight as to what might be on their minds prior to the start of their run, which would be coming up soon. Interviewing riders was a task often fraught with challenges, as it should happen. Some liked to be left alone, deep in their own thoughts, for instance, and weren't afraid to make this fact clear to the person thrusting the microphone mere millimetres away from their faces. Additionally, there were others, despite a friendly warning from the commentators in advance, who were a little colourful in their choice of language — with some repeat offenders suspected of doing it for devilment, and perhaps hoping to promote a reaction and raise a giggle over the airwaves at the commentator's expense.

Listening in, like many down at Quarterbridge, Brad and Chip were giddy with excitement ahead of the first sidecar session. While they'd not known Dave and Monty for very long and had only spoken with them a handful of times by this point, Chip and Brad were already very much invested in their racing journey and thrilled at the prospect of seeing the boys out on track and hopefully capturing some live-action footage of them as well.

"Here you go," said Brad, returning from a trip to the nearby burger van, having taken advantage of the interim between races and now armed with their late lunch.

Chip peered inside the bun at the meagre patty staring back at him. "Hmm," he offered. "Not quite as substantial as a burger back home, is it? But it'll do."

"Christ!" Brad said suddenly, startling his brother in the process.

"What is it?" asked Chip.

"I just realised. I thought I'd gotten the exchange rates wrong, but no," his brother answered, having just performed some quick mental calculations a moment before. "You better enjoy that," Brad added, shaking his head in dismay. "My first car was cheaper than these two burgers!"

"Maybe they have specially-bred cattle over here?" Chip suggested, eying his burger with curiosity, trying to spot any discernible difference between it and American beef.

"What do you mean?" asked Brad, now staring at his own burger as well.

"You know, like that special Kobe beef from Japan? The stuff made from cows that are massaged with sake and fed lots of beer?" Chip explained. "Like that. Except maybe, over here, the cows are fed lots of Guinness or something? Like, instead of whatever kind of Japanese beer they use over in Japan, y'know?"

"Holy shit, you could be right," Brad said in wonder.

As the pair tucked into each of their succulent, now-slightly-mysterious burgers, a not entirely unwelcome problem and surprise presented itself to the brothers in the form of a constant procession of people wandering over for a chat. Word of their upcoming documentary series was heavily reported in the local and motoring press, and identifying the two towheaded twins, near to the course, holding a camera, wasn't proving too much of a challenge. Some of their new friends were clearly angling to make it on film in one form or another, either for a quick visual appearance, or perhaps to share an anecdote or two on camera which they were hopeful would make it into the final cut.

Finishing up his burger, Brad used the back of his hand to wipe away a bit of ketchup that had dribbled onto his chin. As he did so, his eyes were drawn to an elderly gentleman heading their way. The fellow had a noticeable limp, and was currently pointing his cane in Brad's direction. Suspecting this to be another candidate for an on-camera appearance, Brad smiled as the old fellow approached.

"Ere," the old boy called out ahead of his arrival, slowly walking up the pavement towards them. "Ere, you're those two filmmaker chaps what's on the front of the newspaper," he said, providing information that was of course already known to them.

"Yes, that's right," Brad said on behalf of them both, as Chip, not being quite finished with his burger as he was, presently had his mouth full. "Brad," Brad offered, extending his hand, but then whipping it back after spotting the smear of tomato-based sauce across the back of it. He quickly wiped the mess off, and then politely re-extended his hand. "Nice to meet you," he said.

"I know Dave and Monty well," the man said, taking up a resting position stood uncomfortably close to Brad, and leaning in as he spoke as well, as if standing very, very close hadn't already been enough in itself.

"Oh?" said Brad, taking a small step backwards to increase the distance and create a more reasonable gap between them.

"I'm Pat," Pat announced, by way of introduction. "Dave and Monty know me as Pegleg Pat," Pat explained, tapping his right leg like one might ping a glass to demonstrate it was made of crystal. "Prosthetic," Pat added, raising up his trouser leg to provide added visual confirmation to the hollow-sounding noise they'd just heard.

"Nice to meet you, Pat," Brad offered. "So how do you know Dave and Monty?" he asked, wondering if there might be a story involved that they could maybe use.

"From a pie-eating contest," Pat replied, nodding his head in fond recollection. "Greedy bastards, the pair of them," he added.

"I see," Brad replied, smiling politely, and then looking up Quarterbridge Road in hopes that the sidecar bikes might soon arrive and provide a welcome distraction. "So..." Brad offered, uncertain where to go with this conversation. "Did you win?"

"Win what, lad?"

"The pie-eating contest."

"Oh. No, lad," Pat answered, shaking his head solemnly. "No, not a bloody chance," he went on. "You see, Monty, the one with the wonky eye, eats like a bloody gannet. He doesn't swallow, just shovels it in like a fireman stoking the boiler on a steam train," Pat explained. "He can also look down to his plate with one eye, and over to you with the other, without even trying. So it sorta puts you right off your food, dunnit? And Dave, well, the way he eats, I'd reckon he can dislocate his jaw like a snake to accommodate another load. Still, against such formidable opposition, I'm proud to say I *did* still manage to come home in third place."

"Okay..." Brad said, looking to his brother for help, but receiving only a smirk in response.

"I lost my leg during TT week," Pat told them, hopping from one topic to another.

"You did?" Chip asked, entering into the conversation now, interest piqued, as this sounded like a genuinely fascinating story and something they might definitely use. "So you were a racer, I'm assuming? And you got into some kind of terrible accident?"

"A racer?" Pat replied with a hearty laugh. "No, lad. I was a window cleaner."

"Right, so...?" Chip pressed on, looking down, hoping for some clarification as to the origin of the missing leg.

"I fell off a ladder," Pat explained, giving his leg a further tap with his cane. "As I say, it was during TT week."

"Oh, wow," Brad said, disappointed, same as his brother, that it wasn't a race-related incident, but concerned nonetheless. "I'm sorry to hear that, Pat. You must have fallen from quite a height to lose your leg."

"Not too terribly high up, no," Pat replied. "I was cleaning a second-storey window when I fell. So there was a little bit of a tumble, yes, but it could have been much worse, I suppose."

"Ouch," said Chip, offering a sympathetic grimace. "Still, it must have been one hell of a landing, right? I mean, in order to lose your leg like that?"

"Mmm, not really, no," Pat answered.

"No?" Brad asked, just before exchanging puzzled glances with his brother.

"No," Pat said. "Tuck and roll, they always tell you, right? So I tucked and I rolled, just like you're meant to when you have a bit of a fall. But unfortunately, I kept on rolling, yeah? I rolled so much that the momentum carried me all the way down into the road. And that there's when the bus ran clean over my leg."

"All right," Chip replied, reaching down to pick up the camera by his feet. "Anyway, so we need to get ready for the sidecar bikes, Pat. But it was nice to meet you, okay?"

"Ah," said Pat, taking the hint. "Well, I just wanted to pop over and say that it's marvellous that you TV fellas are working with the lower end of the starting grid," he told them. "Usually, it's the glamour riders that get all the airtime. So what you're doing for the underdogs is bloody fantastic, I think."

Brad and Chip both looked at each other, wondering if this was the beginning of another longwinded anecdote, and also uncertain as to what Pat meant by this. "I'm not sure I understand what you mean," Brad said. "Are you saying you don't think Dave and Monty are going to win?" he asked.

"*Win?*" Pat scoffed. "That's what I like about you Canadians. Always such a great sense of humour, you lot," he added, chuckling away to himself as he turned to leave.

"Wait, hang on," Brad said, cautiously placing his hand on Pat's shoulder, taking care not to knock the one-legged man off balance. "Pat, firstly, we're American," Brad gently corrected him. "But, more important than that, you really don't think Monty and Dave have a chance of winning?"

"No, lad. No, I don't," Pat answered. "In fact, there's more chance of me winning a rematch at the pie-eating contest against that greedy pair of gannets," he added. "And that's why I think it's good of you boys to get involved with a team further down the starting grid, as I said."

"But Dave's already a TT winner," Brad pointed out. "So he could do it again, couldn't he?" Brad asked, with a sunny air of optimism.

"Aye, but that win was on a world-class bike, with a world-class passenger," Pat advised. "And neither Monty nor their current bike is world-class, is it? No offence meant, but with a fair wind and a good helping of Lady Luck, hopefully they'll scrape into the top twenty this time around."

Brad slowly removed his hand from Pat's shoulder. "Okay, well, it was nice to meet you, Pat," he said, allowing Pat to be on his way. Brad's thoughts turned to the progress report he'd given earlier that day to their paymasters back home, a phone call in which he'd spoken in-depth about the triumph of capturing the services of a TT winner as the *pièce de résistance* in their project. The same phone call in which he'd expressed great confidence that their new poster boys would be a shoo-in for the top spot in the sidecar class.

"Darn it," Brad muttered to himself, massaging his furrowed brow as he rejoined his brother.

"What's wrong?" Chip asked. "You don't look so good. Are you gonna barf or something? I hope not, for your sake, because the line for the bathroom is really, really long. Just so you know."

"No, I'm not gonna puke," Brad answered. "At least I don't think I am. No, I'm just a little worried now that we may have over-hyped Dave and Monty's prospects of victory."

"It'll be fine," Chip offered by way of assurance, adding, "We're working with a bona fide TT winner."

"Yeah," an unconvinced Brad said, puffing out his cheeks and then exhaling hard. "We've sold the idea of this production to our bosses on the premise that we're working with one of the top teams over here, the best of the best. But if what Hopalong Pat just told me is anything to go by, then..."

"Pegleg Pat?" Chip replied. "I wouldn't worry too much about it, bro. That guy doesn't seem like he's playing with a full deck. Plus, Dave and Monty are two of the most serious athletes I've ever come across," Chip told his brother, using two words — *serious* and *athletes* — likely never before used to describe Dave and Monty. "You'll see, dude, just wait. When the two of them come roaring past us on that motorbike of theirs, you'll wonder what you were ever panicking about, I guarantee."

And they wouldn't need to wait too much longer at all to find out as, soon enough, the first of the sidecars were roaring along Quarterbridge Road, shattering the peace and quiet once more. With a starting number of thirty-six, however, it would still be a good few minutes before Dave and Monty came into view, leaving plenty of time for Chip to adjust his camera positioning once he'd seen the first of the machines come through.

Chip's heart rate increased dramatically, recording the constant barrage of sidecar bikes appearing at speed before braking sharply to navigate the abrupt right-hander and then rocketing away. "These guys are freakin' quick!" he remarked, offer-

FRANK & STAN'S BUCKET LIST #5: ISLE OF MAN TT ACES

ing his commentary on the situation, his eye pressed up against the viewfinder.

Brad watched on as his brother filmed, noting the numbers on the bikes. As sidecar number thirty arrived (and then departed in the blink of an eye), this meant that Dave and Monty couldn't be too terribly far behind. "Any minute now," Brad advised, patting his brother's arm as Chip continued to film. "I can barely watch," Brad added nervously, chewing on his knuckle, looking up the road as both numbers thirty-one and thirty-four burst into view.

Three more machines arrived in quick succession, followed by one bearing the number forty-one. "Where's our guys? Did we miss them?" Chip asked, moving his head away from the camera for just a moment.

"No," Brad answered. "No, at least I don't think so," he added, as another machine numbered in the forties went by. "Maybe they don't send them out in strict number order?" he suggested. "Or maybe..." he went on, trying to think of some other possible explanation. But his thought process was interrupted by the ear-splitting noise of an engine that seemed to be screaming in pain. Most of the machines they'd watched so far all appeared into view following roughly the same optimal path. However, the bike currently wailing like a banshee with a stubbed toe was tucked atypically into the left-hand side of the road, crawling along inches away from the advertising boards.

"I think that's them," Chip said, spotting the distinctive blue paint job with a yellow custard swirl, the bike approaching at what in comparison to the others was a much-diminished pace.

Sure enough, it was them. Machine number thirty-six drew closer, with Monty sat strangely upright, left hand raised aloft.

"What on earth are they doing?" said Brad, straining his eyes. "Monty's not waving at us, is he?" he asked, incredulous.

"He can't be," Chip replied, without raising his head from the camera. "I mean, they don't even know we're filming from here, do they?"

The two of them watched on as Dave slowed further, and rather than negotiating the right-hander, Dave veered to the left, bringing the sidecar to a halt in front of the yellow safety barriers, marshals sprinting towards them.

"Monty must have been signalling that they're having some kind of mechanical issue," Chip surmised, readjusting his camera angle to capture the moment.

The marshals created a temporary gap in the barrier separating the live track from the surrounding area, allowing the machine to be pushed to safety and away from the course. "Come on, let's head over," Brad suggested, starting over towards the spot where Dave and Monty now stood, with Chip following and still filming as they walked.

With helmets quickly removed, Dave and Monty stood with their hands on their hips, looking down at their machine with a marshal talking in their ear. Dave shook his head, swinging his left leg back as if he were just about to launch an attack on their bike.

"Dave!" Brad called out, approaching with caution. "Are you both okay?"

"Ah! Hello, chaps!" Dave replied, changing from completely peeved to entirely cheerful at the flick of a switch. "You enjoying the practice session?" he asked.

"Um... yeah, I guess," Brad answered. "But more importantly..." he added, casting his eyes onto their bike.

"Clutch has gone," Monty explained, running his ungloved hand through his sweat-soaked hair. "It didn't sound right from the start. And then, from the bottom of Bray Hill onwards, the engine was screaming and moaning like a bloody porn star. We had no option but to pull in."

"So that's the end of the practice session?" Chip asked, adjusting his lens for a dramatic close-up shot of Monty, although it was Dave who answered.

"Yeah," Dave said wearily. "Unless you've got a new clutch in your back pocket?"

"I wish we did," said Brad. "Is a replacement going to be expensive?"

Dave shook his head. "Nah, not really," he said, now appearing relatively unconcerned about the mechanical issues, despite nearly taking a kick at the bike a few moments before. "Say, you couldn't lend us twenty quid, could you?" Dave asked, patting his leather-clad frame to indicate the absence of any pockets on his person.

"Of course," Brad responded, retrieving his wallet. "Is it for a new clutch?" he naively asked, handing the note over.

"No," Dave replied with a hearty laugh, strolling away in the direction of the pub. "This is to buy us a nice pint of something cold."

"And a burger?" Monty asked hopefully, skipping to catch up with his mate.

"If there's any change, Monty," Dave said, patting him on the shoulder. "But the beer must come first, yeah?"

Brad watched Dave and Monty disappearing towards the QB with a sense of foreboding, a feeling that their first commission for a major network might also be their last. "Serious athletes," he said softly, under his breath, followed by a sigh.

"What's that?" Chip asked, returning his camera to its case.

"That's how you described them before. Your exact words," Brad answered. "Do they *look* like two serious athletes?" Brad asked, just as Monty unzipped his leathers and removed his sodden t-shirt, revealing the top half of his rotund, now-naked body for all to see and then slapping his protruding belly like a bongo drum.

"No," Chip replied thoughtfully. "No, I don't suppose they do."

Chapter
EIGHT

A solitary tear ran leisurely down Eric Fryer's cheek, wending its way along his pock-marked face like a fly crawling down a windowpane. Then, with a gentle sob, it was released into the hot oil below, sizzling for an instant, after which it was gone forever like the joy in his heart.

Unable to contain his simmering emotions, Eric's shoulders heaved, his pent-up emotion now flowing like raindrops. He offered up a further whimper, moving his well-used spatula around the surface of the frying pan. But there was no conviction in his work.

"For the love of..." Karen, his jaded waitress moaned, noting the stack of order slips lying unattended on the filthy worktop where she'd left them. "Eric," she scolded him, whipping his backside with her serving cloth. "Eric!" she said again. "Not only is that egg being incinerated in month-old fat, but the poor sod who ordered it now has the pleasure of your bodily fluids in his breakfast. Come on, man. I've a café full of hungry builders out there. Chop-chop!"

"She's leaving, Karen," Eric revealed, in between sobs. "The love of my life is heading for pastures new."

Karen made no attempt to hide the consternation written all over her face. "You're not still singing a song about that one that looks like an Eastern European shot-putter with wire hair, are you?" Karen asked, receiving a nod of affirmation in response.

"Eric, she's married to *another man*," Karen added, a statement which resulted only in further sobbing. "Surely that was already enough of a clue for you? I mean, this cannot have come as a surprise, Eric. Even to you."

"Stella's a gentle soul," Eric declared. "A gentle, misunderstood soul. And maybe a little confused."

"What, because she didn't marry you instead? Eric, need I remind you, you tried to get her husband *locked up*, and you destroyed her wedding day in the process. And that's not the sort of romantic gesture that usually wins a girl's heart. I'd suggest going for a box of Milk Tray chocolates next time, yeah?"

"I was blinded by love," Eric responded, dabbing his runny nose on his soiled apron. "Love does strange things to a man, Karen," he said, placing a hand over his ample breast, caressing the tattoo of Stella found there beneath his shirt. It was artwork commissioned as a testament to his devotion and a love that would never fade (unlike the shoddy inkwork that Filthy Barry had etched into his skin for what Eric had hoped would be eternity).

"Strange things? So does hunger," Karen shot back. "So get a bloody move on with those fry-ups before there's a rebellion out there and I get strung up!"

Old Eric may have been blinded by love, but even he could now see that throwing Lee under the proverbial bus wasn't the most ingenious plan he'd ever hatched. By tipping off Rodney Franks' odious private investigator, Terry Scupper, Eric had not only betrayed Lee (who he *used* to be on perfectly friendly terms with) but also succeeded in seriously irritating the object of his affection, Stella, at the same time.

While no police action was ultimately taken against Lee for his criminal intentions to rob the security van, the potential ramifications had been considerable. And yet, even faced with the possibility of serious jail time, Lee had remained more concerned about tarnishing the good name of Frank and Stan's charity, and, of course, the pain caused to Stella when she thought she'd been jilted at the altar. Fortunately, today's headlines become tomorrow's chip wrappers, as the saying goes. But for both Stella and Lee, Eric Fryer was and remained public enemy number one.

Surprising, then, that despite this, Stella still sanctioned his establishment's patronage (though indirectly) owing to the fact that he made a tremendous sausage, black pudding, mushroom & egg sandwich that simply couldn't be equalled anywhere else, according to Stella's discerning palate. Stella did have her principles, but she wouldn't allow her brain to overrule her stomach. And for that reason, Susie was still dispatched at ten a.m. each morning to collect their breakfast under strict instructions that Susie wasn't to engage in small talk with the treacherous, grease-smeared lump of shite, as Stella now liked to refer to Eric.

During a brief lull in business, after the morning rush had passed, Eric rested the overhang of his gut on the shop counter, staring wistfully through the condensation on the front window at the folks passing by. "Oh, you're right, Karen," he conceded, turning his attention to Karen, who was presently wiping down the tables.

"I often am," Karen replied, now using a fork to skewer the discarded chewing gum stuck to the underside of one of the tables, a little gift left behind by an extra-thoughtful patron. "About what, exactly?" she enquired.

"I'm going to snap out of it!" Eric proclaimed confidently, raising his finger in a show of conviction. "I'll respect Stella's wishes and allow her to move on to her new life."

"I'm not sure she really needs or even wants your permission, Eric, but... hurray for you?" Karen replied indifferently, resuming her duties and questioning her career choices.

"I'm still something of a catch," Eric pondered, thinking out loud. "I've still got most of my own hair, for instance," he commented. "Although, granted, a good portion of it is in my ears."

"And you're an entrepreneur, Eric," Karen helpfully pointed out. "Don't forget that."

"Yes, that's right!" Eric said, in ready agreement, completely missing the heavy sarcasm dripping from Karen's words like the grease down his kitchen's walls.

"You should try that internet dating, Eric," Karen suggested, lowering her cloth, and then placing a bum cheek on a table that wasn't much cleaner than before she'd started. "Eric Fryer, entrepreneur," Karen said, running her hand across the horizon, introducing the idea to him. "That could be your profile's headline."

"I should. I really should," Eric told her, nodding like a little plastic dashboard dog while walking out from behind the counter. "I've invested so much of my romantic energy on unrequited love that maybe now is the time to consider other opportunities of the heart..."

Eric held his gaze in Karen's direction a little longer than she wanted or perhaps felt comfortable with.

"Eric," Karen said, rising up from her seated position and extending her index finger. "Eric, if you ever look at me like... like the way you're doing right now. If you ever do that again, I will cut your bollocks clean off. Do you understand me?"

"What? Yes... Yes, of course, Karen. Sorry," Eric said, snapping himself out of his reverie. "No, I was just staring into space, thinking," he said, apologising quickly, as he very much wished for his bollocks to remain intact. "Honestly. I wasn't..."

"*Good,*" Karen replied, narrowing her eyes in his direction. "Right. Now, as to getting yourself out there on the internet," she said, moving on. "The first thing you need to do is to get yourself a decent profile picture," she advised. "There are loads of clever photographic filters you can use these days, which will help to at least give you a fighting chance. Oh, and one quick dating tip in general, Eric. Do spend a little longer in the mornings with your toothbrush, yeah?"

"With... my toothbrush?" Eric asked, confused, not entirely sure what Karen was suggesting. "Doing what, exactly...?"

"Brushing your teeth, Eric! Your breath smells like a mixture of Marmite and rotten vegetables. I don't mean to be cruel, so think of it as constructive feedback."

"What's wrong with Marmite?" Eric asked, though cupping his hand over his mouth and taking a generous sniff, which triggered his gag reflex. "Ah. Fair point," he conceded.

"Or try chewing gum as an alternative," Karen suggested. "Here," she said, tossing over the lump previously skewered on the fork in her hand. "I'm sure there's still plenty of chewing left in it."

"Here's to moving on," Eric said, popping the gum in his gob and chomping away.

Susie knew something wasn't quite right. There wasn't one thing she could pin it down to, but there were differences in Stella's general demeanour over the previous few days. For someone often described as erratic and unstable, Stella was, surprisingly, a creature of habit, so any deviation in the norm was quickly picked up by her observant friend and colleague. There had been subtle changes, like the hairs left unshaven on Stella's jawline, and the absence of her usual afternoon nap on the reception sofa. She'd also stopped having a courtesy fag in the bathroom to counteract the odour she'd produced, and her notoriously short fuse was on a hair-trigger lately as well. In isolation, these little things Susie observed would likely have passed unnoticed, but, cumulatively, they began to paint a picture of discontent.

Returning from Eric's with Stella's usual order, even the alluring scent of her daily breakfast sandwich didn't evoke the ravenous reaction it would ordinarily. Stella would often pace the carpet of the reception area, ready to rip the grease-smeared bag clean out of Susie's hand as soon as she arrived with it. But not today. Today, Stella didn't appear particularly interested, which worried Susie.

"Here you are, Stella," Susie said, placing Stella's breakfast down in front of her. "Eric didn't even come out from the kitchen this time," Susie remarked. "So I didn't have another emotional outburst to deal with, which was a result."

"Dirty get," Stella said in response, with nothing further offered as she reached half-heartedly into the bag.

Susie, who didn't willingly partake in Eric's cuisine and so had no sandwich of her own, took her seat and busied herself tapping away on her keyboard, keeping a discreet eye on Stella. On a typical day, Stella's sandwich would be dispatched in three impressive chomps, and with a fag lit before she'd even licked any spillage from around her mouth. But rather than devouring breakfast in her usual hearty manner, Stella simply nibbled around the edges this time, almost daintily, as if it were a cucumber sandwich and she was a proper lady.

"Right!" said Susie, pushing her keyboard away and spinning her seat round so that she was now facing Stella directly. "Now I *know* something's amiss," Susie announced, pointing a reproachful finger at the barely touched breakfast sarnie. "What's going on, Stella?" she asked firmly, but not so firm as to provoke a physical response, something which Susie had previously witnessed first-hand and which she had no wish to find herself on the receiving end of.

"Eh?" Stella grunted in response, wrinkling her erratically applied painted-on eyebrows.

"What's wrong, Stella? You've not been yourself all week," Susie pressed on, wheeling her chair a few inches closer to her co-worker and colleague, without breaking eye contact.

"Nuffin," Stella replied with a shrug.

"Stella! I've known you too long to believe that. Is it this move to the Isle of Man that's worrying you? If so, I thought you said you were looking forward to a new challenge, especially after Frank and Stan both promoted you to be president of their new company?"

Stella lowered her head, staring at the sandwich she'd barely touched. "It's Commander-in-Chief," she said. "And, yeah, I *am* looking forward to being Commander-in-Chief," she admitted.

"Okay, so what gives?" Susie asked. "Are you going to miss the taxi company? Is that it?"

"Am I shite," Stella replied eloquently. "Stuck in this office dealing with pissed-up idiots all the time? No thanks. It's just lucky that I'm as patient with people as I am, otherwise I'd be cracking skulls daily."

"Right, so if it's not the job, then what's getting you down?"

Stella placed her lightly nibbled sandwich back in its bag, leaving it unfinished. "I s'pose I'm going to miss people when I go," Stella said, rummaging into her bra for her packet of fags.

"Oh," Susie said, surprised by this revelation, as Stella wasn't known for being the sociable type. Not overtly, at least. "Such as...?" Susie asked, fishing.

"The boys at the kebab shop," Stella said in response, without any sort of hesitation.

"Oh," replied Susie.

"Yeah, poor Dirk was nearly in tears when I told him I was leaving," Stella said, sparking up a ciggie. "And I don't even know how I'm going to tell the girls at the launderette."

"Right," Susie answered, eyes fixed on Stella. "Anybody *else* you might miss?" she asked. "Maybe the postman? Perhaps the milkman? Or what about the bloke who stands in the street shouting at busses all day? I'm sure you'll be upset to say goodbye to all of *them*," Susie said with a sniff. "I'm just really pleased you've met so many wonderful people that are going to leave a void in your life when you move on," she added, eyes welling up. "I'm going to put the kettle on," she said, getting up and moving before the tears started, glaring at the back of Stella's head as she headed off.

It'd been a challenging few days in the offices of Frank & Stan's Cabs recently, with the atmosphere tense. Convincing Stella to move to the Isle of Man had been a hard sell on Frank and Stan's part. To sweeten the deal, they'd promoted her three times during the negotiations and, somehow, even ended up agreeing to supply her with free takeaway food upon request anytime throughout her first year of service. It felt very much like Stella was doing the pair of them an enormous favour by even *considering* their offer, much less accepting, or at least that's the way she made it seem, despite the tremendous opportunity they were presenting. At times it would have been easy to walk away, but for Frank and Stan, Stella was like family (not to mention a permanent fixture in their business, almost like heavy, immovable furniture), and they felt a parental devotion to her. So much so, in fact, that no matter how outlandish Stella's contractual demands, the boys would inevitably be compelled to capitulate. Anything for an easy life, they reckoned.

Lee, on the other hand, had required little persuasion. He adored his previous visit to the island and was eager to make a new life for himself and his bride. Gentle walks in the countryside and romantic picnics on the beach consumed his thoughts. Also, his role with the charity was flexible regarding location, but he could still commute if need be, should that become necessary, as the island was only a short twenty-minute flight from Liverpool.

Something that did play heavily on Frank and Stan's minds was the situation with Susie. She was more than just an employee — she was a friend. A friend they hoped would join them on the next stage of their adventure. However, with a family and existing mortgage to consider, Susie didn't have the luxury to up sticks and had therefore reluctantly declined their offer of a position in the new business. Redundancies were not on the table under any circumstances as far as the lads were concerned, and so this had presented Frank and Stan with a few sleepless nights. They'd both agreed from the outset that if their decision to sell resulted in jobs being lost, then they'd simply walk away from the sale. Fortunately, an agreeable solution was found in the creation of an admin role at the charity. Lee had been run ragged for months doing the work of ten people, so he was chuffed at the prospect of some support. In addition, the new position would mean more sociable hours for Susie and the convenience of working from home. She'd need to adjust to the idea of Lee being her manager rather than Stella, but all in all it was a net positive, and a career change she was ready for and happy enough for the most part to embrace.

"There you go," Susie said coldly, returning from the kitchen and placing Stella's cup of tea directly on the surface of her desk rather than on her coaster. Something Susie never did.

"What, no Wagon Wheel?" Stella complained. "You know I can't drink my morning tea without a Wagon Wheel," she said, shaking her head in dismay.

Susie sat down, deliberately keeping her back to Stella. "You could ask Dirk, or one of your other friends over at the kebab shop," Susie answered, tapping away on her keyboard. "I'm sure they'll have plenty of marshmallow biscuits for you if you ask them very—"

But Susie's ramblings were cut short by a wailing noise like a grizzly bear standing on an upturned plug.

"What the…?" Susie said, instinctively ducking in fear, and shielding her head with her hands. Susie moaned in panic, certain that some kind of an attack was imminent. However, when no blows were struck, Susie bravely turned towards the caterwauling, holding out her hands to protect herself should that be needed. "Stella!" Susie called out over the source of the racket, now identified as emanating from Stella herself. "Stella, what are you doing?"

Stella sat wailing with tears streaming down her face like a toddler who'd let go of her favourite balloon, watching it float away on the breeze, gone forever.

"Stella, whatever is the matter?" Susie asked, her mothering instinct cancelling out her sense of panic. "This isn't because I forgot your Wagon Wheel, is it?"

"Nooooo," Stella said between sobs.

Susie wheeled her chair closer once again, wrapping her arms around Stella, which was potentially perilous because Stella was not a cuddler by nature. "There, now," Susie said, rubbing Stella's shoulder. "What's all this about, then?"

Stella blew her nose on Susie's sleeve, taking advantage of its proximity, and then took several deep breaths in an effort to try and compose herself. But try as she might, the emotion took precedent over her words.

FRANK & STAN'S BUCKET LIST #5: ISLE OF MAN TT ACES

Susie, for her part, sat patiently, offering a smile of encouragement until Stella was able to mostly regain her composure. "Stella?" Susie said softly, once the boohoos appeared to be drawing to a natural conclusion. "Stella, what's got you so upset?"

Stella looked directly at Susie, her eyes bloodshot and her nose still running. "It's *your* fault, so you should know," Stella declared, eyeing Susie's other sleeve.

"My fault?" Susie asked, pulling away now, both to give Stella an opportunity to speak, and because she didn't want to give Stella the opportunity to use the one clean sleeve she now had left as a snot rag. "Whatever have I done?" she said, racking her brains for what could have possibly resulted in the extreme outburst she'd witnessed.

"Breaking up the partnership!" Stella responded, staring down at her tea, reaching for the Wagon Wheel biscuit that wasn't there, and then sighing deeply upon remembering her Wagon Wheel biscuit wasn't there.

It took Susie a moment or two to register what Stella was talking about, and then it hit her. "What, you mean about me not moving to the Isle of Man with you?"

"Yes," Stella said, welling up once more at the thought.

"Aww, Stella, I'd love to move over, I really would," Susie told her. "But it's just not practical with the kids being settled in school." Susie stroked Stella's shoulder once again, presently ignoring the phone that was ringing incessantly with punters trying to book a taxi. For somebody as bold and brash as Stella was, there was a childlike vulnerability about her just now. "Stella, you do know how much I'm going to miss you, don't you, luv?"

Stella nodded, eyes still fixed downward.

"And," Susie went on cheerily, "Frank and Stan have already said that I'll need to come over there once a month for charity board meetings."

"Once a month?" Stella said, lifting her head, slightly buoyed by this news.

"At least," Susie was happy to confirm. "And not forgetting

coming over with the family for holidays."

"Yeah?"

"Yeah!"

"Before, when I said I'd miss the guys in the kebab shop and the launderette?" Stella began. "It wasn't them I was going to miss. It was you, Susie," she admitted.

"I know, Stella. I know," Susie replied. "And I'm going to miss you too."

"I don't often tell you this," Stella said. "But not only are you my best friend, but you're my *only* friend."

"Stop," Susie said, fanning her face with the tips of her fingers. "You're going to get me going in a minute."

"Once a month, you promise?"

"I promise," Susie answered, extending her little finger for a pinkie promise to seal the deal. "So does this mean you'll stop being a Grumpy Gus?" she joked, lightening the mood.

"Well, I can't promise anything," Stella said with a deadpan expression, before releasing a gruff laugh, and then sucking on the fag she'd just sparked into life. "Ah, whaddya know," she added, leaning forward to retrieve her breakfast. "My appetite appears to have returned."

"Great," said Susie, giving Stella's arm a final stroke. "I'd best get that phone," she suggested, wheeling herself back over to her own desk. "Oh, one thing," Susie said, pausing halfway over. "Now you're a little perkier, I don't suppose I could ask a teensy little favour, of a somewhat delicate nature?"

"Maybe. Depends," Stella replied, noncommittal, chomping down on her sandwich at the same time as cigarette smoke was billowing from her nostrils. How she didn't choke was anybody's guess.

"When you use the loo..." Susie began. "Well, do you think you could see your way clear to starting up again with the courtesy cigarette once you're finished? Only we've had a few complaints from people waiting in the reception area, and the ciggies seemed to mask the other smell."

"Yeah, all right. For you, I'll do it," Stella confirmed, speaking with her mouth full. "Plus, you know I'm all about the customer service."

"Wonderful," said Susie, reaching for her phone with a contented smile on her face. "I'm sure we'll all appreciate it."

Chapter
NINE

It was another day of rain, and Dave usually liked nothing better than the sound of raindrops pattering steadily down on the roof when he was safely indoors, all cosy with a nice cup of tea. It brought him back to his childhood, taking shelter in the trees while caught outdoors during a rainstorm, and brought a nostalgic smile to his face as well as a sense of calm. Well, ordinarily it did. Just not today. Not in the middle of practice week at the Isle of Man TT races, and certainly not when they'd yet to complete a full lap around the circuit. Unfortunately, varying weather was just one of the island's many charms. Though with limited practice time available, it did create a sense of panic among the riders, with the only consolation being they were all in the same boat, figuratively speaking of course. But ironically, a boat would have had more chance of completing a lap in the current weather conditions.

In a rain-soaked paddock, Dave paced around the interior of their race awning, shaking his head, swearing intermittently. "Bloody clouds!" Dave shouted from the doorway, shaking his ham-hock fist to the heavens. However, one silver lining of the cancelled practice sessions was that the incessant rain had left them plenty of time to get their clutch issues fully resolved. And with little else to fill time, their bike was stripped more times than a prostitute in Prague. Fortunately, their engine was purring like a kitten, fine-tuned earlier by taking advantage of some track time at Jurby. Being seasoned campaigners, though,

Dave and Monty knew the success of any adjustments could only be genuinely measured out on the TT course, travelling at a race pace. The gearing settings, for example, could be perfect pottering around at Jurby but feel completely hopeless once you headed down Glencrutchery Road. Again, these vital adjustments could only be addressed by track time, but sadly, the weather didn't appear to have received this memo.

From his position of shelter inside the awning, Dave nursed a nice cuppa, watching as two figures, outside, travelled in his direction. The pair moved in fits and starts, darting between parked vehicles, stopping here and there to glance over their shoulders before continuing on. As they got closer, Dave could see faces he recognised. Familiar faces.

"Go, go, go!" Frank called out, encouraging Stan to get a bloody move on.

"I'm running as fast as I can, which isn't easy in Gucci shoes!" Stan protested, jumping over a large puddle, giggling like a schoolgirl.

The two of them entered the enclosure, running straight past Dave like he wasn't even stood there, and took cover at the rear of the awning. "Is anybody following us?" Stan asked, struggling to stifle his laughter.

"Like who?" Dave asked, casually blowing the steam from his cup, continuing to look straight ahead.

"Anybody?" Frank said.

Dave leaned forward, craning his neck, scanning the area outside the awning. "Nope. Not that I can see," he announced, after a long, lingering look. "I say again, like who?" Dave asked, turning to face his guests, interest piqued.

"Security guards," Stan suggested to Dave, ruffling out the raindrops from his recently-dyed hair.

"Okay, boys, what's going on?" Dave asked, like a concerned parent.

Frank walked towards the front of the awning, peering outside to confirm for himself that they weren't being followed. "Well, we've just seen that irritating, nasally little pipsqueak,"

Frank whispered, casting his eyes across the paddock.

"Who, Monty?" Dave asked. "Why would you call Monty a—"

"No, not Monty," Frank answered. "Rodney Franks."

"What, again?" Dave asked.

"Yeah. Just now. And we got him good this time," Stan said with an evil laugh, joining Frank and Dave in the doorway, satisfied now that they weren't being tailed. "Ehm, Dave?" Stan said, looking the big guy up and down. "Why is it you're only wearing your underpants...?"

"You just noticed?" asked Dave. "I got caught in a downpour," he explained.

"Okay," said Stan. "But the public regularly walk through the paddock, and the front of the awning is wide open. You do know that, right?"

Dave shrugged his shoulders, taking another sip of his tea. "It's all part of the charm," he suggested. "Race fans like getting up close and personal to the riders, and if this isn't up close and personal, then I don't know what is," Dave advised. "Anyway, so about Rodney Franks...?"

"Oh, yes," Stan said, giggling once more. "Frank and I were walking down to see you when the beer tent called us in for a quick lunchtime libation."

"Just the one," Frank interjected.

"Just the one," Stan confirmed. "Anyway," Stan continued, dragging his eyes away from Dave's white Y-fronts. "From where we were, there outside the beer tent, we spotted Rodney Franks with a delegation of what looked like VIPs wandering around the rear of the grandstand."

"They had a camera crew following them and everything," Frank added. "And, of course, Rodney was front and centre acting like the big I am."

"Yeah," Stan said with a snarl. "So we finished our pint and followed them."

"Which is why we're so wet," Frank explained.

"So," Stan said, picking up the story, "Rodney leads them all into the massive Joey Dunlop Foundation fundraising tent, with us in hot pursuit like Cagney and Lacey."

"Crockett and Tubbs would have been better, Stan, I think?" Frank entered in.

"Who's telling this bloody story, Frank?" Stan admonished. "Anyway, fine. So there we are, like Crockett and Tubbs. And it turns out that Rodney and Co are doing some PR about the work the various motorsport charities do. Frank and I loitered about, pretending to peruse the range of t-shirts on offer in the tent, listening in. That's when Rodney was collared by the shop assistant and asked if he would like to enter a bid in their silent auction. From the looks of Rodney and the way he was prancing about as if he was someone very important, I reckon the woman must've thought Rodney would put in a substantial bid."

"The main auction prize was for a trip in the media helicopter they use to film the races," Frank said, pointing to the sky. "The winning bidder and a guest can ride along in any race at next year's TT."

Stan walked over to fill the kettle, chuckling away to himself. "Rodney joked about not being a fan of flying, trying to worm his way out of it," Stan said, picking up the tale where he'd left off. "It seemed obvious the shop assistant recognised his type, realising he was just a tight arse who didn't want to part with his cash. So she made a point of saying, loud enough for everyone to hear, that it was all for charity and a good cause. At that point, Rodney had no choice but to agree lest he look like the complete prat that he is, so he was ushered into this booth—"

"Like the ones you'd use when voting," Frank explained.

"Right. So Rodney goes into this little booth behind a curtain to write down his bid for the auction..." Stan continued.

"Cheese and crackers, boys, I'm growing a beard here," Dave said impatiently. "Can we get to the punchline while I've still got some life left in me?"

"Ah, okay," Stan answered, not wanting to lose his audience. "Anyway, when Rodney finished up, smiling for the camera on his way back out, Frank and I then went into the same booth a few minutes later, as soon as the coast was clear."

"We took his envelope out of the bucket," Frank told Dave, rubbing his hands in glee.

"I was going to say that!" Stan protested, returning to the others, cuppa in hand.

"Oh, I see," said Dave, his interest returning. "All right, I like where this is going."

"Yeah," Stan said, nodding. "We opened the envelope on top of the pile, and you won't believe how much that miserable, cravat-wearing so-and-so bid for the star prize."

"Dunno?" Dave replied when Stan stared up at him.

"Twenty quid!" Stan replied, shaking his head in disgust. "Twenty measly quid."

"Tight get," Frank said, shaking his head in solidarity.

"So, we felt it was only right to increase his generosity," Stan suggested. "As it was surely a mistake on Rodney's part. What with him being such a benevolent soul and all."

"Yeah. You can stop winking, Stan. I understand what you're saying, and I picked up on this about three minutes ago," Dave told him. "So, how much did you doctor his bid to?"

"Two hundred quid," Stan revealed, rubbing his thumb and forefinger together, counting the imaginary notes that Rodney might soon be parting with. "That'll teach him for crossing us," Stan added, sounding like a cartoon villain.

Frank placed his hands on his hips, turning to Stan. "What? What do you mean, two hundred quid?"

"That's what I changed it to," Stan answered, not understanding the question. "You were stood there right next to me when I did it, Frank."

"Stan..." Frank said slowly and deliberately, "Stan, Rodney had written down a two and zero, yeah?"

"Yeah," Stan confirmed. "And I changed it to two hundred, as I said, and then resealed the envelope."

"No. No you didn't," Frank said with a half-laugh, wondering if his mate was taking the piss at this point.

"I did!" Stan shot back. "I added three zeros, which made it two hundred quid. Did you not do maths at school?"

Frank placed his hand over his mouth as the realisation of Stan's error hit him. He'd thought the extra zeros Stan had added were written down exactly as intended, but clearly they were not. "Oopsie," said Frank, breaking into raucous laughter. "Stan, what number does a two followed by four zeros make?"

Stan offered up an exaggerated sigh. "Der," he said. "Two hundred pounds. Just like I said."

"It would if you'd placed a decimal point after the first two zeros, yes," Frank told him.

"What? Are you saying I didn't?" Stan asked, panic starting to take over. "No, no. I must have. Surely I..."

"You didn't," Frank insisted. "And that's why I was so shocked at what you'd done. Delighted, mind you. But shocked."

"Hang on," Stan said, fingers in the air, writing the numbers on an imaginary blackboard to help him visualise. "Oh, crap," Stan said, once the proverbial penny had eventually dropped. "A two followed by four zeros..."

"Without a decimal point," Frank reminded him.

"That's twenty grand!" Stan said, biting down on his lower lip. "Holy guacamole!"

"Ha-ha, what a plonker," Dave entered in. "It looks like old Rodney is going to have a bird's-eye view of the TT course," he added, with a hearty chuckle. "I'll make sure I look up and wave at the poor, silly sod."

"Surely he'll tell the charity that there's been a mistake?" Stan suggested, flicking his eyes between Frank and Dave.

"Nah," Frank said, unconvinced. "Can you see the headlines? Millionaire businessman shafts hardworking charity? Plus, he made such an effort in getting the cameraman to capture him coming out from behind the curtain, right? So it's not like he can deny making the bid."

"I suppose," said Stan, supposing. "Wow. Rodney best hope someone else comes along and places a higher bid," he added, unable to resist a snigger. "You know, I actually feel guilty for stealing his umbrella now."

"You nicked his brolly as well?" Dave asked, impressed by the impish side being revealed.

"He did," Frank confirmed. "We watched him placing it in the umbrella stand on his way into the tent, and Stan suggested it'd be a hoot if we nicked it so the bugger would get soaked when he went back outside."

"But... you didn't have it with you when you got here...?" Dave asked, a little confused.

"I dropped it somewhere along the way," Stan replied.

"Back when you were puddle-hopping," Frank reminded his partner-in-crime. "But we were still making good our escape, so we didn't want to run back for it," Frank explained to Dave.

"We should really avoid drinking at lunchtime," Stan said, reflecting on their actions thus far today.

"Maybe. Maybe not," Frank said with a laugh, not entirely convinced their efforts hadn't been productive and worthwhile overall. "I'm just picturing Rodney walking around the paddock like a drowned rat with his ridiculous cravat all wet."

"Just imagine his face when the charity calls to give him the happy news," Stan added, setting them both off, happy tears streaming down both their faces.

"Sheesh," said Dave. "Remind me never to get on the wrong side of you two!"

Later that day, the rain eventually started to lift and the big yellow thing in the sky, thankfully, finally came into view. Sadly, though, it was too little too late for that evening's practice session to go ahead as ordinarily scheduled, as there simply wasn't enough drying time before the regularly planned start time. For that reason, the organisers had no choice but to cancel the session for the second evening in a row, reluctant as they were to do so. It was a massive — yet not unexpected, given the circumstances — disappointment for all concerned. Fortunately, the forecast for the remainder of the week made for more pleasant reading. So time enough to catch up on track time, it was hoped.

FRANK & STAN'S BUCKET LIST #5: ISLE OF MAN TT ACES

With folks taking advantage of the improving weather conditions up at the paddock, Dave and Monty's awning was soon like Piccadilly Circus, with race fans milling around, eager to have a chat with the stars of the widely advertised upcoming TV documentary.

It was a terrific atmosphere up at the paddock. Sure, the racing was, of course, the primary draw for all concerned and rightly so. However, there was nothing quite like a gentle stroll around the assembled vans, chatting to the crews and fellow race fans and generally feeling you were part of the action. It wasn't like you were imposing either. Generally, the mechanics, racers, owners, organisers and so on were all delighted to take time and talk to you, time permitting, of course. Granted, it was advisable to give them a respectable distance come race time. But, overall, there was a sense that you were a part of it all. And that felt bloody fantastic.

While Dave and Monty spoke with fans (and with Dave, at this point, fortunately now fully dressed), Frank and Stan were in the garage section of the awning, stood nervously on either side of the sidecar talking to the camera, as Brad and Chip were now present also. Chip and Brad were keen to explore the motivations of team sponsors like Stan and Frank, and what the TT meant to the pair of them.

"And… cut," Chip instructed, raising his thumb above the camera once the interview had concluded. "That wasn't too bad, was it?" he asked, but saying it more as a statement than a question. "You both came across well."

"Well, for some of us, it comes natural," Stan said with a sniff, lifting his chin in the air. Stan paused to wave at the modest crowd of three people stood just outside the garage portion of the awning, a group who were staring in and likely wondering if those being interviewed were famous in any way. Stan flashed a glimpse of his bleached teeth in their direction, appearing ready and willing to sign an autograph should any such autograph be requested. However, following a disappointed-sounding mumbling amongst themselves, the three onlookers concluded there was nothing further to see, with one suggesting a visit to the doughnut stall instead. This suggestion appeared to perk them all up, and off they toddled.

"So," Frank said. "That's us all finished?"

"Yup," Brad was happy to confirm. "Like Chip said, you both came across well."

Stan offered a shrug, indicating that this should never have really been in any doubt, at least in his particular case.

"Yeah, so what we wanted to do," Brad continued, making conversation as he helped his brother pack their equipment away, "is to convey the motivations of people like you. Sponsors and whatnot. Folks who throw a lot of time, attention, and money into a thing like this when there's no real financial reward to be expected, just doing it purely for the love of the race. It's pretty amazing, I think."

Frank nodded along, agreeing with everything being said. "It's like I said earlier, when the camera was rolling," Frank replied. "The thrill of being involved, ringside if you will, is exhilarating. The feeling we get from being a part of a team is worth more than any amount of money. It really is priceless."

"Do... ehm..." Stan said, swirling his fingers around like he was trying to say something but just not entirely sure how to phrase it. "This... documentary series. Might it be seen by those Hollywood types when it eventually airs...?"

"I suppose," Chip replied, not really committing one way or the other.

"Ah," said Stan. "In that case, I just wondered if I should contact my agent," he said, thinking out loud and casually throwing the idea out there. "You know, just in case a casting director liked what they saw?" he said, running his hand up and down in front of him to introduce the entirety of what was on offer.

"Agent?" Frank said with a laugh. "Since when have you had an agent?"

"Spanners Harrison," Stan shot back. "He once said I had a face for the big screen," Stan added, raising his chin again, showcasing his profile for Frank's benefit.

"Spanners Harrison?" Frank answered, delving through the memory banks. "Who the hell is...?" he went on, until a flicker of recognition presented itself. "Hold on. Spanners Harrison, as in the car mechanic? I've not seen him for, what, twenty years, at least."

"Me neither," Stan responded, although pleased his agent hadn't been forgotten about entirely. "After he witnessed my starring performance in that Christmas panto I was in, he said I should call him anytime. With him being a stagehand in at least three sold-out theatrical productions, Spanners told me he could open doors for me. He said I had a jawline to die for. His words, not mine."

"Christmas panto?" Frank said under his breath, not wishing to douse Stan's flames completely but not recalling his friend's performance in any such production. "I'm sure he'll be delighted to hear from you after twenty years," Frank told Stan, though not unkindly, giving his chum a friendly ribbing. "Anyway," said Frank, turning his attention back over to Chip and Brad. "We're meeting our other halves for something to eat, and you'd be most welcome to join us?"

"Thanks," Chip answered. "But we've managed to get in on one of those trike tours that go around the TT course," he explained, reaching for an imaginary throttle, and giving it a little twist for good measure.

"Yeah, should be fun," Brad added. "With the practice session cancelled, they were able to squeeze us in at short notice."

Frank started to chuckle, receiving a confused expression from Brad. "Sorry," Frank said. "I was just thinking about the time Stan and I went on a trike tour ourselves."

"Oh?" Brad asked. "Is it worth doing, or...?"

"Yes, very much so," Frank said. "I just recalled how Stan nearly shat himself during our tour," he added, breaking into another chuckle at the scene replaying in his head.

"Why, do the trikes go really fast or something?" Chip asked, with a worried expression.

"Oh, it wasn't from the pace of travel," Stan explained. "I had something of a gippy tummy when we were out and about," he said, rubbing his stomach. "I got caught short, if you take my meaning."

"Uh... not really," replied a slightly confused Brad, not being well-versed in Brit-speak.

"What Frank means is that I *literally* almost soiled myself," Stan explained.

"It might well be the same trike tour," Frank suggested. "I forget the chap's name who took us around. But if you mention a soppy bloke wiping his bum using a tuft of sheep's wool he found caught on a fence, he'll be sure to remember our Stanley. It's the sort of thing I dare say you'd struggle to forget."

"We'll be sure to give the seats a good wipe-down before we head out," Brad remarked, uncertain whether to be amused or horrified by Frank's little anecdote. Brad then checked his watch. "Yikes, we better get a move on," he said to his brother, throwing one of their rucksacks over his shoulder. "We need to get the recording equipment back to the house before this trike tour thing starts in twenty-five minutes."

"Are you meeting the tour guide at the Sea Terminal?" Frank asked, a bit concerned as he recalled where they'd started their own memorable tour from.

"That's the plan," Chip said.

"Hmm, the traffic's crackers out there," Frank told them. "I don't think you'll have the luxury of heading home first if you want to make it there in time," he advised.

"Crackers," Stan added, by way of verification.

"Good to know. Thanks," Chip answered. "In that case, we'll just head straight to the Sea Terminal," he said, rubbing his hands together in anticipation of their outing around the island. "Thanks again for the interview, guys," Chip added, stepping out of the awning. "You were both awesome."

Brad and Chip offered a quick wave towards the hospitality section of the awning. Dave and Monty, however (Monty having returned from a previous absence after previewing a lovely collection of garden gnomes he wished to purchase), were in deep conversation with a small contingent of passionate race fans. Or, equally likely, it could just as easily have been a small handful of moochers attracted to the beer fridge.

"We need to buy a hand truck or dolly or something," Brad moaned, glancing at his watch and picking up the pace, laden with bags like an overworked packhorse.

But unfortunately, as they were starting to realise, getting anywhere quickly during the TT fortnight was not without its challenges. Even the relatively short walk to their car was like an obstacle course. "Excuse me. 'Scuse me, there," Brad offered, weaving his way through the crowds of people milling around the various retail outlets at the rear of the grandstand. "Coming through," he said politely. But progress was rather like wading through treacle while wearing concrete boots.

Just when Chip had identified and then began forging a path through the merry hordes, a shaven-headed, stocky chap wearing a large, ill-fitting suit blocked their path. Chip offered his apologies, even though he wasn't the one creating the obstruction. "Sorry," he said, polite as always, moving to his left, hoping to sidestep the fellow and be on his way. But the stern-faced chap simply mirrored his movements, once again blocking Chip's way. "Sorry, can I just..." Chip said, pointing in the direction he was hoping to travel.

"You're the filmmakers?" the man asked, flicking his close-set eyes between Chip and Brad, offering up a forced smile.

"Yes. Yeah, we are," said Brad, pulling up next to his brother. "If you wouldn't mind, it's just that—"

"I'll walk with you," the suited chap suggested, stepping to one side, extending his arm. "Please..." he offered, allowing them to continue, and with him now walking beside them. The good thing, at least, was that the crowds were parting much more easily with this oversized fellow in their company.

"Oh...kay..." Brad said, looking to his brother, uncertain if this rather menacing, rough-looking gentleman were somebody they'd perhaps already met and just didn't remember. They had, after all, spoken to a considerable number of people since their arrival on the island (although this particular fellow didn't look like somebody they would have easily forgotten).

"I don't mean to be rude," Brad said, as this man looked like the sort of individual it wouldn't be a good idea to be rude to. "But have we met?" he asked, with a half-smile, not wishing to cause offence.

"What? Oh, no. I don't think so. I'm Vince," explained Vince, matter-of-factly.

"Oh, okay. Well, it's nice to meet you, Vince," Brad replied, continuing in the direction of their parked car, and casting a concerned glance over to his brother. "Is there something... um, something we can..." Brad went on, looking back over to Vince. "Well, is there something we can do for you, Vince?" he asked, cautiously. "I mean, it's nice to meet you, Vince, like I said. It's just that we need to be somewhere in less than—"

"Right, yes," Vince said, raising a stout finger skyward in a knowing fashion. "You're off on your trike tour."

"What? How did you—"

"I overheard you talking in the awning," Vince offered by way of explanation. Though why he was eavesdropping in the first place was a matter he didn't move on to.

"I don't want to delay you from what promises to be a perfectly pleasant evening, so I'll jump straight to the point," Vince said, strolling along, with the twins on either side of him like old friends. "I understand you're filming a multi-episode television documentary about the TT?" Vince asked, looking first to Brad, and then to Chip.

"Yeah, that's right," Brad answered. But as their project had been covered extensively all over the local press, this wasn't exactly inside information.

"And I see you've signed up Dave Quirk and his sidekick Monty as your poster boys," Vince added.

Again, not exactly classified state secrets. But Vince didn't appear to be the sort you wanted to interrupt once he was in his stride, so of course they let him continue.

"And according to your comments in the newspaper article,

you think they've a true chance at a podium finish?" Vince asked, with no attempt to contain his emerging smile. "You do know that's not going to happen, don't you?"

"It might," Chip suggested, unconvincingly. "Anyway, it's been a pleasure, Vince, but, you know..."

"Hmm," said Vince. And for someone stating he didn't want to delay them, he was doing a remarkable job of doing precisely that. "I did smile reading your quote in that interview, talking about the inspiring story of the local underdog who'd made it big, and who was raring to go, ready to do it all over again for this year's TT as well." Vince then laughed, as if he'd just told an especially good joke. Following the long silence from Brad and Chip, he spoke again. "Wait, you don't genuinely *believe* all of that rubbish, do you?" he asked.

"Yeah. Kinda. We certainly hope so," Chip said, lowering his head, a little embarrassed.

"I suppose you've told your TV network, back home, how you've signed up a couple of first-rate, top-notch riders with a real chance at winning this thing?" Vince asked, chuckling away to himself. "You have, haven't you?"

Chip and Brad didn't bother to answer, so Vince answered for them. "Well fear not, boys, as that's why I wanted to talk to you," he told the pair, raising his arms like a bird taking flight, and placing a wing over each of their shoulders. "You see, my gaffer's race team just happen to be the favourites to win the sidecar class," he went on, giving them both a gentle pat. "And my boss thought it'd be just super brilliant to appear in this here documentary of yours. That means you'd get to work with a team that's *actually* got a chance at victory, yeah? And, plus, my employer gets a little publicity for his new logistics business along the way, as well. So everyone's a winner!"

"That's very kind, Vince," Brad said, easing himself free of Vince's grip. "But we're good."

"Thank you, though," Chip added politely, mainly as he was still secured by one of Vince's Popeye-sized arms. "Plus, we don't have any available funds left in the kitty," he explained, hoping to extricate himself from Vince's determined grasp just as his brother had somehow managed to do.

"We don't want money," Vince advised. "Oh no, no, no..." he added, singing the words. "We pay *you*! After all, you'd be doing us a huge honour."

"*You* pay *us*?" Brad asked sceptically. "How much, exactly?"

"Whatever you want," Vince quickly replied, like money was no object. "And, it means you can tell your boss back home that you're working with genuine contenders rather than the potatoes-on-legs that you're currently pinning your hopes on," he told them. "So, it's just a case of you naming your price, then? Show me the money, and all that?" he said hopefully.

Brad looked over to his brother, and then back to Vince. "Look, Vince. I don't know about this," he said. "We've shaken hands with Dave and Monty, and we've already started filming, so..."

"There's plenty of time to play catch-up, boys. And I'll ensure you get whatever access you need to our team. Completely unrestricted," Vince responded. "Also, have you even considered what you're going to record if and when Dave and Monty don't even qualify for race week?" Vince asked them. "That's a distinct possibility, and wouldn't exactly make for riveting viewing, now would it? I'm sure your TV network superiors wouldn't be too happy about that."

"We'll need to think about this," Chip said. "And, we really do have to get going."

"Of course," Vince said, reaching inside his jacket pocket for a business card. "I'll look forward to hearing from you shortly," he said, handing over his details. "There was just one point of order, chaps. There's no room for both our boys *and* Dave and Monty in this equation. So it's an either-or offer on the table."

"Understood," Brad offered politely. "Anyway..."

"Of course," Vince said, waving the brothers on their way. "We'll speak soon!" he called out after them as they hurried away. "Name your price!" he added, allowing the words to float over on the breeze. "Rodney Franks has very deep pockets!"

Chapter
TEN

Wednesday of practice week. Zero laps completed by our boys. Current weather conditions, however, perfectly splendid...

Dave ripped a tear-off strip from his visor on the exit from Ramsey Hairpin and tossed it aside. For the flies splattered across the discarded plastic, their unexpected adventure around the TT course had come to a conclusion. But at least Big Dave could see clearly again in time for the ascent towards the Mountain section of the course now that his temporary lodgers were evicted.

Dave teased open the throttle, breathing heavily, his focus unwavering. He suspected their lap, so far, wasn't quick, but when the machine behind passed them like they were standing still, his fears about their pace — or lack thereof — were indeed confirmed.

Despite their best efforts previously, the gearing was still way off, and the suspension set-up was simply horrendous. Corners that would be taken near flat-out the previous year were now being negotiated at around fifty percent conviction at best. Dave consoled himself with the fact that this was their first proper outing of the year, but, even so, the machine was a long way from being race-ready. The engine, for its part, hadn't missed a beat, but that was to be expected at the relatively leisurely speed they were travelling. Every corner was an effort, however, with the suspension soft in some corners, heavy in others, and this lack of consistency gave Dave what every rider detested: doubt. On a circuit with over two hundred corners to negotiate and speeds of over one hundred and forty mph, you simply had to have confidence in the equipment under your bum. Still, at least Dave and Monty could use the experience of this initial run, and the feedback gathered from the machine, to make further crucial adjustments.

Vital to their hopes of qualifying for race week was having completed laps under their belt. So rather than pushing things, Dave opted to keep it steady and bring the old girl home safely, where they'd soon, hopefully, have completed one of the three required qualifying laps.

All things considered, it still felt bloody good to be out on track with your best mate by your side and along for the ride (quite literally in this case). Dave's cheeks ached from smiling behind the cover of his helmet. He adored the Mountain section of the course. With its sweeping expanse of Manx hillside all around, it was a complete contrast to the tree-lined sector of Glen Helen or the urban roads through Ramsey. Even up here, in the relative wilderness, however, amazingly enough there were still race fans peppered sporadically along the edge of the circuit, all on hand to offer a friendly and enthusiastic wave of encouragement as you sped on by.

The view was simply magnificent, and in these moments of euphoria, all the sleepless nights spent working on the bike, draining cash with each subsequent replacement part, were easily forgotten about. It was this feeling that made all the sacrifice worthwhile and, even in their darkest moments of despair, motivated Monty and Dave to return the following year. It was an addiction, a compulsion, a calling. It was all-consuming and relentless, draining both physically and mentally. There were highs, there were lows. There were tears and frustration. But this was the Isle of Man TT. This was why you were here, doing what you were doing. You were a racer, and if you had oil coursing through your veins, then this was utopia. The sacrifice was worth it. You were racing on the greatest circuit on earth.

Having completed their leisurely lap safely and now back at the grandstand, Dave moved into the return lane, with Monty rising up like a hermit crab poking his head out of its shell.

"Are we heading back out?" Monty yelled, lifting up his visor, trying to be heard over the throbbing of engines. "Dave!" he shouted, tapping his mate on the shoulder. "Are we—?"

But the southerly-pointing thumb Monty received in response told him all he needed to know. There would have been just time enough to head out for another circuit with seven minutes or so remaining in the sidecar practice session. But rather than aiming in the direction of *parc fermé*, from where you headed back out on track, Dave instead turned right, heading in the direction of their racing HQ, confirming their session had been concluded for the evening.

With helmet removed, Monty enjoyed a pleasant stretch once parked up inside their awning, unzipping his protective leathers and peeling off his t-shirt. "Bloody warm out there," he declared, allowing the lovely breeze flowing into the enclosure to caress his glistening breasts. "The old bus was a bit nervous in the corners," Monty suggested, giving their sidecar a friendly tap with the side of his boot.

"A bit nervous?" Dave scoffed, removing his helmet. "She was that bouncy that I was starting to feel seasick," he said, unzipping his leathers and removing his own t-shirt as well, enjoying the fresh air circulating around his bare skin. "That was not the firmest of rides I've ever had."

"Oh? You always said you enjoyed a firm ride," Monty replied with a childish snigger.

"Come here," Dave said, walking around the sidecar towards his half-naked chum. Dave placed his arms around Monty, pulling him in close, and laying a moist cheek on his pal's exposed, equally-moist shoulder. "It may have been a bit of a rollercoaster, Monty. But it was bloody good fun, wasn't it?"

"The best," Monty replied. "It doesn't get much better than that."

"Ahem..." Stan said, clearing his throat. "Are we interrupting a tender moment?" he asked, standing in the awning doorway with Frank by his side.

"Bloody hell, it's like Brokeback Mountain in there, but with sidecars rather than horses," Frank joked.

"Wonderful film," Stan offered, sounding like quite the authority on the subject. "It delivers something different each time you watch it."

"There's room for two more," Dave suggested, without lifting his head.

Stan never needed to be asked twice, what with him being a hugger by nature. "Aww, Team Frank and Stan's Bucket List group cuddle," he said, tugging on Frank's arm, leading the way. "What's the special occasion?" Stan asked, voice now muffled from the skin pressed up against his face. "Not that we need one, of course."

"Just happy," Dave said with a contented sigh.

"And high on life," Monty added, sounding equally contented.

After several seconds and just before things started to get too awkward, Frank peeled himself away first, stepping over to the sidecar. "So," he asked, placing a hand on the bike. "We thought you'd be heading out for another lap...?"

"Nope, just the one, today," Dave answered, shaking his head. "She's running well enough, but the suspension's softer than the springs in a hooker's mattress."

"We've a long night ahead of us," Monty remarked, reaching for his tool belt.

"You know that if we had even a single mechanical bone in our bodies between us, we'd help out, right?" Stan replied.

"Maybe you could get your agent on the case," Frank wryly suggested, laughing to himself. "Spanners would have this fixed in no time."

But Stan allowed Frank's pathetic and hurtful attempt at humour to wash straight over him. "We can go and fetch you something to eat while you work?" Stan volunteered, to both Monty and Dave. "That's something we *can* do."

"Chinese?" Monty replied, licking his lips at the prospect.

"Chinese it is," Stan was happy to confirm, before cryptically adding, "Oh, and we captured some footage of you starting your lap, which we can provide to Brad and Chip. You know, to help them out."

"Right?" Dave said, staring blankly, wondering if there was to be any further clarification on the way. Dave looked at Stan, and Stan looked at Dave.

Sensing this stare-off might conceivably continue for some time, Frank entered in, "You did hear about Brad and Chip…?"

"Did we?" Dave asked of Monty, who was more organised in such matters.

"Is this something to do with their penchant for British women?" Monty asked, torque wrench in hand. "They do love the accent, apparently."

"Oh, you haven't heard, then?" Frank quickly deduced, from the wayward direction of the response. "They've only had their car broken into," he said.

"While they were both out on their trike tour," Stan added. "Blimey, what's the world coming to?"

"Bummer," Monty replied, not appearing overly concerned by the news at hand. "At least they'll be insured," he said with a shrug, grabbing some of the other tools required to commence Operation Stiffen-the-Suspension.

"All of their recording equipment has been nicked," Stan informed them, hoping to garner more of the type of reaction he felt the situation warranted.

"Ah, bugger. That's a bit of a nightmare," Monty said, now grasping the gravity of this development. "They had everything in the car?"

"Unfortunately, yeah," Frank said. "They didn't have time to drop it off at their accommodation before their trike tour, so it was all left inside the car. And now the lowlifes have cleared them out — cameras, HD cards, laptops. Everything."

"What about the footage they've already filmed? Is that all gone?" Dave asked.

"Safely backed up to the cloud, they hope," Stan was pleased to report. "However, the problem is that the passwords for their cloud account are in their laptop bag. Which was also, of course, in the car."

"Bastards," said Dave. "Here, we've got a camcorder we could lend them," Dave offered helpfully. "Monty, we do still have that camcorder, don't we?"

Monty shook his head in the negative. "Nope," he said sadly. "The police never returned it after the investigation. Claimed it went missing from their evidence room, apparently."

"Typical," Dave answered. "Betcha the custody sergeant borrowed it for his summer holiday," he remarked, before turning his attention back to Frank and Stan. "Anyway..." he said to them, pointing to the sidecar. "Unless you know how to adjust suspension..."

"Ah. Right-ho. We'll go and grab you something to eat, as promised, then," Frank said, catching the subtle hint thrown their way. "Come on, Stanley," he instructed. But when Stan didn't move a muscle, he offered Stan a little shove. "Let's get a move on before we get covered in oil, Stanley."

"Yes, but..." Stan said, being gently eased out of the awning.

"But what?" asked Frank, not understanding the source of Stan's reluctance to leave. It was, after all, Stan himself who'd offered to go and get the boys Chinese.

"But what about the camcorder story...?" asked Stan, looking over his shoulder, pushing back against Frank's hand placed firmly between his shoulder blades. "I need to know more..."

※

Further up the TT paddock from where Dave and Monty's awning could be found, there wasn't a rusting van to be seen. Here, the factory-funded teams beavered away next to their shimmering race trucks in awnings of the size and scale a small circus would be delighted to call home. Sure, it was a contrast to the privately funded teams, but the passion and determination were just as fervent. Often, the riders representing these factory teams had progressed through the ranks, having started out as privateers themselves, before being signed up and given the opportunity of throwing their leg over the finest machinery that money could buy. For that reason, you'd struggle to find any inflated egos on display. Those fortunate enough to be a factory rider had, at one time, cut their teeth the exact same way as those further down the paddock.

Of all the expensive race trucks on display, one stood out head and shoulders above its neighbours, owing to the sheer size of the thing. The owner of this particular truck was, it would appear, eager to show his peers just who was boss around these parts, or, to make up for certain inadequacies found within the trouser region, perhaps. And, when talking of little pricks, well, they didn't come much littler than...

"Rodney Franks, gentlemen. His truck is just ahead," an immaculately-dressed Vince announced, extending his arm in the direction of the silver behemoth parked up on the grass before them.

"Holy crap," Brad and Chip said in unison, clapping eyes on Rodney's race team HQ. *"That's* what you call a truck," Chip added.

"Mr Franks should be expecting us," Vince advised, pressing an illuminated button on the truck door, the door then gliding gracefully open, enticing them in.

Two things hit Chip and Brad once they'd climbed aboard: the overwhelming smell of new leather, and the garish nature of the decoration. Sure, the interior of the truck was glamorous enough. But it seemed to lack any class. Absolutely *every* surface appeared to be either polished mahogany or soft, cream-coloured leather, for instance. It was extreme overkill. In fact, if Hugh Hefner had owned a race truck in the late 1970s, he'd have likely employed the same interior designer.

"Brad and Chip," said Rodney, spinning around in a plushly-appointed leather captain's chair, heavy crystal glass hovering teasingly in front of his lips. "Can I offer you a drink?" he asked, raising his glass just a touch and tipping it forward.

"No, but thanks," Brad answered on behalf of them both.

"Please..." Rodney said, introducing them to a large sofa near to him. "So," Rodney continued, once the boys were seated, jumping straight into business and dispensing with any further pleasantries, "I understand from Vince that you're receptive to my offer? That is, you'd like to feature my boys, Jack Napier and Andy Thomas, in your documentary?"

Rodney then took a little sip of what appeared to be whisky.

"Well..." Chip replied, looking first to his brother, and then back to Rodney. "Well, it's not that we necessarily *wanted* to feature them, but—"

"Money talks," Rodney cut across, raising his glass to toast his wealth. "And my offer of fifty grand and unfettered access to the favourites in the sidecar class was obviously tempting enough," Rodney declared confidently.

"Yeah, about that," Brad replied, staring at the crystal decanter on the table next to him. "There's a slight issue," he said.

"It's not about those two absurd orangutans, Dave Quirk and Monty Montgomery, is it?" Rodney asked. "I thought I was quite clear that my offer is dependent on you dropping those two tremendous halfwits from your project."

"I take it you're not a big fan of theirs?" Chip put forth.

"Oh, it's not those two that bother me, necessarily," Rodney offered with a shake of his head. "Although they do grate on me to a certain extent," he added, with a look of distaste. "No, the ones that really make my skin crawl are their sponsors, two cretins called—"

"Frank and Stan," Brad offered up, finishing Rodney's sentence for him. "Anyway, no, it's not about Monty and Dave," Brad went on. "Right now, as it stands, Dave and Monty won't be appearing in the documentary," he revealed. "In fact, *nobody* will."

"Oh," Rodney said, glancing over to an equally confused-looking Vince. "I thought we had something of a deal," Rodney spat out, fidgeting with his cravat. "Vince gave me the distinct impression that you wanted to proceed with the generous offer I'd tabled. And I understood that this was the reason for your personal visit this afternoon."

"Uh, okay. Well, not exactly," Brad said, raising his hands, acutely aware that Vince appeared to be rearing up, or possibly even increasing in mass, as it was obvious Vince didn't like to look bad in front of his boss. "I mean, when we spoke with Vince yesterday, we were only hoping to come see you in person to discuss your offer some more."

"Or at least part of it," Chip entered in, offering an appeasing smile to Vince, before returning the floor to his brother.

"Yes," Brad continued. "We wanted to see you and explain that we can't drop Dave and Monty because they're really nice guys who we've actually become friends with during the short time we've known them. Also, the marketing department over at NBC has spent a fortune creating a PR campaign around them."

"They've got them riding a chariot like Roman soldiers in one commercial," Chip said, cracking an imaginary whip. "It's pretty cool."

"What we wanted to ask, Mr Franks, is if you would consider still allowing us to feature them in the show, but in a smaller, reduced role, maybe?" Brad asked.

Rodney wiggled his now-empty glass in Vince's direction, prompting Vince to jump to attention in response.

"Before you answer, Mr Franks," Brad went on, "I wanted to explain our current predicament."

"Which is?" Rodney asked, although not sounding particularly concerned about whatever their situation might be.

"Someone stole all our equipment," Brad answered, followed by a heavy sigh.

"Broke into our rental car," Chip explained further. "Glass everywhere."

Brad and Chip proceeded to fill Rodney in on all the finer details of the theft and, crucially, what it meant in regard to the progression of their documentary.

"You see, Mr Franks," Brad said in conclusion. "Without our equipment, we're like..." he said, searching for an appropriate analogy to finish his thought.

"A lumberjack without an axe," Chip offered on his brother's behalf, swinging an imaginary axe.

Rodney chewed this over for a moment, reaching for the glass Vince had dutifully replenished for him. "And you can't simply ask your TV network for replacement equipment?" Rodney enquired.

Brad shook his head firmly. "No, Mr Franks. They've loaned us much of it already. So asking them to replace stuff that's already loaner equipment to begin with..."

"It would be kinda awkward," Chip chipped in.

"Hmm," Rodney said, running his tongue over his top lip. "That is unfortunate," he suggested. "And this is your first big break with a major TV network?" he asked, although sounding like a question he already knew the answer to.

"Correct, Mr Franks," Brad replied.

"So, if the television network discovered you'd lost all of their equipment, *and* signed up those two chicken nuggets Dave and Monty as your golden boys, when in fact they're a couple of losers unlikely to even qualify, it's fair to say they wouldn't be too happy," Rodney summarised, thinking out loud. "Oh, and did I mention that those two twits, Montgomery and Quirk, are a couple of losers?"

"Yes, you did, Mr Franks, sir," Vince was quick to confirm.

"That would be a fairly accurate description of the current situation," Brad said, in unfortunate agreement with Rodney's grim assessment.

"And future job offers for the pair of you wouldn't likely arrive thick and fast?" Rodney ventured further. "So," Rodney said without waiting for a reply, "how about I help you out of your present predicament?"

Brad nodded slowly, flashing a smile to his brother. "Sure, Mr Franks."

"How about I offer you..." Rodney said, reclining back in his chair. "The full amount of cash I previously mentioned."

"Very generous, sir," Vince suggested, offering his approval even though it was never requested.

"*And...*" Rodney went on, throwing Vince a look, "I arrange for the loan of replacement equipment to help you finish the project and, of course, give you complete access to my team."

"And what about Dave and Monty?" Chip asked, liking what he was hearing so far, but worried about this one point of contention. "It would really help us if—"

"I wouldn't object if their faces made a very brief appearance, just to keep the network boys happy," Rodney offered, most magnanimously.

"*Very* brief," Vince echoed, wagging his finger.

"All right," Brad said, looking to his brother for agreement, which was duly issued with a nod of approval. "In that case, Mr Franks, we'd like to accept your generous offer," he said, rising up with his hand extended to seal the deal.

"Excellent," Rodney said with a nasal snigger. "Here's to magnificent viewing," Rodney added, raising his whisky glass, and ignoring Brad's hand. "And I'm confident you can find a place in your documentary for yours truly," Rodney said as a statement, not even bothering to pose the request in the form of a question.

"But of course," Brad advised, happy to oblige given the present circumstance, and locking his fingers together like a viewfinder to place Rodney's face in the centre.

"Marvellous. Vince will see you out," Rodney responded, dismissing the brothers with a flourish of his hand.

Watching them leave, Rodney drained the remaining liquid in his glass in one go, unable to contain the grin on his chops.

"You look pleased, boss," Vince suggested, upon returning a moment later.

"Oh, to be a fly on the wall when Team Frank and Stan find they've been consigned to the scrap heap, Vince. They say fame is fleeting, but obscurity lasts forever," Rodney answered.

"Yeah..." Vince said, smiling but not entirely sure what was going on or what precisely he was smiling at.

"You'll need to arrange the hire of some recording equipment," Rodney said.

"No problem, boss," Vince replied before narrowing his eyes. "Do you know the specifications of what they need?"

"How should I know?" Rodney snapped back. "A camera's a camera, isn't it?"

"Right," Vince said, staring down at his feet, appearing uncertain about what to do next. "I was just worried in case, you know, there are lots of different—"

"For God's sake, Vince. Do I need to do all the thinking around here?" Rodney said, stamping his foot down into the lush, shagpile carpet. "If you're not sure what camera to hire, Vince, then you simply cross-reference the order with all of the equipment you've just stolen from the back of their car, yes? Simple."

"Ah," Vince replied, placing an index finger to his temple, offering a sort of improvised salute. "Excellent suggestion, Mr Franks. I'll do exactly that."

Chapter
ELEVEN

Thursday of practice week. One lap completed with two further required. One of which must be within the qualifying lap time (which Stan, no matter how many times you remind him, still cannot remember: 115% of the time set by the third-fastest qualifying team in the class). Weather — warmer than a sumo wrestler's crotch...

There were many perks to managing your own racetrack, chief among them, the ability to test your machinery whenever the mood took. And, as was typical of the sharing nature of the racing fraternity, Dave and Monty had extended the use of the tarmac to their fellow competitors to use when required, an offer that was gratefully received and duly accepted by a steady stream of riders throughout the week. Presently, there were several bikes out on track, and with Dave and Monty having just pulled into pit lane...

"It's skipping a beat, Monty!" Dave shouted, his face strained with emotion. "Why's it bloody doing this to me now?" he went on, clenching his sausage-shaped fingers into a ball.

"There's nothing you can do, old son," Monty replied, in as soothing a tone as he could. "It is what it is."

"But *now*? After all this bloody time?" Dave protested. "It's been running along, smooth as you like, and all of a sudden, it's going haywire?"

Monty walked around the sidecar, taking up a position stood

next to Dave. "It's fine," Monty said with assurance, patting his friend's back. "It's all perfectly normal and to be expected at this stage."

"It is?" asked Dave, eyes filled with hope. "You're certain? I shouldn't be worried?"

Monty shook his head. "Just go with it, my friend. You know what it is, don't you?"

"Dunno?" Dave said, eager for clarification.

"Dave... It's that wonderful thing called *amore*."

"Amore?"

"Yes, *amore*. Dave Quirk, you're in love. Cupid has released an arrow, and it's landed, right there," Monty said, tapping Dave's chest. "That's why your heart's skipping a beat. And it's a beautiful thing. And there's nothing at all wrong. So don't worry about it."

Dave's eyes glazed over for a moment at the very thought of it. "She *is* terrific, isn't she?" Dave said, waving over to the viewing gallery where Becks stood watching on with Tyler by her side. Of course, she couldn't hear Dave from her distance away, but she was happy enough to catch and accept the air kiss dispatched and sent her way by express delivery. That is, however, until Tyler rose like a salmon to intercept the kiss, snatching it away from his mum's hand while giggling away to himself.

"Ha-ha, little tyke," said Dave, blowing another one for good measure.

As far as the bike itself, it wasn't skipping a beat at all, thank goodness. And burning the midnight oil the previous evening had proved rather fruitful, judging by the overall feel of the machine and the improved lap times around the Jürburgring. The real test, of course, would be out on the TT course later on. But they now had increased confidence in the suspension set-up, with Dave joking that he wouldn't need to pop a couple of Stugeron anti-nausea tablets before heading out now that the bike was more stable. It was pretty remarkable that the settings were roughly the same as they'd previously used, but with such wildly varying results in the overall feel of the machine. There were just so many variables to consider at the TT — factors that would have a direct impact on how the suspension and gearing might respond — including resurfaced roads, weather conditions, and the riders' fighting weights that were subject to wild variance, amongst other things. What all this meant was that even small adjustments could make a big difference, and also that it was impossible to predict, beforehand, how the bike might perform or handle when out on the TT course that year.

"A few more laps?" Monty suggested, wiping the sweat from his brow with a greasy rag, leaving an impressive oily snail trail across his forehead. "Or you happy with the old girl?" he asked, giving the bike's fairing the gentlest of taps with his boot.

Dave was distracted for a moment, admiring another machine hurtling along next to the pit lane, zooming past with a roar. "I bloody love that noise," Dave said, offering up a contented sigh, and then filling his nostrils with the glorious aroma of burnt fuel and spent oil wafting over. "Oh, sorry," he said, noticing Monty with one eye trained on him, hopeful of a response. "Yeah, she's singing like a songbird, so we'll call it a day, buddy," Dave advised. "And I promised those two an ice cream," he added, throwing a friendly wave in the direction of Becks and Tyler. "Wanna join us?"

"I could see myself getting an ice cream," Monty replied, bobbing his head. "With a Flake?" he asked.

"Well..." said Dave, putting a finger to his lips, weighing this request up carefully. "Hmm, I dunno. After, hopefully, getting the suspension settings just right, is that an indulgence we can really afford? I mean, do we really wish to tempt fate?"

"Oh," Monty said with a disappointed frown. "I just—"

"Of *course* you can have a Flake!" Dave said with a laugh. "You'll just need to shave your head to cancel out any additional weight that might be gained, yeah?"

While Monty was tucking up the sidecar in the van shortly after, readying it for an afternoon nap, Tyler and Becks enjoyed a kick about in the field as they waited for the boys to do anything that needed doing before they all headed out.

"Just changing out of these!" Dave called over to Becks, walking over to the changing rooms which were, in truth, a glorified workman's hut situated behind the viewing area. Dave and Monty had submitted proposals for a shower block and, ambitiously, a café area, but their request was under consideration by their paymasters, Frank and Stan. So yes, as the new management, Dave and Monty did have big plans for their track. For now, however, they'd need to rough it getting changed in a ramshackle hut with no electrics and no running water and with the permanent and lingering odour of sweating feet somehow attaching itself to every surface.

"Hurry back!" Becks said cheerfully, whilst chasing tirelessly after Tyler.

"I'm hurrying!" said Dave, hurrying, which was no mean feat to accomplish when wearing a set of tight-fitting leathers and a pair of heavy riding boots.

Once at the hut, Dave opened the thin plastic door with a little too much gusto, nearly ripping the flimsy thing clean off its hinges. "Piece of..." he muttered to himself, stepping inside, running his eyes around the drab interior devoid of much natural light owing to the boarded-up window. Dave took a mental note to follow up their refurb funding request, as the small, rickety building appeared to sway with each footstep he took. How it had remained upright, still standing up there in the windy north of the island, was nothing short of a miracle.

Dave cautiously parked his bum cheeks on a red plastic chair, under which he'd stuffed his rucksack, and then proceeded to kick off his boots. He hoped the chair was sturdier than the rest of the place. "Ahhh," he moaned in relief, giving his toes a wiggle. The best thing about wearing boots and leathers was taking them back off again, especially when you'd been throwing yourself around a racetrack for two hours in the midday sun. Dave rose up from his seated position, pulling down on his zip. Then, as he climbed out of his leathers, he suddenly became aware of a damp chill in the location of his left toe area. "What the...?" he muttered, bending down for a closer inspection. Underfoot, previously unnoticed in the murky lighting, was a sodden section of wooden floorboard, with the excess moisture found there now soaking straight through the sock on Dave's left foot.

With the absence of any proper facilities in the changing hut, Dave hoped and prayed this wasn't the result of a fellow competitor too lazy to walk outside to the portaloos. Fortunately, however, this didn't appear to be the case as, after a brief inspection, Dave noted a biscuit-sized hole (the hole being the size of a Jammie Dodger, to be precise, if Dave's expert eye for biscuits hadn't failed him) in the roof directly above his head. One that he'd make sure to plug before heading off for the day.

Dave whipped off his socks, as well as his undies, grateful he'd had the foresight to pack a spare pair of each for himself to change into. "Right, let's get going," he said, clapping his hands together smartly, thinking about the delicious ice cream he'd soon be enjoying. He turned around, reaching for his bag under the chair, but immediately knew something wasn't right. The plywood floorboard felt spongy beneath the balls of his feet, just like it was about to...

"Aaagh!" Dave yelled, when his right foot disappeared beneath him. Slightly dazed, it took him a second or two to figure out what had happened and why his right foot was touching grass even though he was still inside the hut (or at least most of him currently was). He waited for a wave of pain to wash over him, certain something must have broken during the mishap. Thankfully, however, the only thing damaged, aside from his pride, appeared to be the floor.

Dave's right foot had dropped through the floor — as was clear to him by now, at this point — with him coming to a halt at the height of his upper thigh. With the other leg now lying flat across the floor of the hut, his legs formed a perfect L-shape. His flexibility, though presently forced, was to be commended. Indeed, a prima ballerina might well approve of the form being displayed by the acute angle of his limbs.

"Help!" Dave shouted, unable to gain enough leverage to free himself from his awkward position. "Hello!" he called out, hoping the wafer-thin walls would play to his advantage. "I'm stuck in here!" he added, concerned his Achilles tendon was about to rupture under the strain.

Just then, and much to Dave's considerable relief, he heard the gentle rapping of someone's knuckles against the door.

"Oh, Daaavvve," a female voice sang out. "Are you decent?"

"No, not really," Dave was quick to relay, glancing down at his naked form. "In fact, decent is probably the *opposite* of what I am," he made clear.

"That's just the way I like it!" the voice on the other side of the door playfully suggested. "Are you alone?"

"Becks? Becks, is that you?" Dave asked, panic evident in his voice. "Your voice sounds kind of odd through the door," he said. "That's you, isn't it?" he asked hopefully, hopping around on his standing leg in tiny little hops, in what little motion his situation allowed him, until he was facing the door. "I can't move, and yes, I'm alone. I'm also naked and stuck."

"Ooh," the voice replied, appearing not the least bit bothered by Dave's current, awkward predicament. "I'm coming iiiinnn!" in fact, it announced with a titter.

Dave braced himself for the teasing he was sure to receive as the dilapidated door eased open a bit. "Hello, Dave," the voice said, followed by a head appearing from within the open crack.

Now, the lighting wasn't fantastic, and Dave was in some discomfort, but unless his eyes were playing tricks, this wasn't Becks' head before him, as he had wished.

"Gloria?" Dave said, squinting his eyes, placing one hand over his breasts and the other over Little Dave. "For the love of God, don't come any further!" Dave pleaded. "Can you find Monty for me?"

"Oh, now don't be shy, Davycakes," Gloria advised, stepping inside and making sure the door was firmly closed behind her. "Had an accident?" she enquired, looking down at the half-submerged figure in front of her. "You look like a whack-a-mole that's been whacked once too often," she joked. "Don't worry, we'll have you out of there in a jiffy," she told him, just as she reached for and closed over the inside lock on the flimsy door. "And then..." she added suggestively.

"And *then?*" Dave asked, not sure he liked what was being implied, and feeling a mite nervous and uncomfortable right at the present moment.

"And then we can make ourselves comfortable," Gloria explained with a wink.

Now, it wasn't that Gloria was without her charms. In fact, in her day, it seemed like she might well have been something of a looker. But Gloria — part-time marshal/part-time catering stand manager — was currently in her early seventies, and not to mention married as well. So to see her cooing seductively while effectively holding him prisoner had rather taken Dave off-guard, to put it mildly. Still, his present unease did distract him a bit from the throbbing pain he was beginning to feel in his overstretched groin. So there was that, at least.

"Look at you, all naked and magnificent," Gloria said admiringly, unfastening the top button on her blouse, followed by another button, and then another.

"Gloria! Bloody hell, girl, stop unfastening yourself!" Dave squealed, hopping in a clockwise direction so his dangly bits were soon taken off display. "What are you doing in here?" Dave asked over his shoulder. "What would your husband say!"

"Oh, what he doesn't know won't hurt him," Gloria answered. "And you don't need to be shy with me, Dave Quirk," she said. "Not after the way you were flirting with me out there."

"Flirting?" Dave replied, hopping back around to face her, his hands grabbing as much modesty as possible. *"What* flirting?"

"Oh, I don't know," Gloria said coyly, swatting his words away playfully. "Blowing kisses my way, maybe? Shaking your pert bum cheeks in my direction, perhaps?"

"Pert?" said Dave, raising a smile, despite himself, at such positive feedback regarding his posterior region. "Wait, when did I...?" he added, regaining his focus. "Gloria, what in heaven's name are you talking about?"

"Out there, just now," Gloria explained. "You blew me several kisses from the pit lane. I've sensed the raw animal magnetism going on between us for weeks now. So your display of affection came as no surprise," she told him.

"You need to stop," Dave pleaded.

"I can't fight what I'm feeling," Gloria insisted, taking a step closer.

"No, I mean literally stop," said Dave, holding up his palm, and temporarily freeing Little Dave from its finger prison as a result. "Gloria, the floor's knackered, and you're likely to fall."

"Oh, I've *already* fallen," Gloria maintained, placing her hand against her heart.

"No, I mean through the bloody floor, Gloria! The wood's rotten, which is why I'm stuck naked down here doing the splits," Dave explained. "Look, I think there's been some confusion here, luv," he went on. "A misunderstanding, yeah?"

"Oh, bother," Gloria said, reaching up to rebutton what she'd just unbuttoned a moment before, and not looking very happy about it.

"I think you're lovely, Gloria," Dave assured her, hoping to at least partially massage her bruised ego. "But I'm spoken for, yeah?" Dave informed her, and delighted to confirm this information as well. "It's not that you're not a remarkable specimen, and Bert is definitely a lucky man to call you his wife... Not right at this moment, granted, but..."

"You're nothing but a flirt, Dave Quirk!" Gloria spat back, wrestling with the final blouse button. "A right Casanova of the racing world, wantonly stealing poor girls' hearts," she added, which immediately raised another guilty smile from Dave.

"Gloria, I think the blood has stopped flowing to my foot," Dave said, nodding in the direction of the leg still visible. "Can you help me out of this pickle, Gloria? Oh, and if you'd stop staring at me, that'd be marvellous as well, as I'm feeling rather vulnerable right about now. Okay? Cheers."

"I'll see if I can fetch Monty," Gloria suggested, figuring, it would seem, that her pulling Dave from his hole was, on reflection, a job she wasn't adequately equipped to handle. "Hang on. Speaking of Monty..." Gloria said, tilting her head in thought. "He wouldn't happen to be single, would he?"

"Monty? No Monty is..." Dave began, but then reconsidered if telling Gloria the truth was the wisest course of action. "That is... now you mention it... I, ehm, I *do* think he's single, come to think of it," Dave suggested, thinking this would be a good way to redirect Gloria's attention, and hoping that Monty's wife at home would forgive him for this diversionary tactic at poor Monty's expense.

"Is he, now?" Gloria replied, perking up, and recovering quite nicely from her case of unrequited love. "I'll just go and see if I can find him, then!" she said, exiting the hut with a spring in her step, running a hand through her hair as she left.

"Give my regards to Bert!" Dave called after her. "You do remember Bert...? Your husband...?"

"That dilapidated heap needs condemning," Dave said, once dressed, outside, and walking towards his van.

"Who, Gloria?" Monty asked, walking beside him, though it was unclear how serious he was being.

"No, no," Dave answered with a laugh. "But old Bert's got his hands full with that one, that's for sure," he suggested, reaching for his keys. "Though she did tell me I had pert bum cheeks. So she's alright in my book, all things considered, I must say," Dave cheerfully remarked.

"Oh, she did, did she?" Becks entered in playfully, appearing from behind the van, and apparently fully able to have heard the conversation as the boys approached.

"Were you really naked, Big Dave?" asked Tyler, appearing as well, there beside his mum, and unable to stifle a giggle.

"As a newborn babe," Dave replied. "Perhaps that's how she knew I had a pert bum," he added, proudly slapping his rump. "Anyway, that ice cream isn't going to eat itself, now is it?" he said, setting young Tyler off, with him now doing a little happy-dance in anticipation.

"Actually, I think I'm going to pass," Monty replied, scrolling through his phone, his attention drifting. "I need to see a man about a dog."

Monty, who'd arrived in his own car on account of Dave's van being a three-seater, bid the rest of them farewell.

"I hope you like the dog!" Tyler called after him. "I'd be happy to take it for walkies, Monty!"

"Good lad," Monty said, raising a thumb in appreciation.

Peel was a splendid backdrop to enjoy an ice cream, with gentle waves caressing the golden sands, all overlooked by the historic castle as a magnificent centrepiece. The only flaw in Dave's plan was that, with the weather having turned glorious after several days of rain, every bugger on the island had got the exact same idea. Coupled with increased footfall from the TT crowds, Peel was presently bursting at the seams. Still, the bustling crowds only enhanced the energetic atmosphere, offering a glimpse of times gone by when tourists flocked to this charming island in their droves each year before the advent of cheap, foreign travel.

With the queue to the ice cream shop stretching nearly around the block, Tyler was dispatched to the adjacent beach (in clear view of Mum's diligent eye) to make use of the bucket and spade Dave kept primed and ready for action in his van for just such an occasion as this.

"Look at him, Dave," Becks remarked, taking Dave's hand in her own, a beaming smile spreading over her pretty face. "How happy does he look scampering about on the sand," she said, as a statement rather than a question. "I still have to pinch myself, Dave. To think how our lives have transformed in such a short amount of time is... is..."

"The dog's bollocks?" Dave helpfully suggested, receiving a friendly slap on the arm for his trouble.

"I often think I'm in a dream, Dave. Do you know what I mean?"

Dave nodded in agreement, with one eye fixed on the young

fella. "It's a special place," he offered in his considered opinion.

"I sometimes wake in a state of panic," Becks continued.

"Oh? I know I'm a bit rough, first thing in the morning, but really..." he said, feigning an exaggerated sob.

"Not about you, silly," she assured him, giving his shovel-like hand an extra squeeze. "I have this panic that I'm going to wake, and all of this, my wonderful life right now, was just a dream. Like Dorothy returning to Kansas. Except, in the case of Tyler and me, Kansas is a miserable rundown housing estate with a rising crime rate."

The line had advanced, slowly but surely, with Dave and Becks shuffling forward in the queue, until Dave was finally able to clap eyes on the menu displayed behind a perspex screen secured to the wall. He ran his eyes over the enticing array of options designed to lure people in for their sugar fix. "Becks?" Dave said, without breaking his gaze.

"Yes?" Becks said cheerily, snuggling in against Dave's arm so they could both peruse the menu together.

"Now that you know what you want..." Dave said, trailing off, appearing uncertain how to finish his thought.

"Hmm? Oh, I'm not certain yet," Becks answered. "I dunno, mint chocolate chip, maybe?"

"I don't mean ice cream-wise, silly," Dave replied, laughing gently. "No, I mean, now that you know where you want to be in life," he explained earnestly, baring his soul now, "well, you don't need to wake up from your dream, Becks." Then, turning to face her, and in a not-oft-witnessed PDA, Dave planted a kiss squarely on her cheek. "I don't want you and Tyler to go back to Kansas," he told her, oblivious to the people stood around them in the queue enjoying the unfolding soap opera.

"I don't intend to," Becks assured him, administering a quick cuddle. "What's this all about, anyway?" she asked, noting the lingering look of anxiety on Dave's face as she pulled away. "Where's this coming from all of a sudden?"

"You said you wanted to leave the TT farm, and I was just... well, I was just a little—"

"Oh, Dave, you big sillybilly," Becks told him, guessing the direction his thought processes were moving in. "Is this why you've been a little bit glum this week? Are you worried about me and Tyler moving out of the TT Farm? Away from you?"

Dave nodded, shuffling forward as those in front reached the serving hatch.

"Dave, the TT Farm was always going to be just a temporary solution, and one which I'm eternally grateful for," Becks advised. "But when we move out, rest assured that it will be to somewhere local to the job I love, and surrounded by the people I adore. You included," she explained. *"Especially* you."

"Move in with me," Dave suggested instantly. "You and Tyler both. Move in with me?"

"Hmm. Well, we already spend much of the week staying at your place, so I guess..." Becks replied, considering Dave's offer.

"I mean in a place of our own, Becks," Dave told her. "Let's buy a house together, as a family. Then you'd never need to go back to Kansas, ever."

"Oh," said Becks in response, a little startled, and taken by surprise by this, though not necessarily in a bad way. Just then, delaying any further response, however, the young woman behind the counter looked at Becks expectantly, appearing ready to take her order.

"What can I get for you?" the overworked but cheerful server asked, waving her hand over the array of chilled offerings in the refrigerated display case before her.

But Becks' attention remained elsewhere, temporarily distracted as it was by Dave's proposal, and she offered no immediate response.

"Oi!" a gruff-sounding woman behind them in the queue said, appearing inconvenienced by this further delay.

"Oh, I'm sorry," Becks offered, turning to offer her apology.

"It's not that," the woman behind them said. "I don't want you two getting your order and disappearing before I find out what happens next," she revealed. "I've been listening to you two for five minutes, and I'll be damned if I don't know how it all ends up!"

"Me too," an inquisitive chap in a wheelchair asked, as he'd evidently also been earwigging (as were a fair handful of others, with a collection of faces now turned towards Becks and Dave).

"Well...?" Dave asked, all thought of ice cream presently on hold.

Becks looked to Dave, and then back to those in the queue behind them. "Dave," she said, returning her full attention to him. "Dave, nothing would make me happier than to share our first family home with you."

"But..." Dave began, ever the pessimist.

"There is no *but*," Becks promised. "Nothing could possibly make me any happier," she told him.

"What about a mint chocolate chip with a Flake?" Dave jokingly proposed, reaching for his wallet.

"Hmm, that does come close," Becks agreed with a laugh. She then licked her lips, because, well... mint chocolate chip. "Can we tell Tyler?" she asked. "About the house, I mean."

"Sure. You can tell him that Dorothy and Toto are staying in Kansas," Dave replied. "Although, I'm not sure what that makes me. The Tin Woodsman, maybe?"

"The Tin Man? No. Dave Quirk, you're my big... cuddly... lion," Becks answered, wrapping him up in her arms. "But definitely not cowardly," she quickly added, smiling.

Shortly, on Peel Promenade, Dave sat on a wooden bench painted in the vibrant colours of the rainbow, looking out over the bathers enjoying a dip in the Irish Sea. With a smile, he looked to Tyler, sat on his right, and then over to Becks, sat on his left.

Dave could easily be forgiven for the feeling of cheery optimism he was experiencing just now. In fact, it was perfectly warranted. He had a terrific job, good friends, including his best mate Monty, he had the love of a good woman, and now he was making plans to purchase their first family home. And, if that wasn't enough to raise a smile, he was due to take the big blue boiled sweet around the TT course in just a few short hours as well.

The only slight pebble in his shoe, figuratively speaking, was the issue of the money to actually fund the house purchase. Sure, there were irons in the fire in that regard. But a significant element of those plans depended on their success on the track. A fact proving to be something of a niggle in the back of his mind. Still, there was no point in wasting energy fretting about such matters. The bike was running well, Dave and Monty were in rude health (apart from the splinters on the inside of Dave's thigh from his earlier fall), and they had a degree of experience around the course that most competitors could only dream of.

"All right, you first," Becks said, dabbing a napkin with her tongue and applying it vigorously to Dave's chin. "Honestly, I can't take you boys anywhere," she jokingly teased, before leaning over to repeat the very same clean-up operational process with Tyler.

"Oh, *hello*," Dave said, reaching for his pocket upon hearing the familiar Baywatch theme tune he'd set as his ringtone. "It's Monty," Dave announced, glancing at the display on his phone. "He's probably wondering how the ice cream was," he told Becks. "Talk to me," Dave spoke into his phone, placing the device against his ear.

Dave rose to his feet, pacing back and forth, listening intently, making the occasional encouraging noise here and there to let Monty know he was still paying attention. "You don't say," Dave said after a bit, caressing his chin. "That *is* interesting," he added, before glancing at his watch. "Look, I'll be back at HQ in about an hour, and we can chat further, yeah? What's that, the ice cream? Oh yes, it was..."

Dave then proceeded to fill Monty in on each and every detail of the ice cream he'd missed out on, including who had what, double scoop or single, Flake or not, and, if syrup was added, what flavour. Those details were important to Monty, so Dave didn't spare anything in his informational debrief.

"Everything okay?" Becks enquired, once Dave's call had concluded.

"Well, he's upset because I had a cookie crumble without him," Dave informed her. "But other than that..."

"Beyond that, Dave!" Becks playfully admonished.

"It was quite interesting," Dave commented, parking himself down on the bench again, staring in the direction of the castle as he reflected on the contents of the call.

"Well?" Tyler entered in on both his and his mum's behalf, after Dave had failed to continue. "*Spill* it, Big Dave."

"Monty has a plan," Dave replied mysteriously, wiggling his fingers in the air like he was playing a church organ.

"For world domination?" Becks joked.

"World domination is pencilled in for next week," Dave replied, laughing, and without missing a beat. "No, Monty has a plan which could very well see us breaking into a top-ten finish at the TT races," Dave revealed, grinning broadly. "And, if that happens, lovely people, then both of our bank balances, me and Monty's, could swell considerably."

"Ooh, do tell," Becks said, hanging on Dave's every word.

"Ah, I can't really say anything else," Dave admitted. "It's not that I don't want to, mind. It's just that I don't know anything more, right yet. Monty wanted to tell me about the details in person, so..." he said, dangling his van keys. "Shall we go and find out?"

"Yes!" Tyler said excitedly. "And can we ask Monty about that dog he was going to see?"

"The dog...?" Dave asked, taking a moment to work out what Tyler was talking about. "Oh, yes. Yes, you can *absolutely* ask Monty about the dog," Dave agreed happily, giving a little chuckle imagining what Monty's possible answer might be.

Chapter
TWELVE

Stella wasn't a lady often referred to as being a sensitive soul. Never, in fact, that anybody was aware of. However, if you scraped away the abrasive layers — and there would be several of them — you'd eventually find an element of nostalgia residing within her personality. It wasn't that she was sentimental, necessarily. (You'd be unlikely to find Stella with moist eyes watching *Bambi*, for instance, or choked up watching a news report of a long-lost son reunited with his mother.) Rather, it was more the case that she simply wasn't one for change, comfortable with things being just so and as they'd always been. A creature of habit and routine, if you will.

Despite this apparent lack of sentiment on Stella's part, when Stella and Lee had first moved in together a while back, he'd made the grave mistake of tossing out an old lump of rock he'd found collecting dust in the back of a kitchen drawer whilst helping Stella gather up her things in preparation for the move. Stella was devastated when she found out what he'd done, with the news setting her bottom lip wobbling for several days straight — so much so that Lee rummaged through every bag in the wheelie bin. (Which, for Lee, was something of a trip down memory lane, an unfortunate and unpleasant reminder of his times sleeping rough on the street.)

Through an endless waterfall of tears, Stella had explained to Lee that the rock had been a treasured memento of a visit to

Skegness with her gran, Sally (known as Craggy Sally to most). Such was Stella's level of devastation that Lee had even gone so far as to visit the council tip, hoping to scour through the skips for her missing item. However, when he explained to the staff precisely what it was that he was looking for, he was politely asked to vacate the premises, leaving his search to come to a fruitless conclusion.

What this experience demonstrated to Lee, however, was that everybody was wired differently, and what tugged on one person's emotional cords wouldn't necessarily be the same as the next person. And this sentimental air of vulnerability, peculiar as it was in relation to an old, dusty rock stuck in the back of a kitchen drawer, didn't make Lee think any less of Stella. Far from it. No, if anything, it made Stella only that much more endearing, in his opinion, and provided clear evidence that his magnificent dragon queen was in possession of a soft white underbelly.

What this experience *also* demonstrated to Lee was that he ought to be very careful in how he was proceeding in the midst of their *present* move. As such, the process of boxing and packing up their possessions ahead of their current relocation (namely, their big move to the Isle of Man) was proving to be something of a challenge, and a rather more protracted affair. Although they only lived in a modest flat, the sheer quantity of stuff they'd accumulated in a short span of time was staggering, and it was unlikely there'd be sufficient space in the removal van they'd booked. Also, as Lee was no fool (and having learned his lesson that first time around), he was now insisting on double-checking each and every item — asking if it was coming with them, or if he was permitted to dispose of it.

So it was taking a while. Still, they had a fair bit of time left before the taxi business transferred to the new owners, and that gave plenty of time to get things sorted (literally). Time enough, Lee reminded himself several times each day, lest he start pulling his hair out by the roots.

"Do you really need all of these, my love?" Lee asked, nose

currently pressed inside Stella's bedside drawers. "There must be, let's see..." he said, moving aside the various bottles of personal lubricant. "Four... five... six," he counted, surprised by the final tally.

"If I binned any, then I'd only need to buy new ones once we got over to the island. And you said we needed to save money," Stella said, standing in the bedroom doorframe wrapped in a towel that wasn't sufficient enough to cover her modesty. "So that wouldn't make any sense, would it?"

"I suppose you're right," Lee answered, unable to contest the wisdom of her words.

"Plus," Stella went on, delving around the inside of her ear canal with the cotton bud gripped in her one free hand, "they've been with me a long time, and have sentimental value."

"Right, so you've got Guy Martin here, Idris Elba, Ed Sheeran, Ricky Martin, Hugh Jackman, and...?" he said, holding up a slim number with a metallic, chrome-like finish.

"Monty Don," Stella offered helpfully, happy to provide the name of the particular object in question.

"Yeah, but..." Lee said, placing Monty Don back down, and then pulling another of the items out of the lucky dip of sin that was Stella's bedside drawer. "This one. Idris Elba. The tip of this one is starting to wear away!" he said, bravely lifting it up for closer inspection. "Are you sure we want to—?"

"They're coming with us," Stella said firmly, lest there be any doubt on the matter. "If we're short on space in the van, you can bin that crystal vase Frank and soppy bollocks Stan bought us as a wedding present. That way, there's plenty of room for that lot," she said, pointing to the drawer, and losing grip of her towel as she did so.

"Oh, *hello* there," Lee joked, clapping eyes on the splendid, now naked form of his darling wife.

"Back to work, you," she said gruffly, though with a hint of amusement present in her voice. A starkers Stella reached down to retrieve her towel, cotton earbud protruding from the side of her head where she'd left it, leaving her looking like an improperly constructed Dalek. "Two weeks and we'll be gone," she said, grabbing hold of the cotton bud once again and resuming ear-related operations.

"The two of us on our new, grand adventure," Lee offered cheerily, waving Idris Elba in the air for emphasis, and then, upon suddenly realising what it was he was still holding in his hand, quickly dropping it into one of the packing boxes. He then wiped his palm against one of the legs of his trousers, discreetly, giving a little shudder.

Stella stared at Lee for a moment, hard, training her ice-cold eyes upon him. "The *three* of us on our new, grand adventure," she corrected him, slowly shaking her head.

Lee spun around on his knees so he was fully facing her, rather than looking over his shoulder as he had been. "Three?" Lee asked, biting gently down on his bottom lip, eyes misting over. "You mean…?" he asked, daring to dream, looking her up and down, lovingly.

"Yeah," Stella said coldly as if the answer should have been plainly obvious. "Me, you, and Bovril."

"Ah. Yes," Lee answered, lowering his head. "Yes, of course. You, me, and Bovril. How could I forget the cat…?" he said softly, half under his breath.

"Silly bugger," Stella offered with a laugh. "I'm going for a shower."

"Okay, my love," Lee replied, with a sigh heard only by him.

"Oh," Stella added, turning back on herself. "Can you grab hold of that Idris Elba again? You'd better throw it over here, and I'll make sure he's still working while I take my shower."

※

"The fuck you think you're doing?" Stella asked, rearing up from her chair, giving daggers to the startled chap halfway through the taxi office doorway. She placed her hands on the countertop without interrupting her fierce glare.

"Excuse me?" the fellow in paint-spattered white overalls replied, smiling politely, not quite appreciating if the person before him was being serious or not. The man cupped his ear, cocking his head, still smiling, which only served to rile Stella further.

He was a gentleman of a certain vintage, so perhaps his hearing wasn't as sharp as it once was. Unsure if this was the case, Stella repeated her previous question with a little more force. *"The fuck you think you're doing?"* she asked again. But in return, all she received was another polite but vacant smile. "What are they doing?" Stella barked, pointing through the taxi office windows at the ladders propped up against the exterior wall. "What are they doing out there?"

"Erm, I'm John Light," the man said, with an exaggerated smile, stepping forward with caution while reaching into his trouser pocket. "Here," he said, approaching the counter at arm's length and presenting the business card now in hand. "Light and Bright Painters and Decorators, at your service," he explained cheerily, followed by a friendly wink, thickly laying on the charm. "I just popped in because I thought I heard the sound of a boiling kettle...?" he added, optimistically. "A quick brew before I get back to work at lightspeed," he quipped, trotting out a favoured, oft-utilised pun that was ordinarily well received. But not today.

Stella started to laugh. But not the sort of happy laugh you'd hear at, say, a comedy club. Instead, the kind of sarcastic laugh you might offer when you're not sure if someone's taking the piss at your expense. "A boiling kettle?" Stella said, looking across to Susie as she repeated their guest's words back at him. "The only sound *you're* going to hear, John Light..." Stella suggested, looking back over to the gentleman in question. "Is the cracking sound of your vertebrae when I launch myself over this counter, and my knee gets up close and personal with your windpipe."

At this point, the blood started to drain from John's face. "What...? Ehm... it's just that..." he stammered, glancing at Susie, who appeared to offer him a kindly, sympathetic expression in return that may have translated as *run-while-you-can*. "I've been sent to remove the old signage outside and give the wall a lick of paint. You know, spruce her up a little before the new sign arrives," he told Stella, pleading his case.

John sensed a cuppa might not have been on the agenda at this particular time. After years of working with the public, he had a sixth sense for such matters (although not that a sixth sense was especially needed under present conditions, given the swearing and accompanied threats of grievous bodily harm being directed his way). "Right-ho," he said, not wishing to fan the flames further, "I'll just, ehm... I'll just leave you two lovely ladies to your business and crack on with the job, then..."

Stella slapped the palm of her hand down on the countertop, causing both John and Susie to recoil. "If you touch that sign, or anything outside, John," Stella growled. "Then the only thing that'll be getting a coat of paint will be the lining of your colon when I stick a brush right up your—"

"Stella," Susie gently entered in. "Stella, you need to breathe, all right?" she said, slowly and deliberately. "As we practised," Susie added, at the same time using her hand to suggest that now might be a good time for John Light to see the light and bugger off smartly.

"Wait," John bravely ventured. "You're actually Stella?" he asked, incredulous. "I thought the new owners were winding me up when they described... In fact, never mind," he said, stopping himself short before talking himself into further strife. "So, you're off to the Isle of Man, I believe?" he said brightly, hoping a little pleasant chit-chat might help defuse the situation. "I'd love to go for a visit there and try out the roads," he went on. "I ride a Triumph in all weathers, you see. Though not today, of course, as the ladders wouldn't fit on the back." John waited a tick, hoping to garner a laugh, but receiving only a death stare in response instead. "Perhaps I can come and stay with you?" he joked further, figuring a little jocularity was just the remedy needed, evidently not realising the level of jeopardy he was presently wading into, his sixth sense failing him miserably.

"You should probably go," Susie advised, noting Stella's hand reaching for the concealed defensive weaponry secured under her desk. "I didn't think the new owners were taking possession until next week?" Susie added as an afterthought.

"I don't know anything about that," John answered, increasing the distance between himself and Stella, taking several cautionary steps back. "I just do what I'm told. And that was to take the old sign down and give the outside wall a lick of paint," he explained. "Brighten things up, Light 'n' Bright," he added, with what appeared to be his well-worn catchphrase where work matters were concerned.

"You should probably..." Susie advised again. "Maybe you can come back once we've said our goodbyes to the place and packed up," she suggested. "It might be safer then."

"Yes, right-ho," John replied, happy to agree, looking over to Stella who, as far as he could tell, hadn't yet blinked in all the time he'd been stood there. "Best of luck if you're moving onto new challenges," he added, filling the brief silence when there was absolutely no need to do so. "I'll just..." he said, feeling behind his back to locate the door latch. "See you soon, perhaps? And you can keep my business card. You know, just in case you ever—"

"We will, and thanks," Susie said, making sure John closed the door behind him.

"Stella...?" Susie asked, wheeling her chair close to her friend. Over the years, she had, of course, witnessed more of Stella's outbursts than she cared to remember. But this one seemed different, more raw than usual. "Here," Susie said, removing a fag from the packet on Stella's desk for her. "Take this," she suggested, offering it up. Susie couldn't help but notice Stella's trembling hand as she took the proffered ciggie and sparked it up. "Are you okay?" Susie asked, when plainly Stella wasn't. "I've not seen you this... this angry for a long time, Stella."

Stella took a long pull from her fag, staring through the window at their recent visitor struggling to retract his ladders outside. "I'm fine," Stella replied, though the sound of cracking knuckles that followed shortly thereafter suggested otherwise.

"I think you might have given John Light a fright," Susie joked, rhyming, and attempting and failing to thus lighten the mood. "Stella?" Susie bravely persisted. "Stella, what's going on? You looked as if you were going to seriously injure that poor chap, and he was only here to—"

"He was here to change things!" Stella snapped. *"That's* what he was here to do!"

"Ah," Susie said softly, now understanding the nature of her friend's reaction. "You don't want them to touch anything while we're still here. Is that what it is?"

"Yeah," Stella said, finally blinking.

"Oh, Stella," Susie said, moving in close for a quick cuddle. "You're upset about the sign coming down?" she asked, as they both watched John Light throw his ladders over his shoulders. Then, seeing their eyes on him, he scurried away as quickly as he was able, presumably heading back to the safety of his van.

Stella snubbed out her now-spent fag in the palm of her hand, smoke billowing in and around her flared nostrils. "It's the final chapter," Stella said eventually, placing the smouldering dimp atop the fragile stack in the ashtray.

"It's not final, Stella. It's the start of a new and exciting adventure for both you and Lee," Susie told her, trying to get Stella to see the positive side of things.

Stella appeared unconvinced. "None of it felt real," she said. "The sale of the business. The move. Leaving you. None of it. Until now."

Susie watched as Stella, seated in her chair, swung her feet back and forth with the naïve vulnerability of a young child on a swing. "Hey now," Susie said, taken off-guard by the contrary nature of Stella's demeanour: furious one minute, on the verge of tears the next. "You're moving to a lovely new flat on the Isle of Man, where you'll be working with Frank and Stan every day. So it'll be just like old times, yeah? And I've told you that I'll be coming over to see you all on a very regular basis, to the extent that you'll soon be fed up of the sight of me, right?"

"This is my life. Here," Stella said, reaching for her stapler to give her fingers something to do now she'd finished her fag. "I miss Frank and Stan *in there*," she went on, pointing to their empty office. "I want to hear Stan whinging like an old woman about his roots showing or his fake tan fading. I want to hear Frank cracking one of those bloody awful jokes he always thought were brilliant when they were absolute shite. I want to listen to you prattle on about your family when you didn't know I was listening when I really was. I want to walk to work as I've done for years, looking forward to my fried breakfast sandwich, looking up to the sign above the door and knowing I'm part of Frank and Stan's Cabs, Susie. That's all I want. And now that's being taken away from me. As soon as that sign gets taken down, then it's all over. And I'm not ready for that. Not yet."

Susie, for her part, sat listening intently, wiping the tear that fell down her cheek. "Aww, Stella," Susie said, once it was her turn to speak again, fanning her face with her fingertips. "Stella, I always knew you were listening to me when you pretended to be bored, looking elsewhere as I carried on."

Susie wheeled her chair a smidge closer than it already was. "Stella, this building is just that, a building, yeah?" she said. "It's the people inside it that made those memories. Not the sign outside. You'll make *more* wonderful memories in the next chapter of your life on the Isle of Man, right? And, it's going to be a story that I want to be a part of, Stella. If you'll let me, of course?"

Stella permitted a faint smile to emerge. "Yeah, go on, then. I suppose it'd be good to see you now and again," she replied, with a playful rolling of her eyes. "But *only* if you bring over those nice spicy sausages from the butchers I like," Stella added firmly.

"It's a deal," Susie responded, extending her hand to seal the contract.

But, just then, Stella's attention was momentarily diverted by her mobile phone vibrating on her desk. "It's Stan," she said with a grunt, reading the caller's name displayed.

"Do you reckon John Light has reported back to the new owners about his warm reception?" Susie asked with a chuckle. "And you know something else, Stella?" Susie went on, changing the direction of the conversation as Stella's phone buzzed away unanswered. "It's nice to see the other side of Stella. The sensitive side that we only occasionally witness."

"Yeah, whatever," Stella said, rising up from her seat, with no apparent intention of answering Stan's call. "I'm a sensitive soldier, all right," she said. "Now throw me that newspaper, will you, as I'm going for a dump."

Chapter
THIRTEEN

Still Thursday of practice week, but later in the day, after the ice creams had been polished off...

"You still don't understand, do you?" Dave asked, his foot placed ever-so-gently on the sidecar fairing back at race HQ, whilst kneading his forehead with his hand.

"*Pfft*," replied Stan, looking at Frank. "He thinks I still don't understand..."

"But you don't, do you?" Frank asked, though not unkindly.

Stan puffed out his cheeks before releasing a steady stream of air. "Nope," he finally conceded, confirming what the others already knew. "I kinda get what you're talking about, Dave. But mostly, it's just technical mumbo-jumbo that goes *whoosh*," he explained, running his hand through the air illustratively like an aircraft taking flight, right over his head.

Monty raised a finger, indicating he wished to enter into the fray. "Ryan Horsfield phoned me earlier, Stan," Monty said to Stan. "Sadly, his TT effort is over because his passenger has dislocated his shoulder in practice."

"Right. I got that bit," Stan replied. "It was all the technical stuff that came after that where my mind started to wander."

"Okay..." Monty began, talking slowly like he was explaining to a child how you tie your shoelaces. "Okay, it's similar to us humans, Stan," he explained. "Just like us, engines have a brain that keeps everything working, yeah? In the case of a bike, it's things like fuel pressure, oil pressure, air pressure, and so on. Now, just for a moment, imagine that you could lift the brain out of my head and replace it with Albert Einstein's."

"I'm imagining that," Stan dutifully replied. "And it would be something to see."

Monty raised a thumb in appreciation. "Great, so imagine Dave and I could buy an improved brain for our *sidecar*. One that would make everything work more efficiently. Which, in turn, could hopefully improve our lap times significantly," he told Stan. "And that's precisely what we've been offered by Ryan now that he no longer needs his sidecar brain."

"That makes complete sense," Stan said, throwing Dave a look of stern disapproval at his awful teaching skills. "You're a natural at this, Monty," Stan remarked, looking to Monty again and flashing a smile.

Monty waved away the praise bestowed on him. "The brain in question is called a MoTeC ignition system. And the main reason we're not in possession of one already is that they're what's known in the trade as *soddin' expensive*. Ryan has offered us his unit at a slight discount, bless his soul. But even so, it's still very dear."

"Ah," said Frank. "Do you boys need some money, then?" he asked, though the tone in his voice was indicative of a genuine offer rather than an *oh-you-need-more-money-off-us-do-you?*

"No, but thanks," Dave entered in, answering for the both of them. "Monty and I are going to use the sponsorship advance we've received from the gambling company, along with the documentary fee we received from Chip and Brad. Between the two of us, we should have enough to fund the purchase. Still, it would be a substantial investment, and, as that's the case, we wanted to run it past you boys first for a bit of advice."

"Oh, I see," Frank said, happy to have been consulted. "And this MoTeC thingamabob. It will make that much of a difference?"

"Yup!" Monty was pleased to report. "Rather than eyeing a

top-twenty finish, we could realistically push for a top-ten."

"And *that*, lads," Dave added enthusiastically, "is how we'd secure that lovely thirty-k sponsorship bonus from the gambling company."

"So you invest a few thousand to hopefully secure thirty thousand," Stan stated, confirming his understanding.

"The nail on the head, Stanley," Dave replied. "Also, the MoTeC system provides loads of useful track data, which we can use to tweak and improve our settings further," he added. "Once we figure out how to do that, of course."

"And it's also got a cool electronic dashboard display that's like Kitt from Knight Rider!" Monty said, making the *wom-wom* noise that the car was famous for.

"Do it," Stan answered, nodding, and then glancing over to Frank.

Frank pressed out his lower lip, raising his bushy eyebrows skyward. "Yeah, why not? Speculate to accumulate, boys. Makes perfect sense," he said, in happy agreement with Stan. "You're sure you don't need any additional funds from us?"

"No, we're fine," Dave insisted. "Thanks again for the offer, of course. But you already employ us, sponsor us, often feed us, allow us to use your hot tub, and regularly clothe us. We want to do this on our own."

"Wait, we clothe you?" Stan asked. "Since when do we clothe you?"

"I quite like your shirt collection, Stan," Monty chimed in. "They're a little neat on me, but people say I look good in them. I *will* return them once I've washed them. Unless... you want them back unwashed?"

"Right. I'm delighted we share the same dress sense. And I did wonder why the contents of my wardrobe appeared rather light," replied Stan. "Oh, and yes. Wash them, please."

"Perfect," Dave announced, clapping his hands together in celebration now a final decision had been reached. "Monty, get on the blower and tell Ryan he's got a deal. We'll pop round and pick it up first thing tomorrow morning."

"Wait, you can't use it for tonight's practice session?" Stan asked, assuming this to have been the plan. "Would it not help you secure the qualifying lap time you need? Which, if I'm not mistaken, is one hundred and fifty percent of the third-fastest overall qualifying lap?" he said, folding his arms across his chest, smugly satisfied with himself that he actually knew this sort of information for a change.

"Firstly," said Dave, leaning forward to slap Stan's shoulder in fond appreciation, "I'm impressed that you've finally started listening to us. But it's a hundred and *fifteen* percent, not a hundred and fifty. Secondly, we'll need a bit of time to swap the ignition system over, so I'd rather not rush things today. There shouldn't be any problems with it, as they run the same bike as us. But you just don't know in this game. Better to be safe. So, for that reason, we'll go out for practice tonight using the current set-up and hopefully get the qualifying laps we need under our belts."

"Then," Monty entered in, "if we qualify tonight, we can relax a little on tomorrow's final practice session. That way, we can get to grips with the new ignition system before race week without panicking about qualification."

Frank raised the mug of coffee he'd been nursing this whole time. "Well," he said, toasting Dave and Monty. "Here's to a top-ten finish, yes?"

"Bollocks," said Dave, staring intently at the official lap times updating on his phone, sweat dripping down his face from their recent efforts out on the track. The initial elation from successfully completing two qualifying laps in that night's practice session was now waning due to the impressive average speeds of the competitor's lap times displayed. "What was our quickest time, Monty?" he asked, even though he already knew the answer from each time the screen refreshed in his hand.

"Ninety-six-point-six miles per hour," Monty answered him, chin resting on Dave's shoulder as he watched the exact same figures updating.

As things stood, their fastest average lap speed would be sufficient to secure qualification for race week. However, there were still machines out on track and a further practice session the following evening, both of which would likely raise the bar further in terms of the qualifying criteria required. Presently, the third-fastest average lap speed was just over one hundred and nine-point six. But if this increased even by a small margin — which was a distinct possibility based on past experience — then their quickest recorded lap would see them fall agonisingly short of qualification.

"We're going to need to get closer to a hundred-mile-an-hour average lap, Monty," Dave advised, reaching into the fridge for two much-needed beers, one for each of them. Dave then collapsed into their hospitality suite sofa, racing leathers still on. "If we had that new ignition system installed, we'd blitz it," he remarked, taking a long, generous swig of his beer, and then moaning in satisfaction. "Jaysus, that hit the spot," he declared. "Anyway," he said. "We definitely do need to put that MoTeC in there, now, yeah?"

"Do you know what race speed we'd need to aim for to achieve a top-ten finish?" Monty asked, taking a seat next to his mate.

"Dunno? Tell me."

"Tenth place last year was one-hundred-and-eight-point-six," Monty replied, placing his own beer up towards his lips. "Bottoms up," he added, rolling his eyes back in delight as the amber nectar went down.

Dave chewed this bit of information over, staring thoughtfully at the framed picture sat on the table — that picture being the mock-up designed by the TV network featuring Dave and Monty as Roman warriors racing a gleaming chariot. "We can do that," Dave suggested after a moment or two, sounding confident. "With the hours we've already invested in fine-tuning the bike, plus the imminent arrival of our new little upgrade? Not a problem. It'll be tough going, Monty, I won't lie. But we can do it, I reckon."

"I'll drink to that," Monty declared, after which he did exactly that. He wiped his mouth, and then noticed Dave was still looking at the photo on the table. "Ah. We *do* look rather fetching as Roman soldiers, don't we?" he remarked.

Dave nodded his head in happy agreement. "They've done wonders with my codpiece," Dave observed, cocking his head in appreciation as he continued to stare. "Becks has already told me that I need to pop along to the fancy-dress shop and see if they've a similar costume in my size."

"You definitely should," Monty answered, taking another swig of his lager. "Take it from me, you absolutely can't beat a bit of roleplay to spice things up a little, nossir..." he added, trailing off.

Monty was too busy drinking his beer at the present moment to elaborate any further as to how he had come to his conclusion regarding the benefits of bedroom roleplay, and Dave made it a point not to ask. He didn't want those types of images rolling around in his head.

After a bite to eat and an overdue shower, Dave and Monty stripped the sidecar down in preparation for the replacement ignition system. The deal had been done with the previous owner, hands shaken, and cash exchanged. After that, there was no going back. Though he didn't say it out loud, Dave couldn't shake the feelings of nagging doubt rattling through his head like a pneumatic drill. Yes, the new ignition system would be a significant improvement. He knew this, as he'd ridden machinery with it previously. Typically, however, the outfits running with the more advanced systems tended to have a qualified team of mechanics with the technical know-how to get the best from it, and, crucially, know what to do if anything went wrong. Dave and Monty certainly knew their way around a motorbike, but this was a technology relatively new to them. They both knew that what they were doing was a calculated gamble, but whether it would pay dividends remained to be seen. But nothing ventured, nothing gained, as they both often said. And, in this case, the gains could be significant (enabling Dave to place a deposit on a new house, among other things).

They'd not bothered checking the last batch of qualification times for the evening as they came in, deciding it best to crack on with their work instead. To a large extent, it was a waste of time and energy checking anyway, with the qualifying criteria subject to change each time a competitor would cross the finish line. Also, with a further final practice session the following evening, the boys could, and would, drive themselves crazy hitting the refresh button on their phones tonight when numbers would inevitably just shift again tomorrow anyway. The only thing they could influence for sure, at present, was improving their *own* future lap times. So that's precisely what they were focussing their efforts on right now.

"Knock-knock," Brad offered, announcing his and Chip's presence a bit later on that evening, rapping his knuckles on the canvas door of Dave and Monty's temporary garage, and then poking his head inside.

"If it isn't the Spielbergs," Dave joked, as the two brothers entered. Dave wiped an oil-stained hand on his overalls, extending the paw in their direction before then realising just precisely how much muck still remained on it. "Oi, we gave you two boys a wave earlier," Dave added. "That was you two filming at the Creg-Ny-Baa, wasn't it?"

"Today? Yup, that was us," Chip replied. "Your eyesight is pretty good."

"Did you get plenty of footage?" Monty enquired, head still buried in the sidecar, arse in the air, an impressive amount of crack on display.

"We did," Brad was pleased to report. "And we managed to retrieve everything we shot before, too, so that's a relief."

"From the cloud?" Dave asked.

"Yeah," Brad answered. "Fortunately, we remembered the password."

"Uh... excuse me?" said Chip.

"Correction. *Chip* remembered the password," Brad clarified.

"*Thank* you," Chip replied, folding his arms across his chest.

"Ah. That's good news all around," Dave said. "And it's fortunate you were able to borrow some equipment on such short notice. No word on the thieving scumbags who broke into your car?"

"No, not yet," Brad told him, shaking his head. "The police here have been great, though. They're checking all the CCTV footage, they told us, and asking the public for any car dashcam recordings that might help, also. So, fingers crossed."

"Two laps completed tonight, boys," Dave told them. "That means we've completed three qualifying laps and just need to pray to the timing gods that it's quick enough."

"Which means you'll hopefully get plenty of footage of the dream team in racing action next week," Monty suggested, leaning further forward into the bike and just about revealing what he'd eaten for lunch.

Brad and Chip, usually bustling with energy, remained relatively subdued standing near to the doorway, and Dave couldn't help but notice the peculiar look on their faces. "Have you two fallen out with each other?" Dave asked, handing Monty the spanner he was struggling to reach. "You're not your usual enthusiastic selves," Dave said in an overly cheery fashion, hoping to lift their demeanour. "Everything okay, chaps?"

The two brothers looked at each other, both appearing to will the other to open their mouths first. "Not really," Brad offered eventually, eyes fixed towards his feet.

"Oh?" said Dave, his upbeat expression giving way to one of concern.

Brad cleared his throat, giving a fleeting glance over to his brother, hoping his brother might jump in, which he didn't. "The thing is," Brad began. "Well, the thing is..." he added, shifting his weight from one foot to the other. "Okay, as you know, we had all of our stuff stolen," he said, setting his stall out early in his explanation. "And without recording equipment, we may as well have packed up and headed home..."

Dave sighed, resigned to the fact that what he was about to

hear wasn't likely to be news they'd be popping a champagne cork over. "All right, just cut to the chase, mate," he suggested.

"Okay. So we managed to borrow the equipment, like I said," Brad continued. "This allows us to finish our documentary, and, by finishing our documentary, not destroy our future career prospects and reputation, hopefully."

"*But?*" said Dave, sensing there was a 'but' that would follow.

"But..." Brad replied, struggling at this point. "But, the person loaning us the equipment, in return, told us he wants his own team to be the main feature of the show."

"We're sorry," Chip added in, and from the sound of his voice, it was obvious he was being sincere.

Monty raised his head from where it had been buried. "Wait, so we're out of the documentary?" he asked. "You don't need us anymore?"

"No, you'll still be in it, guys," Brad quickly assured them. "Just not as much. Um... and when I say not as much, I mean hardly at all. Like, probably just a quick interview and maybe a wide-angle shot or two of your bike in action."

"So you'll still be in it. Just not as much," Chip reiterated, trying to accentuate what little there was of the positive. "Oh, and you can still keep the money we already paid you to participate," he pointed out.

"We're both so very sorry," Brad told them. "Our hands are completely tied. But without the loan of the equipment, the project would have come to an end anyway, and *nobody* would have been in the documentary."

"Also," Chip added solemnly. "To be completely transparent with you, we're also getting paid to do this. And that's money we can use to replace our stolen equipment, not to mention hopefully kickstarting our careers as well. I only mention this because I don't want you finding out about it later and thinking our decision was based purely on the cash offered. I mean, that's *part* of it, sure. But, like, it's not like we *wanted* to abandon you guys or anything. It's more that..."

"The insurance included with the rental car doesn't appear

to cover the value of the stuff we had stolen," Brad explained. "And without any equipment, neither of us can work. We'd be totally screwed."

"Right," Dave said, placing his hand against his forehead. He was far from happy, but could at least understand and sympathise with the predicament the boys had found themselves in. "Ah, bugger," he added, a grim thought then occurring to him.

"What is it? You thinking about the Roman costume you've just ordered?" Monty enquired. "He's just spent three hundred quid on a replica Roman centurion costume," Monty explained for the benefit of both Brad and Chip. "To spice things up," he told them, from out of the corner of his mouth. "*You* know. In the *boudoir*."

"It's not about the costume," Dave answered. "Though that is a bit of a kicker, I won't lie. But, no, this is worse."

"What is it, then?" Monty asked. "The fact we've told anybody and everybody that we're going to be famous, and now we're not? Is that it? Dave, is that it?"

"Gordon Bennett, I hadn't even thought of that. So, yeah, thanks for cheering me up further, Monty," Dave replied. "But, no, I was actually thinking about the sponsorship contract with that gambling company. If we're not starring in the documentary series, then the deal's scrapped. They were fairly clear on that point."

Brad's shoulders dropped further than they'd already sunk. "Ah, shit," he said, in the absence of anything else coming to mind that he might offer.

"But they only paid the money out if you finished in the top ten, right?" Chip reminded them helpfully. "And by your own admission, that wasn't likely to happen in any case, am I right?" he added. "No offence meant, of course, Dave."

"But you still get to keep the small advance from them, and also the money you've received from us," Brad said brightly, hoping this would in some way soften the pain of the boys not appearing in the documentary to the same extent as originally planned. "So there's that, at least."

Dave started to chuckle to himself, but it was a sad sort of chuckle. "The thing is, we've just invested quite a fair chunk of change in some new, specialised equipment for the bike. Much, much more than we ever would have, had we known about all of this," Dave revealed. Dave then sighed a heavy sigh. "Ahh, you couldn't make it up," he added, more to himself than the others.

Monty placed a consoling hand on his mate's back. "We were hoping to break into the top ten," he explained, looking to Chip and Brad. "So we spent a lot of our money, almost all of it, in fact, on this new, high-tech ignition system, hoping to do just that, break into the top ten."

"Which is now rendered completely pointless," Dave said, throwing his hands in the air. "Because the contract with the sponsors is null and void if we're not starring in your documentary. So we've shelled out all of that cash with no chance of a generous payday in return."

To be fair to Brad and Chip, it was clear they weren't taking any enjoyment from this sequence of events. Instead, they were caught between a rock and a hard place. If they hadn't accepted the offer presented to them there would have been no documentary in any case, and *nobody* would have appeared onscreen. This was scant consolation to the disappointing news they'd just delivered.

"Dave, let us pay for your costume, at least," Chip suggested, reaching for his wallet. "It's the least we can do."

"You're fine," a dejected Dave replied. "The costume will still get used. Several times, I reckon."

"So, who are the new riders in your documentary, then?" an also-dejected Monty enquired, out of morbid curiosity.

"Andy Thomas and Jack Napier," Brad replied. "Do you guys know them?"

Dave screwed his face up in pain. "Ah, you've got to be kidding me!" he said. "In that case, I'm guessing the person who lent you the equipment must be Rodney flippin' Franks?" he added, putting two and two together and coming up with a short-arsed irritant result.

"It was," Brad confirmed, albeit very reluctantly, owing to Dave's current agitated state. Brad looked first to Dave, and then to Monty. "Guys, we're genuinely sorry it turned out like this, and we hope you can see it from our side? But we also totally understand if you might want to run us over with your van," he said.

It looked, for a very brief moment, like Dave was perhaps about to deliver a response of a physical nature. But then he immediately softened up. "Put it there," he said, extending his oily palm. "We get it," he said, getting it. "Don't we, Monty?"

"Yeah," Monty answered, happy to agree, and also extending his own grubby mitt. "We've had a blast getting to know you both, and we're grateful for the cash," he told the brothers. "It's a kick in the bollocks not being featured prominently in your docuseries, yes, but good luck and all that."

Dave raised his finger skyward, a thought presenting itself to him. "On the subject of cash, Monty," he said. "You'd better get on the phone to Ryan Horsfield, yeah? See if we can't talk him into giving us a refund on that new equipment we no longer need?"

"Hmm, about that," Monty said, having no wish to dampen his mate's spirits further, but not seeing any way out of it. "He's already buggered off," Monty revealed.

"As in buggered off?" asked Dave.

"Yeah, as in buggered off. He was catching the ferry earlier," Monty informed Dave, reluctantly. "He's had enough of the TT for this year, I reckon, what with him having to pull out and all," he said. "His mechanic is still here, though, until the end of the week, and has said he'd help us install the new ignition system if we'd like."

"Marvellous," Dave offered, as his considered summary of the situation. "Not ten minutes ago, Monty, we were fearless Roman soldiers headed off for a life of international fame and fortune," he observed, with a resigned laugh. "And now, we've not got a pot to piss in, and I've two hopes of buying a house... Bob Hope, and no hope."

Chapter
FOURTEEN

Friday of practice week. The day of the final practice session with three completed laps under their belt. However, with their fastest lap less than one second inside the qualifying criteria, it proved to be squeaky bum time at Dave & Monty's Race HQ...

"You know who'd kick Rodney's ass for us, don't you?" Stan asked, getting himself all agitated and worked up into a lather. "Henk. *Henk* would," he said, answering his own rhetorical question. "Henk would wrap those huge fingers of his around Rodney's scrawny little throat without hesitation," he remarked, throttling the air in front of him illustratively.

"It's just a shame his team isn't racing this year, then, isn't it?" Frank suggested. "Besides, I'm pretty sure Big Dave could make similar short work of Rodney if the mood took."

"Still, that interview I did with Brad and Chip could have been my big break, Frank," Stan continued. "And I don't see much chance of having any onscreen time now, do you?"

Frank, Jessie, Stan, and Edgar all strolled leisurely along the quayside in Douglas, the island's capital. Yes, they could have parked directly outside their destination. But they wanted to build up the anticipation with a pleasant stroll first.

"Ready?" Frank asked, as they approached the final corner before their goal.

"I'm ready, Frank," responded a smiling Stan. "Let's do it."

FRANK & STAN'S BUCKET LIST #5: ISLE OF MAN TT ACES

The four of them moved forward, deliberately averting their gaze so they could, on command, turn in unison and feast their eyes on what they'd come to see.

"Three... two... one..." said Frank. "Go!"

With that, four sets of eyes fell upon an illuminated glass-fronted building — a car dealership in one of its previous lives — that Frank and Stan could now call their own. Of course, they'd regularly visited during the renovation works, with Jessie, in particular, providing her creative flair to the overall finish. But today was the first time they'd get to see the magnificent, recently installed sign hung over the front entrance, announcing their new adventure to the whole of the world.

"Frank 'n' Stan's Hire Cars," Edgar said, reading the words featured on the sign out loud, bursting with pride. "Chaps, the place looks just splendid. It really does."

Their new place of business had at one time been an auto dealership for a major manufacturer, but for the previous eight years had focused strictly on supplying hire cars. It was a sector that Frank had pondered buying into previously, but the hire car industry was viewed by many as being plagued with unscrupulous practices and substandard vehicles. However, the previous owners of their new enterprise had been a class above. Rather than a grubby backstreet car lot, they'd prided themselves on operating from an immaculate, state-of-the-art facility with a fastidiously maintained fleet of vehicles. Yes, Frank and Stan had paid a premium to buy the business, but they felt confident they were taking ownership of a respectable operation with a sterling reputation. Ably assisted by Stella, Frank and Stan felt confident this was a venture that would thrive under their stewardship and offer significantly more sociable hours (and with a more sober clientele) than they'd enjoyed in the taxi trade.

"Hmm, there are no cars outside at present," Edgar observed, running his eyes along the long row of vacant parking spaces wrapped around the perimeter of what used to be, at one time, the auto showroom. "That's a good sign?"

"Yep. Most of them are booked up weeks in advance," Frank was delighted to confirm. "And the other pleasing news is that the existing employees are happy to remain with the business."

"They've heard about Stella...?" Jessie enquired, though not meaning to sound as surprised as she did.

Stan waved through the window towards the reception area inside. "Yes," he informed Jessie. "There are those two ladies who work on the front desk, plus a mechanic or two, plus a valet. All of whom have been brought entirely up to speed with their new supervisor and colleague."

"Susie's been kind enough to provide some remote phone induction training to the team," Frank added. "You know, let them know what to expect from Stella, such as trigger points, warning signs, and what to do in a range of different scenarios they might expect to encounter. Also, Stella's agreed to a more back-office role, so her face-to-face exposure to any customers should be limited."

"It's generally customers that tend to grind her gears," Stan explained. "So, if we can keep them apart as often as possible, then we should have an easier life and less violence."

Frank directed them towards a flight of metal stairs running up the exterior of the building. "Before we bring you into the new offices, Edgar, let's give you the full guided tour of Lee and Stella's new flat, handily located right here on the upper floor of the same building. Jessie's done wonders with the interior decoration."

At the top of the stairs, Frank unlocked the door, introducing them to the spacious flat within. "By golly," Edgar said, taking a tentative step inside and running his eyes around the freshly painted walls. "It's like a show home," he remarked, taking a gander at the plush, comfortable-looking sofa positioned in front of a widescreen TV sunk into the living room wall. "Can we move in here together?" he joked, looking over his shoulder to Stan.

"I had a few sneaky calls with Lee," Jessie confessed, repositioning a vase on the sideboard so that it was perfectly symmet-

FRANK & STAN'S BUCKET LIST #5: ISLE OF MAN TT ACES

rical with the painting hanging above it. "He told me the types of décor Stella typically likes, colour schemes and such. She doesn't know what we've done here, so she'll hopefully find it a pleasant surprise."

Edgar raised his eyebrows, bobbing his head gently in appreciation. "I'm sure she'll be thrilled, as the overall finish is to an exceptional standard."

Jessie was tickled pink with the generous, positive feedback coming from Edgar, quite obviously a gentleman of excellent character and impeccable taste.

"Is that...?" said Edgar, moving closer to the living room wall nearest and positioning himself in front of one framed photograph in particular that was to be found hanging there. "Oh, it is," Edgar added with a giggle, looking at the two strapping lads featured in the image. "A young, and, dare I say, rather handsome-looking Stanley and Frank."

"Oh?" said Frank, walking over and having a butcher's for himself. "I didn't know you'd done this," Frank added, taking hold of Jessie's hand as she walked over to join them. "Oi! Stan!" he said, calling Stan over from the other room. "Come and have a gander at this!"

Stan wandered in from the kitchen, curious to see what was taking up Frank's attention. "Oh, my," Stan said, upon arrival, smiling warmly. "Did you do this, Frank?"

"Nope, weren't me. It was all Jessie," Frank advised.

The picture immediately conjured up a set of fond remembrances for Stan and Frank, inviting them on a pleasant stroll down memory lane. Without a wrinkle to be seen on either of their faces and a flourishing, luxuriant head of hair apiece, a youthful Frank and Stan were stood either side of Craggy Sally, their longstanding accountant, friend, confidant, matriarch, and often the disciplinarian keeping the both of them on their toes.

"Aww, Sally..." Stan remarked, a wave of emotion taking charge of his voice. "They certainly broke the mould when they made her," he said wistfully.

"Wait, is that Stella, in front?" Edgar asked, raising his finger towards the burly young girl in the image, positioned down in front of the others with a stern expression and apparently no intention whatsoever of smiling for the camera.

"Yes, that's our Stella," Frank replied. "And you'll take note of the decapitated dolly in her hand," he said, which raised a laugh from Stan.

"She had anger issues way back then," Stan suggested, wiping a nostalgic tear from his cheek. "She still does, of course," he added with a chuckle. "Anyhow, what a wonderful surprise," he said, turning to Jessie. "I'm sure Stella will truly appreciate the effort you've gone to," he told her.

"Lee emailed me a scanned copy," Jessie explained. "So I took it to the photographers in town who were able to enlarge the image for me," she said, reaching up to straighten the frame so it was just so.

"You know, what you've all done for Stella is extraordinary," Edgar remarked. "The new job, the new home, and even making sure the flat looks as cosy and inviting as can be. She is very fortunate indeed to have such thoughtful people in her life."

"I'm sure she appreciates us," Stan suggested. "I mean, somewhere, deep down," he added thoughtfully. "Really, *really* deep down."

"Come on," Jessie said, linking Edgar's arm. "Let me show you what I've done with their bedroom," she told him, leading the way. "Lee told me Stella is very fond of a certain, particular gentleman. He said she was often up close and personal with him, although I'm not sure I really understood what he meant, or why he was laughing when he said it. Anyway, so as a further surprise to make her smile, I've also hung up a framed poster of the fellow. I forget his name, but it was a bit unusual, reminding me of Irn-Bru, or something along those lines...?"

Jessie then glanced behind her to make sure Frank wasn't within earshot. "She has excellent taste in men," she whispered with a giggle. "Because he's exceptionally good-looking."

"Idris Elba!" Frank called over, hearing precisely what his

loyal wife was saying about the gentleman under discussion.

Stan waited a long moment until Jessie and Edgar were completely into the bedroom and deep in further conversation. "Did you hear that?" he squealed, to Frank. "Oh my *god*," he said, squirming around like he had to have a wee.

"What?" Frank asked. "Hear what? What did I miss?"

"Edgar," Stan answered, wide-eyed, placing a calming hand against his own cheek. "Earlier," he explained. "When he said he wanted to *move in* together."

"He did?"

"Yes," Stan said. "When we first came in. He said we should move in together!"

"Oh," Frank answered. "Yes, I think he did, Stan. But I'm not sure he meant—"

"He must really be serious about me," Stan suggested, not really listening to Frank's attempted cautionary note in any way. "But *living* together...?" Stan added, drifting away to a happy place, imagining that very prospect for a moment.

"Complete perfection!" Edgar enthused, returning from the bedroom with Jessie on his arm a short time later.

"You think Stella will like the Iris Melba picture?" Jessie asked, smiling hopefully.

"I'm certain she will, as he's quite dashing," Edgar said in response, and being too polite to correct her regarding the name. "But you know what he's not, though?"

"What's that?" Jessie asked.

"He's no Stanley Sidcup," Edgar offered, providing a wink for Stan's benefit.

With the greatly appreciated assistance of Mike, Ryan Horsfield's mechanic, Dave and Monty's new and costly ignition system was fitted without too much fuss and was raring to go in no time at all. As the sponsorship money was no longer on offer for a top-ten finish, the boys had considered selling their acquisition to another team to recoup some of the cash they'd invested. However, selling an expensive ignition system at the very end of practice week wasn't as alluring a proposition to others as the lads might have hoped. They'd received some interest from a handful of riders, but the offers being extended were significantly lower than what they'd spent on the device. So much lower, in fact, that they weren't even worth considering, as far as Dave and Monty were concerned. For this reason, they both agreed to proceed as planned, installing the tech and then carrying on with getting as high up that leaderboard as possible. Assuming they still managed to qualify, of course.

"Good luck, boys," Mike said, once finished, offering Dave a hearty slap on the back. "You've now got yourself some serious equipment under there," he added, glancing down at their significantly upgraded machine. "Go easy at first, though, until you're used to it. The old girl will be quicker than you're accustomed to, yeah?"

"Sure thing, Mike," Dave answered, right before darting over to his van and reaching through the opened side door. "Here you go, mate," he said, handing over the crate of lager he'd retrieved. "Throw that in the back of your truck and have a few beers on us, buddy."

Mike didn't need asking twice. "Much obliged," he said, taking prompt possession of the gift with a contented expression. "Also, my ferry home doesn't leave until late tomorrow, so if you need advice or support after tonight's practice or even after tomorrow's race, then just knock on the side of the van," he told them. "Assuming I'm still conscious, of course," he added, patting the crate under his arm affectionately.

"You're a legend," Monty said, using a clean cloth to wipe off a few leftover fingerprint smudges from their fly-spattered blue fairing as he spoke.

"Oh," Mike said, turning back on himself. "And for what it's worth, gents, I'm sorry to hear you won't be appearing much in that documentary programme."

"Eh, what can you do?" Dave replied with a shrug, accepting of the situation but still clearly disappointed by it. "Word has

FRANK & STAN'S BUCKET LIST #5: ISLE OF MAN TT ACES

spread around the paddock, then?" he asked.

"Well, those colossal hunks of knob cheese, Andy Thomas and Jack Napier, are strutting around the paddock like bloody Robert De Niro and Al Pacino," Mike explained. "They're telling anybody that'll listen how they're going to be the next big thing. And don't even get me started on their goon of a team manager, Rodney Franks. I mean, what kind of twit wears a cravat in the middle of summer? Or wears a cravat at *all*, for that matter?"

"I hear that," Monty said, in complete agreement. "In fact, if our quickest lap gets trumped tonight and we don't qualify as a result, Dave and I are going to cheer ourselves up by throwing old Rodney in the back of our van."

"We're still going for shaving his head?" Dave politely enquired, wanting to make sure their plan hadn't been altered without his knowledge. "We'll get that Rodney all prettied up for his TV appearance, yeah?"

Monty smiled broadly at the thought of it. "Mohican?" he suggested.

"I like it," Dave answered. "I was originally thinking about a complete shave, a true sort of cue-ball, Kojak effect. But I think I like your idea better. More impressive result, I reckon. It's all about the creativity."

Mike offered a hearty laugh. "A pleasure as always, boys," he said, leaving the awning. "And as I say, take it easy, at least initially, yes? You've got a cracking machine there, but you *will* feel the difference in speed with the improved set-up."

With Mike off, there was nought to do at present but wait. Often, one of the more challenging aspects of motorsport was the requirement to simply hang about, waiting patiently until you were next out on track. There was always work to be done on the machinery, of course, tinkering with this and adjusting that. But once you'd done all you possibly could on that front, it was simply a matter of filling the time until you were called into action. Many riders enjoyed this downtime, taking advantage of a nice power nap, or perhaps filling the hours playing video games or by pulling out a deck of cards.

For others, though, Dave and Monty included, minutes often felt like hours before heading out for action. Today, they'd done all the work they could on the bike, drank copious amounts of tea, and virtually worn a path pacing in and around their awning. Fortuitously, one of the neighbouring teams weren't quite as prepared as them, as it turned out, so Dave and Monty were more than happy to don their tool belts to jump in and lend a hand. This welcome distraction also, for a time, took their minds away from the subject of qualification. As it stood, their quickest lap time remained inside the required criteria. But they were both experienced enough, the two of them, to know that things could and would likely change in the evening's final practice session. So rather than leave things to fate, Dave and Monty were eager to go out and post the fastest lap time they possibly could and, it was hoped, ensure qualification in the process.

Twenty or so minutes before the eight-p.m. start time for the sidecar class, Dave and Monty strolled up to pit lane where the machines were all lined up earlier, having been given their final inspection by the scrutineers, now ready and waiting for their plucky riders to climb aboard. Fortunately, but as expected, the new MoTeC ignition system had passed technical muster without incident. So now, the only murky clouds overhead were the actual murky clouds overhead. In typical fashion, the weather on the isle (always subject to change at no greater than a mere moment's notice) had been majestic for most of the day, with race fans, wherever you looked, sporting a collection of beetroot-coloured faces and matching pink arms. But in the late evening clouds appeared en masse, with the forecast suggesting showers were imminent. The good thing about the overcast conditions, though, was the blessed reprieve from the setting sun's glare — that glare being potentially problematic at this stage of the evening, particularly when navigating tree-lined country roads at speeds exceeding one hundred and forty miles an hour.

"Look at that prat, Monty," Dave said, pulling on his helmet.

The source of his ire was the spectacle that was Rodney Franks, there, further up the pit lane, all decked out in a fire-retardant safety suit in front of his team's sidecar and shamelessly playing up for the camera. Either side of him stood his riders, Napier and Thomas, also posing for the benefit of Brad and Chip's camera trained in their direction.

"That should be us," Monty moaned. "You know..." he added, cautiously glancing over his shoulder, and then back to Dave. "You know, I'm almost too embarrassed to admit it, Dave. But do you know what I did last week?"

"Was it another, *ahem*, encounter where you got stuck in your hoover again?" Dave asked, zipping up his leathers.

"That was only the one time, Dave!" Monty protested. "And as I explained then, I'd tripped and landed awkwardly! So you don't need to keep bringing that up," he said, giving Dave the evil yet wonky eye. "And no, it wasn't that. What I was going to say is that I was practising signing my autograph, Dave. You know, just so I was prepared in case I was approached while out shopping or something, after becoming extremely famous. Fat chance of that happening now."

"I know, mate. I know," Dave said sympathetically. "Hey," he added, his voice brimming with optimism, "if we can get this magnificent machine into the top ten next week, you never know, the autograph hunters might be chasing you down in their droves, right? So, come on, buddy, get your helmet on and let's get the job done."

"*Grrr!*" Monty replied with a throaty snarl, ready for action. And then, "Wait, when you said magnificent machine, did you mean you, or the sidecar...?"

"Both!" Dave declared, along with a hearty chuckle. "I'd say definitely both."

Shortly after eight p.m., the first of the sidecars blasted away from pit lane. As each machine headed on its way, those waiting patiently moved forward in the queue to fill the space created, awaiting their turn in a chorus of horsepower from the throbbing engines.

Dave teased the throttle, alone in his thoughts. People often asked him what went through his mind moments before heading out onto the world's most challenging racing circuit. One might imagine concerns such as oil pressure, gearing, or even track adhesion in the sheltered sectors might fill his head. And once upon a time, they did. But now, more often than not, it was rather more mundane thoughts that filled his head. Maybe it was a defence mechanism so his brain didn't register that he'd soon be hurtling down the imposing descent of Bray Hill, the bike mere centimetres from the ground, with his best mate along for the ride, both of their lives held in the palms of his hands. Just now, though, all Dave could see in his mind's eye was the comforting image of a quaint little cottage surrounded by a white picket fence, with Becks and Tyler stood there waving from the porch.

"Ahh," said Dave, muttering a contented sigh at the idyllic thoughts in his mind. Snapping back to the present, he spotted Brad and Chip off to his left, the both of them safely tucked behind a dividing wall in the return lane, thumbs raised.

"You've got this!" Brad screamed in Dave's direction, over the din of throaty, revving engines.

"You guys rock!" Chip added, raising a fist in the air.

Dave offered a quick wave of acknowledgement, right before engaging first gear. He took a deep breath, and then, upon receiving the nod from the starting official, he let out the clutch and opened the throttle. And with that, outfit number thirty-six was on its way.

Despite the requirement for a blistering lap time, Dave remained light on the throttle for the first couple of miles. With minimal grip available from the cold tyres and the new ignition system to think of, Mike the Mechanic's words of caution were fresh in his mind. It wasn't until the exit from Quarterbridge that Dave totally opened her up on the approach to Braddan Bridge.

"Jaysus!" Dave shouted, as the machine responded under acceleration. In that instant, Dave knew the money they'd spent was worth each and every penny. The bike felt tight, responsive, and pulled like a locomotive. "Yes!" Dave yelled further, though his delight was of course heard only by himself, and perhaps Monty. The only other time he'd felt this kind of power beneath him was during his previous TT victory with Harry McMullan beside him.

Heading at a fair old click towards the familiar oak tree at Braddan Bridge, Dave glanced over to his left, ensuring poor Monty hadn't been left behind when he'd opened up the taps. Fortunately, the old boy was still there, tucked in and ready for action as they negotiated a left then right bend in quick succession, passing the cheering crowds watching on from in front of the iconic Kirk Braddan church.

Whilst they weren't necessarily racing just yet, as such — this being merely a qualifying lap — Dave was nevertheless encouraged to catch a glimpse of a machine up ahead on the approach to Union Mills. Either they were running particularly slow, or Dave and Monty were running particularly quick. Dave very much hoped it was the latter, and his confidence increased with every inch of tarmac covered.

In what felt like a glorious blur, the boys were soon flying past The Crosby pub, packed with spectators watching on with pints in hand. It was one of Dave's favourite sections on the course, and he kept the throttle pinned, passing their TT Farm further up on the left-hand side. He knew Becks and Tyler would be watching on from there as well, but didn't want to take his eyes off the road ahead for even an instant considering the current rate of speed they were travelling.

There were rare, wonderous occasions when everything just fell into place throughout his racing career, and for Dave, this was one of them. He'd hit the apex of every turn perfectly, and the bike was handling like it was on rails, balanced and perfectly poised through the corners. Then, passing through the Glen Helen section — around ten miles into the lap — Dave knew from experience they were on for a fantastic overall lap time, even coming from a standing start as they had.

It was, however, approaching the Cronk-y-Voddy Straight when Dave felt a sudden knot in his stomach. Rising up from a tree-lined section of the circuit, Dave had a clearer view of the conditions around them. Typical of the island's rather capricious weather, there was brilliant blue sky directly to his left, but towards the north loomed an ominous-looking cloud formation. And it wasn't clear in which direction the possible rainclouds were heading. Still, as Dave couldn't do too much about the weather, he tucked himself in behind the visor with his mind focussed on the next corner.

Frustratingly, Dave's fears were soon realised on passing the Curraghs Wildlife Park when a solitary raindrop bounced off his visor (as where there was one raindrop, more were bound to follow). A momentary glance skyward confirmed the clouds he'd spotted were heading inland rather than out to sea as he'd hoped. He considered rolling off the throttle just a touch, unsure of the conditions they'd meet on the road ahead. Dave was acutely aware that a damp road and racing slick tyres weren't really a good combination for continuing in the direction you ideally wanted to go. Fortunately, however, the marshals positioned at regular intervals weren't displaying the dreaded red-and-yellow striped "Lack of Adhesion" flags, so Dave kept up the blistering pace, desperate to improve upon the previous lap times they'd already established.

To his immense relief, Dave's visor remained dry, as did the road ahead. He dropped down the gearbox, braking hard to anticipate the tight right-hander into Ramsey's Parliament Square. But his heart instantly sank when he caught a glimpse of a marshal, leaping about in animated fashion, lurching forward and grabbing at something. Dave hoped she was reaching for a flask rather than…

"A red flag! Bollocks!" Dave yelled, slapping the handlebar in frustration, and then decreasing his speed accordingly. He eased the bike to the side of the track, as was the protocol upon receiving a red flag. Dave's immediate thought was one of concern, desperately hoping the resultant halting of the practice session wasn't due to some kind of race-related incident, perhaps an accident.

"You may as well switch her off," the nearest marshal suggested over the sound of the engine, pointing down to Dave and Monty's bike.

"What's going on?" Dave enquired, removing his helmet. "Everything okay?"

"Weather conditions," the marshal replied.

Dave glanced at the bone-dry road, and then back to the marshal. "Weather?" he asked, though not in a confrontational manner. "I had one raindrop on my visor, but it came to nothing," he said with a shrug. "Pissing down elsewhere?"

"It's the clouds," the marshal explained, pointing skyward, as if Dave needed the location of the clouds pointed out to him. "It's too thick for the rescue helicopter to take off or land," the marshal informed them.

The marshal then walked away towards a second machine that had just pulled in behind Dave and Monty, whereupon the same unfortunate news was delivered to another set of equally disappointed riders.

"What a kicker," Monty said, removing his own lid. "We were really flying there, too."

"We were, at that," Dave agreed. "It's just a bloody shame the *helicopter* isn't, though," he added, letting out a sigh, and then a sad little laugh.

Of course, they were both downhearted. But without the medical helicopter's vital service, there was no racing, period. No matter what, safety came first.

The issue Dave and Monty faced now, however, was that the front of the field (those machines who'd started the session higher up the starting order) would likely have had the chance to complete a lap before the red flag had brought proceedings to an end. What this meant for our intrepid lads was that even a slight improvement in the overall lap times of the other riders could mean possible curtains for the two of them, and a premature conclusion for their current TT campaign.

"That's it, chaps," another of the marshals called over, arriving on scene. "They've officially cancelled the session," he said, telling Monty and Dave what, sadly, they already knew. "I've some tea left in my flask if you fancy a swig?" he offered kindly.

Dave raised a hand in gratitude. "Thanks, but I think we'll try and grab a pint," he advised, looking to Monty for approval of this idea.

"May as well," Monty readily agreed. "Other than praying to the racing gods for some type of miracle, there's bugger-all else we can do just now anyway."

"Right. I'll ask around for a phone to borrow so we can ring Frank and Stan," Dave proposed. "See if they can drive the van and meet up with us here in Ramsey when the roads eventually reopen."

"Wanna check on the lap times as well?" Monty suggested.

"Nah," Dave replied, with a shake of his head. "Let's go and enjoy that pint first."

"What, before Stan and Frank pick us up? You've got cash on you, then?" a pleasantly surprised Monty enquired.

"Nope. No pockets," Dave replied with a chuckle. "Hopefully, they'll take an IOU until the boys show up and bail us out."

Chapter
FIFTEEN

An air of exhilaration wafted over the gentle hills around this jewel in the middle of the Irish Sea, for both competitor and spectator alike. For the racers, after a gruelling week of practice, there was no respite. Excitement grew, as this is where the months of preparation and hard work would finally be tested for the riders and their crews. Because this was race week at the Isle of Man TT.

As for the fans, tens of thousands of devotees had completed their annual pilgrimage, desperate to scratch a racing itch that could only be satisfied on this majestic island. Mixed amongst the stalwart regulars were first-timers, drawn to this event by tales of heroic racers tearing through country roads, passing inches from where you watched on in wide-eyed wonderment. But indeed, it didn't matter if you'd been one time or dozens, as the unadulterated thrill you'd experience each and every year simply didn't wane over time.

On a race day, you'd best be up with the lark to secure one of the prime viewing spots around the course, which began filling up from first light. But if you did manage it, your efforts would be rewarded with unbridled adrenalin-fuelled action the likes of which you'd struggle to find anywhere else on the planet. For these early risers, there was always the option to catch up on your beauty sleep *between* the races. More often than not, however, you'd be too busy chatting with your fellow fans, high on endorphins, to catch any proper shuteye!

FRANK & STAN'S BUCKET LIST #5: ISLE OF MAN TT ACES

A certain subset of adventurous spectators were willing to forgo the convenience of seating, toilets, and nearby food outlets for a somewhat more rustic experience. And one of the joys of the Isle of Man TT was the great number of locations out in the sticks open to you, where the only thing keeping you company while enjoying your uninterrupted view was the local wildlife or domesticated livestock. This enviable experience came with a price, however. Often, you'd need to drive to your desired destination before the roads closed early for the day's racing, meaning you'd likely be stuck in situ until the roads reopened later that evening. Fantastic on a warm afternoon (if you'd remembered to bring along your suncream and bug spray, which many didn't). But not so much if the weather conditions soured — a distinctly possible outcome on an island where it could be cracking the flags with glorious sunshine one minute and raining cats and dogs the next.

As for Frank and Stan, having received assurance from Dave that their services as pit crew weren't required, they, along with their collective better halves, ventured to the Mountain section of the course to experience the racing action. (The invite was extended to Becks and Tyler as well, but Becks had reckoned the young chap would've been bored rigid spending several hours in the great outdoors with only the oldies for company, and so had politely declined.)

Acting upon Monty's recommendation, the group had journeyed to Brandywell, located just after the 31st Milestone roadside marker of the circuit. It was one of the highest sections of the course, offering superb views of the riders accelerating away from the popular Bungalow Station vantage point before climbing up Hailwood Rise.

Presently, our merry band of travelling spectators had already enjoyed the earlier and thrilling superbike race when Stan noted an area in the distance he felt confident would offer an even better view as compared to the one they were currently appreciating. So, with the upcoming sidecar race getting underway in about forty minutes, thus leaving a bit of time on their hands, Stan talked the others into a short walk over the rugged moorland to this new location he'd fancied. Just as well, then, that they had all dressed accordingly to trek through the wilds of the Isle of Man...

"Ah, flippin 'eck," Stan remarked, hopping on one foot as he struggled to see the upraised sole of his other shoe. "I think I've stepped in something," he said, waving his new suede loafer in Frank's direction. "Can you see anything, Frank?"

"It's probably sheep droppings," Frank suggested, giving Stan's shoe a quick once-over, but seeing nothing. "Also, are you sure you're dressed for a wander into the wilderness?" he asked, concerned for his mate.

"Whaddya mean?" Stan asked, glancing over his shoulder to see what he may or may not have trodden in.

"Well," Frank continued. "Since when have you seen Bear Grylls, for instance, heading out into the vast wilderness wearing fancy, designer clothing like yours, with brand-new shoes?"

"Loafers," Stan stressed. "Suede *loafers*."

"Which... are a type of shoe...?" replied Frank, unclear as to why Stan felt the apparent need to make such a distinction.

Undaunted, Stan took a lungful of the crisp, clean mountain air. "Besides, the conditions are glorious," he said, extending his arms and spinning around like he was Maria von Trapp from *The Sound of Music*.

"I can't wait to sample your picnic!" Jessie noted cheerfully, eyeing the large basket hooked over Edgar's arm as they set off once again, Stan not having found anything on the sole of his shoe after all.

"You may wish to loosen your belt in advance," Edgar joked. "I may have got a little carried away in the supermarket."

The four of them traipsed over the heath, taking care not to lose a foot down one of the numerous rabbit holes bored in the earth or scratch their legs on the heather gorse. Their destination, described by Stan as about a five-minute walk, had extended past ten, now heading for fifteen, and with further still to go. "It's magnificent up here," Jessie announced, taking hold of Frank's hand, running her gaze over the rolling hills stretching out as far as the eye could see. "It feels like we've got the island all to ourselves."

Frank gave her hand a gentle squeeze in return. "It's days like this that make you glad to be alive," he said thoughtfully. "And there's nobody else I'd rather spend it with," he added, leaning across to deliver a tender smacker on her cheek.

"Cut it out, you two!" Stan called out, looking back from his position ahead.

"Do you want me to carry that basket for a while?" Frank asked over the breeze, though fully expecting the answer to be in the negative. Stan had gallantly taken over carrying it from Edgar, and so Frank very much doubted Stan would wish to relinquish his toting duties so easily.

"You're fine," Stan said, waving away the kind offer.

Frank smiled fondly, observing Stan and Edgar walking a short distance out in front. "Watch him," Frank whispered to Jessie. "When he thinks Edgar isn't looking, he'll have a sneaky glance over at him."

"That's so sweet," Jessie answered, and then watched Stan as instructed. "Aww, he just did it," she said, mere moments later. "He just looked over to him."

"They're like two teenagers on a first date," Frank remarked. "That's why the soppy sod is dressed like he's going out yachting in bloody Monaco rather than mountaineering on the Isle of Man," he said with a chuckle. "It's funny, you know," Frank went on reflectively. "You only have to look at us two, and now Stan and Edgar, to realise that love can come knocking on your door at any stage or moment in life's journey."

"I'm just glad I was in," Jessie said with a smile.

"In?"

"Yes, when you came knocking."

"Ah. Me too, Jessie. Me too."

"Right!" Stan called out, holding his hand directly above his head once they'd reached his desired destination. "This will do," he declared, satisfied, as he placed the basket down in front of him. "Yes, we can definitely set up camp here," he added, after first making sure there was a clear view of the circuit so they could all watch the sidecar action as intended. "Splendid, just splendid," he declared confidently.

Frank nodded his approval, hands resting on his hips, taking a long moment to appreciate the vista laid out before him. "And to think those two selfish bastards, Dave and Monty, very nearly curtailed our plans today by almost not qualifying," he joked, with an audible tut-tut.

"They certainly cut it fine," Edgar agreed, laying out his tartan picnic blanket for their collective comfort.

"Dave said that they scraped qualification by the equivalent of about three one-hundredths of a second!" Jessie offered, with a laugh of disbelief. "Honestly, talk about the finest margins between disappointment and glory."

"I'll drink to that," Stan proclaimed, raising a bottle of chilled white wine aloft to do precisely that.

"To thin margins?" Frank asked, a little confused.

"As good a reason as any," Stan said with a shrug, along with a cheeky grin. "Can I tempt you?" he asked, tilting the bottle in Frank's direction.

"Ehm... I'm driving," Frank hesitantly replied. But his level of resistance was minimal at best, resulting in him staring over, imploringly and with puppy-dog eyes, at his darling wife.

Jessie looked up to the heavens. "Like I didn't see that one coming," she said with a laugh. "Right. Go on, then. I'll be the designated driver," she advised.

"You won't go without, Mrs Cryer," Stan told her, reaching back into his chilled box of tricks. "We've brought along some lovely elderflower pressé as well," he said, holding up the bottle for inspection. "It really does hit the spot, and it's got no alcohol in it at all!"

"I'll tell you what," Frank said, feasting his eyes on the spread Edgar was laying out for them. "When I was a lad, picnics were all about Scotch eggs and plain, lonely ham sandwiches, and little else."

FRANK & STAN'S BUCKET LIST #5: ISLE OF MAN TT ACES

"And maybe a chocolate biscuit if you were very lucky," Stan chipped in, rummaging through the basket.

"Exactly. And this all looks amazingly delicious, and is much more impressive," Frank answered.

"What have you lost?" asked Edgar, shortly thereafter, in response to overhearing several sighs of frustration coming from Stan.

"The corkscrew," Stan replied, double-checking every place he'd already checked.

"They're not twist tops?" Edgar asked helpfully, before then spotting the corks at the top of each bottle, answering his own question.

It was at this point that Frank looked over to Jessie with a concerned grimace. Almost as if he'd just recalled something he might have forgotten. Something important.

"Wait," said Stan, removing his head from the chiller box. "Frank, you said you'd picked up the bottle opener, didn't you?" he asked, turning to Frank. "Back at the house, you remember? You've not forgotten it, have you?"

Frank screwed up his face, looking somewhat pained. "Of course I've not forgotten it!" he replied, appearing offended at the very suggestion. "I mean, I've not *completely* forgotten it," he clarified.

"Right. Pass it here, then," Stan answered, holding out his palm.

"Ah. Well. When you mentioned it, I took it from the drawer and headed straight out to the car, you see, and popped it right in the glovebox so that I wouldn't forget it," Frank explained.

"And that would mean... it's still in the glovebox, isn't it...?" Stan deduced, looking over to the tiny speck in the distance that was their parked car.

"Yes. Yes, it is," Frank conceded, head bowed. *"Technically*, I didn't forget it, though, you understand."

There were two options available to the group at this point — watch the races without wine (horrific to even contemplate), or, somebody needed to go and fetch the corkscrew.

"Bloody hell, if you want a job doing...!" Stan barked, though not appearing too terribly upset, really, as he got up and set foot in the direction from whence they'd come. "Save me something to eat," he added, waving over his shoulder as he sallied forth, like an intrepid explorer.

"Here, do you want me to go get it, Stanley?" Frank offered, though not very loudly, or with too much conviction. "No...?" he asked, when no response was received, although of course Stan was well out of earshot by now anyway. "Right!" Frank said brightly to the others. "Now that's settled, let's get that radio fired up and listen to the action, shall we?"

By the time the picnic was unpacked entirely and laid out before them, the radio commentator was preparing to call away the sidecars leaving from the grandstand, his voice filled with excitement as he attempted to talk over the constant throb of revving engines. It was often mixed emotions for Jessie at this time of year, however. On the one hand, she adored the TT. But having her son Dave competing in it was a constant source of anxiety that only diminished once Dave and Monty had safely crossed that final finish line.

"Don't worry, they know what they're doing, those two," Frank said softly, placing an arm around Jessie's shoulder, recognising the look on her face and well aware of the anguish she was going through.

Jessie smiled in response. She knew Frank was correct, but it didn't relax her completely, or relieve the tension. Something a glass of wine might have a better chance of doing, though she'd have to settle for the elderflower pressé, assuming Stan would hurry back with the corkscrew.

Over the radio, the commentator was still chattering away. It was a bizarre feeling, listening in to the enthusiastic radio commentary and the flurry of action happening over at the grandstand some miles off in the distance, when here, sat upon the tranquil Mountain section in the peace and quiet, there was only empty tarmac at the bottom of the hillside below. One thing for certain, however, was that this would soon change when the front of the pack reached their position in roughly fifteen minutes' time.

The relative calm before the storm would be shortly shattered with the sound of approaching horsepower long before the bikes appeared into view. It was that sense of anticipation that really resulted in Frank's heart racing. The same feeling you get when standing in an empty railway station knowing the express train was due to burst into view at any moment, for instance, but you just didn't know when, exactly. Instead, you'd hear that faint rumble in the distance, which increased steadily in volume with each passing second. It was a giddy thrill, knowing you were about to get the wits scared out of you, but you didn't know just when, and it was something Frank relished.

"I heard something," Frank announced a short while later, reaching for Stan's binoculars and scrambling to his feet. "Here they come!" he shouted, looking into the distance at the first of the bikes that were headed their way.

Edgar placed his half-eaten crab sandwich back on his plate. "Ooh," he said, rising to his feet as well. "Yes, I see it!" he added, as the air filled with the angry snarl of approaching machinery.

"Come on, my love," Frank said, offering a helping hand to a still-seated Jessie.

Seconds later, another machine appeared into view, then another, and then another. Before too long, they were like a trail of ducks moving towards them — that is, if ducks could move at mind-boggling speed! Ordinarily, from the more populated viewing spots, you'd often only catch a fleeting glimpse of the action before the racing bikes were gone again, disappearing as quickly as they'd arrived. From their vantage point, however, Frank and crew were blessed with a much lengthier experience, watching the bikes passing under the pedestrian bridge at the Bungalow Station before climbing furiously towards them, and then disappearing away in the direction of Windy Corner, offering the gang an eagle-eye perspective of the overall action.

Jessie counted down the machines passing by, clenching her fingers into a fist as they moved from the teens and into the twenties. "Won't be long now," she said, gritting her teeth, pulse rate increasing.

"I think I see a familiar-looking blue paint job," Frank said, eyes straining through the binoculars.

"It can't be them yet, can it?" Jessie asked, standing on her tiptoes, peering over Frank's shoulder as if this would improve her view.

"I can't... quite... see..." Frank said, pausing for a moment. The machine in question drew alongside the outfit in front of them, jostling for position, quickly overtaking them, and then opening up the gap between them in very short order.

"It's them!" Frank shouted in delight. "And they left that other bike behind like it was standing still!"

Sure enough, the blue outfit was that of Dave and Monty's machine number thirty-six. The first lap of the three-lap race wasn't yet complete, but they'd already progressed through the field, obviously having caught and passed more than a few of the bikes who'd started before them. "Ooh, there they go!" Jessie said, jumping up and down and waving furiously as the boys passed by (even though, as the track was at least two hundred yards further down the hillside, Dave couldn't possibly have seen her whilst piloting a sidecar at nearly one hundred and fifty miles an hour). "You can do it!" Jessie screamed, long after the boys had disappeared from view.

"Wow. Those boys were going *fast*," Edgar offered, as his considered opinion.

Frank lowered his binoculars, leaving two red rings around his eye sockets. "You're not wrong there, Edgar. Did you see the way they pulled away from that other bike? That speed was staggering!"

They watched on as the remainder of the field passed safely through, starting their descent from the Mountain section of the course, leaving the alluring aroma of exhaust fumes to carry on the breeze behind them. "I need a good drink after that," Jessie said, playfully clutching her chest once they were gone.

"Me too," Frank was quick to agree. "Wait, that reminds me. Where on earth has Stan got to?" he added.

There was a collective silence for a moment or two as the group looked to where Stan could be last observed. A concerned Edgar took several paces forward, in that very direction, hoping to improve his field of view. "How long's he been gone?" he asked, feeling guilty for not noticing Stan's prolonged absence before now.

"Dunno, about twenty minutes, maybe?" Jessie offered with a shrug, but as they'd been consumed by the racing action, in truth, it could've been even longer. "I should think he'd be on his way back by now, though."

"There's somebody down there," Edgar said, finger pointing, and eyes straining. "Frank, could you—?" he asked, looking back over his shoulder. But Frank was one step ahead, stood with the binoculars pressed against his eyes.

"That's him," said Frank, adjusting the focus on Stan's field glasses to get a clearer view. "Yeah, that's him," he confirmed. "But he's not doing anything other than standing there waving the corkscrew above his head. And his bright yellow shorts appear to be covered in mud. At least I hope it's mud."

"We should go to him," Edgar suggested, without hesitation, and proceeded to do just that, breaking into a concerned trot and moving over the terrain with the steady assurance of a mountain goat.

Try as they might, Frank and Jessie couldn't keep up, soon falling behind Edgar's sure-footed pace. "What the heck is Stan doing?" Jessie asked, once they drew a bit nearer and she could see Stan better.

"He's just stood there, like I said," Frank replied as they continued their trek. "Perhaps he's sulking for some reason?"

"He waves a corkscrew above his head when he's sulking?" asked Jessie.

"Hmm. Well, I've found that anything is possible where Stan is concerned," Frank remarked.

By the time they'd reached the foot of the slope, Edgar was

already attending to a distressed Stan. "What the actual hell?" Frank said, breaking into a laugh upon seeing the state of his friend up close.

"Are you okay, Stan?" Jessie added, struggling to stifle her own amusement. "And where's your other shoe...?"

"It's a *loafer*," Stan insisted. "And it's stuck somewhere in there," he added, pointing to a patch of boggy earth that had, by his account, laid claim to his shoe.

"But why do you look like you've been playing rugby?" Edgar asked, in reference to the collection of grass, mud, and prickly gorse covering Stan's previously pristine summer outfit.

"I tripped on a pinecone," Stan explained, gesturing to a point further up the hill. "And this is where I finally came to a halt, landing in a crumpled heap," he explained further, indicating the point substantially further down the hill where they were presently stood. "Which is why I now look like this."

"I thought you told us not to walk this way, as it looked a little swampy...?" Frank asked, playing Stan's earlier words back to him.

"Well, it was a shortcut, wasn't it?" Stan countered. "And I was worried you'd polish off the picnic without me."

"And how did that shortcut work out?" Jessie asked, raising a smile from Frank in the process.

"At least it's only mud," Frank offered, placing a sunny slant on the situation. "From up there," he said, hooking his thumb over his shoulder, "I thought that you'd had an accident."

"I have!" Stan replied, pointing to his dirtied clothes and his shoeless right foot. "Eighty quid these loafers cost me, and forty quid's worth of that is now being consumed by Mother Earth."

Stan stared mournfully to where his footwear was last seen before leaving his foot, receiving a satisfied gurgle from the sodden earth in response.

"And I was shouting for help, Frank!" Stan went on. "I saw you up there, scouring the horizon with my binoculars. I had hoped you were mounting a rescue attempt, so I started shouting up to you to reveal my position... But nothing."

"I was watching the sidecars," Frank told him. "And you think I'd hear you shouting from a quarter of a mile away over the noise of them?"

"Come on," Jessie said, eager to move things along before the bikes came round on their second lap. "There's no permanent harm done, and you appear to have recovered what you went for," she said, noting the corkscrew in Stan's hand.

"Yeah," Edgar added brightly. "A bit of sunshine will dry that mud out in no time, Stan. And I'm sure we can buy you another pair of loafers."

"You might need to give me a piggyback," Stan suggested, with his frown turning into a smile.

"Right, then," said Frank, clapping his hands together in a *let's-get-a-move-on* fashion. "Shall we?" he said, glancing at his watch. "I'm sure I've just heard the sound of an engine."

"Ah," Stan answered, delaying their departure further. "It's just that—"

"Stan. Your shoe is lost for eternity," Frank said, breaking the unfortunate news to him. "Archaeologists will probably dig it up in a thousand years, if that's any consolation."

"Ooh," Jessie said, intrigued by the thought. "They might display it in a museum. You know, behind a glass case?"

"With a tag describing it as *Loafus Soppyius Soddicus*," Frank remarked, already laughing at his own impeccable wit.

"No, it's not that," Stan protested. "Although having it in a museum would be splendid," he added, thoughts wandering off at a tangent in that direction. "No, it's not just my shoe that I appear to have lost," he added eventually, patting himself down to illustrate the point.

"Oh?" Edgar said, looking Stan up and down once again, but noting nothing obviously amiss.

"It's the..." Stan began, though tailing off as he reached the critical bit of his sentence, leaving out the most important bit of information.

"What?" Frank asked, concerned he wasn't going to like what he was about to hear. *"Out* with it, man."

"I've dropped the car keys," Stan finally revealed.

"You've dropped the car keys," Frank said, looking over to the gurgling loafer-eating bog. "Not when you fell in there...?"

"They must've fallen out of my tailored shorts when I tumbled down the hill," Stan replied, continuing to pat down his empty pockets. "I did keep hold of this, though," he said triumphantly, lifting up the corkscrew once again. "So there's that, at least."

"So we're stuck up here, then?" Jessie asked. "In the vast mountain wilderness of the Isle of Man with no way home?"

"Unless we find the keys, yes," Stan answered with a sigh. "Although I've been looking for more than ten minutes without success," he advised. "A-ha!" Stan said, suddenly sounding very pleased, and then crouching down to reach for something.

"What is it?" Frank asked, standing over him. "You've found the keys?"

"No, I thought it was my missing loafer," Stan replied. "But it was only this," he said, holding up a colourful feather he'd just collected from the long grass. "Lovely plumage."

"How can you mistake a feather for a...?" Frank began. "You know what, nevermind," he said, deciding it wasn't worth pursuing an explanation. "But this is all just marvellous," Frank added, his eyes scouring the moorland. "If we don't find those keys, we'll have to wait till late this evening before someone can bring us the spare. And that's *assuming* I can tell them where the spare set of keys are, which I haven't the foggiest."

Jessie didn't want to throw petrol on the fire, but Frank needed to know about the thought that had just occurred to her. "Darling, don't forget we're supposed to be at the theatre at half past seven," she cautiously reminded him.

Frank bit down on his bottom lip, giving Stan daggers. "Oh, for fu—"

But the sound of the sidecars off in the distance, finally coming round on their second lap, served to cut short the rest of what Frank was about to say on the matter.

"Hi. We're here to see..." Brad began, glancing down to his handwritten note. "Police Constable Wright," he declared, flashing a smile at the receptionist who held her gaze a moment longer than was necessary as she tried to place his accent.

"Ah. Canadian," she replied, reaching for her phone. "Who may I say is calling?"

"Brad and Chip Freestone," Brad answered on behalf of them both, and not feeling the need to correct the woman in regard to the nation of his birth, presently distracted, as he was, by the baby-blue eyes staring back at him. "And you are?" he asked, resting his elbows on the countertop, flashing his pearly whites.

"Trudy," replied Trudy, nibbling the tip of her pen, before returning her attention to the task at hand. "It's Trudy on the front desk," she said, speaking into the phone. "I've got Mr Freestone times two in reception for you," she announced. "Thank you, I'll do just that," she said to the person on the other end, replacing the handset a moment later. "If you could both sign the visitors' book and then take a seat over there, and she'll be out to see you soon," Trudy told Brad.

"Typical," Chip moaned, walking towards the bench seat at the rear of the reception area once they'd signed the visitors book as instructed. "We're identical twins, and yet there's the pretty receptionist falling all over you like you're the freakin' messiah or something while I don't get hardly a second glance. And fercryinoutloud, doesn't anybody on this island know the difference between Canadians and Americans?"

"You should take it as a compliment," Brad advised.

"I should?" Chip asked, looking suspiciously at the mysterious staining where he was about to park his rear end.

"Of course you should," Brad replied. "We're twins, right? So if Trudy looks at me and likes what she sees, that means she must also like you."

"Right..." Chip answered, sounding unconvinced by the logic of this supposition. "So, why didn't she look over at me? It was like I didn't even exist."

"She's efficient," Brad put forth. "By only looking at me, she cuts her workload down by fifty percent, therefore saving herself time!" he proposed.

"What's that smell?" Chip asked, switching off from his brother's ramblings and changing the subject.

Brad flared his nostrils. "Dunno," he replied, gagging when the unpleasant scent caught the back of his throat. "It's like when an overfilled trashcan full of rotting garbage has been sitting in the sun for too long."

Chip shifted uncomfortably in his seat, giving the stain on the bench beside him another worried glance. Aside from the slight discolouring there, the place looked clean enough, for the most part. But the reception area at police HQ had no doubt seen its fair share of unsavoury characters parading through, judging by the pungent odour hanging in the air.

But before Chip could dwell on this too much longer, the door signposted as 'Custody Suite' opened, and a uniformed officer appeared from behind it. "I'm PC Wright," she said, giving them a genial smile. "If you'd like to come through?"

Brad and Chip followed the constable through a maze of corridors, swopping nervous small talk with her along the way. Even though they were both invited guests, it was difficult to shake irrational feelings of guilt while being in a police station.

"Here we are," PC Wright said eventually, opening the door to an interview room. "Please, take a seat."

Brad and Chip did as directed, though Chip couldn't stop himself from investigating the surface first, wondering who might have sat in the plastic chair before him and what kind of condition they'd possibly been in.

"So," said PC Wright, taking a seat across the table from them. "Firstly, can I once again offer our apologies that you were the victims of crime while visiting our little island."

"It could happen anywhere," Chip offered magnanimously, despite the fact they were discussing something that had very nearly cut their burgeoning careers short. "Back home, the thieves would've probably also taken the car, *and* shot us both to death as well," he pointed out with a laugh, though only half-joking, actually.

"I... see..." PC Wright replied, before swiftly moving on. "So, as I explained over the phone, gentlemen, we made a public appeal for information, and I'm pleased to report that we've succeeded in securing some dashcam footage of the incident in question."

"Ah! Nice!" Brad said, leaning forward in his chair, eager to learn more.

The constable reached down and produced an iPad from her effects. "I must apologise right up front, as the footage is a little grainy and not the best quality," she told them, managing their expectations in advance. "Here," she said, loading the footage and then sliding the iPad across the table. "It's not ideal, but at least it's a lead we can work on."

"That's our rental car," said Chip, pointing to the screen. He and Brad watched on as a black motorbike pulled in alongside of it at the car park, coming to a stop. The rider dismounted, looking about them suspiciously, and then walked around the vehicle while stealing periodic, furtive glances inside.

"Do they ever take the helmet off?" Brad asked, receiving a negative shake of the head in response.

"And there's no number plate on the bike," Chip remarked. "Where's the number plate?"

"Unfortunately, it's not there," PC Wright answered. "We suspect they must have removed it beforehand in order to avoid being identified. Which, in this case, worked as planned."

The relevant portion of the footage concluded when it was clear the dash-mounted camera recording it had continued past, the area no longer in view as the car filming the scene moved along its intended path.

"That's it?" a dejected Brad asked, disappointed at the brevity of the clip, and looking up from the screen. "There's no more?"

"That's it. However, we are reviewing all available CCTV footage in the area, and so remain optimistic," PC Wright advised, reaching over and retrieving the iPad. "Anyway, I don't suppose the footage jogs your memory at all? For instance, perhaps you saw the motorbike in the vicinity before the theft?"

"No," Brad replied blankly, followed by a similar dejected response from Chip.

Disappointed by their largely fruitless trip to the police station, and that this was the only reason they'd been called in, Brad and Chip followed PC Wright as she escorted them back out to the reception area. "We'll keep on the case," she assured them, offering a confident smile before returning to her duties.

"Everything okay?" Trudy asked from behind the reception desk, noticing the look on their faces.

"Not really, no," Chip answered. "We hoped to get our laptop and cameras back, but no luck."

"Don't get the wrong idea," Brad entered in. "They weren't confiscated," he was quick to point out, laughing nervously. "I mean, the police didn't take them for evidence, or anything like that," he clarified. "They were stolen. As in stolen by thieves. Not seized by the police. And that's why we..." he said, trailing off, worried he was starting to look like a fool now.

"Oh-kay," replied Trudy, her demeanour turning decidedly more guarded. "If you'd like to sign out before you leave?" she suggested, pointing to the register, and then suddenly finding something very interesting there on her desk to occupy herself with while they complied.

"I don't suppose... you know..." Brad said, leaning over the desk and turning on the charm. "That is, I wondered if you'd like to—?"

"No. But thanks," Trudy replied curtly, lifting her head just long enough to deliver what looked to be a very insincere smile, cutting him off mid-flow.

Outside in the evening sun, Brad kicked his brother in the ankle.

"Ow! What the hell! That hurt!" Chip said.

"She was totally going to give me her phone number until you started babbling on about having our laptop seized and stuff," Brad insisted.

"Me? *You're* the one who said that," Chip protested.

"Well that's what it must have sounded like. Because there she was, looking at me like I was some kind of creep or something," Brad complained. "What a complete waste of time that was," he added with a sigh.

"Not *entirely* a waste of time," Chip suggested, rubbing his hands together.

"Are you taking pleasure in me striking out back there?" asked Brad. "Is that what that stupid grin is for?"

"No. I mean, partially. But no, it's not just that."

"Then, what?"

"You didn't recognise who that was on the motorcycle?"

"What, you mean the person dressed all in black, with a blacked-out visor, captured on a dashcam that looked like the lens hadn't been cleaned in years?" said Brad. "No, I can't say I did recognise the person."

Chip sensed a distinct element of sarcasm in his brother's response, which he didn't let bother him in the slightest. "I think I know who it was," Chip said, eyes sparkling.

"What do you mean? How could you possibly know?" Brad answered, his brow furrowed. "And why didn't you say anything before?"

"It didn't hit me until just now," Chip replied. "The person riding the bike wasn't wearing gloves."

"So what?" Brad said, though, in fairness, this was a point he'd not picked up on himself. Still, he didn't understand how it could be in any way relevant.

"*So,*" Chip replied, pausing for a long moment to build up the suspense before continuing. "So, even though the image quality wasn't that great, I'm pretty sure I could still make out a fairly distinctive mark on the back of the thief's left hand, even from a bit of a distance," he said, hoping for an enthusiastic reaction that didn't arrive. "A black mark, dear brother," Chip pressed on, fluttering his eyebrows in an excited flurry of flapping. "That, if I'm not mistaken, is a *tattoo*," he continued. "And one I think

I recognise."

"Okay," said Brad, raising his own eyebrows in response, interest now piqued. "But you didn't think this was important enough to mention to the cops a few minutes ago? When she asked us if the video jogged any memories?"

"It didn't click in my head right away, like I said before," Chip answered. "Besides, I've got a much better idea," he said.

"Better than telling the police? You're making no sense whatsoever, *dear brother*," Brad told him, using the same affectionate form of address his brother had just used a moment ago. "And if you think you know who stole our stuff, then who the hell was it?"

"Well," Chip began, running his tongue over his top lip in anticipation of what he was about to say. "It was—"

"Mr Freestone!" someone called over, from just outside the police station.

Brad and Chip, each of them having the same surname, of course, both turned in response, seeing Trudy.

"You forgot this!" said Trudy, waving a small piece of paper, and then skipping down the police station steps.

"What? I don't think I forgot anything. What's this...?" Brad asked, taking receipt of the hand delivery thrust promptly in his direction.

"That's my number," Trudy explained.

"But I thought—?" Brad began.

"PC Wright confirmed to me that you weren't a criminal or any sort of pervert," Trudy was happy to report. "Call me!" she said, raising her thumb and pinkie to the side of her face in the universal *give-me-a-ring-sometime* signal, before then turning round and heading back inside.

Brad stood with a simple smile on his face, looking lovingly at the now-empty steps. "And you thought I'd lost my touch," he said, turning to Chip after a moment and shaking the piece of paper in his hand in triumph. "Once you've got it, you never lose it, my friend," a very pleased with himself Brad declared. "Not ever."

Chapter
SIXTEEN

Stan limped through the kitchen area of his and Frank's house, exaggerated whimpering noises emanating from him each time anybody cared to look his way due to the fuss he was making.

"Ehm, you okay there, Stan?" Monty asked, taking hold of the toast that'd just popped up from the toaster.

"Me?" said Stan, wincing as he came to a halt, turning to face the inquisitive Monty.

"Oh, don't set him off again," Dave joked, already tucking into his breakfast at the kitchen table.

"Well I don't really like to talk about it," Stan advised, even as he prepared to do precisely that. "Likely third-degree burns, the medical staff said," he explained valiantly. "They even told me I must have an exceptional tolerance for pain," he added with a sniff.

"Medical staff?" Dave scoffed, once the contents of his mouth had passed down his gullet. "You told me earlier that you had Ivan at the back of the grandstand check you over."

"Ivan from the hotdog stand?" Monty enquired, butter knife held at the ready. "I do like his hotdogs, but..."

"Yes, Ivan from the hotdog stand," Stan confirmed. "Ivan has several first aid certificates from St John's Ambulance, I'll have you know. And what Ivan doesn't know about medicine isn't worth knowing."

"Ah, is that so," Dave replied. "Well if that's the case, then what's he doing running a food stall that failed its last several food hygiene certifications? Did he somehow just get bored of medicine and settled for running a dodgy hotdog stand?"

"Wait, hang on, so what part of you was subjected to third-degree burns?" Monty interjected, anxious to hear more about whatever was presently ailing Stan, as he could see no evidence of said burns, although he did remain sympathetic.

Stan, very gingerly, removed his left foot from his slipper for Monty's inspection. "This," Stan moaned, eyes falling on the slightly reddened (that is, *very* slightly reddened) skin covering the top of his foot. "Agony," he added, succinctly.

"It does look a *bit* red, maybe...?" Monty offered, appearing thoroughly disappointed by the minor nature of Stan's medical mishap. *"Anyway,"* Monty said with finality, bringing his plate of toast over to the table, and turning the focus of his attention back over to his grumbling tum.

"I lost one of my new loafers, along with my sock as well," Stan explained, despite no further explanation being requested at this point. "So I ended up wandering around the hillside, half barefoot, for over three hours!"

"When you were looking for the car keys?" Monty responded, having been kept abreast of the unfortunate incident from the day before.

"Bloody hell, is he still harping on about his foot?" Frank asked, entering the room and marching over to the kettle.

"I think I can see a blister," Stan remarked, foot poised in the air in case there was any further interest shown, which sadly for him there was not.

Frank shook his head dismissively, letting out an exasperated sigh (his bedside manner being somewhat lacking). "So, have you told these two yet why we missed the majority of their epic race?" he asked.

"They already know," Stan replied, carefully sliding his foot back into the soft, protective casing of his slipper.

"Three hours we were looking for those blasted keys," Frank

commented. "We must have scoured every single blade of grass in the area amidst searing heat."

"And that's how I fell victim to my injury!" Stan offered up. "Barefoot in the crippling heat!"

"You found them, though, right?" Monty asked, hoping to bring this story to an expeditious conclusion. "I mean, judging by the car being parked outside when I arrived a few minutes ago, I'd say you must have," he remarked.

Frank shot Stan a look, and then turned to reply to Monty. "Well..." he said, pausing, the unpleasantness of the prior day's fiasco still fresh in his mind. "Well, eventually, after three long hours, we decided to call the recovery truck to tow us home. Unfortunately, as one might expect, they could only come out after the roads had reopened post-race... meaning the fee would go up to double-time evening rates, naturally."

"But they did get you on your way, yeah?" Monty replied, attempting for a second time to draw the discussion to a close. "You know, what with the car being outside and all."

"Stan, do you want to finish up?" Frank asked, pursing his lips.

Stan reluctantly obliged. "The recovery man was excellent," Stan recalled. "For a modest fee of only four hundred quid, he was able to gain access to the car, once he arrived, in a matter of mere seconds. Which is good value for services rendered, if you ask me."

"In a matter of seconds?" Dave said, amazed. "Who was it, Harry Houdini?"

"No," Stan advised. "He was just a professional, and knew what he was—"

"Stan had left the keys lying on the roof of the car all along," Frank cut in. "It's the one place that none of us thought to look because, I mean, why would we? So we all wandered back over to where the car was parked, delighted to see Tommy, the tow truck man, as he pulled up to rescue us. And that's when old Tommy spotted the keys lying right there on the roof of the car. He took the keys, unlocked the door for us, and then that was

FRANK & STAN'S BUCKET LIST #5: ISLE OF MAN TT ACES

that. All for the princely sum of four hundred quid."

"I thought they'd fallen out of my pocket when I took what was a very nasty fall!" Stan protested, wincing once again, hoping to attract the sympathy vote. "It was an easy mistake that any one of us could make."

Frank's stern expression softened. "It *was* pretty funny, I suppose. Not funny *at the time* funny, but funny when you look back on it funny," he said. Frank then reached into his pocket, retrieving and then throwing a small item in Stan's direction.

"The chemist was open?" Stan asked, deftly catching the article in question.

"Not the first, this early in the morning, nor the second or third one I went to," Frank advised. "But I pressed on, knowing my pal was in at least a moderate amount of discomfort."

"Ah!" Stan said excitedly, kicking off his slipper and taking a seat, staring lovingly at the tube of Savlon antiseptic cream now in hand.

"I'm not rubbing it in for you, though, so don't even think about it," Frank joked. "My friendship only extends so far."

"Ahhh," said Stan, moaning in relief. "It's like pouring cold water on a hot fire," he declared, massaging the soothing salve into his mildly pinker-than-usual skin.

With Frank and Stan's house only a short walk from the racing paddock, Dave and Monty were both regular visitors. Even though the pair were ostensibly roughing it by camping in their van/awning, it didn't stop them sauntering over periodically — for breakfast, lunch, toilet breaks, showers, internet access, washing of their clothes, and catching up on the happenings on Coronation Street, amongst other things. In fact, even though they were technically camping to immerse themselves in the overall TT experience, Frank and Stan had never seen so much of the boys. In other words, their visits weren't strictly periodic as much as they were constant.

"Finishing in fourteenth place?" Frank said with a proud smile, in response to what Dave had just informed him. "That's deeply impressive," he added, raising his freshly-brewed mug of tea to toast the two of them.

"Even if you did miss most of it," Monty commented, ripping the plaster off that particular wound once again.

"We did see you leaving another bike for dust coming out of the Bungalow section," Frank added, with an appreciative nod.

Dave raised his mug as well. "The old girl was like a rocket ship, alright. There was more in the tank, too," he said.

"Yeah?" Stan asked, wiping the excess cream on his hand onto his forehead, for good measure, even though his forehead didn't really seem in any way pinker than usual. "You reckon she could go quicker?"

"If we were able to keep hanging onto her, yeah!" Dave said with a laugh. "That new upgrade is a game-changer, that's for certain."

"After the day's race, Mike plugged the bike into his laptop," Monty explained. "And the sheer amount of data and analytics he was able to gather was a wonder to behold."

"Yep," Dave agreed. "He was like a schoolteacher marking our homework. He told us which corners we rolled off prematurely, improvements we can make to the setup, and even showed us the optimum approach angle for specific corners and such by virtue of the item's GPS."

"Wait, hang on. Are you talking about the MoTeC device?" Stan asked. "I thought it was just an ignition system...?"

"Ah, it's much more than that," Dave advised. "It records a whole shedload of useful information."

"Wow," said Stan.

"Yep. And Mike was helping us interpret all that data. That boy is worth his weight in gold," Dave replied.

"But he's already gone home on the ferry by now?" Frank asked, recalling an earlier conversation about Mike's imminent departure.

"Yes, sadly," Dave answered, nodding his head mournfully. "But before he went, he did spend some time with us making last-minute adjustments, and then gave us instruction as to how to interpret the data in order to hopefully improve our lap times even further."

"Ah. At least you can pull that data off for yourselves now," Stan remarked. "So that's a bonus, yeah?"

Dave was amused at the idea of Monty and himself hunched over a laptop, extrapolating reams of complex data for detailed analysis. "Not a bloody chance," he said with a chuckle, raising a laugh from Monty as well. "What Mike told us went into one earhole and right out the other."

"In one and out the other," Monty cheerfully agreed. "You may as well have placed us in the cockpit of a spaceship," he added. "Lights flashing, fancy graphs, and calculations coming out from every direction?" he said, running the palm of his hand over his head and accompanying it with a *whoosh* sound effect. "That Mike must be the love child of Bill Gates and Mark Zuckerberg the way his brain works."

"So you've got this all-singing, all-dancing upgrade, but you don't really know what you're doing with it?" Stan asked.

"Not one single clue," Dave confirmed. "He's left us with an instruction manual the size of an encyclopaedia, but it was really dull, so we just ended up using it to prop up one short leg of a table there in our awning. Besides, Mike's already got the bike running a treat, so we'll just leave things as he left them."

"And we're probably just going to sell the new equipment after this year's TT concludes anyway," Monty explained. "The only reason we upgraded in the first place was to try and win that sponsorship cash. And with that no longer on offer, we don't really need all that technology going forward. We'll be happy with the old girl back as she was."

"It's worth selling just so we don't have to read that manual," Dave added, yawning like a tired hippo.

Monty stood up to bring his now-empty plate to the kitchen sink, and pulled his phone from out of his pocket when he felt it buzzing. "That's odd," he said, glancing at the screen, then to Dave, and then back at the screen. "Why on earth does Gloria want to see me?" he asked with a shrug, wandering out of the kitchen and in towards the living room. "And why the hell is she referring to me as Sugar Tits?" he wondered aloud, moving the phone closer to his one good eye to confirm he was seeing what he thought he was seeing.

"Who's Gloria?" Frank asked of Dave.

"Dunno?" said Dave, the name not ringing any immediate bells. "Oh, wait," he said a second later, a thought occurring to him. "Oh, shit," he added with a wicked laugh.

"Dave...?" Stan pressed, wondering what the evil laugh was all about.

"It's *Gloria*," Dave whispered. "The catering lady from over at the racetrack," he explained with a snigger.

"Okay?" said Stan, not really understanding why this would present an issue for Monty.

"Well, it turns out old Gloria is filthier than a coalman's fingernails," Dave explained, with a mirthful grin. "After I rebuffed her overly enthusiastic advances, I just *may* have indicated to her that Monty was single and ready to mingle."

"Even though he's obviously not?" Frank asked.

"Even though he's obviously not," Dave confirmed. "Ahh," Dave went on, smiling at the scene unfolding in his head of a hapless Monty confronted by an exceedingly randy and ready-for-action Gloria. "What?" he then asked, noting the two looks of disappointment and disapproval aimed in his direction.

"You're going to warn him?" Stan asked, though suspecting he already knew the answer to his question.

"Am I buggery," Dave shot back. "We all know he'd do precisely the same thing to me given half the chance."

"True," Frank conceded.

"Totally fair," Stan agreed.

Dave and Monty found themselves with a fair bit of spare time on their hands, as could often be the case between races. Ordinarily, the boys would fill some of this time tinkering with the bike, adjusting this or tuning that. However, they now had no cause to tamper with the bike as Mike the Mechanic had left it in a better condition than they could ever achieve. So, with the next race not until the following Friday (on Senior Race Day) and no documentary work with Chip and Brad to occupy them, they could kick back, relax a little and absorb themselves in the TT atmosphere. Also, the respite should give the two of them ample opportunity to scrutinise the data provided to them by Mike the Mechanic, if they were so inclined. It would absolutely be time well spent, as the long hours used poring over the technical analysis could definitely serve to shave vital seconds off their lap times. Thus, for two elite racers such as Dave Quirk and Monty Montgomery, it was an opportunity most certain to be taken advantage of...

"Would you rather live in Oz, or Gotham City?" Monty asked, laying there stretched out on the grass, leisurely enjoying the late afternoon sun warming his skin.

"You mean Oz as in Australia? Or Oz as in the Land of Oz?" Dave replied, lying on the grass as well, near to Monty.

"Yeah, the Land of Oz," Monty replied.

"Ah. It's funny you should ask, then, as Becks had only just mentioned Kansas the other day," Dave answered. "I dunno," he went on, turning over and pushing himself up on his elbows so he was looking down at Monty. "Hmm, I'd say there's probably going to be too much crime in Gotham City for my liking," he mused, giving Monty's question the type of serious consideration it fully deserved. "Plus, I did always have a thing for Glinda when I was younger. So, on reflection, I'd go for Oz, I reckon."

"The green one with the big nose?" a shocked Monty asked, pushing himself up as well, and looking over to Dave.

"No, you big lummox! Although, if I'd had a few pints..." said Dave, giving the idea a brief moment of thought. "No, mate. Glinda is the *good* one," Dave clarified a moment later, lest there be any doubt as to which witch he'd once harboured adolescent feelings for, making his trousers tight as a teen.

"Are you saying you can't be good, *and* green, at the same time?" Monty asked. "Because I'm not sure I follow your logic."

Dave was just about to answer Monty's ridiculous question,

when suddenly a figure stood over them, blocking the sun's rays from bronzing their two topless torsos. "Oi!" Dave said to the interloper. "You're creating a shadow!"

To be fair to the person standing over them and creating the unexpected eclipse, Dave and Monty were sprawled out on one of the main, common areas of the paddock, and one that was perfectly open to foot traffic. It was also an area that enjoyed a steady supply of uninterrupted sunlight. At least until now, that is.

"I've been looking for you two for bloody ages," the breathless figure above them now said.

"We've not gone too far, Spanky," Dave suggested to their friend and fellow Manx racer, Spanky McFarlane, recognising the voice of the person looming over them. "That's our awning right over there," Dave said, pointing to the awning only a very short distance from their current location. "And here we are, not even a stone's throw away."

"We gradually move down the length of the path to follow the sun," Monty explained helpfully. "If you'd appeared in an hour, we'd be all the way down there, by the perimeter fence."

"Right," a flustered Spanky said, positioning himself by their feet so he could talk to them without them appearing upside down, and so he wasn't backlit by the sun, with them shielding their eyes and trying to get a look at his face. "Right, lads. I have news. *Important* news," he announced dramatically.

"Oh?" Monty said, sounding interested now, and wondering what good (or possibly bad) tidings Spanky might have come to deliver. "Spit it out, Spanks."

Spanky pointed in the general direction of where he'd arrived from. "Okay, so you know this international documentary series you were telling me about before? The one for the telly?"

"Yeah," said Dave, inspecting his sweat-soaked navel and plucking out a few blades of grass that had somehow managed to find themselves a home there. "What about it?"

"Well, I don't quite know how to break this to you," Spanky told them, the poor chap appearing on the verge of tears. "But

FRANK & STAN'S BUCKET LIST #5: ISLE OF MAN TT ACES

I've just heard you've both been dropped from the project. And as if that weren't bad enough in itself, those two giant nits you don't like, Napier and Thomas, have both been signed up in your place!"

"I'm shocked..." Monty commented.

"I *know*, right?" Spanky offered sympathetically. "I came to tell you the instant I heard, which is why I'm out of breath from running all over the paddock looking for you!"

"But why would you run all over the paddock?" Dave asked, slightly puzzled. "Why wouldn't you just come straight here, to our awning?"

"I'm shocked," Monty commented again, repeating his remark from a moment ago. "Shocked that it's taken you this long to find out, that is," he clarified, reaching casually for his vintage 1980's Sony Walkman. "We do appreciate your concern, though, Spanks. It's nice to know you've got our backs," he said, popping his earphones on. "Anyway, I've got Kylie Minogue's greatest hits to listen to, and about another good half hour or so of sunshine left to enjoy," he advised, pointing to his ears.

And with that, Monty settled himself down again, lying on his back, getting comfortable on the grass once more.

"Anything else for us, Spanky?" Dave enquired. "What with you being the man with his finger on the paddock's pulse?"

"Nah," Spanky said, disappointed his investigatory prowess hadn't invoked the sort of astonished reaction he'd imagined, and unhappy he didn't have any additional knowledge he could perhaps impart. And then another snippet of information presented itself to him, wandering its way up to the front portion of his brain. "Oh, by the way, I was up at Jurby taking in a few laps just the other day, and guess what," he said.

"What?" asked Dave.

"You know old Gloria?" Spanky said, lowering his voice a smidge. "The one with the wandering hands," he added, in case there was any confusion.

"Yeah?" Dave said, suddenly liking where this conversation was going. "What about her?"

"Well, she was asking about Monty," Spanky informed Dave, glancing over at Monty, who lay with his foot tapping to a beat heard only by him, oblivious to all else.

"And?" Dave pressed, eager to hear more. "What did she say?"

"Quite a bit, actually," Spanky answered, scratching his nose as he tried to recall all of the details. "But the overall theme, at any rate, was that she intended to ride our Monty here like a Harley-Davidson. Low and slow, she said, as I recall."

"What's that?" Monty asked, freeing one ear, fairly certain he'd just heard his name but not entirely sure. "Were you speaking to me, by any chance?" he asked, looking first to Spanky, and then to Dave.

"No, mate," Dave immediately replied. "You get yourself back to Kylie, and tell her I said hello," Dave advised. And then, once Monty had resumed listening to his music, Dave quickly used his heels to drag himself a little further away, sliding along the grass like a dog scratching its arse on the carpet. "Ah, hell, this is perhaps getting out of hand," he muttered to himself. "I think I'll maybe need to have a quiet word with that frisky old goat."

Dave then extended his hand to Spanky. "Pull me up, buddy, would you?" he said. "Any other gossip for us?" he asked. "Shall I put the kettle on?"

"Yes. Yes, there *is* something else, now you mention it," replied Spanky, following Dave inside the awning for the promise of a cuppa.

"Oh? Is there?" Dave said, passing a packet of lovely HobNob biscuits over in Spanky's direction. "You're on a roll today, my old son."

Spanky glanced over his shoulder, before leaning in close to Dave. "Napier and Thomas, yeah?" he said.

"Yeah," replied Dave.

"I overheard them talking about you lot. And I don't mean about the documentary TV thingy," Spanky told him.

"Saying what?"

"They said..." Spanky went on, taking another quick, cautionary glance over his shoulder. "What they said was that Team

FRANK & STAN'S BUCKET LIST #5: ISLE OF MAN TT ACES

Frank and Stan were in for another pleasant surprise. And an expensive one, at that, one that would really piss them off."

Spanky held his gaze as Dave digested his words. All that was missing was a dramatic crack of thunder, accompanied by a flash of lightning.

"And I don't think they were sincere when they said *pleasant*," Spanky felt the need to clarify, tapping the side of his nose like he was privy to the inside track.

"Ah, those two tosspots couldn't knock the skin off a rice pudding," Dave suggested, dismissing Spanky's concerns and returning his attention to making their cuppa. "There's nought those two could do that would interest us."

"Yeah, but they were talking to Mike the Mechanic at the time," Spanky added promptly, sensing he was quickly losing his audience. "Mike, who's been working on your bike," Spanky reminded him. "It all smells a bit fishy to me."

"Mike the Mechanic, you say?" Dave answered, setting their freshly brewed tea on the table and having a seat, reflecting on what he'd just been told. "Mike the Mechanic," he said again, his soft expression hardening. "You don't think they'd use Mike to sabotage our bike, do you? I mean, they wouldn't seriously sink that low, would they?"

"Oh, I never thought of that," Spanky replied, shaking his head in wonder.

"You didn't?" Dave asked, incredulous. "Well what were you implying just then, when you...?" he began. "In fact, don't worry about it," he said, deciding it wasn't worth it. Spanky may have had his ear to the ground, but the sharpest tool in the box, he was not. "That's not good news, Spanky," Dave observed, picking up his teaspoon and stirring his tea. "Not good news at all."

"How so?" Spanky asked vacantly, still yet to catch up.

Dave allowed Spanky a few more seconds, but it was no use, as Dave likely would have spent the entire rest of the day waiting. "Because, Spanky," Dave explained slowly. "If those two nitwits, Napier and Thomas, wanted to ruin our TT, then throwing a snake into our tent would be the perfect ploy."

"Oh, yeah!" Spanky said, absolutely horrified at what he was hearing, as he truly hated snakes.

"You don't know what I mean, Spanky. Do you?" Dave asked.

"Not really," Spanky confirmed. "Biscuit?" he asked, ripping open the packet of delicious HobNobs.

Chapter
SEVENTEEN

The Isle of Man basked in Mediterranean-like weather over the next several days, resulting in exceptional conditions for racing and spectating alike.

In the warm evenings, the streets were packed to the gills with punters soaking up the various organised entertainment and wandering around to each of the local watering holes, all with grins as wide as their faces. With many having arrived on bikes, motorcycles were parked up wherever you looked, filling every available parking space, and even then, spilling over onto the pavements as well. It was a delight to observe bikers fawning over both modern machinery and classic bikes, with such classics likely having adorned many a bedroom wall back in the formative years of these motorsport enthusiasts.

There was no trouble to speak of, no fights, and no arguing other than to decide whose round it was next. Watching the races by day, and socialising by night with like-minded motorsport devotees. It was heaven. Washing down a greasy burger with a beakerful of beer, then heading over to the fairground to bring it all back up again on the spinning Waltzer rides.

It was these wonderful times that visitors to this charming little rock remembered, and it was these experiences that made it difficult not to return year after year. Sure, there were occasions when your camping tent was in danger of washing clean away in a rainstorm. But that didn't matter. Not really. When you reluctantly headed home on the ferry, the negatives were already forgotten. The memories that remained were much more likely to be you, in the sunshine, there at the side of the road, watching your heroes racing by mere inches from where you sat in the grass. Sharing a pint with friends you'd just met. Friends that would, like you, head home with a sense of disappointment that it was over for another year, yet filled with exhilaration knowing that it was just shy of one year until you'd be heading back to the Isle of Man to do it all over again. And it couldn't come quick enough.

Despite the current, marvellous weather conditions and such, there were, however, two fellows with the name of Grumpy Gus over at race HQ at present. The sidecar which Dave and Monty had previously been perfectly content to leave untouched was now stripped, with pieces lying all over the floor of their awning like the contents of an upturned Lego box. Twice that week they'd driven up to Jurby to put the bike through its paces, hoping to discover if they'd been the victims of sabotage. But as far as they could see, there was nothing amiss. So why had Napier and Thomas laughed with Mike the Mechanic about some supposed unpleasant surprise that was due to befall Team Frank & Stan? It was torture suspecting something was afoot but not being able to figure out what it was. Especially when the next race was less than forty-eight hours away.

Dave was all for marching up to Thomas and Napier's workshop and asking them outright, using a pair of heavy-duty pliers to extract the information from them, removing a fingernail or three during the procedure. But as Monty, the voice of reason, was quick to point out, they only really had Spanky's third-hand account to go on. And as far as credible witnesses went, he was, without being unkind, perhaps not the most reliable of sources. In addition, they'd not as yet found anything untoward with the bike.

"Maybe you're right," Dave conceded. "What if it's all a big ruse?" he said, looking wearily at all the mechanical bits they needed to reassemble. "Imagine if Napier and Thomas happened to see Spanky wandering in their direction and decided to just make some flippant remark about us for a laugh, knowing he'd likely repeat it to us."

"Yeah, that's what I'm saying," Monty answered. "They know as well as we do that old Spanks is the nosiest git around the paddock, and that their comments would inevitably reach our ears in no time at all."

"It's genius, now I think about it," Dave said, reflecting on that scenario. "Just by uttering a few words, they've had us running around in a state of paranoia, spending hours in a panic stripping down a bike that was running perfectly in the first place."

"But why?" Monty asked. "Why would they bother with us, I mean?"

"Because they're a couple of cockwombles," Dave replied, in absence of anything more specific to go on.

"They could be jealous of our good looks and athletic prowess?" Monty proposed.

"There's that as well," Dave was only too happy to agree. "Aagh," he quickly added, a short moment later. "But what if they *have* done something? In fact, what if their bluff is really a *double*-bluff?"

Dave then lurched forward, reclaiming the set of pliers resting on the workbench. "That's it. There's only one way to know for sure," he declared, heading for the doorway at pace.

"No, no, Dave!" Monty said, grabbing him by the shoulder, preventing his departure. "Relax, mate. Breathe," he instructed. "Remember what Brad told us he'd learned at his yoga class? Breathe in through the mouth, and out through the nose. Or, erm... was it the other way around?"

"I know how to bloody breathe, Monty," Dave insisted, large pliers still in hand. "But the same won't be said for that pair of twits Thomas and Napier by the time I've finished with them."

Monty tightened his grip, but trying to contain Big Dave whilst on a mission was like wrestling a water buffalo covered in oil. There was nothing that could stop Dave once he'd made up his mind, and so out the door he went...

"Gloria!" Dave said, once outside the awning, drawing to an immediate halt.

Dave *could* be stopped in his tracks, apparently. And all it took was a frisky pensioner wearing a ridiculously low-cut top and a matching leopardskin-print skirt.

"That's a very big tool indeed," Gloria remarked, spotting the outsized set of pliers in Dave's right paw. "You're not going to give me a good going-over, are you?" she joked.

"No, Gloria. No, I'm not," Dave replied, with a polite smile. "Just passing, are you?" he asked, flicking his head in the direction he hoped she was heading. That direction being away from their awning.

"Relax, you," Gloria said, attempting to look past Dave's hulking frame. "You had your chance, butterballs. And you blew it."

"*Anyway*," said Dave, glancing down to the watch he wasn't wearing, hoping it would expedite matters.

"Where's Monty?" Gloria asked, undeterred. "Is he in there?" she said, trying once again to look beyond Dave.

"Look, Gloria," Dave said impatiently, dispensing with his usual charm. "We really don't have the time to deal with your... your, ehm... rampant libido, just now."

Right then, Monty appeared from the awning, hoping for a second attempt at protecting Dave from an impending assault charge. "Oh! Gloria!" he said, upon seeing their guest. "You're looking..." he added, searching for an appropriate word to use, but failing miserably.

But before Gloria had a chance to say anything in response, Dave turned to face Monty, taking a step closer so that he was in clear violation of Monty's personal space. Monty looked up at him, fearing something was about to happen but not sure why, and uncertain as to what to do about it.

"We can't hide it, Monty," Dave implored, moving in even closer and scooping Monty up in his arms.

"Em... what? How's that?" a panicked Monty enquired.

"Don't worry, that's just a very long spanner in my pocket,"

Dave advised, only a second before placing his lips firmly but tenderly against Monty's own.

Monty tried to protest, but his speaking hole was obstructed by Dave's mush presently being mashed into his. *"Erlmf!"* was all Monty could manage, through occupied lips, startled, his wide eyes conveying his sense of shock.

Dave continued with the lingering smooch for several extended seconds. Several seconds which must have felt like all but an eternity for Monty.

"You see, Gloria," Dave concluded, wiping the saliva from about his mouth once he'd eventually severed his and Monty's intimate connection, "Monty and I are both off-limits to you, forbidden fruit, as it were, as we only have eyes for each other. So I'll thank you to keep your hands off my man, if you please."

Dave then punctuated his performance by reaching for and giving Monty's bum a gentle squeeze.

Gloria, for her part, started to laugh. "Thanks for the show. But I only came to apologise to Monty," she explained. "Once he told me he was happily married, I agreed to lay off the saucy text messages and stop with the nude pictures," she advised. "As I was passing, I thought I'd say sorry in person and clear the air. And I'm glad I did, as I wouldn't have missed that presentation of yours for anything."

"Oh," said Dave. "Oh," he said again. "I, ehm... I thought you were here to proposition Monty or something, no...?"

"Not at all," Gloria said with a cackle. "And on that note, I think I'll leave you two fun boys to get on with whatever you'd like to get on with," she added, breaking into another chortle.

Dave and Monty watched on as Gloria wandered off through the paddock, her high heels digging into the soft turf, sending her careening off balance with every step.

"Sorry about that, mate," Dave said, turning his attention over to Monty. "I was just trying to protect you from that one's unwanted advances, and it's the only thing I could think to do," he explained. "Although, one question, if I may?"

Monty nodded, appearing dazed and still in a state of temporary shock.

"When I kissed you, just then. Did you really need to use your tongue?" Dave asked. "I mean, really?"

"Ah. Sorry. It's an automatic reaction, I suppose. I couldn't help myself, could I?" Monty replied with a shrug. "And you know what?"

"What?" asked Dave.

"Becks is a very fortunate girl," Monty said with a wink. "If you kiss her with only half as much passion, then you must be a very kind and generous lover."

"Yeah. Let's never speak of this moment again, Monty, shall we?" Dave answered.

"Fine," Monty agreed. "But... can we just hold hands for a little while?" he asked, fluttering his eyelashes.

"No, Monty. No, we can't."

"How about a cuddle...?"

Burning the candle at both ends that week were the industrious yet sleep-deprived Brad and Chip. Altering the focus of their docuseries wasn't ideal, as they had to reshoot hours and hours of footage in order to make sure the narrative of their story flowed properly. A further challenge to their creative process was the requirement to now work with Team Rodney Franks. As 'stars' of the show, Andy Thomas and Jack Napier were eager to scrutinise each shot, ensuring that the camera captured just the right angle like the couple of jumped-up prima donnas they were. And, if the shot wasn't to Thomas and Napier's precise satisfaction, the pair would insist it was redone until it was just so. The other major issue was that the camera didn't really like them, and the camera wasn't alone in that fact. In other words, they didn't come across as a team you were rooting for or hoped would succeed. Rather, they came off as a couple of arrogant tosspots, strutting around like they owned the place.

As for Rodney Franks himself, well, he was no better, and was in fact proving himself to be a complete pain in the backside. It was easy to see where his riders picked up their irritating ways (or, it could just as easily have been a case of like attracting like). From the get-go, Rodney revealed himself to be a rude, condescending, and offensive little prat. It was clear his required outcome from this vanity project was purely to promote his business interests, with less-than-subtle product placements in every shot that he was involved in. And never had Brad and Chip witnessed one man with the unique ability to irritate and annoy every person he came into contact with and accomplish the task with such consummate ease and apparent pleasure. He was a master at it.

For Chip and Brad, it was turning out to be a genuinely soul-destroying experience. Their dreams of creating a gripping, intimate, right-there-in-the-midst-of-the-action style portrait of the TT races was morphing into an unnatural, scripted mess, only missing a cameo appearance by one of the Kardashian clan to be the final nail in their creative coffin.

Still, at least Rodney delivered one thing into the mix that had proven helpful (well, two if you included his deep pockets). Napier and Thomas had won the first of the sidecar races and were now hot favourites to secure the second. And having the champions on board *did* make for great publicity for the show.

But contributing to Brad and Chip's overall stress levels was the network's desire to premiere a series trailer/preview on the island later that week at the TT awards ceremony. The TV studio was, understandably, eager to strike while the iron was hot and showcase the docuseries in front of the motorsport glitterati and assembled press pack. It was simply too good an opportunity to pass up. However, the difficulty in this plan was that condensing hours and hours worth of footage into a single compelling snapshot wasn't as easy as it sounded. That, and also the fact Chip and Brad hadn't even started in on the process yet.

Here on the ground, they knew they were dealing with an odious collection of buffoons. But all Brad and Chip had to do was smile politely and suck it up for a while longer, and their future careers would very likely be forged on the back of this

FRANK & STAN'S BUCKET LIST #5: ISLE OF MAN TT ACES

production. Just grin and bear it for a little longer, they reminded themselves again and again...

"Only us, Mr Franks!" Brad said as he opened the door to Rodney's stately motor home, with Brad announcing he and his brother's presence clearly and loudly, as he had no wish to catch Rodney in a state of undress as they'd done the previous day. It was an image that was now burnt into their retinas, and the only thing they could see whenever they closed their eyes. Today, thank goodness, Rodney was fully dressed, for the most part, cravat and all, leaving the boys never so happy to see a stupid cravat in all their lives.

The boys didn't know if it was a control thing or a genuine interest in the show's progress, but Rodney's insistence on face-to-face daily reports was eating into the time they simply didn't have to spare.

"Hello, Mr Franks," Brad said, approaching a seated Rodney. There was a woman on her knees before Rodney, servicing him, who Brad noticed (with a great sense of relief) was merely performing a pedicure.

"Ah, very good, my production team are here," Rodney announced, sounding very much like he was trying to impress the unfortunate young lady attending to his trotters.

"We wanted to drop this back off to you, Mr Franks," Chip offered, as the first point of order for today's meeting. "It's some of the equipment you were kind enough to lend to us, but that we're now finished with," he explained, placing the box of items in the corner and out of the way.

"Excellent," Rodney said, paying more attention to the present condition of his toenails. "So..."

"Ah, okay," Chip said, as eager to draw this meeting to a swift conclusion as Rodney appeared to be (despite Rodney insisting on the darned meetings in the first place). "Okay, well, we've had word from the TV studio about the name of the show, so it's official now," Chip informed him. "Isle of Man TT Aces," Chip said, running his hand through the air as he said the words, rather pleased with himself as he was the one who'd originally come up with the title in the first place.

"Yes, yes, very good," Rodney said. "And you've all the footage you need?"

"Pretty much, yeah," Brad entered in. "A few final pieces here and there, and of course some film from tomorrow's final race."

"Footage that will hopefully cover my team claiming their second trophy of the week," declared Rodney, followed by a loud snort through his nose that gave the poor girl at his feet a bit of a start, as she thought Rodney had just sneezed on her.

"Of course," Brad allowed, offering a smile of sympathy to the young lady for the obvious misery she was having to suffer. "Oh, and the studio would like us to air the show's initial trailer at tomorrow night's prize presentation. So we'll just need the green light from the people in charge, in order to—"

"Leave that to me," Rodney cut in, appearing quite delighted by the prospect of throwing his weight around and thus making himself feel important. "A global premiere of the show's trailer in front of the world's motoring press?" he said, a giddy sneer taking over his face. "And I'll be in it?" Rodney asked, though not sounding like a question as much as it was an edict.

"Of course, Mr Franks," Chip confirmed, even though they'd not yet started work on the trailer as yet.

"I can see myself," Rodney said, seeing himself. He lifted his chin, staring dreamily into the distance. "A large image of me in soft focus..." he began, describing his daydream. "Surrounded by cheering race fans lifting me onto their shoulders as my race team cross the finish line, receiving the chequered flag." And then he thought for a moment. "Hmm, and after that, perhaps you could have a shot of just my head, floating on a cloud?"

"Like a *god*...?" asked a flabbergasted Brad.

"Yes!" Rodney immediately replied, unaware of the sarcasm present in Brad's voice.

"Um... that's maybe a little over-indulgent. No offence," Chip entered in, hoping to temper Rodney's thoughts of becoming a racing deity. "And also not really our style, either, to be honest," he added.

"See what you can do," Rodney not-so-gently suggested.

"Of course, Mr Franks," Brad answered, hoping to appease him, though of course having no genuine intention of doing as Rodney wished. "And that's as much of an update as we have today, Mr Franks. So, other than to wish you good luck for tomorrow's race, we'll leave you to your... your... Um, well, yeah, we'll leave you to it."

"Oh," Chip said, one parting thought occurring to him, and something he'd been waiting for just the right opportunity to say. "Mr Franks," he went on, smiling in anticipation of what he was about to reveal. "Mr Franks, you'll be happy to know the police have been in touch with us, giving us an update regarding the progress they're making about our stolen goods."

"Ah... excellent..." Rodney said hesitantly, leaning forward to inspect the pumice stone just about to be applied to the underside of his foot. "They've recovered your stolen items, I hope...?" Rodney asked, without looking up, and without sounding especially confident that the items being recovered should actually have been the case.

"Not yet, Mr Franks. But they've managed to procure some dashcam footage of the actual incident. So, yeah, they're definitely making progress in the case, and sound very positive," Chip informed him. "Fingers crossed, they'll soon find the people who did this," Chip added, and then watched intently, waiting to see what kind of reaction this comment might generate.

"Yes, fingers crossed indeed," Rodney replied, echoing Chip's words. "Now, if we're done?" said Rodney. "Because I really need this troublesome corn on the pad of my right foot attended to."

"Alright. Well, again, we'll leave you to it, then," Brad replied, shuddering at the idea of having to witness such a display, and happy he and his brother wouldn't be there to see it. Brad gave the girl having to perform the unfortunate procedure another sympathetic glance, as did Chip, at which point they both took their leave.

Once outside and clear of the motorhome, Brad gestured with his finger like he was going to stick it down his throat to induce vomiting. "Chip," he said, "if I ever whine or complain about an awful day at work again, please remind me about that poor girl having to sand down that douchebag's corn, will you?"

"Will do," Chip replied. "And you'll do the same for me?"

"Agreed," Brad agreed.

Chapter
EIGHTEEN

Sleep eluded Dave as it often did the night before a race. So often seen as nothing more than a big cuddly joker, rarely letting anything dampen his spirits, there was, nonetheless, a serious, seldom-seen side to him. The casual observer might easily be forgiven for assuming Dave must treat racing in the same laid-back, relaxed manner he usually carried himself with his customarily jovial approach to life.

However, that perception couldn't be further from the truth. From the moment Dave Quirk pulled his helmet over his cauliflower ears, he was in race mode, with the pressure firmly resting on his broad shoulders. He was the captain of their little ship, and each time he set sail, Dave assumed the responsibility for all souls on board, those souls of course being himself and his best mate Monty.

Dave did have complete and utter faith in the abilities of his passenger, though, and hoped the sentiment was shared. His competitive spirit meant that he often pushed the boundaries during a race, but he took care never to exceed what he thought he was truly capable of, as the consequences were simply too grave to even consider.

Tonight, he'd tossed and turned for most of the wee hours, disturbing Monty, who slept next to him in the van (and probably dreaming of garden gnomes and such, if Dave knew his mate). Usually, Dave was pumped, eager to get out on track and do what he adored, assured that the machinery under him was the best it could possibly be. But right now, sadly, Dave didn't have that confidence. And the nagging doubts bouncing persistently around his head kept sleep at an unfortunate arm's length. They'd completed virtually an entire nut and bolt rebuild of the sidecar, with nothing untoward discovered. But what if there *had* been foul play? What if they'd voluntarily opened their gates, unwittingly inviting a Trojan horse into their camp, disguised and hidden in their new ignition system? After having found nothing obvious to that effect, Dave knew he was perhaps being a bit paranoid at this stage. Still, there was no point lying there wide awake, he supposed, looking at the rusting metal interior of the van listening to the constant soundtrack of Monty snoring. So, he threw on some clothes and climbed over Monty, deciding a nice early-morning cuppa to be a most splendid idea.

And so, soon armed with a steaming mug of lovely Earl Grey, Dave found himself stood in the doorway of their awning, looking to the heavens, where the first signs of a new day were just starting to break through. Then, with gentle steps, he headed out for a leisurely stroll through the maze of assembled tents, awnings, vans, and motorhomes which collectively formed the temporary pop-up community that was the TT paddock. Dave enjoyed having a gander at all the motorhome windows as he wandered. Not because he was a voyeur, as Monty had once previously suggested, the cheeky bastard. No, it was because Dave liked to appreciate the stickers that most of the teams displayed there on the glass. Spread out over the windows, you could see which countries they'd visited and which circuits they'd raced, all courtesy of the souvenirs proudly stuck there. In addition, many festooned their awnings with the flags of their homeland, like the large Saltire flag of Scotland Dave observed presently flapping on the gentle morning breeze as he passed by.

But, despite the early hour, the paddock wasn't in complete silence. With Senior Race Day being a local bank holiday, revellers from the previous evening could be heard making their way merrily home after a night on the tiles, giggling as they recalled the evening's events. And while some of the awnings were cloaked in darkness, their occupants no doubt satisfied they'd done all the preparation they could, others, like the one Dave walked past, appeared to be a hive of activity. Dave smiled upon hearing the stressed voices from within, sounding like tipsy parents on Christmas Eve desperately constructing their child's new bike in the dead of night.

Dave ambled towards pit lane, brew in hand, absorbing every sight and sound, enjoying the relative calm. It was difficult to comprehend that this place would erupt in only an hour or so, bursting with activity. Every blade of available grass would be covered by teams furiously making last-minute preparations while jubilant spectators wandered by to catch a glimpse of what was going on, pinching themselves that they were here.

For the fortunate race fans who'd made the journey, they'd soon be rewarded by waking to find themselves in the Isle of Man on the Friday of race week. Of course, there were other major sporting events to be had in the world (or even here on the Isle, for that matter), each with its own particular charms and attractions. But this was different. To be here, today, well, it was like your birthday, wedding day, Christmas morning, and even your christening, all rolled into one. You were here. You were on the Isle of Man on Senior Race Day. It really didn't get any better than that.

"Whaddya doing?" a squeaky voice called out, nearly sending Dave falling backwards over the wall in pit lane where he'd just sat himself down.

"Gordon Bennett!" Dave shouted, wiping the tea he managed to spill all over himself. Then, just as he was about to admonish what he assumed to be an overzealous security guard on his morning rounds, Dave caught sight of a familiar face in the darkness, one that was currently sporting a toothy grin. "Jaysus, Spanky," Dave moaned. "I nearly had an unscheduled pit stop in my pants just then."

"You're up and about early," Spanky observed, taking a seat

on the wall next to Dave. "Monty snoring again?"

"No. Well, yes, actually. Loudly," Dave answered. "But it's not that, Spanky."

"Nerves?" Spanky suggested, in a knowing, assured tone. "I can never sleep the night before a big race," he confided. "My mind's whirring like a large troupe of miniature monkeys have gathered in there," he said, tapping his head. "All riding around on unicycles whilst playing the cymbals. That's why I like a nice little walk, first thing, to clear my mind. Know what I mean?"

"Well, not necessarily that part about the monkeys," Dave replied. "But, yeah, I do, Spanky. I know precisely how you feel, mate." And Dave meant it. Indeed, there actually weren't many who'd shared the experience that Dave would soon once again find himself in. Frank, Stan, Becks, and his mum all knew the strains the event placed on the riders, of course. But only if you'd sampled it for yourself could you truly understand what the emotional rollercoaster felt like. Even Monty, as his trusty passenger, would likely have a different outlook to Dave even though they were racing the same bike. As the pilot of his own particular ship, however, Spanky was more qualified than most to understand what was going through Dave's head, even more so than those closest to him.

"You'll be all right," Spanky suggested, giving Dave a hearty thumbs-up to emphasise the point. "Just take it easy and don't let the adrenalin take over," he said. "Because if you do, Dave, that's when you end up peeling yourself off of a wall."

"Wise words, my friend. Wise words," Dave said with a smile. "Say, do you ever have concerns about your bike?" Dave asked, turning to face his colleague. "You know, doubts and that?"

"When? Before a race?" Spanky asked.

"Yeah," Dave answered. "Like right now, for instance. A feeling that something's not quite right, yet you don't know exactly what?"

Spanky shook his head. "If I had any doubts about the bike, Dave, then I wouldn't even race," he advised. "Even if there was nothing actually wrong, you wouldn't be in the moment because you'd be too overly worried about things."

Dave released a pained sigh. "Yeah, that's what I'm thinking, Spanky."

"You're thinking of sacking the race off?" Spanky ventured, reading between the worry lines on Dave's weary face.

"I think so, mate."

Spanky hopped down from the wall, taking up a position directly in front of Dave. "Here, is this because of what I told you about those two muttonheads, Napier and Thomas?" he asked.

"It is," Dave replied. "I just can't shake the thought of that pair boasting about ruining our TT to the mechanic who just fixed our bike. Do you reckon I'm being irrational, feeling this bloody disconcerted about it?"

"Disconcerted? I don't know what that means," Spanky said. "But I do think you're being bloody stupid."

"You do?" Dave asked, surprised, as Spanky himself was the one who'd delivered the news to he and Monty, after all.

"Do you remember my bike misfiring in practice a couple of years ago?" Spanky asked.

"I do, yeah," Dave replied, indeed remembering. "It sounded like an old lawnmower, as I recall."

"And I'll never forget you dropping what you were doing to try and help me fix it," Spanky commented.

"I'm not sure we didn't make it worse," Dave joked. "Anyway, you're a mate, so of course I'd help you if I could."

"But many wouldn't," Spanky was quick to point out. "Then, when we couldn't fix it, and I was on the verge of calling it a day, Mike offered to look her over, remember?"

Dave nodded, and Spanky continued...

"Right. But then when Mike's team called him back to work on their own machinery, that's when I thought my TT was over for the year. But Mike had other ideas, didn't he? He came to my awning at two in the morning and spent four hours stripping my bike to get it up and running for the final practice session just so I could try and qualify."

"Amazing," said Dave, raising his now-empty mug (as most

FRANK & STAN'S BUCKET LIST #5: ISLE OF MAN TT ACES

of the tea had previously been spilt) in appreciation. "And he fixed the issue for you, I take it?" Dave asked, unable to recall any further details of the situation.

"Yeah, but the point is, I never got to take her out again that week," Spanky explained. "See, I thought our TT was over for the year, right? So like a complete dunderhead, and to wallow in my bloody misery, I ended up getting completely sozzled. And I only found out what he'd done the next day, when I was too hungover to even *consider* heading out on the practice session. And, still, you know what? Our Mike wouldn't take even a single penny for all the work he'd performed."

"Right," Dave replied. "So what you're saying is—"

"Don't worry about Mike the Mechanic, is what I'm saying," Spanky replied firmly. "He's one of the good guys. And I know for an absolute fact that he thinks Thomas and Napier are a right pair of gormless gits," he said, slapping Dave on the arm encouragingly. "So my point is, if Mike's worked on your bike, you should see it as a distinct advantage, Dave. Just like a doctor would never cause harm to humans, he's the same with bikes, yeah? Similar to that Hippopotamus Oath them doctors have."

"Is *that* what it's called?" Dave said with a grin, pushing himself down from the wall.

"Yeah. So my point is..." Spanky said, having yet another point to make, it would seem. "My point is, don't make the same mistake I made, right? Don't be a silly sod, yeah?"

"Thanks. I needed this, Spanky," Dave told him, pulling him in for a quick cuddle. "I really needed this."

"Anytime, Dave," Spanky said, casually walking away down pit lane once released from Dave's grip, free to continue his own early-morning wander.

"Oh. And Spanky?" Dave called after him.

"Yeah?"

"You ride safely out there today. You hear me, pal?"

"I hear you, Big Dave. I hear you."

Chapter
NINETEEN

P arc fermé, situated at the top of the paddock adjacent to the TT start line, was rammed. It was reminiscent of a Marks & Spencer's carpark on late Christmas Eve with vehicles strewn everywhere and folk running around with panic etched on their faces. However, this was organised chaos. Granted, to the uninitiated, it wouldn't have seemed so. It must have appeared like utter mayhem to those spectators packed in and watching on from the nearby grandstand.

Finally, those teams that were waiting were invited to exit parc fermé in groups of ten and thus move onto the starting grid ahead of the official Sidecar Race 2 start time of 10:30 a.m. It was at this precise moment that Dave's sphincter muscles began twitching like Elmer Fudd's trigger finger every time he aimed to make hasenpfeffer stew out of poor Bugs Bunny. It wasn't fear for the race, necessarily, but rather a concern that if something went wrong at this late stage in the game then there simply wouldn't be any time to fix it. Fortunately, however, he and Monty managed to safely manoeuvre machine number thirty-six through the throngs and secured her in place towards the rear of the long line of other outfits making up the collective queue of racers.

The circus soon followed, as crew, friends, well-wishers, and hordes of media all lined the starting grid, flashing their all-access passes for an enviable experience walking in and around the bikes, immersed in the intoxicating environment.

As they waited for things to get underway, Dave and Monty sat on the pavement, backs resting up against a stone wall, soaking up the unfolding spectacle before them. Monty flicked his one good eye to the electronic board displaying the countdown. "Fifteen minutes to go," he remarked, whereupon he puckered his lips and began whistling a happy little ditty.

"Look at those two prize plums," Dave said, pointing an extended finger towards the front of the grid. There on the tarmac, in full view of everyone, and for the whole world to see, Napier and Thomas were sat on yoga mats performing a series of stretches — something they'd never, *ever* done previously in all the time that Dave had known the pair.

"If that was anybody else doing that, I'd probably think it was a bit odd but quite cool," Monty suggested. "In fact, I'd probably head over there and join them."

"I sense a *but* coming..." Dave ventured.

"But, seeing *them* two sat there doing it makes me want to walk over there and place them in a bloody chokehold," Monty clarified. "The only reason they're doing it is for the benefit of the cameras, just to put on a show."

"I hear that," said Dave, hearing that. "Brad and Chip look absolutely thrilled to be involved," Dave commented, noticing the two of them capturing this clearly staged, pre-race exercise regime and appearing not the slightest bit happy about having to suffer through the ordeal of filming it.

"They'll be glad to get back home after a week of working with those two tools," Monty remarked. "Although..." he went on, giving the matter before him a brief moment's consideration. "Although, those tools *did* win the first race. So maybe we should consider having a little stretch as they are as well...?"

"If you insist," Dave dutifully replied, reaching for the sky. "You're the boss," he added, enjoying his pleasant little stretch, though of course not the sort of stretch Monty had just been referring to.

"Not what I meant, but it's better than nothing, I suppose,"

Monty said with a shrug, and was just about to perform his own little stretch when the early morning sun interrupted his plans. "Are you trying to blind me up there?" Monty protested, shielding his eyes from the sun's burning rays. "Oi! You!" he said to an attending Stan. "Move the brolly over this way, will you?" he instructed, tut-tutting his disapproval at Stan not anticipating his every move and leaning in quick enough to compensate.

"Sorry about that, Monty," Stan replied, adjusting his stance so the umbrella in his hand diverted the sun's rays away from Monty's delicate skin. "How's that?" asked Stan, looking down to the seated Monty.

"Perfect," Monty was pleased to report, satisfied, and then relaxing back against the wall.

"Frank, I personally think you're doing a *tremendous* job up there," Dave advised, not wishing Frank to feel either left out or underappreciated.

Standing either side, like umbrella-wielding bookends, were an attentive Frank and Stan, tasked with keeping their leather-clad charges cool and protected from the sun. Unfortunately, Dave and Monty's budget didn't extend to the provision of attractive, Lycra-clad ladies to hold their umbrellas, looking all seductive and smouldering. So, rather than brolly dollies, Frank and Stan had been put to work, just as they had in previous years, as the team's very own brolly wallies, as it were. (And a rather bang-up job they were doing, Monty's minor complaints notwithstanding). Frank was always up for a joke, of course, but when Monty introduced them on live radio at one point this morning as such (that is, as their own personal "brolly wallies"), scoring points at their expense, Frank had seen fit to set him straight, giving him the very gentlest of reminders afterwards as to who it was that signed their paycheques each month. Stan, on the other hand, was a bit more accommodating, and had in fact even embraced the role...

"Fancy a cooling breeze?" Stan asked, reaching for his pocket fan the instant a bead of sweat formed on Monty's brow.

"I'm good," Monty said, curtly waving away the offer like a

spoilt Roman emperor. "Though perhaps you could peel me a grape...?" he suggested.

"Unbelievable," Frank said with a laugh.

Just then, a weary-looking Brad was spotted navigating his way through the mingling crowds, offering apologetic smiles as he brushed past first this person and then that. "Ah, there you are. Good morning, gentlemen," he said, once eventually presenting himself before Team Frank & Stan.

"You've finished your yoga class, then?" Dave asked playfully.

"Finally, yes," Brad replied, rolling his eyes in exasperation. "The dizzying highs of being a documentary filmmaker are practically never-ending, as you can clearly see."

"Looks like they're on board with the idea," Chip said to his brother, arriving a moment later with his phone pressed to his ear, conveying the information he'd just received. "Morning, fellas," he added, before returning his attention to his call.

Brad swallowed with anticipation, squatting down so he was at eye level with Dave and Monty, and then resting his arms on his thighs before he spoke. "We have news," Brad told them, looking to each of them, and then glancing up to the two brolly wallies as well (though Brad likely wouldn't have been familiar with that term).

"Hmm, probably don't have too long for the dramatic pause," Monty suggested, noting the flurry of activity on the starting grid behind Brad.

"Sorry, yeah," Brad continued. "We hoped to meet up with you guys earlier this morning, but we've literally just received confirmation right now."

"Of what?" Frank asked, allowing his brolly to fall just a few millimetres askew. "Sorry, Dave," he quickly added when the sun pierced through the resulting gap, at which point he just as quickly set the brolly right.

"Well, Chip's on the phone with the company who offered Monty and Dave that sponsorship money for getting into the top ten."

Dave and Monty both leaned forward, pricking up their ears.

"Yeah...?" Monty said, now hanging on Brad's every word.

"We've just gotten approval that the deal's back on," Brad was pleased to report. "It's the same conditions as before. If you can finish in the top ten, the cash is all yours."

Dave and Monty allowed that splendid little morsel of info to digest as Brad continued talking. He outlined how awful he and his brother had felt about pulling the documentary rug out from under them and, as a result, the opportunity of the thirty grand sponsorship money. Of course, it would take a fair amount of creative editing on their part to ensure that Dave and Monty were featured a bit more prominently again. But Brad appeared confident that they could keep all interested parties happy, and, as he said, they would make it happen.

"Blimey," Monty responded, scarcely able to believe what he was hearing. "That's brilliant news, mate."

"We weren't sure if we should mention it beforehand, just in case it hampered your race prep, you know?" Brad told them. "But, in the end, we figured you'd want to be informed."

Dave waved away Brad's concerns. "Hey, don't sweat it," he said. "We're just happy to be spotlighted a bit more. And having a shot at the cash is a real bonus as well, of course!"

Brad smiled, conscious that he was now being called over by somebody in Team Rodney. "After seeing how well you did in the first race, it was obvious you had a real shot at hitting the top ten today. That's when we knew we had to reach out to that sponsor of yours and make this work for you," he said, at which point Brad dispensed a series of high-fives. "Good luck, guys," he said. "Go out and destroy the competition."

In that exact instant, Dave's attention drifted, taking him away from the moment. In his mind's eye, he reached down, sweeping Becks off her feet and into his arms. Then, using his foot, he teased open the gate on his white picket fence, stepping inside and then twirling the both of them around so they could each admire the glorious blooms in their lovely, manicured garden. At the top of the path, Tyler jumped for joy, proudly holding up the key to their new house like it was an Olympic torch.

That was when Stanley, their new dog, came bounding out of their spacious garage with a yellow rubber chicken clamped between its teeth, squeaking with every stride.

"Right! Let's smash this shit!" Dave shouted, snapping himself from his idyllic reverie. "And, incidentally, remind me to purchase a yellow rubber chicken," he added. "Oh, and a dog named Stanley."

"Sounds good," Monty answered. "And speaking of Stan, by the way, before we get to any smashing, might I take you up on that offer of a cooling breeze, Stanley?" he asked, with a snap of his fingers, in reference to another bead of perspiration that had just started forming on his brow.

Stan immediately reached for the aptly-named pocket fan held at the ready, as one might reasonably expect, there in his pocket. "Of course," Stan replied, flicking the switch and positioning the device several centimetres away from Monty's face. "And would you like a face cloth?" he asked.

"I'll have to think about it and let you know," Monty replied imperiously, having not yet decided such measures should be required, but leaving open the distinct possibility.

"Bloody incorrigible," Frank suggested, shaking his head and laughing again.

Chapter
TWENTY

The starting grid was soon cleared of any extraneous persons ahead of the official start time, leaving the riders alone with their thoughts. All eyes in the grandstand were directed towards the long line of sidecars stretching up Glencrutchery Road, the atmosphere tense with anticipation. Engines throbbed, desperate to be let loose onto the track. Finally, the first machine was allowed to move forward, coming to a halt under the starting arch as it made ready to depart, raising a collective cheer from the excited, expectant crowd. Several rapid twists of the throttle followed until the clutch was released and the first bike was away, hurtling onward towards the upcoming St Ninian's Crossroads in a deafening roar.

The bikes were set on their way at ten-second intervals, meaning Dave and Monty still had at least three anxious, butt-clenching minutes to wait. As each machine left the start line, those outfits behind shuffled forward like hungry diners waiting in a lunch queue.

While they waited their turn, Dave couldn't help but reflect on Brad's most excellent news. It was, after all, life-changing money on the table. He considered his overall strategy for the race in light of this information and, crucially, if it would impact on his thinking. The last thing he needed before the start of the race was uncertainty. Then, in a moment of clarity, the answer hit him — it wouldn't change things a jot, other than what he and Monty had already discussed. The reason being that they'd given it their all in this year's previous race and had secured a highly respectable fourteenth position. Using Mike the Mechanic's technical data, they'd already identified several corners where Dave had rolled off the throttle too early and places where an incorrect gear choice may have cost them valuable seconds. And so, already armed with this information, Dave would give it everything he had, and, if that didn't turn out to be good enough, then what was meant to be was simply meant to be. But what Dave wouldn't do, under any circumstance, is push them beyond their limits. Yes, the money would be lovely, but getting home safely was lovelier.

It's funny how one's mind works in moments of extreme duress. Here was Dave, easing towards the start line of the most challenging road race on the face of the globe, and all he could do was stare at the starting official who'd soon tap them on the shoulder and send them on their way. It was the same chap who'd tapped Dave's shoulder several times before. But this was the first time Dave had ever really looked at him, due to usually being so utterly focussed on the empty road ahead. Did this mean he was more relaxed? So comfortable they'd done all they could with their preparations, giving him the confidence to just go and enjoy it? Whatever it meant, Dave took a deep breath, edging forward in order to take up his own position under the starting arch.

Knowing the familiar hand would soon land on his shoulder, Dave teased the throttle instinctively, his other fingers poised above the left handgrip, ready to release the clutch the instant he felt the expected tap. Then, when Dave did indeed register the contact on his shoulder, with the reactions of a sprinter hearing the starting gun, he opened the throttle, tearing away from the start line on the first of three laps of this, Race 2 of the year's Isle of Man TT.

Despite the quick start, Dave often felt it wise to exercise some small degree of caution, relatively speaking of course, on the opening few miles of any race. With a full tank of fuel, cold tyres, and two riders still trying to regulate their breathing, it made sense to settle themselves in a bit. On the approach to Quarterbridge, even for a seasoned campaigner, Dave was staggered to see the sheer volume of spectators crammed into the popular viewing spots when he lifted his head. As he moved down the gearbox before the sharp right-hander, Dave tuned his hearing into the engine note, listening out for any early indications of trouble. However, he needn't have worried as she was warbling like a choir girl quite beautifully, and with the suspension feeling tight as you like and gobbling up the challenging corner with ease.

"Come on!" Dave said aloud, opening the taps, his confidence growing with each passing mile. The weather conditions out on track were perfection as well, and couldn't possibly have been any better as far as Dave was concerned. A touch of cloud cover meant the awful glare from the sun was greatly reduced, and without any rain for days the tarmac was bone dry — both great comfort when heading towards a blind corner on racing slicks.

Coming through Union Mills with the Methodist church on the right, Dave caught a glimpse of two machines jockeying for position. Encouraged by the distance he'd already clawed back on them, Dave tucked himself in for the fast run up the Ballahutchin Hill, thoughts already turning to the bowel-opening corner that was Ballagarey rapidly approaching.

"Don't roll off, don't roll off, don't roll off," Dave warned himself, overtaking the first of the two bikes in front. "Don't roll off," he repeated, passing the busy campsite on the left, meaning Ballagarey was next up. "Don't you do it!" he shouted as he approached the deceptively quick right-hander. But a self-preservation instinct overtook him, resulting in the throttle being released ever so slightly despite his best efforts. It was one of the corners which Mike the Mechanic identified as directly impacting their lap times, so he knew this was important. And Dave also knew from experience that he *should* be able to take the corner flat out, but it still didn't stop him from rolling off, as he had feared. "Wanker!" Dave admonished himself as the other sidecar in front increased the gap, having not rolled off, Dave had to assume. Even by losing a fraction of your speed, you lost your slingshot into the long straight through Marown and, with it, valuable momentum.

Fortunately, by the time they'd reached The Crosby pub, however, they'd caught and passed that bike, rewarding them with a clear road ahead and a chance to glance over to their very own, much-beloved TT Farm where stood an animated contingent heartily cheering them on.

They didn't come across any additional traffic until the Glen Helen section of the course, which meant smooth sailing of course, but also worried Dave. Had they dropped the pace, for instance? That was the concern racing through his mind. But, on the other hand, it certainly didn't *feel* like they had. Indeed, his considerable experience suggested they were going like the clappers, but it was impossible to know for sure.

Many riders, as it should happen, particularly those regularly found further up the leaderboard, would have folks dotted around the course displaying pit boards. This gave the riders valuable, real-time updates of their current position, and would detail the time between them and their closest competitors. If you knew you were leading by two minutes, for example, you might choose to use this knowledge to settle things down just a touch, perhaps reducing the demands on the bike. Of course, if you were two minutes *down*, you'd use the information on the timing board to really give her dixie. For that reason, a pit board could be a valuable tool to have in your arsenal.

Unfortunately, Dave and Monty didn't have this luxury. If they'd prior knowledge of the sponsorship cash being back on the table, they'd likely have been able to drum up some willing volunteers. But, as it was, all they could do was carry on with more of the same strategy. That strategy being to go as fast as they bloody could and race like the dickens.

To Dave's immense relief, they caught up with the next bike on the road just before the iconic Sarah's Cottage landmark. He tucked in behind the machine in front rather than immediately outpacing it, choosing to cleverly use their slipstream for a tow up to the Cronk-y-Voddy Straight, at which point Dave finally pulled out to overtake.

Dave's heart smashed against his chest. "Yes!" he yelled, every one of his senses in a state of heightened awareness and absolute euphoria. He couldn't see himself smiling, of course, but his grin was so wide he could feel it pressing against the inside of his full-face helmet. This was the Isle of Man TT, and there was, unequivocally, nothing else like it, anywhere, that could possibly compare.

The challenge of attempting to watch the racing action from anywhere around the pit lane area of the grandstand as opposed to, say, watching from a grassy roadside bank in the middle of the countryside, was the sheer, constant commotion all around you. Yes, it was spine-tingling to be in the thick of it, but if you wanted an unobstructed view, then there were, arguably, more suitable options available to you around the circuit. Presently, Frank and Stan were stood behind the wall dividing the active pit lane area and the return road leading through to parc fermé — the route the riders would travel after their race. With no scheduled fuel stops in the sidecar race, the area wasn't as busy as it would be during a solo's race but was still hectic enough.

Stan didn't like to admit it, but his hearing wasn't what it was. So listening to the radio commentary over the sound of bikes tearing by was proving something of a challenge. In addition, by being jostled about, viewing the live scoreboard on their phone app was also proving troublesome.

"Should we go and get a pint?" Frank shouted over to Stan as another outfit screamed by at the start of their second lap, all but drowning out his words. "We can get comfortable and listen to the commentary!" he added, slowly and deliberately, and at the same elevated volume, but it was useless.

"What?" asked Stan.

"I fancy a pint!" Frank said, pointing in the general direction of the beer tent.

"You dirty get!" Stan shot back, shaking his head in mock disgust.

Frank paused for a moment, trying to determine what Stan could possibly have incorrectly interpreted from what he was saying.

"So, you don't fancy a pint?" an exasperated Frank asked, curling his fingers and thumb into the shape of a crescent moon to simulate holding onto a glass, and then jiggling this in front of his mouth illustratively.

"Oh. I thought you said something else," Stan replied during a brief lull in the action, laughing away to himself, and with Frank appearing somewhat grateful he wasn't bothering to elaborate as to precisely what that something had actually been. "Anyway, yes, I could certainly go for a pint," Stan added, nodding in appreciation of Frank's most excellent suggestion.

The two of them strolled through the array of delicious-smelling catering stands at the rear of the grandstand whose staff were enjoying a period of relative calm, what with the majority of fans enjoying the action at the current moment. As they walked along, Stan had his nose pressed to his phone like a moody teenager at a family function. "They've broken that timing thingamajig at Cronk-ny-Mona," Stan informed Frank, watching intently as the race positions updated themselves.

"*Well?*" Frank asked, shuffling close behind and trying to get a good look over Stan's shoulder at the screen being held in his mate's hand. "What position are they in?"

"They're in eighteenth position," Stan said, once the app updated itself. "If I'm reading the details correctly, that is."

"Oh," said Frank, uncertain how to react to this news. "Is that good, or—?"

"I reckon so," Stan offered. "Their start number was, what, thirty-six? The fellow on the radio said there were a few non-starters, but, even so, that must mean they've moved up the leaderboard...?"

"Hmm, I imagine you're right," Frank answered. "Lager?" he

asked, once they'd arrived near the beer tent.

Stan parked himself down on the first unoccupied wooden picnic bench nearest, with several stacks of uncollected plastic beakers strewn about, left there mainly by thirsty, pre-race drinkers. "Yes, please," Stan said, in answer to Frank's question. "Bugger off!" he demanded, swatting away a wasp attracted by the sticky residue left there in the cups, with Stan then looking around for another, perhaps emptier table, but to no avail.

"Who, me?" Frank replied, feigning offence as he headed off to procure their lagers. "I haven't even fetched our beers yet!"

From their repositioned location, Stan could now hear the radio commentary with greater clarity, at least. Unfortunately, as a result of the sheer number of competitors in the race, only the higher-placed outfits tended to receive a mention as they circulated around the course. And it was for this reason that the official TT phone app (of which Stan was canny enough to possess, his mother having raised no fool) was a godsend. With six official timing points, you could immediately see which timing beam any given team had broken and thus what section of the course they were presently at. In addition, lap times and current standings were displayed. And even though it was just a series of numbers flashing up on a screen, it really did make for compelling viewing. Especially if you had an interest in a particular outfit, as Stan and Frank obviously did.

"Little demon!" Stan said, lashing out at the wee, winged devil, which was now shifting its attentions between any small remaining quantities of lager in the empty cups on the table and the styling gel in Stan's hair, which it seemed to find especially enticing much to Stan's continued consternation. "Bugger off, you!" Stan instructed once more, swatting away with his hand but his strike landing frustratingly wide of the mark.

With the wasp off to vex somebody else, at least for the time being, Stan glanced down to the app on his phone once more, but the boys hadn't yet reached the timing point at Glen Helen. "Come on," Stan said, urging the two of them on.

"Who'd have thought there'd be a queue at this time?" Frank

FRANK & STAN'S BUCKET LIST #5: ISLE OF MAN TT ACES

announced jovially, placing the circular tray he was carrying down onto the table. "I purchased us both a little snack as well," Frank added, scanning Stan's face for a reaction.

"Little snack?" said Stan. "Those are the two largest wieners I've ever seen, and I've seen my fair share!" he added cheekily.

"It's a bratwurst," Frank advised, handing Stan his pint. "And if I'm not very much mistaken, it's possibly the most *expensive* bratwurst ever sold," he remarked, along with a resigned, you-only-live-once sort of shrug.

"Prices here are indeed the würst," Stan agreed, resulting in a moan, but also an appreciative chuckle, from Frank (as a good pun was of course always welcome). "Hmm, it's not even..." Stan remarked, checking his watch, "quarter past eleven, and we're already having a pint." Stan then inspected the individual tube-shaped meat treat that Frank passed him. "Ah, jolly good, we've got loads of ketchup here," he observed, impressed that Frank would remember his predilection in this regard. Some people considered it sacrilege to put anything other than mustard on hotdogs and such, but Stan much preferred the tomato-based condiment (haters be damned), and plenty of it.

"We're proper party animals," Frank commented.

"I don't think proper party animals have an afternoon nap like we do these days," Stan replied.

"Or have their cuticles done bi-monthly?"

"They do look fabulous, though," Stan said in answer, raising both hands in front of him and wiggling his fingers like a puppet master. "Ah, lovely, they're through Glen Helen," Stan observed, spotting a change on his phone and informing Frank. "Still eighteenth place, though. Although that particular bit of information appears to be in need of updating. Or maybe it's frozen...?"

Frank took a mouthful of lager, looking around, taking in the sights and smells.

"You love this, don't you?" Stan enquired fondly. "The TT, I mean. It makes me smile to see the smile it puts on your face, old pal."

Frank nodded, releasing a peaceful, contented sigh. "Yeah... it's not half bad, is it?"

"The best," Stan said. "Also, other than perhaps an airport, where else can you have a pint at this time of day without being judged?" Stan then took a grip on his oversized hotdog, ready to tuck in, holding it to his mouth like a trumpet. "I'll need a brisk walk to burn all the calories off from ingesting *this* bad boy," he suggested, starting to chomp down...

"Soddin' thing!" Stan yelled, before his porcelains had even caressed his elevenses. The wasp was back, and with buzzing near his ears, Stan spun his head around, darting his eyes every which way, this way and that, like a WW2 gunner trying to zero in on a target. "Shoo!" he commanded, much to Frank's great amusement.

"There it is!" Frank said, in a tone suggesting he wasn't, in fact, actually sure where it was. "Just there!" a devious Frank added, throwing a wadded-up piece of napkin across the picnic table, hitting Stan on the left side of his beak.

"Aaah!" Stan wailed, flapping his hotdog-wielding hand in the area of the perceived threat. But, whilst Stan maintained a firm grip on his bread roll, it wasn't sufficient to prevent his flailing momentum from launching the bratwurst out of its floury casing, just like a circus clown being shot from a cannon.

Frank's face crumpled like a dropped towel, mouth agape as the overly expensive meat missile sailed away, over both their table and the next, heading directly towards the t-shirt vendor plying his wares from the nearby pop-up stall.

"Noooo!" Stan said like a budget ghost, as the well-lubricated ketchup-covered projectile bounced off a metal clothing rack, sending a crimson splatter all over the merchandise displayed there, before finally coming to a rest atop a pile of motorcycle-themed baseball caps on the countertop.

Horrified, Stan quickly turned around, picking his phone up off the table and staring at the device as if he'd been looking at it the whole time. "Oh, would you look at that. The boys are at Ballaugh Bridge..." he said casually, taking a long, lingering look at the screen, his back to the scene of the crime.

"It's no use, Stan," Frank informed him, somewhere between sympathy and mirth. "The bloke is already headed this way, carrying a collection of items it seems you'll soon likely be paying for."

"Bloody wasp," Stan moaned. "Bloody wasp."

Dave ripped clear a strip of optically compromised tear-off visor, one giving the appearance of a gruesome battle having occurred between the island's midge and fly population against said visor, with all lives being lost and not a single soul left to tell the tale. Surely, however, those perished were currently being whisked away to Valhalla, the lot of them, as they'd all seen glorious deaths this day sacrificing themselves for the good of the Isle of Man TT.

Crossing the start/finish line on the beginning of their third and final lap of the race, Dave felt strong, like he had plenty left in the tank. But it was whether there was plenty left in the tank of their *bike* that now occupied his thoughts. Dave was acutely aware that all their efforts could come undone by something as simple and straightforward as an empty fuel tank. It was the stuff of nightmares for any racer, giving it your all for three gruelling laps only for the engine to splutter, gasping for life as the final drops of precious fuel drained away. But it was pointless concerning yourself as there was nothing to be done other than sending off a prayer to a higher power — in this case, the racing gods — an activity Dave dutifully performed.

As for the bike itself, though, everything about the machine was magnificent. The handling, gearing, and acceleration all hadn't missed a beat. Not a one. And when all those ingredients came together precisely right, it made for a rather delicious cake, Dave was thinking just then. Perhaps not the best analogy, Dave reckoned, but cake was something he was particularly fond of, and it at least took his mind off worries about fuel depletion. Anyway, Mike the Mechanic had truly worked wonders, and for even doubting the man's professionalism, Dave felt a pang of guilt. Even the new electronic dashboard made him smile each time he sneaked a glance at it.

Dave and Monty were having the race of their lives in near picture-postcard conditions, and Dave was absolutely loving it. Even if he didn't have a clue where they were currently placed. He'd lost count of how many bikes they'd passed this run, but he did know the number was fairly significant. Certainly more than he recalled doing during previous campaigns. And with each little victory, it spurred him on a bit further.

Monty, for his part, appeared to be rolling back the years. With the agility of a Russian gymnast, he threw himself around the passenger compartment in a masterful ballet, ensuring the bike remained precisely balanced, using his weight to deliver optimum grip to their tyres as a result. Rarely in any sport were two people so dependent on each other to achieve a common, shared goal. And here, today, Monty and Dave were operating in perfect harmony.

On the approach to the iconic Ballaugh Bridge, Dave shifted down the gearbox under heavy braking, intent on reducing their speed before tackling the challenging, humpbacked structure. It was too little too late, however, as Dave soon realised he was coming into the bridge far too hot. "Aww, bollocks," he said, as their bike jumped the bridge with the grace of a gazelle, yet landed a split second later with the grace of an elephant falling out of a tree. Dave's head snapped forward, taking his attention off the road ahead momentarily, which wasn't ideal.

He'd check later to see if he'd lost any teeth, but for now, he was straight back on the throttle. However... there was nothing there. Rather than the throaty roar that'd accompanied their race so far, there was only an eerie silence. With no vibrations shaking his core, Dave knew immediately they'd lost power, with their only option to coast to a halt on the left-hand side of the road, sadly, and remove themselves from the live track, which is what he did. Nearby marshals leapt into action, waving yellow flags to warn approaching machines of the potential hazard.

Once stopped, Dave immediately jumped off the bike, reaching for the R-clip securing the seat unit in place and lifting the seat off. Dave raised his visor, running his eyes around the usual trouble spots he knew might account for their present predicament. "The kill switch...?" he mumbled to himself, moving his attention to the right side of the frame, but quickly discounting it as the issue as there didn't seem to be anything amiss there.

Like an emergency room doctor, Dave carried on with his patient's diagnosis, remaining calm under pressure, shifting his focus now towards the fuses, which were notorious for shaking loose. And sure enough, he spotted the casing of the fuse box had flapped open, likely a result of the heavy landing, just as suspected. "Bastard!" Dr Quirk screamed, throwing his gloves to the ground in a fit of rage, the cracks of a challenging shift at the hospital beginning to show.

A concerned marshal sprinted over, with one eye remaining on the approaching traffic. "What's the damage?" she asked upon arrival, pressing for a quick answer so she could radio in any potential retirement to the clerk of the course.

"Well, my marbles took a bit of a hammering on landing," Dave joked, desperately hoping the marshal wouldn't enforce their premature retirement. Laughing nervously, Dave turned back to the bike, hoping there was something he could do.

Monty, who'd also climbed off the bike, stood with his hands on his hips. He knew not to get in Dave's way at this point, just hoping the big fella could fix whatever needed fixing.

"Bloody hell!" Dave yelled, turning to Monty and shaking his head.

"Game over?" Monty enquired.

"There's an issue with the fuse," Dave whispered, hoping to delay the extent of their mechanical woes from the marshal's notice just a moment longer.

"That one there?" Monty asked, inspecting the particular spot where Dave had his finger pointed.

"The master ignition fuse. Exactly," Dave said. "It must have bloody shaken itself loose."

With no spare fuse on hand, retirement was now the only alternative, it would seem. What was devastating was that they had dozens of the darned things back at race HQ — a fact that offered absolutely no consolation right now. All of their blood, sweat, and tears were going to be undone by a simple missing fuse not costing more than a few measly quid. Meaning that a heavy, mistimed landing was now going to deprive them of not only a finish at the Isle of Man TT, but also any hope of ever seeing that lovely thirty-k sponsorship money as well.

"A bit of a problem here, lads?" someone called out from on the property of the home adjacent, the voice originating from an elderly gentleman by the sound of it.

"No," Dave replied cheerily. "We just stopped to admire your lovely garden," he said, though the sarcasm of his words wafted away like the exhaust fumes from their interrupted engine.

"No spare fuse, you say?" the old boy enquired, peering over his garden wall like an inquisitive child at the zoo. "What you need..." he went on, chomping down on the biscuit he'd been enjoying just prior to Dave and Monty's arrival. "Is a piece of tin foil," he declared, his weathered face breaking into a knowing grin. "It worked wonders on my tractor back in the day," he suggested, raising his eyes in fond recollection of that memory.

Dave, who was now on the verge of tears, stared back at the chap. "Tin foil?" he said, repeating back what he thought he'd heard, wanting to make sure he'd indeed heard correctly. "What are you on about?" he asked, though not in an unkind way, necessarily. More the way you'd question someone attempting to convince you the world was flat.

In possibly the Manxest accent Dave had ever heard (and Dave *himself* was Manx, and not from across) the chap continued with his educational session. "Trust me, bay, it'll do a mighty job," he said, liberating what was left of his KitKat from its wrapper. He then rolled the tinfoil into a ball. "Take this, yessir," he said, throwing it towards Dave. "Stick that ball of foil in the gap and secure it in place, alright."

"Ehm... all right. With what?" Dave asked, wondering if his chain was presently being yanked.

"A stone, yessir. A small one, bay. A small one, mind," came the reply.

In the absence of any other available options, Dave did as instructed, stuffing the ball of tinfoil in the housing of the fuse box. "We need a stone," he said to Monty. "I can't see any stones. Actually, what we need is more like a pebble, I guess."

Monty dropped to his knees, running the palms of his hands over the smooth tarmac, but nothing. Then, in a eureka moment, he looked to where he thought he might possibly find one. "There, stuck in the tyre," Monty said, noting several small stones lodged in the warm rubber, just as he'd suspected. He managed to dig out one of them using his fingernail, presenting it to Dave like a cheap wedding ring.

Dave accepted the gift, glanced over to the old boy, shrugged, placed the stone on top of the tin foil, and then secured the lid of the fuse box. Dave flicked the ignition switch without much hope, not one to believe in old wives' tales or something taken from the script of a bloody *MacGyver* episode, but...

"Well bugger me sideways," Dave said, when his shiny new dashboard lights came on, and the fuel pump whirred into life, sounding like a free-flowing stream after a downpour as the vital fluids began circulating.

Tentatively, Dave pressed the start button, located near to the throttle, and in a glorious moment that would remain with him for all of his days, the engine roared furiously into life once again.

Dave carefully replaced the seat unit, threw on his gloves, and the two of them, Monty and Dave, climbed back aboard their rocket ship. "I owe you a large drink!" Dave said, giving a hearty thumbs-up to the sweet-toothed chap in the garden. "Can we go?" Dave then asked, looking over his shoulder towards the marshals, and receiving a vigorous wave in return to send them on their way.

Dave had absolutely no idea how much time they'd lost, sat

there stationary at the side of the road. He reckoned three or four minutes at least. With all their hopes of finishing now resting on the integrity of a crumpled-up KitKat wrapper, Dave's concerns moved away from the contents of their fuel tank, that being the least thing on his mind just now. Over each and every bump in the road, Dave held his breath for a moment, panicking that the temporary fix would shake itself loose. Dave kept the bike smooth and steady, happy the pace was similar to how they were travelling before pulling in. He would have given anything right about now for a couple of well-placed pit boards on the run into Ramsey. With that information, he would have known if he possessed the luxury to roll off just a touch, therefore reducing the stresses on the bike, or if he needed to give it one final push.

Dave tried to clear his mind of all distractions on the climb up the Mountain Mile section of the course, but the recurring image of Becks and Tyler jumping around the garden of their new dream house had other ideas. "Come on," said Dave, moving out to safely overtake the machine in front.

Passing over the electric railway tracks at Bungalow Station, Dave was spurred on by the sight of hundreds of happy spectators waving their programmes, cheering as each and every rider rode past. *Not long now*, he told himself, glancing up at the pedestrian bridge connecting both sides of the road.

Rapidly approaching the highest point on the course, fierce crosswinds buffeted their bike. Dave, as large as he was, often acted like a sail in conditions such as this. So, being no idiot, he tucked himself down, hugging the bike, making as small a target of himself as humanly possible.

Like him, the tyres were now starting to show signs of fatigue. Understandable after three laps around the place. On the previous two laps, the sweeping bend at Windy Corner was handled with aplomb, the bike feeling like it was glued to the road. This time, Dave felt the bike twitch, concerning him that the tyres were about to give up their valiant quest. *Five more miles*, Dave said, willing him, the bike, the tyres, and even the tinfoil, to hang on in there for just a few more minutes. After all, they'd come this far together.

Up ahead, Dave caught a glimpse of a familiar red fairing just before it disappeared around the rapidly approaching corner. It was Spanky, which pleased Dave, as Spanky had his own concerns about his bike's reliability, and yet there he was, clearly on his way to another finish. Dave caught up with Spanky just before the familiar Kate's Cottage landmark, hanging back a moment longer until the road straightened out, descending to the famous Creg-Ny-Baa pub at the bottom. Then, Dave passed Spanky's machine on the inside line, briefly raising his hand, partly in greeting and partly in appreciation of his words of encouragement earlier — without which, Dave might still be sat in his awning feeling sorry for himself, *listening* to the race rather than *competing* in it as he presently was.

A little over three miles to go, and everything was performing as it should, if not better. The old girl hadn't missed a trick. There were always mixed emotions moving in on the finish line towards the end of the second sidecar race. On the one hand, riders were delighted to cross that finish line, a monumental achievement in and of itself. On the other hand, however, it was tinged with sadness knowing you wouldn't grace this hallowed tarmac until the TT festival the following year. Still, there was always the temptation of the wonderful Southern 100 races in July (held down in Castletown, the island's former capital) if you had withdrawal symptoms from racing sidecars at the TT and needed to scratch that same itch again.

Dave was delighted to see Glencrutchery Road stretching out before him, offering a deep sigh of relief, pinning the throttle with the chequered flag awaiting them at the start/finish line.

"Get in there!" Dave screamed. "Bloody get in there!" he said, the stress evacuating his weary body in a moment of glorious relief as he made it through, sailing across the line. He applied the brakes, dropping down the gearbox, slowing sufficiently to double back on himself up the return lane.

The lower-numbered competitors at the TT weren't the

glamour boys of the sport, necessarily, far from it in some cases. But that didn't stop hundreds of appreciative fans lining the route of the return lane, cheering you on, waving furiously in acknowledgement of what you'd just accomplished. Of course, you may not have been vying for a spot on the podium or even the top twenty, for that matter. But each rider had their own personal goals and motivations, and even if you fell short, you could still lay claim to something that not many others were entitled to say: you'd raced the Isle of Man TT.

Sidecar Number Thirty-Six, battle-scarred and weary, arrived proudly back in parc fermé under its own steam — something neither Dave nor Monty thought possible only half a lap earlier. But she was a warrior, was their bike. Drawing to a halt, Frank and Stan were first on hand to rush over and congratulate them for making it home.

Dave and Monty dismounted their trusty mechanical steed, grateful to remove their helmets and appreciate the breeze. "Well...?" Dave asked with a grimace, almost afraid to hear the answer.

Frank and Stan stood there gravely, their faces deadpan and revealing no emotion.

"Wait, is this one of those moments where you look all serious, then break out the jazz hands, telling us we've made the top ten?" Monty asked, scanning their faces for any flicker of a reaction. "It is, isn't it? Frank?"

"Ah, sorry, boys," Frank replied softly, shaking his head. "Fourteenth place again," he was pained to say. "Assuming none of the other guys still out on track bump you down," he added. Frank could see the utter disappointment on both their faces. "For what it's worth, boys. We're each very proud of you both," he told them.

"Very," Stan agreed.

Dave puffed out his cheeks, exhaling a solid burst of air. "Ah well, Monty, my old son. We couldn't have gone any quicker," he said, leaning down to place a well-earned peck on the side of their bike.

"Nope, you're right," Monty was quick to agree. "I think we've earned ourselves a cheeky pint, yes?"

"I'd gnaw my arm off for one," Dave joked. "Yours too," he said, nibbling the air like a gerbil. "Oh, and we'd best get on the phone to our brand-new sponsors."

Monty smiled, but he didn't know what his mate was on about. "New sponsors?"

"Yes, that's right. Team Frank and Stan's Food Stamps, powered by KitKat," Dave replied, though it was an inside joke that neither Frank nor Stan were yet privy to.

Chapter
TWENTY-ONE

Initially, Dave and Monty had absolutely zero intention of attending the post-racing awards ceremony at the hospitality suite that evening. None whatsoever. They'd relaxed with a beer or several watching the Senior TT race in the afternoon sunshine, and next on their itinerary was a shower and shave, followed by a couple more beers, and then a wander into town for a nice curry to finish the day. The fact that Brad and Chip were premiering the trailer to their documentary series — featuring Captain Ballbag and Major Dipshit — was further reason to give the event a very wide berth, though no disrespect to Chip and Brad of course.

However, Stan took great delight in reminding them of an excellent reason to attend. Well, twenty thousand reasons as it should happen. Because also being announced that evening were the generous winning bidders in the charity's silent auction. And Stan harboured a quiet confidence that their dear old chum, Rodney Franks, was a shoo-in for the helicopter ride! And so, with four tickets allocated to their race team for the glittering event and no desire to waste the remaining two, Frank and Stan made the short walk from their house to the hospitality suite, stopping to collect Dave and Monty from their race HQ en route.

"Knock-knock," Stan said brightly, buoyed by a smug sense of impending satisfaction and the two glasses of prosecco he'd

FRANK & STAN'S BUCKET LIST #5: ISLE OF MAN TT ACES

downed just earlier. "Are you decent?" he joked, opening the flap of Dave and Monty's awning.

Dave rose reluctantly from his seated position. "We're ready to rock 'n' roll," he said.

Stan stopped in his tracks, throwing a quizzical glance at Frank before looking back over to their two friends they'd come to fetch. "Ehm... boys? We need to be there in about, oh, seven minutes or so?" he advised.

"Yeah," Monty replied. "As Dave said, we're ready to rock 'n' roll."

"Any plans on getting changed?" Stan asked, running his hands up and down the sides of his body, showcasing the smart grey sports coat and matching slacks he was wearing.

"Do I need to repeat the rock 'n' roll thing again, Stan?" Dave asked, reaching for his wallet sat there on the arm of the sofa.

Stan fumbled for the event tickets in his pocket, holding one up for inspection. "It says the dress code is smart-casual," Stan confirmed, tapping a manicured fingernail on the embossed card.

"Yeah," Monty said, introducing the shorts and hoodie *he* was wearing with a flick of the wrist. "And I'm casual and feeling smart," he told Stan. "And I even put on a clean pair of socks."

"Eight days straight we reckoned he'd been wearing the previous pair," Dave proudly announced. "Originally, we thought the smell in the van was a piece of cheeseburger that'd escaped down the side of our bed and gone off in the heat. Then my nose ended up near his shoes, and that shocking little mystery was soon solved."

Frank raised a laugh, questioning his own choice of attire. "I suppose it *is* a bit warm for a blazer and such, isn't it?" he considered, fidgeting with the collar of his dress shirt. "Maybe we should head back and change into our shorts...?" he asked to no one in particular.

"We'll do no such thing!" Stan barked in response. "I've already made *significant* sacrifices by dressing without a tie," he pointed out, indicating to the top of his sternum. "Okay, let's get a wriggle on, as I want to savour every minute of watching that cravat-wearing cretin get his comeuppance."

A short traipse through the paddock was often never a quick affair. At every turn, race fans congregated, having a chat with the riders, or simply wandering around awestruck, reflecting on all the majesty and wonder they'd experienced over the previous few days. In addition, there was usually a friendly face or three at this awning or that, eager to drag Dave and Monty in for a bite to eat or to share a beer. And indeed...

"Look at you two dressed for a night on the tiles!" Spanky remarked, his lanky figure appearing from his awning in an oil-stained vest and a pair of denim shorts that were bordering on indecent on account of the unfortunately-placed holes worn through them.

Stan was about to graciously accept Spanky's compliment until he realised it was, bizarrely, directed to Dave and Monty. Still, a pair of shorts and a hoody was at least an improvement over a tatty, oil-covered vest, Stan consoled himself.

"We're being dragged along to the awards ceremony against our will," Monty replied, directing his lazy eye suspiciously at Stan.

"Well, if you need to escape..." Spanky said, but then nothing further.

"Yeah?" Monty answered, anxious to hear the rest of Spanky's master plan, but Spanky just smiled.

"You looked good out there today," Dave said eventually, breaking the silence. "And thank you, mate."

"No problem... for what exactly?" replied Spanky.

"The little pep talk we had beforehand," Dave reminded him, wondering if Spanky had forgotten already. "You remember? We spoke about how Mike the Mechanic came to your aid like Florence Nightingale. Except instead of a thermometer, he had a spanner."

"Oh, yes!" Spanky said, hitching up his shorts. "Yeah. Yeah, actually, that was a load of flannel," he told Dave.

Dave waited for a punchline that didn't arrive. "Sorry? What was?" he asked eventually.

"Mike the Mechanic fixing my bike," Spanky explained.

"Jesus, can we go?" Stan said, stamping his foot like a child eager to hurry their parents along at the supermarket.

"So he didn't fix your bike?" Dave asked, ignoring Stan's plea.

Spanky shook his head, a wry smile emerging. "Nah..." he said, now grinning broadly, showcasing an absent tooth. "Nah, he *did* offer. That much is true. But when he got called away, he never did get an opportunity to come back. So that part was bollocks."

"Oh," said Dave, looking not especially pleased he'd been lied to. "Oh," he said again.

"But it *did* give you the boost you needed, Dave, am I right?" Spanky countered.

"You bastard," Dave replied, though he had a smirk on his face when he said it. "That it did, Spanky. That it did," he conceded. "Thanks, pal. We'll get out for that beer soon," he promised.

"Come on, Stan," Monty said, giving Stan a gentle shove, indicating he was ready to be on his way. "We're always bloody waiting for you, aren't we?" he teased.

"You know," Frank whispered to Dave once they were underway. "Your friend Spanky looks the sort who'd sit in a rocking chair on his porch, bloodhound by his side, arguing with the moon."

"Ha-ha! That's our Spanky to a tee," Dave answered. "And I'm not sure who'd win the argument, him or the moon."

The temperature inside the hospitality suite was warmer than a welder's armpit. Fortunately, Team Frank & Stan's table was at the rear of the building near the opened door. In fact, any further south of the stage and they'd have been sat outside in the paddock from where they'd just arrived.

"From the distant position of our table, I get the impression we're not honoured guests this evening?" Frank gamely ventured, removing his blazer and placing it there on the back of his chair.

"And this table's got one leg shorter than the rest," Stan said, tipping the table back and forth to illustrate his point.

Frank glanced around the room, smiling happily to each set of eyes he met on the way. "I think we're the only bozos overdressed for the occasion," Frank remarked through the corner of his mouth.

"Well, that's their lookout then, isn't it," Stan replied. "If they want to appear like slobs on their big night, then so be it. No offence, boys,"

"None taken," Dave replied.

Even the MC on stage finalising his soundchecks appeared remarkably understated in the way he was dressed, which did not go down well with Stan. "He's wearing *flip-flops!*" Stan observed in a rage. "On stage in bloody flip-flops! Honestly, how standards have slipped."

Stan's eyes then fell on the table in front of theirs, whose seated guests were busy deciding aloud whether they wanted a glass of red or white. "Ah. Where are they getting the wine?" Stan asked, raising his hand at the same time as he said this in hopes of attracting the waiting staff.

"I'm pretty sure they don't have table service," Dave advised, recalling that fact from previous functions he'd been dragged along to.

"Oh. So where do we...?" Stan asked, now at a loss.

"Just there," Dave directed, pointing out the long line of thirsty people running the length of the building and snaking back on itself.

"Please tell me that's not the queue for the bar?" Stan moaned. "It's probably quicker to run back home and raid our bloody drinks cabinet," he remarked.

"Your friend Spanky said he had a few in the fridge, didn't he, Monty?" Frank suggested, though not appearing entirely serious. "Mind you, it's probably moonshine, and I quite like being able to see."

Just then, like two American angels sent from the heavens, Brad and Chip parked themselves on the vacant chairs around the table.

"Oh, hello, boys. So you're gracing the cheap seats?" Dave asked. "I'm surprised you could see us all the way over here."

Brad placed two bottles of red wine on the table. "Courtesy of Rodney Franks," he told them, as Chip then produced four wine glasses.

"Rodney Franks bought us wine?" Stan asked, needing a drink at the very suggestion.

Chip unscrewed the lid from one of the bottles, filling the row of glasses laid out before him. "Well, we borrowed them from his table," Chip explained. "So he *kinda* bought them for you, I guess you could say, even if he doesn't know it."

"We had to get away from the insufferable fool," a jaded Brad added. "We just left him arguing with one of his associates about which country produces the finest caviar."

"Well in that case, I'd like to propose a toast, then. To Rodney Franks, the insufferable fool," Stan proposed, raising his glass.

"The insufferable fool," the others agreed, raising their own glasses and each of them repeating Brad's apt description.

Sadly, two bottles of wine didn't last so very long, especially when you had the pleasure of Dave and Monty's company. So with one eye on the bar area, Stan had just begun to contemplate whether he should mosey on over and join the queue when the compère for the evening kicked things off with several firm finger taps on his microphone. "Welcome, welcome, welcome!" the chirpy fellow announced, allowing the audience to take their seats.

"I'm finally at the front of the queue!" an agitated woman of generous build heckled him from the head of the drinks line. "Thirty minutes I've been waiting here, and now you decide to bloody kick things off? Well, you can just wait!"

"Ooh," the compère offered in response. "You look like you've had enough already," he quipped, raising a cautious laugh from the braver element of the audience.

"I'll wrap that microphone cable around your throat!" the woman shot back, before turning her attention to the harried, overworked bartender. "Nine vodka and Cokes," she said. "No," she quickly added, perhaps reflecting on the time it'd taken her to arrive at this point. "Make it twelve," she said, rummaging in her purse for her money.

"That's what you get when you invite the wife along," the compère said with a sigh, expecting another laugh from the audience but getting only groans in return as this was, after all, the modern 21st century. "Okay, back to business, then. We've another wonderful evening in store for you all!" he said, hoping to whip the audience into a frenzy that didn't arrive. "Right..." he pressed on. "Okay, first up, we're going to announce the generous winners of the silent auction before you're all too legless to remember. And then, we'll move on to the awards..."

"This is it," Stan said, tuning his ears out from the rest of the agenda being announced, nudging Frank in the ribs. "I can't wait to see the look on that smug get's face."

Stan moved his seat slightly to the right, just a touch, so he was now able to enjoy an unobstructed if somewhat distant view of Rodney Franks' table. He rubbed his hands together so furiously he was in danger of starting a fire. "Ooh, I cannot wait," he reiterated.

"Um... what's going on?" Brad asked over the table, trying to follow Stan's line of sight. "You okay, Stan...?"

"Oh, I'm simply wonderful. Never better, in fact," Stan told Brad, not breaking his intense stare from where it was being directed.

The compère worked his way through the selection of silent auction prize winners, resulting in a steady stream of benefactors making their way to the stage to accept their prize and bask in the warm appreciation of their generous patronage. But, in truth, some of the prize items were distinctly average, including such treasures as a wheelbarrow modified with a motorsport-themed paint job, and a three-course meal with the scintillating company of sidecar aces Andy Thomas and Jack Napier.

FRANK & STAN'S BUCKET LIST #5: ISLE OF MAN TT ACES

"I'd rather have a Pot Noodle and an early night," Dave suggested, though the generous applause drowned him out.

The compère congratulated the lucky winner of the painted wheelbarrow, before waving a white envelope teasingly for the crowd's benefit. "And now for the star prize, as you've all been waiting for," he said, extracting an audible *oooh* as the situation correctly demanded. "To remind you, the winning bidder and a guest will have the thrill of accompanying the TV helicopter as they fly above the course recording one of next year's races. It really is a prize that money cannot buy. Apart from, that is, the person's name inside this envelope."

"Get ready," Stan said, hanging off the edge of his seat and gripping Frank's knee tightly.

"And to present the very generous winner of the helicopter flight, I'm delighted to bring upon the stage a guest of honour. A man familiar to us all in racing circles and, as he told me earlier, one of the stars of the upcoming TT documentary, a preview of which will be aired this evening for the very first time. Ladies and gentlemen... Rodney Franks."

Rodney graciously accepted the invite, waving to his appreciative audience with such fervour that you'd be forgiven for thinking he was collecting an Oscar rather than simply opening an envelope.

"I don't understand," Stan said, hand still on Frank's knee. "They must know who the winning bidder was, so why would they have Rodney Franks up there, unless...?"

"Unless he's not the winning bidder," Frank said, finishing Stan's thought for him.

Stan swallowed hard. So hard his larynx looked like a golf ball being forced through a hosepipe. "I don't like this," Stan said, shifting nervously in his seat, and with beads of perspiration starting to appear on his forehead.

"What if that little ruse of yours has been uncovered?" Frank whispered, looking around to see if security were perhaps heading over to their table right then, as they spoke.

"I think we need to go," Stan said, making as if he was about to rise from his chair. But before he could even lift his bum cheeks from the seat, Rodney pressed the microphone to his lips. He shielded the stage lighting from his eyes, running his attention around the room. For a frightening moment, it even appeared he'd stared directly at Stan's table.

"It's an honour for me to be up here on stage," Rodney said. "For you lot, at least," he quickly added, releasing a laugh that sounded like an asthmatic donkey. "I really wanted to present the winner of the silent auction simply because the generosity of the bid has astounded us all. I even joked that with a bid so generous, the winner could just as easily have purchased their own helicopter."

"I'm starting to feel ill," Stan said, elbows now on the table, head resting in his hands. "This isn't going to be good, is it?"

Rodney peeled open the envelope on stage, flicking his eyes between it and the audience, unable to contain the satisfied grin spreading over his face. "And the winner of the helicopter ride for two, with an unbelievable bid of twenty-five thousand pounds, is..." he said, shaking his head in mock disbelief, or it could just as easily have been delight. "Stanley Sidcup!" Rodney announced, starting the applause and causing a ripple effect. "Get yourself up here, Stanley!"

Stan, for his part, cowered over the table, trying to make himself as small as possible, and very much hoping that one of those sinkholes he kept reading about in the news would be kind enough to appear just now and swallow him up whole.

"Don't be shy!" Rodney called out, directing the half-soused spotlight operator as to where his shaking beam should now be trained.

Stan often liked to be the centre of appreciation, but right now he would've been more than willing to pass that attention along to someone else. *Anyone* else.

"More money than sense, that one," Monty remarked with a chuckle, shaking his head as he reached for one of the two open wine bottles on the table which both, to his regret, remained sadly empty.

FRANK & STAN'S BUCKET LIST #5: ISLE OF MAN TT ACES

Stan now realised that he'd been stitched up like a kipper, and with no other options on offer, he reluctantly rose to his feet, smiling bravely, though legs shaking like a shitting dog. He desperately wanted to crawl into some dark recess, but the spotlight following him had other ideas. Several people offered their sincere congratulations as Stan passed by, but their words of kindness washed away like the stream of sweat currently running down his back.

"Stanley Sidcup, ladies and gentlemen!" Rodney said as Stan approached, with Rodney clapping, microphone in hand.

The next few minutes skipped by in a surreal blur. Stan even managed a rambling acceptance speech, but with him on the verge of tears throughout and constantly tripping over his words. He remembered little of what he said, but he did know it wasn't his finest theatrical performance, that's for sure.

As the compère stepped forward, anxious to bring Stan's largely incoherent moment in the limelight to a close, Rodney handed over the microphone, placing his arm around Stan and moving his mouth within kissing distance of Stan's ear so that only Stan could hear him. "And that's what you get for crossing Rodney Franks," he whispered, giving a little giggle. "You didn't really think I'd fall for that pathetic plan, did you? I saw you and your idiotic acquaintance hanging around that day and knew you were up to something. So, after you'd left, I amended your handiwork, making *you* the winning bidder. Oh, and with an extra five grand for good measure."

"Is that why you wanted Monty and Dave out of the TV documentary?" Stan asked weakly. "For revenge?"

"That's part of it, yes," Rodney said, patting Stan's back. "But mostly it's that I just really don't like you lot," he added simply. "And we couldn't have people like you becoming famous, now could we? That's better suited for someone of my standing and impeccable breeding."

There was no fight left in Stan, so he retreated from the stage with the world's most expensive white envelope to keep as a souvenir. Then, passing Rodney's table near to the front, Stan reached over the vacant seat and swiped another bottle of red to keep him well lubricated on his long walk back home to the cheap seats.

Try as he might, Frank was doing a pretty substandard job of cheering his mate up in his time of need, once Stan got back to their table. Unfortunately, the sporadic bouts of laughter at his mate's expense didn't appear to be helping matters any. Compounding Stan's pain further was Dave and Monty humming the theme music to *Airwolf*, the old American TV series with Ernest Borgnine and Jan-Michael Vincent, a friendly little reminder of his helicopter adventure that awaited him.

"This must have been what Spanky overheard," Dave said in a moment of realisation. "There was never any issue with the bike, or any plans of sabotage, I reckon. Rather, the expensive issue they mentioned was Stan winning the helicopter ride, though Spanky wouldn't have known that."

Monty grinned in response. "That's a relief," he said.

"Not for Stan," Dave replied.

"No, I'd dare say it isn't," Monty answered, and with the both of them laughing.

"I'm *right here*, guys," Stan sulked.

The awards portion of the evening's proceedings came and went without incident. Well, apart from the distinct displeasure of witnessing a snivelling Rodney Franks, arms draped over his riders as they collected yet another set of awards to add to their ever-expanding trophy cabinet.

"Can we just go?" Stan moaned, placing his eye on the mouth of the upturned wine bottle in his hand and seeing nothing at all coming out of it.

"You might want to give it another ten minutes or so," Brad suggested from across the table, accompanied by a cheeky grin.

"Okay," the compère called out, signalling the end of the brief comfort break. "It's not often we can boast about hosting a worldwide premiere, of sorts, but that's precisely what we've got for you this evening," he said. "Brad? Chip?" he called out, running his eyes around the room until he caught sight of the

FRANK & STAN'S BUCKET LIST #5: ISLE OF MAN TT ACES

brothers. "If you'd like to come on up?"

Brad and Chip headed up to the stage, offering a series of polite waves in response to the warm applause aimed their way. "Thank you," said Brad, taking possession of the microphone once on stage. "My brother and I have both been overwhelmed by all the positive support we've received here during the filming of our production," he told the crowd. "For that, the two of us are sincerely grateful. And our colleagues back home have been burning the midnight oil to help us quickly finalise the trailer for our documentary series, which is due for release later this year."

"Yes," Chip entered in, taking the microphone handed over to him. "Our docuseries wouldn't have been possible without the support and cooperation we've received from the moment we stepped foot on this beautiful island. And, in our minds, there is no finer, more exhilarating sport on the face of the planet than the Isle of Man TT. Which is of course why we chose it as our subject." Chip paused for a moment to allow the applause to settle down. "From the outset, we wanted to tell the story of the heroes that are the heart of this captivating event. Those dedicated folks for whom this event is not merely just a hobby, but a way of life," he said. Chip turned, extending his arm towards the screen behind him. "Ladies and gentlemen, we're delighted to give you the story of the Isle of Man TT Aces."

Dramatic music boomed from the speakers, shaking the audience to attention. The introduction was pure Hollywood: dramatic, sweeping action shots of bikes hurtling past, inches from the kerb. A montage of race fans watching, jaws swinging low in response as to what they were witnessing. It was all very thrilling. Even Stan managed to snap out of the doldrums for a while to appreciate it.

"Just because you're breathing, doesn't mean you're alive!" an enthusiastic, rugged-sounding male voiceover artist declared in typical, bombastic fashion and a distinctly American accent, moments before another burst of racing action. "Two men with one dream! A dream of competing amidst the greatest sporting show on earth! Coming to your television screens this fall! This is the story of Dave Quirk and Shaun 'Monty' Montgomery! This is the story of the Isle of Man TT Aces!"

A hushed silence filled the hospitality suite as the preview progressed, with the trailer eventually drawing to a dramatic conclusion with a final parting shot of a sidecar leaving the start line and snaking its way into the distance until it disappeared from view.

Rapturous applause erupted the moment the presentation was finished. It was evident from this response that Chip and Brad had captured the emotion well that only came from this fair isle's world-famous sporting event.

What was also evident was the obvious absence of Rodney Franks, anything associated with Rodney Franks, or anything even *remotely* Rodney Franks-related to be found within the highly anticipated preview. This, of course, as one might anticipate, did not go unnoticed by Rodney Franks...

"Oi!" Rodney called out. "Oi, you two!" he protested, shaking his fist, incandescent with rage, his cheeks scarlet. "I'm talking to you!" he said, but his protests went unanswered as the two of them scarpered off backstage, completely ignoring poor old Rodney.

"You know..." Stan remarked happily, after watching events unfold. "Tonight might not be that bad of an evening after all!"

Chapter
TWENTY-TWO

The Saturday after Senior Race Day was often something of an anti-climax for many people involved in the racing. Awnings were being taken down, vans packed up, and farewells issued to friends you might not see for another year. The vibrant paddock was transforming from a bustling community and back into an unassuming patch of grass. But if this grass could talk about what it'd been a party to, it'd tell tales of dreams fulfilled, friendships forged, late nights, early mornings, tears of laughter, and sadly, perhaps for some, the pain of friends who wouldn't return.

Spectators were headed off for home as well, heads buzzing from both the memories made and the absence of a good night's sleep in they didn't know how long. And, as the ferry pulled away from Douglas Harbour, the rear of the vessel was packed with folks desperate to enjoy the island for just that wee, tiny bit longer. As the isle slowly disappeared from view, thoughts turned from sadness to optimism. Yes, their time on the island had drawn to a conclusion, but they now had exactly fifty weeks to save some dosh until the next TT races when they'd be back to do it all again.

Back at the paddock, Dave and Monty had packed up most everything, leaving only a patch of faded grass and clover where the awning that was Team Frank & Stan's race HQ had been home for the last two weeks.

"What are we going to do with this?" Dave asked, patting the arm of their manky sofa.

"Throw it in bloody Rodney Franks' awning," Monty insisted, rubbing the bruising around his eye.

"Does it hurt?" Dave asked with a chuckle, not entirely without sympathy and yet still seeing plenty of mirth to be had in the situation.

Monty prodded the tender, orbital flesh like he was inspecting a steak to see if it was properly cooked, checking it for doneness. "Yes, it does!" he said.

"You know, you may not want to make too much fuss about this," Dave advised.

"But I was assaulted!" Monty protested. "I was the victim of a vicious, unprovoked assault!"

This allegation set Dave laughing once again. "You tried to grab his cravat," he had to remind his friend.

"I just wanted to see if it was tied in a knot, or something he slipped over his head. And he didn't have to bloody punch me, now did he?"

"Ahh, Monty," Dave said with a delighted sigh. "You must be the only man in history who could lay claim to being physically assaulted by that little pipsqueak of a rodent, Rodney Franks. You know, when he squared up to you, it reminded me of a small boy shouting at someone for stealing his shoes outside of a bouncy castle."

"You can laugh—"

"And I will."

To suggest Rodney Franks hadn't taken his omission from the official trailer particularly well would have been something of an understatement. He'd marched over to Brad and Chip, jabbing fingers into each of their chests, demanding to know what exactly the pair of them were playing at. Threats were then issued regarding the cash Rodney had paid them, and the well-worn edict of "you'll never work in this town again" was issued, drawing a burst of laughter from those sat nearby, only serving to wind Rodney up even further.

Stan, especially, was enjoying the unfolding fracas, taking

particular delight in witnessing Rodney's fury and frustration. Unfortunately, when Monty grabbed Rodney's cravat and fists started flying, security had to be called over. And that was when Team Frank & Stan were ejected from the venue, unable to enjoy the conclusion of the developing mêlée.

Presently, with the absence of an awning surrounding them or any neighbours to speak of, the image of two blokes sat on a sofa in the middle of a mostly empty field must have appeared quite amusing to those passing by. "Oh, incoming," Dave said, offering a hearty wave across the grassy pitch.

Approaching with rucksacks slung over their shoulders, Brad and Chip marvelled at the difference a few hours made to the place. "It's like the circus has came and went," Chip called over, shaking his head, incredulous. "Mind if we join you?"

"Please, take a seat," Dave replied with a smile, pointing to empty space, as there were of course no seats in the immediate vicinity left to take.

"Thanks, but we'll stand," Chip joked, as it wasn't like they really had any other choice. "How's the eye?" he asked, turning to Monty.

"We think the impact might have lined them back up," Dave replied on his mate's behalf. "I'm pretty sure both pupils were finally working in unison when he looked over before, believe it or not."

"Hilarious," Monty said in reply to Dave's commentary. And then, in response to Chip's query, "It hurts," he said. "I was, after all, subjected to a most vicious assault."

"Oh? It was more of a girlish slap, though, wasn't it?" Chip suggested, having been there and seeing it for himself. "Anyway, let's see," he offered, moving in for a closer look. "Huh. You know what, they *do* look straighter," Chip remarked, waving his finger this way and that, back and forth, and watching how Monty's eyes tracked.

"So what happened after we were all hoofed out?" Dave asked, smiling at the thought. "Did Rodney get his lawyers on a conference call?"

FRANK & STAN'S BUCKET LIST #5: ISLE OF MAN TT ACES

"Rodney Franks can kiss our Yankee doodle asses," said Brad, slapping his derrière for effect. "After his little hissy fit, we politely informed him that neither he nor his race team were going to be the primary focus of our documentary. We told him we'd feature *some* footage of Napier and Thomas, since the TV studio was pretty clear they wanted scenes of the TT winners included in there. So, them picking up the trophy, obviously, and maybe a few action shots, we said."

"And he was agreeable to that?" Monty asked.

"No, he absolutely wasn't," Chip answered. "At that point, we thought the dude was going to have a freakin' aneurysm. He reminded us about all the money he'd given us, and told us, in no uncertain terms, that he'd very much like to have it back. In addition, we were not, under any circumstances, to use any footage of his race-winning team in action. If they weren't going to be the stars of the production, he told us, then we didn't have permission to show them at all."

"But you're going to use them anyway?" Dave asked.

"Oh, sure," Brad said.

"And you're not giving him his money back?"

"Oh, no. No, not at all," Brad added brightly. "Not a chance."

Dave reflected on this for a moment, and as pleased as he was to hear it all, he was left a bit confused. "So, Rodney Franks paid you a shedload of cash for his team to feature prominently in your TV documentary, but, aside from the occasional appearance here and there, you've all but cut them out? Is that right?" he asked, wanting to make sure he understood things correctly.

Brad nodded. "Yup!"

"Yet you've taken his cash?" Monty entered in. "And, we're now reinstated as stars of the show?"

"Yup!" Brad said again. "Nailed it on the noggin," he added.

"Right. As much as I admire anyone getting one over on that miserable sod," Dave said, "I'm not sure Rodney's the sort to let you get away with that, lads, if I'm honest. Surely he'll just call the rozzers? I mean, as much as I like the two of you, is that not fraud or something?"

"Okay," said Brad, perching himself on the end of the sofa. "It's probably a good idea if we take you back a little ways and fill you in on everything that's been going on. Then, all will become clear..."

Brad began his story by once again apologising for cutting Dave and Monty out in the first place. Of course, it was never their intention, but with their camera equipment stolen, there simply wouldn't have been any way to continue had Rodney Franks not intervened. But, as it should happen, Rodney had intervened in more ways than one. Brad then went on to explain how the police had got in touch with them regarding the dashcam footage they'd received.

"When the police showed us the clip, I was pretty sure I knew who'd broken into our rental car, since I recognised a tattoo on the thief's left hand," Chip entered in.

"Oh? Who was it?" Monty asked, eager to hear more, and all thoughts of the searing pain around his eye forgotten.

"Well..." Chip went on, pausing to wet his lips, building the anticipation for a moment. "It was that big sack of meat, Vince. The gorilla who works for Rodney Franks."

"Rodney arranged for your equipment to be nicked?" Dave asked. "Holy crap. But why...?"

"So he could conveniently come to our rescue, and then use the situation as leverage to kick the two of you out as stars of the docuseries and insert his motley crew of dickwads in there as the leads instead," Brad explained.

"*Bastards*," said Dave. "But you didn't tell the cops that you recognised Vince as the thief?"

Chip shook his head. "Nah," he replied, "Rodney would've just denied knowing anything about it, so it wouldn't have been worth the hassle. Besides, we came up with a better idea."

Chip went on to explain the next stage of the plan. One which was always going to be a calculated gamble. But with their future career as filmmakers on the line, the boys pressed on with the production of their series, using the equipment Rodney had loaned them. In the beginning, of course, they'd

FRANK & STAN'S BUCKET LIST #5: ISLE OF MAN TT ACES

had every intention of honouring their agreement with Rodney and in fact had spent a considerable amount of time and energy retooling the script and capturing additional footage of the new cast of characters. However, once they'd eventually realised that their saviour, Rodney, was actually the *instigator* of their potential downfall, the boys immediately changed tack. Oh, they still carried on with making their programme, but they were now back to making it *their* way. And as far as ensuring this could happen, they decided to take matters into their own hands. All they needed, then, was proof of Rodney's guilt.

"So," Chip said, "that's when we decided to return some of the recording equipment he'd lent us. Specifically, radio mics and such. While we were in Rodney's motorhome, we happened to mention — well, very *intentionally* mentioned, I should say — that the police had procured some fantastically useful footage of the original theft. And then, we amscrayed and left him to his own devices."

"Like, literally, his own devices. That *we* planted there," Brad added in, with a laugh.

"You left one of the radio mics on to record the prat?" Monty suggested, getting the gist of this scenario, and rubbing his hands together in appreciation of the boys' cunning.

"Exactly!" Brad said. "All we needed to do was set things in motion. And sure enough, next thing you know, Rodney's on the horn instructing Vince to dispose of our equipment. A conversation we now have on tape. So we then follow Vince, and catch him on video emptying a storage unit where all our stolen gear is being kept."

"What a horrible, horrible little man," Dave remarked, looking across to Monty. But again, Dave couldn't help but laugh when he saw Monty's black eye.

"Stop it! I'm in pain here!" Monty protested, turning away from Dave in a huff. "So..." Monty said, encouraging the two brothers to please continue their tale.

"So you remember how upset Rodney was the other night? At the awards ceremony?" Brad replied. "Well, he came blowing over like a hurricane, eventually catching up with us. We let him run his mouth for a few minutes. And then we sprang that recording on him, the one we made of his conversation with Vince, his oversized minion."

"And *then* we showed him the video we made of Vince at the storage locker," Chip entered back in, grinning widely. "That's when we gave him two options," he added. "First, we could give him back his money like he asked. *Or*, he could shut his piehole, let us do our show the way we wanted, and maybe, just maybe, we wouldn't turn over the evidence we'd collected to the boys in blue. Or whatever you call them over here," he said. "Anyway, naturally, he went for option number two."

"So where's your equipment now?" Dave asked. "Did you get it back?"

Chip offered a shrug. "No, we didn't," he said. "And no idea where it all is, either. We watched Vince drive away with it, so it's probably in some landfill, or somewhere at the bottom of the ocean by now."

"But all is not lost," Brad said, perking up. "We've figured out how much we'll need to replace everything, even factoring in some nifty upgrades, and the money we got from Rodney will *totally* cover it, even leaving us with lots left over. So him not getting his money back is the very least Rodney could do after nearly ruining our careers."

"Bingo," said Dave, raising his hands for a celebratory high-five. "Every time you hit the record button on your new camera, you can think of Rodney squirming."

Monty noticed the two rucksacks lying on the grass. "That you boys packed up and ready to leave?" he asked.

"Those?" Brad answered. "Naw, those are just the rest of the borrowed equipment that's being returned to Rodney. That huge motorhome of his is still parked around here someplace, so we're just gonna go dump the stuff on his doorstep."

"Don't want to be accused of robbing him," Chip said with a wry smile. "In answer to your question, though, we *are* packed and ready to go, yeah. But we just wanted to stop by and say thanks. Thanks, that is, for being a part of our great adventure here, and hopefully we can now count you guys as friends...?"

"As if that were even in doubt," Dave answered, smiling as he stood. "Come here, you lot," he said, ushering them both in for a cuddle. "You too, Monty," Dave instructed, waving Monty over.

"Just mind my eye, will you?" Monty cautioned, rising up from the couch and extending his arms to join the group embrace. "Only it's still extremely sore, and Dave here's not taking it very seriously at all!"

The boys enjoyed a snuggle in the middle of a virtually empty field. "I'm going to miss you two," Brad said, once freed. "Please pass our best wishes on to Stan and Frank?"

"Of course," Dave said. "And we look forward to seeing our mugs on the telly soon?"

"Probably late September," Chip advised. "Depending upon scheduling and the final edit."

Brad remained quiet for a moment, looking to his brother, as if waiting to see if he could be the one to say the bit that needed saying next, and then receiving the nod. Brad cleared his throat. "Okay, well there *was* something else to tell you guys," he said, desperately fighting a losing battle with his emerging smile. "The money we got from Rodney was actually pretty substantial," he told them. "We've figured out exactly how much we'll need to purchase our new equipment, replacing what he stole from us. But there'll still be a whole lot left over."

"Yeah," Chip said. "We felt really terrible for you guys getting screwed over. Which is why we contacted that previous sponsor of yours once we knew you were back in the game. Of course we hoped you'd win the money they were offering, but when you didn't, we couldn't help but feel it was partly our fault. Like, for not giving you proper time to prepare and stuff."

"*Pfft*," Dave said, waving their concerns away, but liking the sound of where this conversation might be heading.

"What my brother and I would like to do," Brad said, "is to offer you a bit of cash. Now, we know you're proud individuals, and that we'd probably need to force you to—"

"No, no!" Monty cut across. "We're proud, yes, but we still need to buy new tyres, and fuel, and, well, loads of other things. So any contributions are greatly appreciated, is what I'm trying to say," he told the two brothers.

"Great. The money will be forwarded to the same account we sent your advance to," replied Brad. "Oh, and it's the exact same amount you would've gotten from the gambling company," he advised, adding this casually as if it were no big deal. "But we want first dibs on you guys for a sequel to the series, agreed?"

Dave was definitely pleased. But he was certain the boys had made a mistake and couldn't have meant what it seemed like they were saying. "No, lads, they offered us thirty thousand pounds," Dave gently advised, wishing to correct the apparent misunderstanding. He was absolutely appreciative of whatever amount the boys had been planning to send over, of course, but he knew it couldn't possibly have been that.

"Yup, that's right. And that's what'll soon be warming your bank account," Brad informed Dave.

"Done," said Chip, looking up from his phone.

"You're joking?" Dave said. "Tell me you're joking."

"We're not," Brad was happy to report, and with Chip standing there smiling, phone still in hand. "Just check your bank account, and you'll see it's there, assuming Chip's just done his job."

"You'll see two transfers, actually," Chip relayed. "I messed up the first one, forgetting to do the dollars-to-pounds conversion thing. All set now."

Dave placed his hand over his mouth, scarcely daring to believe what he'd just been told. "I can put a deposit on a house!" he said, jumping for joy, setting his breasts a-wiggling. "Monty, I can buy a house!" he screamed in delight, stepping forward and scooping his best mate up in his arms. "I can buy a house, Monty!"

Monty, for his part, was equally as thrilled, even if he couldn't exactly breathe right at present due to him being subjected to a patented Dave Quirk bearhug. "Mind... my... eye..." Monty cautioned, through laboured breaths, though his broad smile suggested he wasn't completely worried.

Brad and Chip patted the boys on the back and felt genuine sadness as they bid their farewells. They'd had an absolute blast on the Isle of Man, meeting a great group of characters. Of course they'd met some real knuckleheads along the way also. But, in the end, it all balanced out, as it often does in life's rich tapestry.

Brad and Chip headed away to return Rodney's equipment, leaving the boys jumping up and down on their sofa behind them. "Oh, hey!" Brad called over, turning around, and walking backwards as he spoke. "Hey, you guys!"

"Yeah?" Dave said breathlessly, between bounces.

"The studio wants you over in Boston to perform some PR work ahead of the show's premiere!"

"Piss off!" Dave shouted back, assuming they were now the object of a gentle ribbing.

"We're serious! They said they'd pay for four of you to come over for a month!" Chip offered, raising his thumb. "So we'll be in touch, real soon!" he added, wandering in the vague direction of Rodney's motorhome.

The aged springs in the sofa did a remarkable job of withstanding the onslaught they were presently being subjected to, with Dave and Monty hopping up and down like two kangaroos on a trampoline. If there were any fleas left on the sofa, they all would have been bounced right off, clearing them out.

"There's something I was going to tell you," Monty said, once they finally came to a stop.

"Yeah?" Dave said, climbing down from the sofa.

"Mavis across the road has just put her house on the market. I wanted to tell you before, but when we didn't win the cash, I didn't want to dangle that carrot."

"We could be neighbours?" Dave said, catching his breath.

"We could be neighbours," Monty confirmed, repeating his mate's words back to him.

"We could be neighbours!" they both screamed in unison.

Chapter
TWENTY-THREE

John Light loitered with intent, stealing a series of furtive glances through the window of the taxi office. He hadn't seen Stella inside for a good while. But after his previous experience — one he'd yet to entirely recover from — he'd wait outside until the official handover point in a little over twenty minutes, at four p.m. Of course, it meant he'd have less time to replace the signage, but you could never put a price on personal safety, he reckoned.

Inside the office behind the reception desk could be seen new staff, appointed by the new owners, now sat there ready for action. It was a changing of the guard. No longer would the passing public look through the large glass windows to catch a glimpse of Stella, fag in mouth, bringing order to chaos amidst Frank and Stan's empire. The two new operators on hand were fairly young, by all appearances, with still quite a few years ahead of them to look forward to. Bright and well-presented, they sported their new uniforms of matching polo shirts and a generous smile apiece.

Stella had been tasked with training the two young women, upskilling them to her own methodical and particular standards. Initially, Stella had been uncooperative, even belligerent, building a defensive fortress around her considerable frame (metaphorically speaking, that is) to prevent any information from being either transmitted or received. After all, why should she spend long hours of her precious time training the new staff when she was being ousted from the job she adored, were her thoughts. However, as Susie was quick to point out, it wasn't the girls' fault, and it would be their customers that'd suffer in the long run.

Once the selfish mist cleared, Stella knew Susie was talking sense. The taxi business had been her life for years, and she wouldn't let standards slip at this late stage. For that reason, in the final few days of her tenure, Stella set about teaching her students everything she knew about the orderly operations of a bustling city centre taxi business. The girls sat rapt, listening to the secrets of a grandmaster being revealed. They were like two young Luke Skywalkers being given life lessons by Yoda, and it was an education they wouldn't soon forget.

Some elements of the curriculum the girls chose to safely disregard, such as what biscuit went best with what time of day, and which air freshener spray worked best in the bog when those biscuits would eventually be vacated. Other aspects were of particular interest, though, including the self-defence tutorial. Working all hours in a busy taxi office exposed you to all sorts of unsavoury sorts. Even the type who liked to expose themselves, as Stella spoke in fond recollection. So, the girls watched on, awestruck, as Stella explained, in detail, how to incapacitate a drunk using their own kebab against them (with Stella pointing out that you were perfectly free to eat the kebab afterwards as well). It was a real eye-opener, and information the girls hoped they'd never be required to use, but relieved that the knowledge was there, stored in their memory banks should it ever need to be deployed.

It's fair to say their business relationship was brief and, for the girls, often frightening. But once they'd climatised to the acrid stench of stale tobacco and occasional bursts of uncontrolled aggression, there was a hidden side to Stella that they rather enjoyed, they found. Indeed, the girls were eventually sorry to see her go as their working environment wouldn't be quite the same without her.

Eventually, at 3:50 p.m., Stella emerged from the toilet one last time. She hadn't needed to go, necessarily. But, she'd felt one last poignant attempt for old time's sake was in order, and sure enough, there'd been success. It had been a struggle, but one that was important to her. And then, upon completion, all matters finally being settled to her satisfaction, she placed her well-thumbed newspaper atop the reception countertop. "You should probably—" she started to say.

"Give it ten minutes before going in?" Debbie, one of the new recruits, said fondly in response, cutting her off mid-flow. "We will, Stella," she added quickly, diligent student that she was, remembering precisely what she'd been taught.

"Twenty to be safe," Stella advised, tapping her nose like another life lesson had just been delivered.

Stella was disappointed that her last day was spent without her able and longsuffering wingman, Susie, for company. Yes, a gippy tummy wasn't the nicest thing to be off ill with, but still. Her absence didn't stop Stella feeling even more down in the dumps than she already was. She paced slowly around the office, having one last look around, allowing her finger to trail across the various surfaces. Finally, she eased up in front of the coatstand. It was unexpected, but a wave of emotion surged through her, resulting in a shudder.

"You okay?" Marlayna, the other of the two day-shift girls, called over, unsure if she should approach or keep a respectable distance, as she'd been cautioned in the handover notes (and as she'd learned from her own experience working with Stella these last few days).

"That coatstand used to be full," Stella said, without turning. "Stan had some bloody awful coats over the years," she went on, allowing the memories to come flooding back. "He once had this leather number with a fur-lined collar. Bloody awful it was. I told him he looked like a seal, and threatened to club him like one on several occasions. Frank, his soppy mate, used to be married to this right stuck-up tart. For a time, she made him wear one of those parka, Liam Gallagher-style coats. From what he

FRANK & STAN'S BUCKET LIST #5: ISLE OF MAN TT ACES

told me, she thought he was looking old and said this would take years off him."

Stella held that thought a while longer, running her hand up and down the coatstand. Neither of the girls had met Frank or Stan, but they sat silently, allowing their mentor ample time to reflect.

"When Frank came in wearing that ridiculous jacket, all the drivers were laughing at him behind his back, weren't they?" Stella continued. "So I marched right in with my scissors and cut the bloody arms off of it, completely ruining it so he couldn't wear that horrid thing anymore. After he'd taken it off, and hung it on *here*," she said.

Still with her back to the girls, Stella wiped the tears from the side of her cheek. "She treated him like dirt, that money-grabbing slapper," Stella told them, her voice hardening. "She'd saunter in here like Lady Muck, swanning around like she owned the place. One time she marched into his office, furious because the new hot tub he'd ordered didn't have Bluetooth. She used to scream at him that much that I caught him crying in his office once. I remember, on this one particular occasion, when she came in here with her shopping bags and dumped them right in the middle of the reception area. She was meeting up with friends for the afternoon, and she *ordered* me to have one of the drivers take her shopping home. The cheek of her! She was all done up, just back from the nail place and with her fake tits popping out her blouse. She didn't like it one least little bit when I told her she could fuck right off. Said I was above my station, and that she'd have me fired. So you know what I did? There are two industrial-sized bins in the back lane, right? So I grabbed hold of her by this tacky, god-awful scarf she was wearing, marched her through the reception area, back through the rear, kicked open the back door, lifted her up, and then dumped her headfirst into one of the bloody bins. *Nobody* makes my friends cry. Not even if that friend happens to be a dunderhead like Frank."

Stella moved away from the coatstand and into Frank and

Stan's empty office. It was a shell of its former self, with the personal possessions now removed. She closed her eyes and could hear the two of them in her mind squabbling over something or other. But there were good times, of course, aside from the pleasure of listening to those two silly sods bicker like the prats they were. It may have been an office and a place of work, but Stella's resounding memories were of laughter, awful jokes, and people apologising on her behalf. She'd been happy here. She took a seat on Frank's desk, trying desperately to keep her emotions in check.

"Sorry to interrupt," Debbie offered, leaning against the inside of the doorway and keeping a respectful distance. "I meant to say, earlier. We were having a clear-around, and we found this under one of the desks."

Stella scrunched up her eyes, straining to see what it was that Debbie was holding in her hand. "That's a metal bolt," she declared, distinctly uninterested.

"I know," Debbie pressed on, approaching the desk. "We were going to throw it away, but Susie had stopped us. She said it reminded her of a special night, and asked us to show it to you. I'd clean forgotten about it until just now," she said. "Here you go," she added, passing the item over.

Stella took hold of the short metal bolt. It had a very distinctive shape, and Stella half expected it to be a practical joke and blow up in her hands in a cloud of dust. But then, seeing it there in the palm of her hand, a memory jumped into her head, resulting in an immediate and exuberant burst of laughter. "Frank and Stan wore these on our Christmas party one year," she managed to get out in between a fit of the giggles. "The silly sods dressed themselves up as Frankenstein. The monster, that is. Not the doctor. You know, the big green bloke? Anyway, the bolts were attached to plastic straps that went around their necks like a dog collar. The two of them ended up having too much to drink, with Stan climbing into a shopping trolley once outside, and Frank pushing him around in it like a baby in a pram. It was all fun and games until a shop assistant started chasing after them wanting the trolley back. Anyway, they must have been going some speed when they hit the kerb and overturned it."

"Ouch," Debbie responded with a grimace. "I take it there was no lasting damage?" she asked. Debbie could have listened to Stella reminiscing for hours. It was nice to see Stella like this, she thought, smiling and content.

"One of the wheels snapped off," Stella replied with a cackle. "Stan went face-first into a phone box, and I found that bolt later on, lying there on the ground next to one of his teeth. Aah, happy times."

"It's nearly knock-off time for us," Debbie said kindly. "Do you want to maybe go for a quick drink after the evening shift arrives? You know, to say goodbye?"

"Thanks," Stella answered, wrapping her fingers tightly around the metal bolt. "But I think I'm going to get going," she said, pushing herself off the desk. She gave Debbie's shoulder a pat as she walked by, making her way back to the reception area. "You two look after this place, yeah?" she said, voice breaking. "Otherwise, I'll be back to crack your heads together!"

"We'll look after her, we promise," Marlayna assured her, struggling to contain her own tears. "Oh, and before you go, you might want this...?" she offered, reaching under her desk. "You nearly forgot it," she suggested. And with that, she produced, and then handed over, Stella's miniature cricket bat, which had lived under the desk for those times when Stella's fists didn't quite fit the bill and something a little extra was required.

Stella caressed the hard, seasoned wood affectionately, but then ended up returning the bat, shaking her head firmly. "You keep it. It belongs in this office, keeping you both safe," she insisted. "I'll see you soon, yeah?"

Stella took a deep breath, opening the front door one last time before stepping outside into the warm evening air. She wanted to look back, just for a moment, but reckoned her fragile emotions wouldn't be able to handle it. "Goodbye, old friend," she whispered to the place, placing one hobnail boot in front of the other, looking down at the pavement as she began walking away, entirely consumed in her own thoughts.

"Oi! You there!" a brusque voice suddenly called out, serving to divert Stella's attention. "You order a taxi, sweetheart?" the person added, surly yet welcoming, snapping Stella firmly back into the present.

She glanced up the street in the direction of the familiar voice, which she well recognised. "If I was going to phone for a cab, I wouldn't have asked for *you*, Albert," she said with a cheerful snarl. "You're the worst bloody taxi driver in Liverpool," she told him, walking in the direction of his idling cab a short distance away, with Albert standing there beside it. "The absolute worst," she added. "Always getting lost, aren't you?"

"I blame it on the sat-nav, Stella," Albert insisted. "Now get yourself over here for a quick cuddle before you go, you grumpy old witch. Right this instant."

Stella offered a half laugh, doing as instructed, throwing her arms around Albert, the company's longest-serving driver, and very nearly suffocating the poor chap with her ample bosom in the process. "I'm going to miss you, you daft old bugger," she said, stroking the back of his head.

"Do you need a lift home?" Albert asked, once set free from Stella's tight embrace. "Seriously, though," he said, patting his vehicle's front wing to show he was indeed serious. "And no cost, of course."

"Naw, I'm good. I think I'll walk," Stella said, offering him a friendly wink.

Just then, Stella observed John the painter, who was lurking nearby, waiting patiently for the coast to be clear so he could commence work. "Well? Get on with it, then," she commented. "And if I learn you haven't made a decent job of it, you'll bleedin' hear from me later on, yeah?"

"Right-ho," John dutifully replied, reaching for his ladder. "I'll soon have the place looking fresh and new," he promised, collecting his things.

Stella hadn't walked more than five paces away, however,

when Albert called out to her once more. "Oi!" he shouted, standing half in, half out of his taxi, door opened.

"Yeah?" Stella growled back, turning on her heel. "Whaddya want *now*?"

"You honestly didn't think we were going to let the queen of taxi rank leave just like that, did you, without any fanfare?" he asked, reaching in and placing the flat of his hand over the car horn, giving it a long, robust toot, scaring the hell out of a nearby cat passing by and sending it skittering away in fright.

Stella screwed her face up in response to the ear-splitting sound of his horn. But before she had a chance to try and admonish him, another car drove slowly up the street with its horn blasting at liberal intervals as well. A moment later, another car pulled up behind it, and then another, and then another. More cars joined the convoy in no time, all filling the air with the sounds of their blaring horns.

Stella glanced back over to Albert, trying to make sense of whatever it was in the blue bloody blazes that was happening. Eventually, the procession of cars drew to a halt, and finally, peace was thankfully restored, all horns now drawing silent. Stella couldn't count them all, but there were thirty, possibly forty taxis all lined up, parked on either side of the road. Their drivers stepped out, taking up a position next to their vehicles, forming a guard of honour the length of the street.

Commuters walking home after a hard day at work slowed, wondering what on earth was going on and the reason for all the previous, recent racket. Then, adding to the intrigue, a regal, maroon-coloured Rolls-Royce appeared into view, weaving its way through the gap left by the parked taxis. Those people watching on would, at this point, surely have thought they were witnessing a Royal visit.

Stella offered a thin smile as the Rolls drew up, coming to a stop directly in front of her. There, the door eased gracefully open, with an immaculately dressed Frank climbing out. "My lady," Frank said, reaching in behind him and offering Susie a helping hand in exiting the vehicle. Next, Susie was followed by Stan emerging, and then finally Lee appeared from inside the sumptuous vehicle as well.

"What's all this?" Stella demanded, rummaging for a fag with her trembling hand. "And I thought *you* had dodgy guts," she said, throwing an accusing eye at Susie.

"I had other matters to attend to," Susie remarked. "Namely, helping to arrange all of this, amongst other things," she added, stepping forward and giving her friend a cheerful peck on the cheek.

"We didn't want you to be on your own today, Stella," Frank said to Stella, uncertain of the reaction he was going to receive, but carrying on regardless. "So, me and Stanley flew over to be with you on your final day."

Stan raised his hand, resulting in the waiting cabbies all falling into line and standing to attention in what appeared to be a pre-planned, expertly performed routine. With their shoulders pressed back, chin raised, not a word was uttered.

Stan offered his hand to Stella. "All present and ready for inspection, ma'am."

Stella accepted the hand, following Stan as he started the parade up the line of taxi drivers, Stella casting her hardened eye over each and every one of them as she went along. Then, sucking the life out of a fag, she came to a temporary halt in front of Albert's car, looking him up and down like an antique dealer appraising a Ming vase. "Straighten that tie!" she barked. "And would it kill you to get some deodorant on you?"

"I'll get right on it!" Albert replied, offering a quick salute, and then reaching to the base of his throat to attend to his tie, as instructed, before realising he wasn't even *wearing* a tie. But he straightened it up anyway, just to be on the safe side, after which he then gave another smart salute.

Stella continued her inspection, first heading up the street and, once satisfied, crossing over the road and heading back the way she came. These people were the drivers she'd worked with for longer than any of them cared to mention. Yes, Stella was a taskmaster, tearing them a new one when they were slacking off, taking too long to pick up a fare, or simply letting company standards slip by turning up to work in a dirty or unwashed car. She may have been a cantankerous, crotchety old so-and-so at times, but she was *their* cantankerous, crotchety old so-and-so. She was a large part of the business's success and, as a result, their employment was down to Stella's eye for detail and enviable ability to take not the slightest bit of guff from anybody, ever. She may have upset people along the way loads of times here and there, but they'd still miss her, by Jove. Likewise, they'd even miss hearing her voice crackling over the radio, chastising and berating them whenever they dared step out of line.

Once Stan and Stella were back at their starting point and standing beside the Rolls-Royce again, Stan glanced around to the others. As a result, Frank, Susie, and Lee all took Stella in their arms. "To the Queen of the taxi rank!" Stan called out, just before joining in with the group cuddle himself.

"The Queen of the taxi rank!" each and every one of those taxi drivers shouted back, right on cue. And then, after giving off one final salute, the assembled drivers, many of them misty-eyed, climbed inside their waiting cars.

"Come on," Susie said. "We need to get a move on."

Stella did as instructed, wiping a tear away with the back of her hand. "Where are we going?" she asked, once inside their elegant transport.

"We're going to the Frank and Stan's Cabs leaving party," Susie was delighted to advise. "It's where I've been all day, blowing up balloons and making sandwiches. I've even managed to print out and enlarge some photographs of us all in the office over the years."

"We've about seventy drivers in all, past and present, coming along as well," Stan explained, fastening his seatbelt. "So if people want to order a taxi anytime soon, I suspect there will be something of a delay."

Frank leaned forward in his seat, looking Stella, across from him, straight in the eye. "This isn't the end, Stella," he told her. "Stan and I are bursting with excitement about what's next in our adventure."

"Bursting," Stan happily agreed.

Frank smiled, placing his hand on Stella's knee. "We're going to have an absolute blast on the Isle of Man," he said. "Just you wait and see."

"We really should warn them in advance?" Stan suggested, with devilment in his eyes.

"Who?" Frank asked.

"The good people of the Isle of Man, Frank. It's only fitting that we let them know Stella's on her way."

"We could take out an advert in the local paper," Lee gamely suggested, receiving a stern glare from his beloved, though one delivered in good nature.

Stan laughed along at Lee's joke, but then kept his gaze fixed on Lee for perhaps a moment longer than was comfortable for Lee. In fact...

"You, ehm, okay there, fella?" Lee asked, wondering if there was something stuck to the side of his mouth.

After a bit of further consideration, Stan tilted his head to one side. "You're an XL t-shirt size?" he asked.

"Large on a good day, Stan," Lee answered. "It just depends on who's been doing the cooking at home. Why?"

Stan rubbed his hands in anticipation. "Well, this could be your lucky day," Stan replied, setting out his stall. "You see, after an unfortunate incident with a flying bratwurst, I've come into possession of thirteen very lovely t-shirts," he revealed. "Which, after a hot wash, have next to no staining on them at all," he added. "And I've got some in your size, which, for a small fee..."

"Yeah. Let me think about that one, will you?" Lee responded, not committing one way or the other to Stan's tempting offer.

"The silly bugger is just trying to recoup some money to pay for his expensive helicopter ride," Frank was quick to point out.

Frank then reached beside him, opening a hidden, leather-lined compartment tucked away between the rear headrests. Like something from a James Bond movie, he then retrieved a chilled bottle of Bollinger. "Stanley, if you'd be as kind?" Frank suggested, prompting Stan to distribute the champagne flutes found concealed there in the secret compartment as well.

"Now, I know our good friend Susie isn't moving with us, but she's still going to be part of the family, and we hope to see her each and every month," Frank said.

"She bloody better!" Stella barked. "Or I'll be on the next flight over, won't I?" she said, raising a clenched fist and a smile.

"So, with that promise..." Frank continued, removing the wire muselet from the bottle and taking a grip of the cork. "I'd like to propose a toast to our next, great adventure in the Isle of Man," he declared, setting the cork free.

"To the Isle of Man!"

The End?

(If you'd like to read more Frank & Stan, please leave feedback on Amazon and let me know. Your wish is my command!)

To browse the author's other uplifting titles, please visit his website at:

www.authorjcwilliams.com

Printed in Great Britain
by Amazon